Copyright © 2025 by Hayley Turner

All rights reserved.

No part of this book may be reproduced in any form or by any electronic or mechanical means, including information storage and retrieval systems, without written permission from the author, except for the use of brief quotations in a book review.

This book is a work of fiction. Names, characters, businesses, places, events, locales, and incidents are either the products of the author's imagination or used in a fictitious manner. Any resemblance to actual persons, living or dead, or actual events is purely coincidental.

Cover designed by Selkkie Designs.

Edited by Jeanine Harrell.

❀ Formatted with Vellum

LIGHTGUARD

DAUGHTER OF SUN DUOLOGY

1

HAYLEY TURNER

To anyone else who has battled that insistent inner voice that tries to convince you to believe the worst of yourself.

You're more than that.

CONTENT WARNINGS

LIGHTGUARD depicts the following:

Graphic: intrusive thoughts, anxiety, panic attacks, violence, torture, religious abuse/indoctrination (physical and mental), consensual sexual acts
Moderate: nightmares of parental death, sexual repression/shame
Mild: sexual harassment/unwanted physical contact, alcohol use, physical abuse (parent to grown child)

MAP OF ASHERA

THE LIGHTGUARD'S CREED

Light by Light and stone by stone
I am conduit alone
This I vow, to be Her hand
And never will I seek a throne

CHAPTER 1

Stay the course. Be the Light.

Corinne dodged a blast of light magic hurtling straight for her face. When a second one came for her an instant later, she caught it, absorbing the attack with her own light before launching it back toward her opponent. The golden markings along her lightly tanned skin glowed steadily from the backs of her hands up her arms, filling her with warmth as she executed another perfect counterattack.

One of the three Lightguards fell, blasted off their feet and into the dirt of the training enclosure.

Corinne blew one of her short chestnut curls out of her face and fought a smile. The sun was setting over the surrounding Asheran Mountains, and power radiated from her, her body moving with the precision of a trainee on the verge of earning their Anointing. She easily ducked another attack and flung her own magic outward in a wide, golden arc.

Another Lightguard hit the ground while the final one rolled out of the way. It was difficult to quell the pride that bloomed within her. *Focus, Corinne.*

The final Lightguard attacked her at close quarters, forcing her to dance backward to avoid a sharp blow to the face. When he shot light at her, she was ready. She let the energy meld with her own as it hit her open palms, and she lifted her hands to the sky before thrusting them toward the ground again. The earth quaked with a shimmer of light, throwing the Lightguard off-balance.

An instant later Corinne was on him, twisting his arm behind his back and forcing him to the dirt. He struggled, but she had him pinned.

Bells rang out as her chest rose and fell rapidly. She released the Lightguard, who threw her a rather unsavory glare. Corinne bit her lip to keep from smiling again.

She'd done it. She'd completed her final Test.

In the far right corner of the training grounds, the four Priestesses stood tall in their flowing white robes and hooded cloaks beneath a veranda. The purple blooms of wisteria swayed around them in the breeze. Mother Creita, the High Priestess, bent her ear to Priestess Chala, and Corinne could have sworn a little smile touched her pale face.

"Well done, Corinne." One of the Lightguards Corinne had defeated, Erla, approached her with a nod. "We all knew you'd pass, but that was one of the best Tests I've seen."

"Thank you," Corinne said as Erla patted her back and headed for the exit. Corinne looked to the pink-hued sky as the other Lightguards departed, neither offering her congratulations, but she didn't care. She'd be leaving the stucco walls and red clay roofs of the monastery soon enough, headed for an assignment of great honor once she was Anointed tomorrow.

The Goddess Helaera had blessed her. Corinne took a deep breath, closing her eyes.

"Congratulations, Corinne."

Tia, one of her fellow trainees, had entered the sparring enclosure and was standing several feet away. Unlike the other four in their training class, there was never a hint of jealousy or resentment on Tia's dark brown face when she looked at Corinne. There wasn't often any emotion on Tia's face as the most reserved of them, but Corinne at least never felt on edge around her.

"Thank you," Corinne said. "Are you next?"

"I am." Tia's braids blew gently in the late spring breeze as she adjusted the sleeve of her white tunic and checked the golden laces at her front. All trainees wore the plainest white tunic with ochre pants and simple leather boots for their final Test, a reminder of their modesty before Helaera. Corinne's tunic was now covered in dirt and sweat.

"May Helaera bless you," Corinne said, folding her arms over her upper chest, and Tia returned the greeting with a slight bow of her head. "What are you hoping for?"

It had been a question on all the trainees' minds who had turned twenty-five in the past year. Tia's mouth lifted slightly on one side.

"The Boundary watch," she said. "Hopefully by the sea."

Corinne nodded—she wouldn't mind that, either, though she preferred the mountains. "May you earn it."

"You too, Corinne."

Corinne walked toward the veranda, passing by several onlookers who had come to watch the Tests. A few warriors, several Acolytes, and a handful of Attendants in white robes similar to the Priestesses' had gathered on the outside of the fenced training enclosure.

They all know your secret.

A bit of Corinne's joy faded, her throat constricting. *Stay the course. Be the Light.* She repeated it to herself four more times, and the tightening in her chest eased.

"...The best light mage I've seen in decades."

Voices drifted past as Corinne approached the Priestesses, singing her praises in hushed tones.

They couldn't know. If they did, they wouldn't be watching Corinne with admiration and approval.

She pushed those thoughts away as she stood before the Priestesses, greeting them the same way she had Tia before kneeling and bowing her head.

"Corinne Anastos," Mother Creita said. She hesitated just long enough for a trickle of panic to skitter up Corinne's spine. "You have passed your Test. Helaera's Sun shines upon you."

"May the Goddess guide my path," Corinne said, lifting her head.

Mother Creita and the three other Priestesses raised their arms toward her, and their markings alighted with Helaera's Light. A moment later, the light turned to gentle fire along their skin. Corinne swallowed hard. The flames were the mark of exceptionally powerful Lightguards, but they always made Corinne uneasy.

"We will see you at the Anointing tomorrow," Mother Creita said, lowering her arms. Several wisps of her silvery hair escaped her hood as she offered Corinne a gentle smile. "Prepare yourself to receive your charge from the Goddess."

Corinne stood and crossed her arms over her chest once more before taking her leave, headed for the doors behind the veranda. Three more Lightguards passed her, nodding as they took their places for Tia's Test.

The moment Corinne stepped inside the training hall corridor, a shriek echoed down the narrow stone passage, followed by a flash of brown hair before two strong arms encircled her.

"You *did* it, Corinne," Vera said, her head barely reaching Corinne's chin as she squeezed her tightly.

"Vera, I can't breathe—"

"Sorry." Her best friend released her, her fair face flushed with excitement as she looked up at Corinne with wide blue eyes. Vera was dressed almost as plainly as Corinne, though her white shirt was made of a finer material. "I'm just so happy for you. I've waited for this for two years."

"You really think they'll assign me to the Boundary?" Corinne asked, walking alongside Vera as they headed for the living quarters. She desperately needed a shower. And food. Her mouth watered as she thought about the freshly baked yeast rolls the Attendants made.

"They're not going to assign you anywhere less important," Vera said, nudging her as they turned a corner into an open hall with tall windows on either side. They stepped through the doors leading outside into the monastery's central courtyard, then headed for the building to their right. "There's a good chance your assignment will be near mine."

Corinne would be lucky if that happened. If her outpost was close to Vera's, she'd be in the most beautiful part of Ashera, up in the western mountains, and she'd get to see Vera more frequently.

"I don't want to get my hopes up," Corinne said, even as her heart yearned for it.

"Probably wise, so I'll hope for the both of us," Vera said, winking at her as they entered the dormitory. "Now go get cleaned up and I'll meet you at the dining hall in an hour."

Huffing something between a laugh and a sigh, Corinne hurried up the steps to the second floor and her room. A few younger trainees passed, offering their congratulations to her.

Just before she reached her door, an older Attendant walked by, nodding silently. Corinne recognized him, forcing herself to keep her eyes from going to the partially healed handprint-shaped burn on his forearm.

She suppressed a shudder, wondering what he'd done to receive such punishment. But that was between him, the Priestesses, and Helaera, and they would fully heal it once he'd paid his penance.

Pushing the curiosity and pity out of her mind, Corinne stepped into her room to retrieve fresh clothes, heading for her small dresser full of white and gold attire.

The showers were mostly empty when she arrived, only one of the dozen or so stalls occupied. Corinne quickly scrubbed herself clean and prayed to Helaera yet again as she closed her eyes beneath the hot water.

Please let me be assigned near Vera. Or, at least, she hoped, along the Boundary. It wouldn't be terrible to be assigned as a village guardian or traveling scout, but if she were placed as a monastery guard, she wasn't sure how she'd handle that disappointment.

A bit of shame crept up the back of her neck. *Any assignment is an honorable one.*

Corinne dried herself and dressed quickly, successfully avoiding the attention of the other occupant showering, and headed into the dormitory corridor.

THE DINING HALL WAS FAR NOISIER THAN NORMAL, ABUZZ IN a way that only meant it was Testing day. Corinne quickly retrieved a plate of spiced rice and chicken—and three yeast rolls—before walking past several rows of tables to join Vera. One of the Lightguards from Vera's training class was seated next to her already, a woman with golden-brown skin and long, dark brown curls.

Corinne had only found herself attracted to a handful of people in her life, and the first time she'd met Sana when she was fifteen, she'd prayed to Helaera for forgiveness for a week. She'd also avoided looking too long at one of the librarians she'd met when she was eighteen, but he'd been transferred to another location only a few months later.

That was years ago, though, and the infatuations had long passed. Corinne's mind was far more disciplined now. Her heart belonged to Helaera, as did the hearts of all Lightguards.

"Hi, Corinne," Sana said, flashing a bright smile. "Congratulations."

"Thank you," Corinne said, taking a seat across from her and Vera. Both of them had already eaten the majority of their food, so Corinne devoured her meal in peace as they chatted. She melted into the bliss of basil and garlic and butter until the loud clang of dishes and cutlery caught her attention from several tables over.

A fellow trainee, Greer, had shoved his plate away, sending it crashing into Tia's and several others' before he stood from the bench and headed for the exit. Corinne accidentally made eye contact with him as he passed, and he paused, fists clenched at his sides.

"Congratulations, Corinne," he said bitterly, his fair face pinched as he regarded her, his light brown hair falling in his eyes. "You've always thought you were better than the rest of us, and now you have proof."

Before Corinne could respond, he stalked off, pushing through the double doors a few feet away. Corinne's stomach went leaden as she noticed all the eyes on her. She looked down at her plate again, cheeks burning.

Chatter started up once more, filling the hall, and Corinne looked to Vera and Sana once she was sure she'd purged any emotion from her face.

"I heard he failed his Test," Sana said, her voice low. "Don't take what he said to heart."

Vera nodded, her eyes narrowing. "If he's going to talk to his fellow trainee that way, then he wasn't ready to become a Lightguard anyway. He can learn more discipline and try again next year. Don't listen to him, Corinne."

Corinne took a deep breath and smiled softly at them, but the leaden feeling remained pinned in her gut. She didn't think she was better than the others in her training class.

She *knew* she was, because she'd worked at it harder than any of them, to prove to herself, to everyone, that she deserved to be here. She wouldn't let Greer take the victory of today away from her just because he felt inferior.

"Come on," Vera said, standing. "Let's go to the roof."

Corinne nodded; getting away from the noise and energy of the room was probably best.

They bid Sana farewell and headed outside. Dusk had fallen, and the stars would be out soon. She followed Vera to the dormitory building again, and they quickly climbed three flights of stairs before clambering out of an old window and vaulting onto the roof above. It wasn't terribly difficult to get to, but only she and Vera ever seemed to venture up here. That was fine by Corinne.

Their boots clacked on the red clay shingles as they made their way to a flatter area of the roof where they could comfortably lie down without the fear of tumbling off. The shingles were still pleasantly warm from the heat of the day, and Corinne sighed as she lay near Vera, gazing at the pinpricks of stars as they began to appear.

The night sky always made her feel small, reminded her how vast the world was. Tomorrow she would find her place, her purpose in that vastness, and that was what mattered more than anything. Still, that heavy feeling returned. All these years she'd only truly trusted Vera, and now that she was faced with leaving, a bit of regret settled within her.

"Vera," Corinne said quietly. "Do you think the others hate me?"

Vera sighed. "Is this about what Greer said?"

"Maybe."

Vera reached over, grabbing Corinne's hand and squeezing it. "They don't hate you, Corinne. No one could hate you. Even Greer doesn't, not really. He just doesn't understand you."

Corinne frowned at the sky. "How could he when I've never let any of them really know me?"

"You've been cautious and disciplined," Vera said, sitting up on her elbow. "Which is exactly how you should be. And Helaera knows you, which is what matters most."

Corinne closed her eyes and breathed in the cool night air. "I suppose you're right."

"Of course I am," Vera said. "Put that out of your mind for now. Tomorrow is your day."

It was her day tomorrow. Tomorrow, she would become a Lightguard.

CHAPTER 2

The earthy, hot tea burned Corinne's throat as she choked it down, just as she always did on the first day of the week. Fifteen years of this ritual and she still wasn't accustomed to its bitterness. She squeezed her eyes shut as she knelt before the little altar in her room and finished her prayer.

Guide me, Goddess Helaera, as I enter your service.

She stood once more and checked the ties at her forearms for the fifth time since donning her armor, ensuring the vambraces were secure. She'd waited weeks to put this armor on, gazing longingly at it in her modest room at the monastery. The gold-accented steel and the white hauberk with the sun emblazoned on the chest would mark her as the recipient of the highest honor in the nation of Ashera.

Today, she would become a Lightguard.

It would've been nice if they'd held the ceremony in the morning, though. Not a single part of her was visible below her chin, and she would be sweating by the time Vera arrived to retrieve her. She'd left her chestnut curls unbound after washing them earlier that morning, but they remained out of her way, falling just below her jawline and cut so they wouldn't obscure her vision.

A knock at her door sent her heart beating so fiercely she thought it might rattle the armor.

"Corinne, are you ready?"

Corinne glanced in the mirror one last time to ensure not a fiber of fabric was out of place before grabbing her sword belt and fastening it around her waist.

Vera waited for her in the hallway, her dark brown tresses pulled back into a braid. She was dressed in a white tunic with a little sun embroidered over her heart. Her brown leather boots fell far more softly on the stone floor than the heavy steel that wrapped up Corinne's shins and knees.

"Corinne," Vera said, stepping forward to take Corinne's hands, eyes welling with tears. "I'm so proud of you."

Corinne couldn't suppress a smile. "Let's just get going, shall we?"

"Aren't you excited?" Vera asked, crossing her arms as Corinne closed the door to her room.

Sunlight filtered through intermittent windows in the second-floor hallway of the dormitory, shining in Corinne's eyes each time they passed one of them.

"I'm more excited about finally being assigned my post." Corinne nodded as they passed two other Lightguards before arriving at the stairs. "What if I say the wrong thing during the ceremony?"

"You won't. You've trained for this for years, Corinne. And I'll pray to Helaera you get assigned near me."

Corinne subdued the hope that Vera was right. "All posts are of great honor."

Vera nudged her shoulder, her smile wry. "They are. You'll get an esteemed placement regardless. I know it, Corinne."

Corinne shook her head as they entered the main courtyard, headed for the tallest structure at the heart of the monastery. The sky was a beautiful clear blue as it spanned above them, the sun bright and blazing. Even in the foothills of the Asheran Mountains, where the monastery was nestled, the temperature climbed high in late spring and summer.

Vera held the door open for Corinne to step into the Great Sanctuary. As they entered, joining a dozen or so others who stood down the aisle at the front, they fell silent. The ceiling was tall in the sanctuary, the stone bathed in sunlight from the six massive windows. Rows of wooden chairs sat neatly on either side of the aisle that led to the front, many of them occupied for the Anointing.

Corinne tried again to suppress her pride and excitement, forcing herself to focus on her steps as she and Vera approached the front of the sanctuary. The five other Lightguard trainees who were being Anointed today stood in a line before a large marble altar. A shaft of sunlight beamed down from a skylight in the ceiling high above, making the altar and their armor gleam.

Corinne took her place among them, to the left of a trainee named Oskar, and Vera left to join the Lightguards seated behind them.

The doors at the back of the chancel opened, tall and gilded, and the four Priestesses entered the sanctuary. Everyone in the room stood. Once the Priestesses were before the trainees, a Lightguard behind Corinne instructed her and the others to kneel on the marble steps, and they did so in unison, heads bowed.

"We gather today to anoint six," Mother Creita said, her voice echoing around the room.

Corinne nearly shook with anticipation as they began the presentation of swords. How many times had she imagined carrying that beautiful blade in her hands?

"Tia Niaron," Mother Creita said. She stood before Tia with her sword held aloft, the golden pommel in one hand and the flat side of the blade in the other. "Today Helaera takes you into her service. You will serve the Goddess at the Boundary on the Gleaming Shore."

An excited murmur ran through the crowd behind them as Tia lifted her hands to receive her sword.

Please, Corinne prayed. Of course she was the last in line, and it became more difficult to conceal her nerves as each trainee was Anointed and given their assignment. Finally it was Oskar's turn, and they assigned him to the Monastery Watch. *All posts are of great honor,* she told herself.

"Corinne Anastos," Mother Creita said, her voice booming above Corinne. Corinne lifted her head, as was expected of her, and gazed into the High Priestess's porcelain face as she presented the sword. "Today

Helaera takes you into her service. You will serve the Goddess as the personal guard to Prince Aryel Serra."

Another murmur rippled through the crowd, one of uncertainty this time, and Corinne herself blinked at Mother Creita. *Personal guard to the prince?* Since when were Lightguards assigned to the royal family? The High Priestess gave her a hard look, and Corinne remembered herself, lifting her hands to receive the sword. Her stomach sank, her lungs constricting as she took the exquisite weapon, hardly noticing its weight in her hands as she stood alongside the others.

"Light by Light and stone by stone..."

Corinne forced her lips to move, almost forgetting to recite the Creed alongside everyone in the room.

"I am conduit alone.
This I vow, to be Her hand,
And never will I seek a throne."

Her breath was shallow as she placed her sword in its sheath at her waist, glad the movement was so practiced that she hardly had to think to do it in perfect synchronization with her fellows at the altar.

"Servants of Helaera, stand and welcome your new siblings," Mother Creita said, her arms outstretched.

Corinne turned with her fellows as all the Lightguards behind them stood and crossed their arms over their chests, their fists tight at their shoulders.

"May we be Her hands and Her swords," they said in unison, and each of their arms lit up with the markings of their magic—the sun's magic. Helaera's magic, bestowed upon them at birth and honed as trainees in the monastery.

Corinne had been born with such magic, same as the rest of them. So why was she being relegated to guard duty for a spoiled *prince*?

That wasn't fair, though. She didn't know he was spoiled, just assumed as much about anyone with an exorbitant amount of riches at their disposal.

CHAPTER 2

The storm of emotion in her chest began to rage as the ceremony concluded and Lightguards came forward to congratulate her and the other new appointees. Corinne felt as though she were watching the scene unfold from outside her own body as she plastered a smile on her face and accepted everyone's well-wishes. The Priestesses exited the same way they'd come, and Corinne tried her best to find some calming thought.

Stay the course. Be the Light. "May Helaera bless you as well," she said to another Lightguard. *Stay the course. Be the Light.*

Where was Vera?

"Corinne, did you know being the guard for the prince was even an assignment?" a Lightguard asked her, and Corinne forced herself to focus on the woman's fair face. She recognized her, but didn't recall her name.

"No," she said, failing to hide the strain in her voice.

"The royals have never had Lightguards in the castle, have they?"

"I wonder if it will be dangerous," another Lightguard said.

"Perhaps," Corinne said, hardly looking at them. She was lost in a sea of faces, but finally the one she sought appeared several feet away.

Vera approached her as the other Lightguards dispersed to either leave the sanctuary or talk amongst themselves, several of them glancing in Corinne's direction.

"Come," she said quietly, her voice soft and her eyes full of understanding.

She shepherded Corinne to the side exit of the sanctuary, and as soon as they were in the relative privacy of the little corridor, Corinne let the panic come forth.

"It's all right, Cori," Vera said, placing a hand on her armored forearm. Corinne hated that nickname, mostly because Vera only used it when she pitied her. "Just breathe."

"Why would they…I thought I…what am I supposed to…?" Corinne forced herself to take several breaths, furious at her lack of control.

"I don't know," Vera said. "But it will be all right."

"Do you think it's because—?" Corinne couldn't bring herself to say the words out loud, but Vera understood. Vera was the only person besides the Priestesses who would understand.

"No," Vera said, taking Corinne's hand. "Why don't you go speak with Mother Creita? If that's the assignment they chose for you, it must be important. There's something they know that we don't."

It took Corinne a few more seconds and several more deep breaths to calm her heart and racing mind.

She nodded. "You're right," she said. "I'll go find her."

CHAPTER 3

Corinne lifted her hand and lowered it about five times before she finally knocked on the door to the High Priestess's private study. An airy "Enter" sounded from within, and Corinne stepped inside, bowing quickly.

"Corinne, dearest," Mother Creita said, standing from her desk in a fluid movement, her white and gold robes billowing around her. "I was just going to send for you."

"You were?" Corinne asked, her feet heavy as she accepted the High Priestess's invitation to sit at the chair before her desk.

Mother Creita followed suit, steepling her fingers in front of her nose as Corinne awkwardly adjusted the sword now at her hip.

"I'm sure today was a shock," she said, her green eyes sparkling with understanding.

Her silvery hair was braided around her head like a crown, gold ribbons woven within. She, like many of the older Lightguards, aged more slowly than those without Helaera's gift, but a few lines still peppered her beautiful face, a testament to her wisdom and experiences.

"I..." Corinne swallowed hard. "I am not ungrateful, Mother Creita, just...I want to make sure it wasn't because of my...upbringing."

"I worried you would think that," Mother Creita said. "You have done remarkably well for having come to the monastery later than what is usual. You have overcome the circumstances of your childhood and hidden that past well. You're exceptional, Corinne, and your assignment should reflect that."

That damning pride rose in her chest again, and Corinne tamped it down. She didn't know what the right response was, so she remained silent, and Mother Creita leaned back in her chair.

"The truth is, the Priestesses and I changed your assignment only this morning," she said. "When we received word from Vytanos that the prince's life has been threatened by Nightrenders."

Corinne went rigid, blood freezing in her veins. "Nightrenders? Have they breached the Boundary?"

Mother Creita shook her head. "None who bear the dark magic themselves. But somehow a message made it through to the royal family. The safety of the Crown is paramount. We offered to assign guards to the king and queen as well, but they insisted we not call too much attention to it. We must, however, protect the heir of Ashera at all costs, and I would trust no one more with this task, Corinne."

The knot in Corinne's chest loosened, some of her disappointment fading. It wasn't an assignment that would have her gazing at the seas or standing in the mountains every day, but Vytanos, she'd heard, was a beautiful city, the castle a marvel of their forebears' ingenuity.

"I am honored by your faith in me, Mother Creita," Corinne said, bowing her head.

"I'm glad to hear it." The High Priestess stood once more, and Corinne did the same. "You report to Vytanos immediately. They will want you on duty as early as tomorrow morning."

Corinne blinked. She had to leave *now*?

"The Attendants have already begun packing your things and preparing your horse." Mother Creita went on, oblivious to Corinne's dismay. "You're already fully dressed in your armor, so no need to change. You may visit the dining hall before you depart, and I suggest you eat something—the journey to Vytanos is a several-hours' ride."

She approached Corinne, who schooled her face into neutrality as the High Priestess took her hands.

"The royal family and nobles of Ashera are used to luxury and

CHAPTER 3

indulgence," she said, sniffing. "This is the first time they have allowed a Lightguard to be at court. You will not only provide protection, Corinne, but also be an example of how the Goddess wishes for us to live our lives. May Helaera guide you, child."

"Goddess willing," Corinne replied, forcing her voice not to tremble.

She bowed to Mother Creita again before taking her leave. Every part of her wanted to sprint back to her room and lock herself inside, but she kept her pace at a brisk walk until she found Vera waiting just outside the sanctuary.

"How did it go?" Vera asked, almost jogging to keep up with Corinne.

"I have to depart as soon as possible," Corinne said, her voice hard.

"What?" Vera grabbed her arm, forcing her to slow down. "Why?"

Corinne stopped just as they reached the entrance to the dormitory.

"I don't know if I can say," she said quietly.

Vera's face hardened. She glanced around to ensure no one would overhear before stepping closer to Corinne.

"Is this about the Nightrenders' attempted breach of the Boundary?" she asked.

Corinne's eyes widened. "You know about it?"

"They informed us earlier, before I came to retrieve you for the ceremony." Vera frowned. "But what does that have to do with the prince?"

"There was a threat to his life," Corinne said. "The royal family expects me there as soon as possible."

Vera stared at her for a long moment.

"This is...this is such an *honor*, Corinne," she breathed. "To entrust the heir's safety to you against the threat of those shadow-wielding heretics."

It *was* an honor. So why did Corinne feel so dismissed, so pushed aside?

"Mother Creita told me to eat before I go," Corinne said, heading up the stairs. "But I don't think I could eat right now if I tried."

And, if she was honest with herself, she couldn't bear the stares that would certainly follow her in such a crowded space.

Vera lingered at the base of the stairs, her eyes narrowing.

"What?" Corinne asked, pausing on the landing.

"Go get your things, and I'll meet you outside the dining hall."

"Vera, what are you—?"

But Vera had dashed off already.

Corinne sighed and climbed the next flight of stairs to the second floor.

The Attendants had indeed already packed her things, which wasn't much, in truth. A brown knapsack sat neatly on her immaculately made bed. She peeked inside quickly to make sure they'd included her most precious item—a gold ring inlaid with opals along the band. She pressed her lips to the cool metal and placed it safely back in her bag between an undershirt and her favorite pair of pants. She wasn't allowed to wear jewelry as a Lightguard, but they were kind enough to let her keep the ring that had belonged to her mother.

Memories of the night she'd died sometimes still plagued her nightmares, but Corinne had been ten years old at the time, and the terror had mostly faded. The Lightguards were her life now, her family, her purpose, and she owed them everything. They'd embraced her and trained her for fifteen years, and now it was time for her to repay that debt.

No tears. No feeling sorry for herself. Corinne hoisted the pack onto her shoulder and glanced around her room one more time. Would a new little light mage arrive soon to claim this space for the next fifteen, twenty years? Would they be an orphan, like many of them were, or brought here by parents with teary but dutiful farewells?

She hoped whoever they were, they weren't a latecomer like she'd been. With a bracing inhale, Corinne turned and headed back outside.

∽

Vera looked close to bursting with excitement when Corinne arrived at the dining hall entrance, smiling widely. Several Lightguards passed them, glancing at Corinne as they stepped inside. The noise from within grew and then faded once more as the doors closed.

CHAPTER 3

"I've been given permission to ride with you to Vytanos on my way back to my post," Vera said. "I can't stay, obviously, but I figured it would be nice for you to have a—"

Corinne cut her off with a fierce embrace, and Vera returned it, patting her back.

"I grabbed a few rolls and two apples," she said as Corinne released her, holding up a small travel pack. "Since you said you couldn't eat now."

Gratitude warmed her, and she couldn't help a small smile. "Thanks, Vera."

"Don't mention it," Vera said. "Come on, we ought to get going so you can arrive before nightfall."

Just as Corinne's belongings had been packed, a horse was indeed saddled and prepared for a journey. She was a gorgeous dappled gray mare who huffed when Corinne patted her neck.

She and Vera rode through the monastery, their horses' hooves heavy on the dirt beneath them. They passed by the main courtyard on the path leading to the exit, more wisteria climbing the limestone walls, and finally rode by the training grounds where younger classes of future Lightguards honed their skills. A boy shot an orb of light at a dummy several feet away, and his companions cheered him on. An ache formed in Corinne's chest.

As much as she'd wanted a post outside the monastery, she would miss this place, with its high walls and chiming bells and everyone united under a single mission.

A Lightguard stationed at the gate whistled, and the portcullis rose. The path into the forest stretched ahead of them.

The path to Vytanos.

CHAPTER 4

By the time the capital city appeared in the distance, Corinne was ravenous. Vera tossed her a roll, and she tore into it with little decorum.

"Goddess, Corinne, *eat* the roll, don't inhale it."

Vera laughed atop her brown mare and retrieved some bread for herself. Corinne shrugged and finished it off, turning her eyes back to the looming city walls that interrupted the green, mountainous landscape. What awaited her within them? She'd hardly left the monastery aside from a few trips to villages as a trainee, the journey to get her tattoos, and the pilgrimage to the mountains she'd taken on her birthday last autumn. She rubbed the heel of her hand absently over her left thigh.

The castle naturally towered above everything else, its spires silhouetted against the sunset. Corinne was glad for her armor now—the mountain city boasted cooler temperatures than what she'd become used to at the monastery.

The road dipped into another patch of trees, hardly big enough to classify as a wood, and when they emerged from the tree line, it ran steeply uphill. Their horses slowed as the incline increased, and Corinne gripped her reins tighter. They were nearly to the eastern gate of the city.

The gate was designed similarly to the one at the monastery, but far larger. They stopped their horses when two city guards came forward with spears in hand.

"State your name and business," one of them barked, and Corinne nearly jumped in her saddle.

She swallowed. "Corinne Anastos, Lightguard and Servant of Helaera," she said, mustering up as much confidence as she could. "I've been summoned to the castle."

The guard nodded, then looked to Vera. "And you?"

"Vera Bronan, sir," she said with a dip of her head. "Lightguard and Servant of Helaera. I'm not entering the city."

The guard barked another order at the wall behind him, and the portcullis began to open with a rattle of chains. Corinne dismounted quickly alongside Vera, who took her hands and squeezed.

"Helaera guide you, Corinne," she said, tears welling in her eyes. "You are blessed."

Corinne couldn't speak past the lump in her throat. How was she going to survive here without Vera, without anyone she knew?

Vera released her hands and climbed back on her horse as the portcullis finished its ascent. Corinne steeled herself and swung back into her own saddle, urging her horse into the city.

The main road ran up little hills and around curves, taking her past numerous shops, cafés, and other buildings she assumed were residential. She'd lived most of her life in a monastery full of people, but the sheer number of city-goers bustling in the streets, even as night fell, was overwhelming. A young man was dashing around, lighting lanterns, when someone bumped into him, and the little flame at the end of his pole snuffed out against the cool stone of a nearby building.

"Oh, Goddess, I'm so sorry, lad!" the older man said, scratching his head.

The closest lit lantern was a moderate distance back up the street, a rather steep incline.

"Watch where you're going, why don't you?" the young man snapped, and Corinne balked. "You going to pay me for lost time?"

"Now, listen here, boy—"

The two were almost nose to nose now, looking tensed to get into a physical altercation.

Corinne hopped down from her horse. "Can I help?" she asked, approaching them and gesturing to the pole.

The lantern lighter and the older man looked at her, puzzled, their anger defusing.

"Have you got a lantern hidden in that armor or something?" the boy asked.

"No, but I can relight that for you," she said.

Cautiously, the boy held out the pole.

Corinne placed two fingers on the wick at the end and summoned her light. She let it build and funnel into her fingertips for a moment before releasing it, creating enough pressure that it sparked against the wick and set it aflame once more.

The two men gaped at her.

"Well, fuck me, that was incredible!"

Corinne nearly choked. She knew some people used such vulgar words, but she'd never heard them spoken aloud. She could only nod as the young man shook her hand and thanked her before sauntering away to continue lighting his lanterns, all anger forgotten.

"You're a Lightguard, aren't you?" the older man asked, and Corinne nodded. "I've never met one of you before! What's it like having magic? How often do they let you out of that monastery?"

Discomfort prickled at the back of Corinne's neck. "I'm sorry, sir, but I must be on my way. I'm expected by th— someone."

"Ah, of course, of course," he said. "Well, thanks again for saving my blunder!"

Corinne hurried to remount her horse. No more detours or speaking to strangers.

Somehow, she made it to the castle gates without getting lost in the side streets that branched off every few buildings, and her jaw nearly dropped at the sight of the castle this close, even in the growing darkness. It was so impossibly tall—white stucco walls smattered with ornate windows and beautifully carved swirls. The gates themselves were open and manned by two guards on each side, standing stoically with

CHAPTER 4

spears or swords in the torchlight. As she led her horse through, two stable hands hurried forward to help her dismount.

A figure dressed in a deep blue tunic with a crescent moon and stars embroidered on the chest approached as they led Corinne's horse off, one hand on the hilt of their sword. The torchlight shone on the man's deep brown face, reflecting off his dark eyes.

"Are you Corinne Anastos?" His voice was deep and warm, and Corinne found herself craning her neck to look at him as he stopped before her.

She'd never met anyone so tall, and she was rather tall herself.

She nodded once. "I am."

"Welcome to Vytanos. I'm Captain Ekhana," he said. "I'll show you to your room."

He turned on his heel and headed up the stone path to a pair of the largest doors Corinne had ever seen. She hurried after him, clutching the pack on her shoulder tightly. Two guards opened the front doors with a heave, and Corinne's eyes widened. The entrance hall stretched to a tall archway, lined on either side with statues and works of art. She trained her eyes on Ekhana's back when she realized the statues were all nude depictions of people. Her face burned. *Stay the course, Corinne.*

The archway led into a perpendicular corridor covered in thick blue carpet, intermittent sconces with bright lanterns lining the walls. Ekhana turned right and led her to the end of the hallway and around a corner.

"The prince's chambers are in the south wing of the castle," Ekhana explained over his shoulder. He nodded to several servants who passed by, and Corinne did the same. "Your room will be right beside his for safety purposes, and you'll dine with the rest of the castle guards at times of the day when your presence is less necessary. Our matron of servants will have more information for you in the morning about Prince Aryel's schedule and yours."

Ekhana approached the end of the long corridor and began ascending a spiral staircase. The carpet was so lush that even Corinne's armored footfalls weren't terribly loud. They exited at the second floor, and Ekhana led her through a maze of additional hallways with stained glass windows and more art and statues before approaching a pair of dark brown double doors. The brass doorknobs were ornate, the wood polished to perfection. He opened them and led Corinne onto a breezeway lined with vine-wrapped pillars on either side. Purple blooms swayed in the evening air, and the scent of the wisteria brought Corinne right back to the monastery. It was her favorite part of spring—when the climbing vines of wisteria bloomed all over the walls.

Beyond the pillars, though, was a view of the entire city of Vytanos. Lanterns flickered in the night, winding through the streets, and beyond that, the mountains stood resolute against the darkness. A bit of hope flickered in her heart. She wasn't assigned to a place where she could explore the mountains and forests, but at least she'd have a view of it all.

Ekhana led her through a stone archway, and three sets of doors stood in an expansive outdoor alcove. He paused, and Corinne stopped beside him.

"Those are Prince Aryel's chambers," he said, pointing to the large wooden door at the far left. He moved his hand to gesture to the much smaller door several yards to the right. "And those are yours. You'll spend a lot of time outside his door, I expect."

Corinne nodded, and he pressed forward, leading her toward her room. Just before she could step inside, stumbling footsteps approached them from behind, and Corinne whipped around, one hand aloft and shining with her magic.

"Whoa, that'ssss'awfully bright." A man stood before her, his brown eyes narrowed to slits, his dark brown hair tousled, and his white shirt half unbuttoned. Dark ink designs on his chest and shoulders were partially visible, intricate celestial moon tattoos that were stark against his fair skin. He swayed on the spot as Corinne lowered her hand, and the smell of liquor wafted through the air. "Who the—*hic*—hells are you?"

"Prince Aryel," Captain Ekhana said, "this is Corinne Anastos, the Lightguard they've assigned for your protection."

Corinne could barely process what she'd heard. This foul, drunken mess was her charge?

"Ahhh," Aryel drawled, patting Corinne's armored shoulder. "Fantastic. My devout royal babysitter."

"Your Highness—" Ekhana started, but Aryel darted back to the

CHAPTER 4

breezeway and heaved over the side of it, emptying the contents of his stomach.

Corinne could only stare, horrified. A roaring started up in her ears.

"I'll get him to bed," Ekhana muttered. "You get settled in your rooms."

"I'm *fine*, Captain," Aryel said, stumbling back into the alcove. "I've been drunk before and made it back to my rooms alone just fine! Or, wait, that's *her* job now, isn't it? To follow me around and never give me a moment's peace?"

The roaring in Corinne's ears grew louder. Aryel slung an arm around Ekhana's shoulders, and the captain kept the prince upright. He trained an unfocused eye on Corinne.

"Do you speak, oh righteous one?" he asked.

Corinne scowled. "I speak, Your Highness."

"Why don't we get you to bed, Your Highness?" Ekhana said, shepherding the prince toward his chamber doors.

Aryel let out a dramatic sigh. "Fine, fine, Captain. Lead the way."

Corinne stood rooted to the spot until they'd disappeared into the prince's rooms, hoping that if she didn't move, she wouldn't fall headfirst into the waiting abyss of despair. But she couldn't just stay out here all night. With a shaky hand, she opened her door and entered her room.

It was spacious, with a bed large enough to fit three of the one she'd had in the monastery, two tall windows, and even her own private washroom through a door on her right. She removed her armor in a daze, as if she were watching someone else do it, all the while chanting to herself. *Stay the course. Be the Light.*

After riffling through a nearby wardrobe and extracting a plain white nightgown, she curled up beneath the admittedly luxurious blankets of her bed and let the tears come. Perhaps if Prince Aryel hadn't been exactly what she'd expected of a royal and worse, this assignment might have been bearable. But what she'd seen tonight...he *was* a spoiled prince, and an irreverent brat.

And Corinne hated him for it.

CHAPTER 5

Corinne's sleep was fitful, and when she woke, it felt as though her chest were caving in. In a single day, she'd become a Lightguard, left her home of fifteen years, and decided within five minutes of meeting the prince that she hated him.

Perhaps you are the irreverent brat.

Her stomach sank to her toes. Panic burned through her insides in waves she tried to subdue, but the thoughts wouldn't cease, the voice insistent.

You want to stray from your path, you want to give in to the darkness. You'll end up just like your father, and Helaera will spurn you.

Corinne squeezed her eyes shut and curled in on herself. No, she didn't want any of that. *Stay the course. Be the Light.* She repeated it four times, then again five more.

A brisk knock at her door startled her out of her spiraling panic. The tightness in her chest didn't entirely fade, but she managed to stumble out of bed and answer the door. Before her stood a woman with olive-brown skin and light green eyes. Her dark hair was braided into a bun at the top of her head. She was almost at eye level with Corinne, but not nearly as muscular.

"Good morning," she said, her voice gentle and friendly. "I'm

CHAPTER 5

Orana, head matron of servants. Did you need, eh, a few minutes to freshen up?"

Her eyes darted down Corinne's scantily clad form and then back up, and Corinne's face warmed.

"Yes, one moment," she stammered out, and closed the door again.

Clothes. She needed fresh clothes, and probably needed to wash her face. The simple act of cleaning up and dressing herself was enough to make her earlier panic subside entirely, and she sighed in relief. It had been a while since she'd had an episode like that.

After fastening her sword belt over her white and gold tunic, Corinne checked her reflection in the mirror and grimaced. Deep circles shadowed beneath her hazel eyes, and her curls were a mess. She turned on the tap of the sink in her washroom and did her best to re-tame them. Her tunic was secured, her sword in her belt, boots laced tight. She was as ready as she'd ever be.

Orana was waiting patiently outside, humming to herself when Corinne opened the door.

She offered a soft smile. "No armor today?" she asked.

Corinne shook her head. "The armor is mostly for special occasions," Corinne told her. "My magic is usually protection enough."

"Fascinating," Orana said, tilting her head to the side. "Well, shall we go?"

Corinne glanced at the double doors just down the alcove, where a castle guard stood watch. "Am I not supposed to guard the prince?"

"Oh, yes, dear, but he won't be up for hours, and I need to show you where things are around here so you can properly navigate the castle. And I imagine you'll be wanting a bit of breakfast, yes?"

Now that the knot had dissipated from her stomach, Corinne *was* quite hungry. The rolls and apple Vera had brought on their journey yesterday had hardly been a true meal. Corinne gave Orana a tentative nod, and the matron smiled brightly at her.

"Follow me, then."

∽

Corinne had never seen such opulence and luxury in her life. Orana and everyone else in the castle were used to it all, going about their morning as if they weren't walking through hallways covered in intricate carvings and past some of the most beautiful art in Ashera. Corinne tried her best to memorize how to get everywhere, but some places in the castle were practically a labyrinth.

"Now, most days, Prince Aryel's schedule will have you in those four main locations, but twice a week he has archery training and once a week he has pianoforte lessons."

Imagining that drunken fool of a man she'd met last night doing anything that required coordination was a challenge.

Orana led Corinne through the western wing, and Corinne nearly stumbled when the view from the window caught her eye. Gardens spanned the entire western perimeter of the castle, perfectly kept flower beds of tulips and daffodils smattering the ground in a sea of color. Willow trees and well-kept hedges lined the outside edges, and stepping stones wound through the greenery and flowers to meet at the center, where a large stone fountain bubbled in three tiers. Pergolas stood at each of the four corners, covered in wisteria and other climbing vines.

"Are you a gardener?" Orana asked wryly, eyebrows raised.

Corinne hadn't realized she'd stopped entirely to stare out of a tall window.

"No." Corinne shook her head and cleared her throat. "I just love flowers and trees. Well, most nature, really."

"Well, you're welcome to visit the gardens whenever you're off duty," Orana said. "They are especially lovely in spring and summer."

Corinne nodded, and Orana continued on. They returned to the southern wing and the breezeway faster than she'd expected, and dread settled within her. She'd have to face Prince Aryel again soon.

Orana knocked gently on the prince's door before entering, beckoning Corinne. She wasn't sure why she'd expected anything less ornate in the prince's chambers, but even the antechamber to his bedroom was larger than Corinne's entire room at the monastery. A deep blue upholstered couch stood beneath a long mirror mounted on the wall, and beside it was a large flower arrangement with an

CHAPTER 5

assortment of the same bright pink tulips and yellow and white daffodils that she'd seen in the gardens.

Orana strode directly into Aryel's bedchamber, and Corinne remained behind, unsure if she was meant to follow. She truly didn't *want* to follow, but Orana called for her anyway. Corinne took a deep breath and stepped inside.

A large dining table stood to the immediate right, and beyond it lay another couch and two chairs by a large fireplace. Two massive windows let in the midmorning light on either side of a balcony designed just like the breezeway outside. On the far left of the room was a bed even larger than Corinne's, covered in plush pillows and blankets that matched the dark blue couches. Orana was hefting the prince out of that bed despite his protests.

"All right, I'm up, I'm up, Orana!" he groused, clutching his head as he sat up and swung his legs over the side of the mattress.

Corinne's face heated at the sight of his naked torso, his abdomen defined and his upper arms, chest, and shoulders covered in those detailed tattoos. Moons and stars connected by delicate lines spanned his chest and shoulders, ending at interconnected crescent moons that formed a spiral around the defined muscles of his upper arms.

Corinne had tattoos herself—the Sun of Helaera on her upper back, which she and all Lightguards received during their final year of training, and geometric designs around her upper arms. Those weren't typical of a Lightguard, but she remembered her mother having them, and it was a way to carry her with her since she couldn't wear the ring.

"Oh good, you're here," Prince Aryel groaned, catching sight of Corinne. Any mild appreciation she may have had for his appearance vanished. "And so begins my personal hell."

"Your Highness, don't be rude," Orana said, tossing a dark blue shirt at him. "She is here to protect you."

"Right," Aryel muttered. He stood, then grimaced. "Fuck, my head hurts."

Corinne winced before she could stop herself, but neither he nor Orana seemed to notice. She'd have to get used to hearing such colorful language—people outside the monastery clearly didn't mind sprinkling those words into their everyday speech.

"There's a remedy already waiting for you in the library," Orana called from his washroom. A moment later, a tap began to run from within. Orana appeared in the doorway. "I assume you have enough wits about you to bathe yourself?"

"Goddess, yes, Orana," he said. "I'm hungover, not gravely injured."

"Then get to it." Orana stepped out of the way as he passed. "You'll be late for everything today."

Corinne stood awkwardly in the doorway to the antechamber, watching as Orana tidied up a few things in Aryel's room. It was surprisingly clean, given the state he'd been in last night.

To his credit, he bathed quickly and emerged from the washroom fully clothed in the deep blue shirt Orana had tossed at him and a fresh pair of black trousers tucked into boots. His dark brown hair had a bit of wave to it, the longer strands on the top falling into his face when he leaned over. His facial hair was neat, too, well-kept and as dark as the hair on his head.

"Shall we go, then?" he asked, looking at Orana instead of Corinne.

"I won't be going anywhere," Orana said. "But Corinne will accompany you starting today."

Almost reluctantly, Aryel turned his gaze to Corinne. He huffed. "Fine."

Corinne stood aside to let Aryel through, and from there, she followed him at a respectable distance. His walking speed wasn't terribly slow, she was glad to discover; he was a few inches taller than her, and his natural stride didn't make her own gait awkward. She tried to make note of the corridors they walked through and the turns they took to reach the library, but eventually she gave up and just followed the prince.

He pushed through the doors with a great shove and quickly headed for a table at the far end of the stacks, where a glass filled with some green, sludgy liquid waited. He ignored the stack of books on the table, downed the drink, and winced as he set the empty glass back on the table.

"All right," he said, putting his hands on his hips and looking around at the other empty tables. "That's enough of this place for today."

CHAPTER 5

Corinne stopped short as he turned on his heel and headed back in her direction, toward the library exit.

"Aren't you supposed to study here for an hour?" Corinne asked, following him once more.

"Perhaps," Aryel said without turning around. "But I don't want to. So, I'm not."

Corinne caught the door that he let swing back on her and hurried after him. "Isn't that part of your schedule? How will people know where you are?"

"They don't need to know where I am," Aryel said over his shoulder. "That's why you're here, isn't it? You can offer me plenty of protection."

"But I—"

"Look, spare me the sermon, Sunshine," he said, fully turning around and walking backward. *Sunshine?* "We can't all be as disciplined and righteous as you."

Corinne bit her tongue against the slew of retorts that came to mind. He wanted her to spare him her input, then so be it. Perhaps if she followed him in silence, *he* would speak less too.

Prince Aryel's next destination was one Corinne hadn't been shown by Orana. He ventured down several flights of stairs before emerging into a stone corridor with dim lanterns. She might have thought it was headed into a dungeon if not for the absolutely mouth-watering smell of baking bread that hung in the air. Aryel stepped through a swinging door at the end of the corridor, and Corinne sped up to keep him in her line of sight.

Heat and noise and busy servants met her as soon as she crossed the threshold into the kitchens, which, unlike everything else in the castle, were a reasonable size. The monastery kitchens were equally as large, responsible for feeding hundreds of Lightguards, trainees, and Attendants. Though, Corinne had to admit, the smells coming from these stovetops and ovens were richer and more enticing than anything she'd ever consumed.

Aryel snatched several pastries from a basket and piled them onto a plate alongside some bacon slices. One of the cooks turned around just in time to see him swipe a piece of toast, too, and playfully reprimanded the prince. Aryel flashed him a smile and a wink, and the cook shook his head and turned back to his work, but not before Corinne saw the blush creep across his face.

The rest of the day passed in a series of hallways, servants bowing, and waiting outside doors while Aryel was in meetings with nobles or councilors. He'd thankfully kept his snide comments about Corinne's presence to a minimum, opting instead for the occasional long-suffering sigh.

Stay the course. Be the Light. Corinne would not let this impudent man-child antagonize her into being ungrateful for this assignment. This was her duty, her chance to truly prove her loyalty and devotion to Helaera; perhaps his goddess-forsaken attitude was meant to be a test of sorts. Corinne had always excelled at tests, and this would be no different.

It was certainly a test of her physical stamina as her feet began to ache from venturing through the castle corridors, followed by prolonged periods of standing in one spot. She'd have to heal them tonight if she didn't want to be miserable tomorrow.

A few nobles passed by, two of them staring at her unabashedly and whispering to one another. Her cheeks warmed. *Just focus, Corinne.* Though she was running out of things to focus on after she'd already counted the number of sheep in a painting on the corridor wall opposite her.

"Oh, fucking hells, I forgot you were out here."

Corinne scowled at Aryel, who'd just exited the council chamber.

"Must you use that language?" she asked, the question hissing through her teeth before she could stop herself.

Aryel stopped in his tracks, turning to face her. He was close enough that she could see the mischievous twinkle in his brown eyes.

"Are you offended by swearing, Sunshine?" he asked, the glee in his voice barely suppressed.

It was too late to deny it now, but Corinne attempted anyway. She lifted her chin. "No," she said, one hand gripping the hilt of her sword.

Aryel grinned. "Good," he said. "Because I fucking *love* to swear. I wouldn't want you to have to listen to the foul shit I say on a regular basis. Can't have my hells-damned mouth corrupting your virtuous ears."

Helaera help her, how was she supposed to protect this man's life when she wanted to throttle him herself?

Corinne took a deep, steadying breath and plastered a mask of apathy onto her face. "After you, Your Highness," she said, gesturing down the hall.

He raised an eyebrow and gave her a nod of concession, but before he could walk off, the door to the council chamber opened again. A man with warm russet skin appeared, his dark gray robes nearly swallowing his slender form. At the sight of Aryel and Corinne, he nearly dropped the load of scrolls overflowing in his arms.

"Oho, Prince Aryel, is this the Lightguard the monastery sent for you?"

"Ah, yes, this is..." Aryel paused.

Had he *really* forgotten her name?

"Corinne Anastos," she said with a dip of her head.

"Lovely to meet you, Corinne," he said. "I'm Councilor Toro. I believe I speak for us all when I say it's an honor and a relief to have you here."

"The honor is mine, Councilor," she said.

He offered her a bright smile. "I look forward to continuing our conversation with Councilor Leta tomorrow," Councilor Toro said, addressing Aryel. "Good day, Prince Aryel, Corinne. May Helaera bless you."

Councilor Toro headed off toward the north side of the castle, and Corinne followed Aryel as he set off in the opposite direction. The glee from before had dissipated, his body language rigid and his fists clenched at his sides. He practically seethed with frustration, and Corinne wondered what had set it off. Perhaps he disliked Councilor Toro.

Figures. The councilor seemed perfectly respectable to Corinne.

Night had fallen by the time they returned to the breezeway and the prince's alcove. Another castle guard was waiting at the prince's door, ready to relieve Corinne of her duties.

"Well, I suppose I'll see you in the morning, Sunshine," Prince Aryel said, every word dripping with resentment.

Corinne forced a tight smile as she paused several paces from his door and bowed, every part of her raging against this show of deference and respect.

The prince snorted a laugh. "That's the worst fucking bow I've ever seen."

Corinne swallowed her annoyance. "Apologies, Your Highness, I'm not used to being in the presence of royalty."

"Clearly," Aryel said, eyeing her up and down. "Doesn't matter. I don't give a damn if you bow to me or not."

Corinne waited until he'd disappeared into his room before breathing, afraid her exhale would give away her chagrin.

She was, mercifully, allowed to sleep after the prince retired to his chambers. If anything were to go wrong in the night, she was close enough to provide aid. Corinne almost wished it were the other way around—if she guarded his room at night, she wouldn't have to follow him around and listen to him talk.

She scrubbed away the day in her private shower, which was, like everything else here, designed with peak luxury in mind. The tiles lining the walls of her washroom glittered in all sorts of colors until the steam from the hot water clouded them. There were at least a dozen bars of soap to choose from, and she went with one that smelled like lemongrass and basil, wrapping it in a cloth and breathing in deeply as the scent enveloped her. With a great sigh, she let her forehead hit the tiles, closing her eyes as the hot water washed over her head and down her body.

Tomorrow will be better.

CHAPTER 6

The next day wasn't better. Nor was the day after that. On the fourth night, Corinne had been woken to guard the prince's door while the castle guard sought Orana. He'd evidently drunk himself into a stupor again and was in need of a tonic that couldn't wait until morning. Both she and Aryel were excessively moody that next morning from poor sleep, and it was entirely his fault.

"Follow me at a greater distance today, would you?" he snapped at her as they crossed the breezeway.

Corinne halted and let him walk several steps before continuing, her blood boiling. As always, he let the door nearly slam in her face after crossing the threshold. She shoved her way through it.

"You know, it would be much easier to protect you if you didn't try to take me out with a door every time you use one," she bit out.

Aryel whipped around. "If a door can take you out, Sunshine, you're not a very good Sword of Helaera, now, are you?"

Corinne clamped her teeth together to prevent herself from saying something that would get her thrown out of the castle, but her glare said plenty. It didn't help that she'd skipped breakfast to try and sleep a little longer. Aryel held her gaze for several heartbeats and then sighed, pinching the bridge of his nose.

"Once we arrive at the throne room, I'll be in there for the next four goddess-damned hours if you'd like a reprieve," he said, turning away from her and beginning to walk again.

Some of the fire within her cooled. A break from him would be welcome, and she was itching to get some training in—she hadn't had a moment to actually use her sword since it had been given to her.

The throne room was on the third floor of the castle in the north wing, its doors nearly as large as those at the castle entrance. Two guards opened them for Aryel, and Corinne hung back, glancing quickly around the room. Two silver thrones stood at the far end of a blue-carpeted aisle, lined on either side by six guards. That must be why Corinne wasn't needed here.

Footsteps approached from behind her, and she turned just in time to face a woman and man who couldn't be anyone other than Queen Erina and King Theo. The queen's dark brown hair was intricately braided, and a silver crown sat delicately atop her head. Her deep blue gown was cut low, revealing her own celestial tattoos on her chest. The king, a tall, robust man with a full beard and crystalline-blue eyes set into a pale face, was dressed more simply in a blue tunic with silver embroidery, and a matching silver crown lay on his brow. Queen Erina was Aryel's mother through and through, with the same shade of brown eyes and the same cool undertone to their fair skin. Her eyes widened, and Corinne remembered herself and sank quickly into a kneel, bowing her head.

"Are you Corinne Anastos?" the queen asked, and Corinne looked at her. "Stand, child, please."

Corinne did, trying to ignore her sweaty palms. "I am, Your Majesty."

The queen came forward and held out both hands. Was Corinne even allowed to touch her? She couldn't very well deny a queen, so she placed her hands in Queen Erina's. She was close enough now that the tiny silver stars and sapphires in her crown were distinguishable.

"I don't know Lightguard customs," she said, squeezing Corinne's fingers. "But I'm grateful you're here. Should we pray, perhaps?"

Corinne hoped to Helaera her surprise was not painted plainly on her face.

CHAPTER 6

"I'd be honored, Your Majesty," she said, her voice sincere even if her sentiment was not.

The queen bowed her head, and Corinne followed suit, trying not to think about the eyes of the guards that were surely glued to them.

"Goddess Helaera, Mother of us all," Corinne said, fighting to keep her voice from trembling. "Guide my hand in service to the Crown, your faithful servants, and let us not fall prey to Arytalis and her wicked shadow wielders. Let the Light guide us."

She opened her eyes, and the queen did the same, squeezing her hands before dropping them.

"Well, that was something, wasn't it?" Queen Erina said, gazing at Corinne with something between amusement and fascination. "How charming."

The queen stepped past her, and the king merely gave her a curt nod before joining their son in the throne room. He'd stopped halfway down the aisle to watch the exchange. Corinne caught Prince Aryel's eye just as the doors closed, and the disdain on his face reignited her need to go hit something. It wasn't *her* fault the queen had asked her to pray in such an unexpected, abrupt manner.

Training would definitely do Corinne some good.

Breakfast first, though, her stomach loudly reminded her as she stalked off.

After braving the awkwardness of the dining hall for a late breakfast—where she ate at a table off to the side, avoiding the other servants and castle guards—Corinne found her way to the training grounds. She breathed in the midmorning air as she stepped onto the path leading to the various sparring circles. Each had a different terrain—grass, stone, dirt, or sand—and an attendant who could set up dummies or targets. The ring with grass terrain was occupied by two guards training with spears, and beyond the combat rings, several guards trained at an archery range. Prince Aryel was supposed to be here for archery lessons that afternoon, once his meeting with his parents had finished.

Corinne approached the attendant at the ring with dirt terrain, and the young man dipped his head in a quick bow.

"Hello," Corinne said, crossing her hands over the pommel of her sword. "Could you set up all targets and four dummies?"

"Sure thing, miss," he said, and hurried to do so.

This circle, like the others, was surrounded by a waist-high wooden fence, and the four targets were locked into place on hinged poles, evenly spaced apart. The entire ring was large enough to accommodate three, maybe four fighters in combat, but Corinne would be glad for the space. She needed to expend the energy.

Once everything was in place, the four dummies spaced out within the ring, Corinne entered and drew the sword at her hip. For a moment, she admired the gold pommel and crossguard, the wickedly sharp, sleek steel that had the Lightguard's Creed etched into it. These swords were only wielded by Lightguards, their impeccable craftsmanship a centuries-old secret of their blacksmiths. The balance was perfect, the black handle so comfortable beneath her fingers it was like an extension of her body.

She breathed in, then out, and summoned her light. Her arms lit up with those ancient, sacred sun markings, golden and bright even in the light of day. She sent an orb of light blasting toward the target on her right before dashing forward to deal a fatal slash to the nearest dummy's torso. Fatal, that is, if it were alive. She kept moving, taking out two more targets with her magic before somersaulting forward to cut out another dummy's legs from beneath it.

Goddess, this sword was exquisite. She found herself grinning as she kept going, twisting behind one "dead" dummy to fling her magic at another, and finally she took out the last target. With a flourish, she drove her sword through the heart of the final dummy and yanked it back out, her chest heaving.

Speaking to strangers and handling a petulant prince were not her strengths, but fighting? The rush of magic funneling through her veins, coupled with the racing of her heart? Corinne finally felt at ease. She'd hardly broken a sweat, so she brandished her sword and prepared to ask the attendant to reset the targets and dummies.

She repeated her exercise twice more, executing different strikes and pushing herself to move faster without sacrificing accuracy. She was grinning again when she drove her sword into a fallen dummy's chest, letting it bear her weight as she caught her breath.

"Goddess, that was impressive."

Corinne's head snapped up. A guard was standing at the edge of the ring, their forearms propped on the fence as they smiled at her. They had the same russet skin tone as Councilor Toro and silky black hair braided from the top of their head down their back. Their leather armor was typical of the other guards she'd seen around.

"Uh, thank you," Corinne said, standing and sheathing her sword.

"I'm Danai," they said, their face open and friendly.

"Corinne," she said.

She wasn't sure if it was expected that she move closer to Danai, and she didn't want to be rude by walking to the circle's exit, so she remained awkwardly in place.

"You're Prince Aryel's new guard, yeah?"

Corinne nodded once.

"I've seen you around the past few days," Danai said. "Do you want to get lunch? I was just heading to the dining hall."

Corinne wasn't really hungry yet, but she had no other plans until she had to retrieve Aryel from the throne room. And something about this guard's sunny demeanor reminded her of Vera. Her heart ached.

"All right," she said, and Danai smiled brightly.

Corinne headed for the sparring circle's exit and thanked the attendant before joining them.

CHAPTER 7

"So you're a Lightguard?" Danai asked as Corinne fell in step beside them.

After the continuous disappointments of the past five days, Corinne didn't feel much like a Lightguard, but she couldn't very well say that to someone she'd just met.

"I am," she said.

"You grew up in the monastery to the west?"

Corinne nodded.

"Incredible. I've only ever met one other Lightguard, and she was only in Vytanos for a few days. But I never got to see her train, and she wasn't as pretty as you are."

Corinne's face heated. Was she doomed to be permanently red in the face here? She'd known that life outside the monastery was different, but she wished Mother Creita or *someone* had warned her about it in greater detail.

Danai hardly took a breath as they walked, leading the way to the dining hall, and Corinne's head was spinning with the effort to keep up. She caught something about guard training being rigorous but surely nothing like Lightguards, and somehow by the time they stepped into the dining hall, Danai was finishing a story about how they tripped and fell into the massive garden fountain on their first day four years ago.

"Oh!" Danai said, making Corinne jump. "My friend and partner are here. Come on, I'll introduce you."

Corinne followed Danai between the long tables and their accompanying benches, full of guards and servants who were sitting down for a meal. It was always easy to tell who was on duty and who wasn't, depending on how long they lingered at their table. Danai approached the fifth table on the left, the one closest to the tall windows and the largest fireplace Corinne had ever seen. She supposed it was a welcome source of heat in the colder months, but if it had been lit now, they all would've been baking alive.

Danai sat next to a man with deep umber skin and circular spectacles adorning light brown eyes. His black hair was braided in rows along the top of his scalp and tied with a ribbon at the crown of his head. His food was half untouched, his nose buried in a book until he noticed Danai and smiled.

"You've been at the training grounds," he said, wrinkling his nose.

"I have," Danai said. They gestured to Corinne. "Please, sit. Nik, Iliana, this is Corinne."

On the bench to the left of where Danai invited Corinne to sit was another castle guard. She wore a tunic similar to what Captain Ekhana had worn the night Corinne had arrived, deep blue with the Serra family crest on the chest. A thin scar ran down the left side of her pale, freckled face from her eyebrow to her chin. She smiled softly at Corinne, her amber eyes kind, and brushed her unbound auburn hair over her shoulder.

"I'm Iliana," she said. "City guard turned castle guard."

"Nik," said the man beside Danai, setting his book down. Two kitchen servants placed plates before Corinne and Danai, piled with bread, cheese, and a bit of fruit. "I'm assistant to the head librarian."

"Nice to meet you," Corinne said.

"She's a Lightguard," Danai said, nudging Nik as they dug into their lunch.

"I can see that," Nik said, rolling his eyes. "No one else carries a sword like that."

"What was it like, training to become a Sword of Helaera?" Danai asked, inhaling another piece of cheese.

Corinne nearly cracked a smile. *Goddess, Corinne, eat the roll, don't inhale it.*

"Goddess above," Nik said, looking from Danai to Corinne. "Please ignore them, they have entirely forgotten any sense of decorum, it would seem."

"You probably fooled the poor woman into following you here," Iliana said, crossing her arms on the table after a servant took her empty plate.

Danai shrugged innocently. "I asked her if she wanted to get lunch, and she said yes."

Iliana turned to Corinne, her face apologetic. "If Danai dragged you here against your will, you can tell us."

Corinne actually smiled now, something warm and light settling in her chest. "It's fine. I haven't met many people since I've been here."

"Well, now you've met us," Danai said. "And you're welcome to join us here any time our shifts align. Same with training too."

"Thank you," Corinne said.

"Iliana, you'll want to spar with her," Danai said, pointing their fork at Corinne. "Never seen anything like it."

"Spar with a Lightguard? I'd be on my ass in two seconds."

Corinne choked a bit on the piece of cheese she'd just bitten into, and was grateful the sound passed as a laugh. She *really* had to get used to all this swearing.

"Exactly why you should train with her," Danai said sagely. "We both should, it would be a challenge."

"How have things been for you since your arrival?" Nik asked, cutting Danai off before they could continue making plans for their supposed training with Corinne. "I can't imagine it's been easy not knowing anyone here."

Corinne did not understand many things about the culture outside the monastery, but this unexpected, immediate kindness was something she didn't mind at all.

"It's been—" She wanted to answer, but how could she answer

CHAPTER 7

honestly? "An adjustment. But I'm learning my way around." And learning how insufferable the prince was.

Danai glanced around before leaning in closer and lowering their voice. "I hear Prince Aryel is a bit of a rogue."

"*Danai,*" Nik hissed, elbowing them.

"What? I've heard stories about him and some of the other young nobles. Late-night parties, no shortage of liquor, spats between lovers..."

"He was quite inebriated the first time we met," Corinne said slowly. "I have not been witness to any of the rest of...that. But it would not surprise me."

Danai snickered. "Well, may the Goddess be with you, then."

Corinne spent the better part of the next two hours with Danai, Nik, and Iliana. Nik had to leave after a while to return to work, quickly kissing Danai on the cheek before departing. Danai sighed as Nik walked away.

"Goddess, I love that man," they said, propping their cheek on their hand.

"Eugh, spare us," Iliana said, taking a sip of water from her cup.

"He's your partner?" Corinne asked.

"He is," Danai said. They blinked and refocused on Corinne. "That's right, Lightguards aren't allowed to have romantic attachments, right?"

Corinne nodded. "Our hearts belong to Helaera entirely."

"I fear I'm not strong enough for that," Danai said. "Helaera is great and all, but not being able to love Nik would break me."

"It would break the rest of us, too, because you'd never shut up about it," Iliana said, and Danai stuck their tongue out at her. She giggled, finishing her water and standing. "I've got to leave myself, get some sleep before I'm on night shift. Corinne, it was nice to meet you."

"You as well," Corinne said.

"Hey, what I said about training earlier," Danai said after Iliana walked off, their voice a little uncertain for the first time. "I would like to train with you, if you're up for it. But more importantly, I wanted you to feel welcome here. You looked awfully lonely in here the past few days."

A little piece of Corinne's Goddess-owned heart cracked open. "I... thank you, Danai."

~

Corinne fully expected Prince Aryel's mood to have gotten even fouler after spending four hours in the throne room, but when he emerged from the doors, he avoided her gaze entirely, his shoulders sagging and his face drawn. He didn't even offer her a snarky quip before setting off down the corridor.

Fine by her. Though between his contempt for his mother's prayer earlier and this defeated demeanor, Corinne couldn't help her curiosity.

They ventured to the ground floor of the castle, and for once, Corinne recognized where they were as they approached the training grounds. Perhaps she'd eventually find her way around this place more easily.

Aryel still said nothing as they stepped outside, and Corinne glanced at a group of castle guards in the ring with stone terrain. Two were sparring while two others leaned on the fence, and as the prince passed, they bowed quickly. Aryel hardly glanced at them.

Corinne frowned. Was it normal for royals to act as though their subordinates were beneath their notice and acknowledgment? Even the revered Lightguard Priestesses would offer a gracious greeting to the humblest Attendants at the monastery.

At Aryel's approach, a handful of guards at the archery range vacated the space, also bowing. Captain Ekhana strode forward, handing the prince a bow made of fine dark wood and a quiver of arrows with a respectful nod. Aryel took them wordlessly and headed for the farthest end of the range. Corinne exchanged a glance with the captain, but he merely gave her a nod before walking off, hands clasped behind his back as he faced the training rings, watching the guards.

Corinne tried to force down her disdain as she stood off to the side, watching the prince string the bow. Or rather, watching him attempt to. His fingers slipped several times, and he huffed in frustration. Corinne fought the urge to roll her eyes as she took a step forward.

"Would you like some help?" she asked, trying and failing to sound patient.

Aryel threw her a withering glare as he finally got it strung, and Corinne cursed herself for saying anything. He resented her mere presence, and her assistance would be no different.

The target in the area he'd chosen was placed quite far away, but he nocked an arrow and took aim with confidence, letting it fly after only a few moments. Corinne's eyebrows raised as it found its mark close to the center of the target.

"Don't look so surprised, Sunshine," he said, and Corinne looked back at him. "I'm not completely fucking useless."

She fought a wince. "I never said that, Your Highness."

"But you've thought it."

Corinne had no reply. She *should* deny it, but being dishonest had never been her forte.

Aryel snorted, rolling his eyes. "That's what I figured," he muttered, and pulled another arrow from his quiver.

It didn't take long for him to empty the quiver, each arrow lodged in the target with varying degrees of accuracy. His skill wasn't equal to that of a Lightguard, but she had to admit it was impressive.

Heaving a great sigh, Aryel trudged down the field toward the target to retrieve the arrows. Corinne followed.

"Goddess above, you don't have to follow me down the archery range," he snapped, turning around and coming to a halt.

Corinne stopped, her grip tight on the hilt of her sword. "Apologies, Your Highness," she said, anger and embarrassment heating her cheeks in equal measure.

He turned and began walking again, and she backed away several paces, returning to the place she'd been standing before. Resentment only grew as she watched him painstakingly wrench each arrow from the target and replace it in the quiver.

Aryel shot another round of arrows before returning the bow and quiver to Captain Ekhana. He seemed slightly less downtrodden now, at least. Not that it made a difference in how he behaved toward Corinne.

They'd nearly made it back to Aryel's chambers without uttering a single word when the prince suddenly slowed, muttering a curse Corinne barely heard. A woman was standing halfway down the breezeway, her golden hair flowing in the afternoon breeze. Half of it was pulled back in intricate braids, leaving the rest to fall down her back, ending at her petite waist. She turned, and Corinne had to master herself so she didn't gawk.

She was the kind of beautiful Corinne had only read about in books, with striking green eyes set into a delicate face. Her peachy complexion was complemented by the aquamarine dress she wore, which dipped low between her breasts and boasted a slit all the way up her right thigh. She smiled broadly at Aryel's approach.

"Aryel," she said, walking up to him and taking his upper arm. "Lovely afternoon, isn't it?"

"I'm not in the mood, Lana," Aryel said, shaking her off as he continued down the breezeway.

Lana glanced at Corinne quickly before hurrying after him. "You were certainly in the mood two weeks ago," she said, and Corinne's entire body heated. She should *not* be privy to this conversation...

Aryel turned as they entered the alcove, once again removing Lana's hand from his arm. "I told you then I was done, and I meant it. Go find Janus if you're so desperate for attention right now."

Lana stiffened. "Are you so pathetic you can't handle it if I spend time with another man?"

Fire ignited in Aryel's eyes. He looked to Corinne, who looked away, pretending as though she couldn't hear. He lowered his voice. "I told you I'm not in the mood for this," he said. "Leave. Me. Alone."

Lana scoffed. "What, are you going to have your new golden brute of a guard toss me out?"

Her derision should mean nothing to Corinne, but the word *brute* stung her in a way she did not expect. She'd never been particularly concerned with the way she looked, and for the first time in her life, the shame of inadequacy fell into her stomach like a brick.

"Perhaps I will," Aryel hissed, and Corinne's eyes flew to his face. It was still filled with that fiery displeasure. "Now get out."

With a huff, Lana swiveled, her dress flowing gracefully as she stalked back down the breezeway. She gave Corinne a scathing once-over

CHAPTER 7

before barging through the doors and slamming them behind her. Aryel heaved a sigh before turning toward his room and disappearing without another word. Corinne took up her post outside his door, furious at the threat of tears in her eyes, at the prince for his poor choices in company, at the High Priestess for sending her here, and, most of all, at herself for her own silly pride.

CHAPTER 8

The bitter ceremonial tea of the Lightguards did not taste any better in Vytanos than it did at the monastery, and in fact, it was far worse since Corinne had to steep it herself. Orana had been kind enough to send a servant up with hot water and a teapot that morning, so Corinne was at least spared the awkwardness of venturing down to the kitchens for a request she knew they'd find odd.

It was the dawn of her second week at the castle, and she wasn't sure if things had improved or if she'd simply resigned herself to misery for the rest of her life, but she didn't feel quite so hopeless. Having the occasional meal with Danai, Nik, and Iliana certainly helped, and she looked forward to training with them this week on the day Aryel had that weekly council with his parents and the nobles of Vytanos.

Wincing at the aftertaste of the lukewarm tea, Corinne finished her ritual.

"I will stay the course. I will be the Light. May Arytalis never find me. May Helaera guide me."

She blew out the two white candles she'd set up on her nightstand, which she'd dragged beneath one of her windows as a makeshift altar. A bit of sadness touched her heart; she missed the feeling of connection when participating in the weekly collective ritual, the sound of the

CHAPTER 8

Lightguards singing as one. Her room's walls were thick enough...it should be safe to sing freely in here. Corinne took a breath and closed her eyes.

Goddess of all light and life,
Lend your ear to all our strife;
Let us move both bold and brave,
To bring peace to the world

We will carry what you teach,
And our hearts will not be breached—
By our faith we'll bring your Light,
And guard the realms from falling night.

She'd always felt closest to Helaera when she sang, though she'd never admitted it aloud. Lightguards were supposed to find connection through magic and direct action on the Goddess's behalf. Prayer and song were important, but being Helaera's Sword was the epitome of devotion.

A knock startled her, and she stood too quickly, bumping her thigh on the corner of the nightstand. Her vision went white with pain—the wood had connected with an old scar, and deep shame and anguish flooded her at the reminder of its presence on her flesh. She breathed through it as a second knock sounded, corralling her thoughts before her mind unleashed a torrent of panic.

The face that greeted her in the doorway washed those thoughts away.

"Corinne!" Vera flung her arms around Corinne and squeezed her tightly, and Corinne let out a shocked laugh.

"Vera, what are you doing here?" she asked, leaning back to look at her friend. She had to make sure Vera was truly here, and she wasn't merely dreaming.

"They sent me to check in with you," Vera said, stepping past Corinne and plopping down on her bed. "Wow, Corinne. This place is incredible."

Corinne sighed. "It's not bad."

Vera pursed her lips. "I would be ecstatic if I were you."

Cold crept into Corinne's chest. She heard what Vera didn't say. *How could you be so ungrateful?*

"I'm trying, Vera," Corinne said, sitting on the bed beside her. "I really am."

Vera's face softened. "I know, Cori." Corinne held back a grimace. "Listen...I have news from others at the Boundary."

Corinne forgot her personal troubles at the urgency in Vera's voice.

Vera looked at her door. "We can't be overheard here, right?"

Corinne shook her head. "No, the walls are thick, so the guard outside shouldn't be able to hear, and the only other person nearby is the prince. He'll be fast asleep at this hour." He'd be fast asleep until at least midmorning, and it was only an hour past dawn.

Vera nodded. "We suspect there's a spy in the castle," she said. "Not a Nightrender, because we would have sensed that at the Boundary, but someone who works for them."

Corinne's blood ran cold. "Am I meant to uncover their identity?"

"No," Vera said firmly. "But Mother Creita wanted me to tell you and ask you to report the prince's movements and anything else you might notice to me on a biweekly basis. With you on the inside and the rest of us keeping watch from the outside, we should be able to keep him safe."

"Can you not station additional Lightguards within the castle?" Corinne asked, a bit of hope sparking in her heart. "Does someone need to guard the king and queen too?"

Vera shook her head. "It would call far too much attention to him, and to us." Vera stood and walked over to one of Corinne's windows, gazing out at the city below. "The last thing we need is to push them into accelerating their plan before we can uncover it."

Corinne didn't like it, but she understood. She'd just have to be extra vigilant. Goddess, she was so self-absorbed she might have missed something suspicious this past week. And though more Lightguards wouldn't be joining her here, at least she'd see Vera every two weeks.

"I'm sorry I can't stay longer," Vera said, turning back to Corinne. "But I have to go by the monastery before I return to my post at the Boundary."

CHAPTER 8

"I understand." Corinne stood and wrapped Vera in another embrace.

"Have you made any friends here, Corinne?"

Danai's smiling face appeared in her mind, and Corinne gave a soft shrug. "Some acquaintances, I suppose."

Vera nodded solemnly. "Good, you don't want to become too close with those who aren't virtuous. But I don't want you to be alone all the time either."

After a final embrace, Vera took her leave, and Corinne went to look out the window herself. Shame overtook her fully now. She'd been gone from the monastery for a week, and she'd already let her steadfastness and commitment flounder. What kind of devotee to Helaera was she? She *should* be ecstatic at her accommodations, at the honor of her post, and she should hold Danai, Nik, and Iliana at arm's length.

Icy fear shot through her center. What if one of *them* was the spy? They'd all seemed friendly and kind, but she didn't truly know any of them.

Corinne watched the city come alive as the sun continued to rise, steeling her mind and heart. She'd keep a wary eye on her three new acquaintances. She would recommit herself to her task and do it well, and Prince Aryel could despise her all he wanted.

He had archery training again later that day. Though he was a decent shot, a bow was near useless against a close-quarters attacker. Perhaps it would be wise for him to learn basic self-defense if there really was a spy in the castle. She fastened her sword belt around her waist and adjusted her tunic in the mirror, resolving to mention it to him later.

Corinne forced her face into stony apathy as she approached the dining hall for breakfast, but Danai, Nik, and Iliana were not inside. Even if she knew it was best to keep some distance from them, it was a small relief that she wouldn't have to be cold to them this morning. Training would be fine—it was far easier to avoid talking and contain emotions when the task was physical and formulaic.

She ate her breakfast quickly and hurried back upstairs to relieve the guard on duty outside Aryel's rooms. Orana would arrive soon to wake him with a tonic again, surely.

But Aryel's door opened before Orana appeared, and the prince stepped into the alcove, fully dressed and, by the scent of pine and mint as he walked past, freshly bathed.

"Morning," he said, voice low, and Corinne blinked.

"Morning, Your Highness," she said.

As they made their way to the library, Corinne braced herself. Perhaps this meant he was good-humored enough that he'd be amenable to her suggestion.

"Your Highness," she said just before he reached for the library door.

He paused, raising an eyebrow.

Corinne hesitated for a moment before taking several steps closer to him. "I know you have some skill with a bow, but I wondered if you'd consider training in hand-to-hand combat."

His brow lifted higher. "And why would I do that?"

Corinne's resolve faltered, but she pressed on. *This is your duty.* "With a cryptic threat to your life, I'd assume an attack would be stealth-based, which means close quarters. It would be prudent for you to at least have a basic knowledge of self-defense."

Those brown eyes scrutinized her in a way that made her feel painfully perceived.

"And who would teach me such things?"

Corinne mustered every ounce of confidence she had. "I would."

Aryel stared at her for another long moment, then smirked. "All right, Sunshine. This afternoon, instead of my archery practice, you can show me how to duck a punch."

Corinne nearly sagged with relief. She fought a self-satisfied smile as she nodded, and the prince stepped into the library. She ran through what she'd start with later as she waited in the hallway.

"Oh, hi, Corinne."

She hadn't heard Nik approach, but he stopped right in front of her, a pile of books in his arms.

"Hi, Nik," she said stiffly.

"Is Prince Aryel in the library?"

"He is."

"Ah. Probably speaking with Danai's father, then."

CHAPTER 8

The resemblance between Danai and Councilor Toro suddenly clicked. "Danai is Councilor Toro's child?"

Nik nodded. "Lovely man. Danai's mother, Selana, is lovely too, they have us over for dinner once a week. Her cooking is divine. I'm sure they'd be delighted if you joined us sometime."

"Oh," Corinne said. "I...I wouldn't want to intrude—"

Nik laughed. "There is no intruding in the Mykotas family. Just consider it an open invitation."

Corinne smiled despite herself. "All right." For the first time, she glanced at the pile of books in his hands. Her eyes widened. "Is that *The Songbird and the Raven*?"

Nik's eyes lit up. "It is! One of my favorites."

"Mine too," Corinne said. "How did you interpret the ending?"

An hour later, Corinne and Nik were still talking and laughing, his stack of books placed on a nearby table with an ornate vase. The door opening startled them both, and Prince Aryel appeared.

"Your Highness," Nik said, bowing.

Aryel looked between him and Corinne. "Hello, Nik," he said. "I was just on my way to see your father."

"Ah, archery today?"

"Actually, I'll be learning some hand-to-hand combat basics from Sunshine over here," he said, pointing a thumb at Corinne. "I'm headed to tell him he's got the afternoon off."

Confusion crossed Nik's face, which he failed spectacularly at hiding. "I see. Well, I hope it goes well."

"I have no doubt," Aryel said, shockingly chipper.

Perhaps Councilor Toro had put him in a good mood.

Corinne bid Nik farewell, a bit of guilt nagging at the back of her mind as she and Aryel set off. *You don't want to become too close with those who aren't virtuous.* She'd lowered her guard around him again.

They arrived at the training grounds in no time, the walk not far from the library. Aryel had Corinne wait for him by the ring with grass terrain while he approached the archery enclosure to speak with Captain Ekhana. Another connection clicked in Corinne's mind; Nik was Captain Ekhana's son. A bit of relief settled within her; surely the son of the man responsible for the royal family's safety wouldn't be a Nightrender sympathizer. Unless the Captain himself was, and that made little sense. Ekhana would have had numerous chances to kill the prince himself before Corinne ever arrived.

"All right," Aryel said, clapping his hands together as he returned to Corinne. "Lead the way."

Corinne didn't entirely trust this enthusiasm of his, but she wasn't going to question it. She removed her sword, and he flinched back.

"I thought you said we were doing hand-to-hand," he said.

Corinne couldn't suppress a small laugh. "We are, I'm just taking this off."

Aryel's body relaxed, and Corinne removed her sword belt, handing it to the attendant nearby. She felt almost naked without it, but she couldn't very well risk smacking the prince with a rogue sword at her hip. She led him to the center of the grassy ring, only realizing when she turned that he'd removed his tunic, leaving just a thin white undershirt covering his upper body. Those tattoos of his stood out beneath the fabric in the afternoon sun. He'd rolled up his sleeves, too, stopping just below his elbows, and Corinne's mouth went dry. He certainly had the arms of a trained archer.

She kicked herself mentally. *Focus, Corinne.*

"All right," she said, clearing her throat. "First, I can teach you the most effective dodging techniques for when you see your attacker coming, and then we can go through how to break a hold."

Aryel nodded, his face serious, and Corinne walked him through how she was going to attack him and how to avoid her.

"Ready?" she asked.

"Ready."

She lunged for him, and he executed the move perfectly. Corinne turned to him, impressed.

"That was...well done," she said. "All right, next one."

Again, on the first try, Aryel dodged Corinne with ease, as if his steps were practiced. The third time he did it, he was grinning from ear to ear. His cheerful willingness to go along with her suddenly made perfect sense as he dissolved into a fit of laughter.

He already knew the basics of hand-to-hand combat, and he wanted to make a fool of Corinne. Ire ignited in the pit of her stomach, blazing up her spine. She was doing this to *help* him, and he was making fun of her.

Fine. If he was so confident, she would make this lesson more of a challenge.

Moving twice as fast as before, Corinne dove at him, cutting off his laughter as she tackled him to the ground. In a blink, he was pinned beneath her, his left arm shoved into his side by her knee and the right forced to the grass with her fingers around his wrist. He blinked at her, their faces inches away.

"Well," he said slowly, grunting as he tried and failed to break her hold. "I must say I've never been in this position with this much clothing on."

Corinne leapt off him with a growl, certain her face was violently red yet again. She stalked away several feet. "*How* is it possible for you to be so insufferable?"

She regretted the words immediately, cursing her own mouth for her lack of self-control, but Aryel sat up and burst out laughing.

"You know, you're far better company when you're less polished and stoic, Sunshine," he said, getting to his feet and brushing the grass off his trousers.

Corinne crossed her arms and glared at him. "Can you tell me what you *don't* know so this lesson is actually helpful?" she asked.

Aryel studied her for a moment. "Well, clearly I don't know how to get out of that hold you just put me in, so why don't we start there?"

Corinne narrowed her eyes. "No more jokes about nudity."

The prince pressed his mouth into a thin line, fighting a smile as he lifted both hands in surrender. "On my honor."

PRINCE ARYEL CAUGHT HIS BREATH ON THE GRASSY TERRAIN nearly an hour later, one hand resting on his sternum.

"I think that's enough for today," he said.

Corinne couldn't help her smug satisfaction as he struggled to sit up. He planted his palms on the ground to lift himself, but then hissed in pain. A splintered piece of wood, hidden in the grass, had cut into his palm.

"My sincerest apologies, Your Highness," the attendant said, rushing over with Corinne's sword and belt still in hand. "The terrain is supposed to be thoroughly inspected, I—"

"It's fine," Aryel said, waving the boy off even as he winced. "I'll just go to the infirmary."

"I can heal it," Corinne said.

Both Aryel and the attendant stared at her. It wasn't uncommon for Lightguards to heal their own minor injuries during training, and Corinne had healed kitchen burns for monastery Attendants and even once helped when a younger trainee broke their leg. But these two had likely never seen healing magic.

"I-if you don't mind," she added quickly.

Aryel looked to the boy holding Corinne's sword and then back to her. "It's not going to hurt, is it?"

Corinne almost snorted. "No."

Aryel held her gaze for another moment before nodding and holding out his hand. Taking it softly, Corinne knelt beside him on the grass.

The part of her magic that healed was gentler than the part used for combat, and she cleared her mind to call upon it, coaxing it into her fingers. Her hands and forearms lit up with her markings, and Aryel's eyes nearly popped out of his head. She pushed the light into his hand, and in moments, the cut sealed itself, his palm good as new.

"Goddess," he breathed as Corinne's healing light faded.

She'd been so focused on his healing that she only just noticed the smooth skin of his hand in hers, the veins that ran from his wrist up his toned forearm. Her pulse jumped, and she released him quickly.

"There," she said. "Hopefully there will be no unexpected wood next time."

Aryel swallowed hard, meeting Corinne's eyes with a pained look. It took her a moment to realize he was holding back laughter again.

"Hopefully not," he said, his voice trembling with the effort.

Did she have something on her face? She hadn't said anything particularly funny...and if she had, she didn't want to know.

CHAPTER 8

She stood, offering her hand to help him up. "Come on," she said. "You've got a formal dinner tonight, and I'm sure you'll want to clean up first."

Aryel grimaced as he took her hand and got to his feet. "Thanks for the reminder."

His tone suggested he was anything but thankful, and Corinne resisted the urge to sigh. She couldn't win with him.

But, she reminded herself as they trekked back to his rooms, she could keep him alive. That was all that mattered.

CHAPTER 9

Flames surrounded Corinne, unbearable heat licking at her skin, up her arms, smoke burning her throat.

"*Corinne!*"

Mother. Her mother was screaming for her, calling from the next room. She couldn't move—she was trapped here, on the floor of her room in the little house, a fallen beam trapping her legs beneath its weight. Her fledgling magic was enough to keep her alive, and she tried not to inhale the smoke, but she wasn't strong enough to lift the charred wood.

"*Corinne!*"

"*Mother!*" she tried to call, but her voice wouldn't work either. She couldn't speak, could hardly see. A great crack echoed around the room, and the ceiling began to collapse—

Corinne shot upright in bed, gasping for air, covered in sweat. She was still burning, her magic lighting up not just her hands and arms but her chest and neck too. She stumbled out of bed and managed to get to her washroom, fumbling for the tap on the shower and turning it to the coldest setting. The frigid water shocked her back to reality, and she forced herself to breathe slowly, until the gasps waned and she could pull her magic back under her control. She curled up on the floor of the shower as she trembled, waiting for the horrible images of her nightmare to fade. A ragged sob fell from her lips. It hadn't been that vivid, that visceral in several years.

It had been two decent days in a row with Prince Aryel; minimal snipes on his part and several breaks where she'd been able to return to the library and speak to Nik about books they'd both read. As nonchalantly as she'd been able, she'd also borrowed a tome outlining the names of all the nobles in Ashera, perusing the family information to search for any potential indicator that one might be connected to the Nightrenders. Today, she was supposed to train with Danai and Iliana.

So why now? Why had her mind betrayed her like this? She'd done her duty, sought out information that could help her keep her charge safe, and she'd continue to keep Vera's warning in mind and keep her eye on the path.

It always felt like the panic, the grief, the terror would never cease, but eventually it did, and Corinne started running warmer water so she'd stop shivering violently. The tremors eventually abated as she stood there, still in a nightgown that was now plastered to her skin. She crossed her arms over her chest, her hands gripping her upper arms right over her tattoos.

Stay the course. Be the Light. Helaera help me. Be the Light.

That wasn't the right prayer, the right order. Corinne gritted her teeth and started over.

Stay the course. Be the Light. Stay the course. Be the Light. Three more times with the right inflection in her head this time, the right order.

Her heart slowed to a normal speed, and she turned off the shower before groping in the dark for a towel. She peeled off the soaked nightgown and squeezed the excess water out before hanging it on the rack by the towel. All she wanted to do was crawl back into bed, but the mundanity of the tasks anchored her further in the calm of reality. She looked outside one of her windows as she exited the washroom. Dawn hadn't broken yet, the sky still a deep indigo littered with stars. She let out a shaky breath. She should try to sleep more.

Without bothering to put anything on, she climbed into bed again, nestling in the blankets. She tried to focus on good things over the past few days: Danai approaching her and introducing her to Nik and

Iliana, Vera's surprise visit, Nik's excitement when he spoke in detail about a book he thoroughly enjoyed, Aryel's laughter at her outburst—

Corinne's eyes flew open. Where did *that* come from? She must truly be sleep-deprived if anything about the prince was a comfort to her.

Though, she had to admit, sometimes things that seemed negative in the light of day provided some solace when her mind drifted to such dark places.

Corinne let her eyes droop shut again and allowed her mind to wander where it would in those lighter moments, eventually finding sleep again.

~

Corinne's body ached as though she'd gotten into a brawl the day before. With a groan, she hauled herself out of bed and made her way into the washroom to assess the mess that was surely her hair. Half her curls were misshapen and flattened. Helaera help her, she looked like she'd been plucked out of the fifth realm of hell.

First things first. She summoned her healing light and let it spread throughout her body, easing her exhausted, stiff muscles. She peeked out of the washroom and checked the time quickly—she still had a few minutes to try and tame her hair, so she ran it beneath the shower and quickly applied the concoction she'd brought with her from the monastery. It usually held things in place nicely, and she prayed this rushed version of her routine was enough to make her presentable.

Her hair was still damp when she finished, but it would have to do. She dressed quickly, opting for a sleeveless tunic. She couldn't bear the idea of getting overheated again, especially while training with Iliana and Danai later, and the morning sun blazing on the rooftops of Vytanos promised a warm day.

When Aryel emerged from his rooms, he started past her with purpose, but stopped short when he caught sight of her.

"I didn't expect you to have tattoos," he said, nodding to her upper arms.

"All Lightguards have tattoos," Corinne said. Not *these* tattoos, but he didn't need to know that.

With a shrug, he carried on, and Corinne fell into the familiar rhythm of trailing after him. He slowed at the doors this time, not allowing them to fall back on her, and Corinne took it as a step in the right direction.

Despite Vera's warning to keep her distance from Danai and the others, and despite her increased trepidation about their trustworthiness, Corinne was looking forward to their training session that morning. A long reprieve from following Prince Aryel like a shadow and a chance to spend time doing something she enjoyed would be most welcome after her horrific night.

Corinne was ready to bolt the moment the doors to the throne room closed behind Aryel, but before she could, a voice called from within.

"Wait a moment," Queen Erina ordered, and Aryel paused, following her gaze to Corinne. "Have the Lightguard join us. I wish to speak with her."

Corinne's heart sank. She was no stranger to frequent prayer, but she desperately hoped the queen wouldn't subject her to that public display again. Prayer, like song, was intimate for Corinne; it felt strange to engage in it with someone outside the monastery.

"Well, come here, girl," King Theo barked, and Corinne flinched.

Queen Erina placed a hand on her husband's arm and stood from her throne, walking down the dais and past her son. Aryel had stiffened, his fists clenched at his sides. Corinne forced her feet to move and tried not to wince when the doors shut behind her with a resounding *thud*.

Queen Erina approached her with a warm smile, her midnight blue dress billowing gracefully with each step along the carpeted floor. Corinne didn't know whether the guards on either side were staring at her, but it certainly felt that way.

"Come, Corinne," she said kindly, holding out her hand.

Corinne took it and followed the queen back toward the thrones, dropping into a kneel once she reached the base of the dais. Aryel said nothing, standing in stony silence to her right.

"My dear, we hoped you might share any news from the

monastery," Queen Erina said, taking a seat upon her throne once more. "Have they made any progress in identifying and apprehending the party behind the threat to our son's life?"

Corinne wasn't sure she was qualified or authorized to speak on behalf of the Lightguards, but the queen was asking her a direct question, and she couldn't simply lie to her.

"All we know is that whoever delivered the message is working with Nightrenders," Corinne said, fighting against a tremor in her voice. "And...they suspect a spy may be within the castle walls."

The queen nodded solemnly. "We would not be surprised if that's the case. We'll begin a thorough re-vetting process for all in the castle's employ. You see, Aryel? You must be careful and stay vigilant. No more of your late-night excursions, and I *mean* it this time."

The tension exuding from the prince was nearly palpable. "Yes, Mother."

Something about the queen reminded Corinne of Mother Creita. Queen Erina had a gentle, motherly spirit, but there was a certain sternness to her that made Corinne feel small.

"Thank you, Corinne," Queen Erina said. "You may go."

Corinne stood, offered another quick bow, and forced herself not to sprint for the doors. Her heart hammered in her chest as she made her way to the training grounds. She'd have to ask Vera on her next visit how much information was appropriate to share on behalf of the Lightguards. She'd assumed Vera or someone else from the monastery was keeping the queen and king informed, but perhaps not.

Outside, Danai and Iliana were waiting for Corinne at the edge of the ring with dirt terrain, leaning on the railing of the wooden fence. Danai's face lit up at Corinne's approach.

"Corinne!" they said, straightening, but their smile faded to befuddlement as she drew nearer. "What's wrong?"

Come on, Corinne. Once again, her emotions were plastered on her face like she'd stepped into a room and bellowed exactly what she was feeling. *Control.*

"Nothing," Corinne said, shaking her head and forcing a small smile. "I had to speak to the queen, is all."

Danai's eyes widened, and Iliana let out a low whistle.

CHAPTER 9

"I'd have shit my pants," Iliana said, and a laugh burst from Corinne's mouth.

"I think I'd be less terrified to face Helaera herself," Danai said. "Although I suppose Prince Aryel isn't much better. He hardly ever speaks to anyone who isn't a noble."

"He spoke to Nik several days ago," Corinne said with a shrug, and Danai's mouth popped open.

"I can't believe him. Why wouldn't he tell me the prince spoke to him?"

"Probably because he knows you'd interrogate him and try to find out all of Prince Aryel's dirty secrets," Iliana said.

"Well of course I would. I live for gossip."

"And Nik respects the privacy of others."

Danai sighed and crossed their arms. "He does. The noble bastard."

Corinne took a deep breath—*they're just words, Corinne. Don't be a child.*

"Are you not a noble, Danai?" Corinne asked.

"My father is officially noble by merit and station," Danai said. "So my family holds certain prestige and privileges, but we're not included in the social gatherings of nobles by birth."

"That feels unfair," Corinne said carefully, gauging Danai's reaction.

"Lucky, more like," Danai said lightly. "I much prefer the company of guards or scholars to highborn nobles. And it's nice to have no obligation to show up to their parties."

"Agreed," Iliana said.

"The queen also mentioned a re-vetting process for all employed within the castle, given the recent threats," Corinne said, feigning indifference.

Danai and Iliana exchanged a look, and Iliana let out a long-suffering sigh.

"Well then, we can expect the barracks to be overturned by the time we get back," she said. "And I'm sure they'll interrogate us all again."

"Again?" Corinne asked.

"We're all thoroughly questioned prior to becoming guards," Danai said. "It's an intense process."

"Do you think it's possible a guard or servant could be a spy?" Corinne prompted.

"I suppose," Danai said, frowning. "Goddess. I hope that's not the case."

"If a guard or servant is a spy, then they're a fool," Iliana said. "We stay busy and we're paid well. Not much to complain about."

"You underestimate us, Iliana," Danai said solemnly. "We can always find something to complain about."

Iliana laughed. "That we can. Like wasting good sparring time. Corinne, what are you comfortable with showing us today?"

Right. The reason she was here. Her mind settled again as she fell into the familiar pattern of preparing to train.

"Why don't we start with a basic spar so I can get an idea of your fighting styles?"

The two guards agreed, Danai eager as ever. Corinne beckoned Danai into the ring first. Their weapon of choice was a longsword like Corinne's.

Danai held their own against Corinne, but was not as quick. Corinne was glad to find she didn't need to hold back much with them, her skill pushing them to their limits, and Danai's defensive maneuvers clean enough to give her a challenge. Corinne executed a final twisting strike that ended with her sword at their throat, and Danai held up their hands in surrender, breathing hard, wisps of hair falling from their braid. Clapping sounded from outside the ring, and both Iliana and Captain Ekhana waited there.

"Well done, Danai," Ekhana said. "You did better than I thought you would."

Corinne lowered her sword as Danai laughed. "Such confidence in me, Captain. I thought you were glad to finally have a son who enjoyed a fight."

Captain Ekhana chuckled. "Keep practicing with *her*, Danai, and then I'll be impressed."

He walked off, and Corinne looked to Danai again, puzzled. "I thought Nik was his son?"

"He is, and he is a scholar through and through," Danai said. "Nik and I have been together for four years now, and I'm Ekhana's honorary...well, sometimes a son, sometimes a daughter. Depends on the day. Usually I am both."

Corinne understood, then. There were a few monastery Acolytes who identified as such, blessed by Helaera. In another life, she and Danai may have known one another in that way.

"All right, my turn," Iliana said, leaping over the fence and approaching Corinne and Danai.

She was several inches shorter than Corinne but no less muscular, and she whipped out a pair of thin, slightly curved swords like she'd been born holding them. Corinne had already begun mentally adjusting her technique, and as Danai jogged to the edge of the circle, she sank into her starting stance.

Iliana was slower than Danai, but the brute strength behind her blows made Corinne's arms vibrate as she caught them on her blade. Corinne didn't need to hold back with her, either, and even grinned as they fought. An exhilarated laugh left her throat when Iliana nearly cut through her defenses, forcing her to employ a different strategy to overpower her. Using the weight of one of Iliana's blows against her, she darted out of the way and lunged, sending her to the ground, disarmed.

Corinne held out a hand for her, but Iliana lifted a finger, closing her eyes as she caught her breath.

"Nice work, Iliana!" Danai called. "You lasted longer than I did!"

It wasn't right to be so prideful about her skill in fighting, but Corinne wanted to bask in this feeling, in the enthusiastic affirmation of who she was.

She spent the next two hours offering suggestions to Danai and Iliana, and asking them to break down their own techniques so she could learn from them too. Danai had executed a defensive move she'd never seen before, and Iliana's footwork was impeccable. Even if one of them was somehow the spy, Corinne didn't see the harm in learning how to fight them, in gaining their trust.

Though, she desperately hoped neither of them was trying to deceive her.

"By the way," Danai said as the three of them headed inside, bound for the dining hall. "Your tattoos are beautiful. What village are they from?"

Corinne lifted a hand to one of them, her brow furrowing. "Cara Talle."

"In the forests to the north?" Danai asked, eyes sparkling.

Corinne nodded. "My mother was from there."

"What about your father?"

"Danai," Iliana hissed. "Leave her alone."

"Sorry! I'm just curious."

Corinne was glad for Iliana's admonishment, even if she didn't necessarily blame Danai for their curiosity. She would not, could not speak of her father. The mystery of why he'd kept her from the Lightguards as a child had caused her more turmoil than she'd ever wanted to endure. As if to remind her, the scar on her leg throbbed.

"Are things a little better this week?" Danai asked instead as they entered the dining hall. The smell of roasted potatoes made Corinne's mouth water. "Easier to get around the castle and all?"

"Yes, actually," Corinne said. She didn't consider her episode last night to be "better," but she'd at least found a routine here now.

After eating quickly, Corinne decided to clean up before retrieving Prince Aryel. She'd sweated quite a bit during training, and her trousers had sustained a few encounters with the dirt of the sparring circle. She ought to stick with the grassy terrain on days she might run into the king and queen.

Corinne showered and put on an identical sleeveless tunic, but this time with ochre trousers. A folded pile of freshly laundered clothing had been left on her bed in her absence, all the garments she'd worn last week. It was terribly strange to have such tasks done for her, but she hadn't had the time here anyway. She hastily put them away in a chest at the foot of her bed.

Halfway across the breezeway outside, Corinne ran into Orana.

"Prince Aryel sent me," she said. "His meeting with his parents ended early, so he had a guard escort him to the music hall. You can find him there."

"Oh, I'm sorry, I should have—"

"Calm yourself, Corinne," Orana said with a kind smile. "You aren't expected to know when the prince strays from his schedule if you aren't with him."

CHAPTER 9

Corinne nodded. She was right; that would be absurd. She thanked Orana and set off for the music hall, which was up three flights of stairs but mercifully still in the south wing of the castle.

At the fifth floor landing, Corinne's hurried steps faltered. A light, sweet melody was drifting from an open door at the end of the short hallway, and a castle guard stood outside it without a flicker of emotion. Corinne returned to her previous speed and quietly relieved the guard, who nodded once at her before departing. At this angle, Corinne could only see part of the music hall, but the ceiling was high, and sunlight streamed in from what she assumed were equally tall windows.

The piano music cascaded into a deeper, richer timbre, the melody turning more mournful than sweet, but still breathtakingly beautiful. When it rose again, building to a grand cadence, Corinne thought her heart might leap from her chest. Only after the song ended with three soft, repeated chords did she realize a rogue tear had escaped down her left cheek.

It had sounded like a lullaby and an aching plea all at once.

The music ceased altogether, and the sound of approaching footsteps made Corinne hastily wipe at her eyes. Aryel appeared in the doorway a moment later.

"Oh, it's you," he said, those brown eyes widening.

Corinne blinked rapidly as she cleared her throat, hoping he couldn't tell she'd been crying. He stared at her for a moment, a bit of color creeping into his cheeks. Was he embarrassed that she'd heard him?

"I relieved the guard who'd come with you," she said quickly.

He glanced down the hall, then back at her. "Yes, I see that," he said. Another beat of silence. "I'm going to stay here for a bit longer."

Corinne nodded once, and Aryel returned to the music hall, shutting the door this time. She could still easily hear his playing, and wished she weren't on duty so she could simply close her eyes and let the music wash over her. Prince Aryel was still a spoiled prince with a foul attitude, but there was no denying his playing was lovely. Orana had said he had lessons each week, but judging by the artistry in his musicianship, he'd been studying the instrument for many years now.

Not that Corinne was an expert in music, but she'd always appreciated it at the monastery. Studying music herself had never been an option, and her heart had been set on becoming a warrior since she was ten years old anyway.

Her mind wandered along with the music, losing track of time, and when it cut off after another softer piece, Corinne forced herself to refocus. Aryel emerged moments later and set off down the hallway without a word. It wasn't until he turned a corner that she noticed the bruising on the back of his left arm.

"Is that from training?" she asked. Aryel stopped mid-stride, brow furrowing in confusion when he turned to her. "Your arm. I'm sorry, I could've healed that too—"

Corinne cut off at the look of panic in his eyes as he twisted his arm to look at the bruises. He quickly rolled his sleeve down.

"It's fine," he said.

"I could still heal it if you want—"

"I said it's *fine*," he snapped, and Corinne nearly flinched. "Don't worry about it."

Seething, Corinne traipsed after him as he stalked off. *Helaera give me strength.* If he didn't want her help, she'd just stop offering it.

CHAPTER 10

"Iliana won't be here today."

Corinne frowned as she and Danai prepared to spar again two days after their first session, this time entering the ring with grassy terrain.

"Is she all right?" Corinne asked. For the first time since she'd met Danai, they looked troubled.

"The last couple of days have been challenging for her at home," they said. "It's...well, it's not my place to share, but some days she keeps more to herself, and I try to give her space."

Corinne, of all people, could understand that. Her empathy warred with the remaining fragment of distrust she'd harbored since Vera's visit.

"I hope things get better for her soon," she said, and she meant it.

"Me too," Danai said. "All right. What are we covering today?"

Corinne didn't want to admit it, but training with Danai was pure fun. When had she last uttered that word, or considered it worth her time? They spent half the session laughing and exchanging quips, and when Corinne accidentally nicked Danai's upper arm with her sword, she healed it quickly, trying to ignore Danai's flabbergasted expression the whole time.

"You can channel your magic into that sword, right?" Danai asked, hopping off the edge of the fence after Corinne had successfully mended their arm. She nodded, and Danai's eyes sparkled. "Can you show me?"

Corinne knew Danai wouldn't have asked if Iliana had been present to chastise them, and it made it all the more endearing. With a smirk, she took a step back and held her sword at her center, blade facing the heavens. Her magic flashed along her arms with Helaera's blessing, lighting up the blade in brilliant golden light. Corinne swung it out to the side, taking off a dummy's head in an instant, leaving behind only charred edges of straw. In a breath, her magic receded, and Danai stared at her with wonder in their eyes.

"Incredible," they said, arms crossed as they shook their head. Corinne sheathed her sword as she fought a smile. "If I'd seen things like that growing up, I might be more inclined to visit the sanctuary every week."

"Is there a sanctuary in the castle?" Corinne asked, brow furrowing.

Only a Priestess or designated Lightguard could lead a service of worship, and she was the first Lightguard to reside in the castle in living memory, as far as she knew.

Danai nodded as they vacated the training grounds, heading inside for lunch. "It's usually empty, but it's on the fourth floor in the east wing. Iliana goes there sometimes. Nik, too, to light a candle for his mother."

Corinne's heart sank. "Nik's mother has crossed the horizon of the Goddess?"

"That's a very beautiful way of describing death," Danai said with a sad smile. "But yes, she died when Nik was sixteen, about thirteen years ago now. An illness took her."

"I'm very sorry to hear that," Corinne said. She was quiet for a moment as they walked. "I...was a Lightguard unable to heal her?"

"They weren't able to get to Vytanos in time," Danai said. "It took her swiftly and suddenly."

"That's terrible."

Danai nodded. "And Lightguards, I hear many of you are orphans?"

Corinne kept her face impassive. "Many, yes. Myself included." Before Danai could offer condolences or ask questions, Corinne gave them a bracing smile. "Most come to the monastery as very young children. They are my family."

"Leaving them had to be difficult for you."

As they arrived at the dining hall, Danai's eyes were full of understanding when Corinne looked at them.

"They are always with me," Corinne said, forcing her smile to stay in place as she opened the doors. "As the Goddess is."

"Say that again!"

Corinne and Danai froze the moment they entered the dining hall. Four tables down, two guards stood almost nose to nose, one of whom was Iliana. She grabbed the front of the other guard's tunic, a man who was a head taller than she was, her face incensed. He shoved her away, sneering.

"I said *mud-dwelling beggars*," he spat, and Iliana lunged at him.

The room erupted, servants scattering, some guards watching with interest, a few cheering. Danai raced forward, and Corinne followed, pushing around bodies to reach Iliana and the guard she'd tackled.

They were on the floor between two tables, Iliana straddling the other guard and delivering a heavy punch to his face. Danai shoved several onlookers out of their way and dove for Iliana, hauling her off the man. Corinne jumped in to restrain the guard as he shot to his feet and made to attack Iliana. She grabbed his upper arms and immediately received an elbow to the ribs, dislodging her hold on him. Stars burst in her vision. Her shock turned to anger in an instant, and her magic surged within, easing her pain.

Just before the guard reached Iliana and Danai, Corinne grabbed hold of his arm, yanking him back. He started to throw a punch at her, but Corinne dodged and used his momentum to send him to the ground, his arm pinned behind his back.

"You won't like how this ends if you try to attack me again," Corinne hissed in his ear.

The guard squirmed for a moment, rage blazing in his eyes as blood ran heavily from his now-broken nose. Iliana spit on the ground at his feet, still held firm by Danai but no longer struggling to break their hold.

"Fuck you, Antin," Iliana growled.

"ENOUGH!"

Corinne's head snapped up at the furious bellow. Captain Ekhana appeared at the end of the tables, disapproval painted across his face.

"Antin, Calais, you're both working double time for a week starting today," Captain Ekhana said.

"Captain, he insulted my family—"

"I don't care if he cursed your entire bloodline to the fifth gate of hell, Calais," Captain Ekhana said, turning to Iliana and Danai. "Brawling in the dining hall? You disgrace yourselves."

Iliana held her tongue, but Corinne could tell she wanted to argue.

"And as for you, Antin," the captain said. Corinne released him, her markings disappearing as she reined her magic in. He lifted himself from the floor, wiping blood from his nose onto his sleeve as he scowled at Captain Ekhana. "Insult a fellow guard's family again and I'll send you packing back to your rich aunt in the city."

A murmur rumbled through the crowd around them.

Captain Ekhana turned to leave. "As you were!" he barked to the room at large, and guards and servants who hadn't finished eating returned to their places at the tables, while others quickly vacated the room.

Corinne waited until Antin stalked off with two other guards before turning back to Danai and Iliana. They spoke low to one another, Danai patting Iliana's shoulder as Corinne approached, trying to ignore the stares of those surrounding her.

Iliana gave her a sheepish smile. "Thanks, Corinne," she said. "Are you hurt?"

Corinne shook her head. "I'm fine. You?"

Iliana grimaced. "My hand hurts like hell, but I suppose I deserve that."

"I can fix that," Corinne said. She glanced around at all the eyes still on the three of them. "Preferably not here, though."

"Come on," Danai said, beckoning to them.

Danai led Corinne and Iliana out of the dining hall and down a quick series of short hallways Corinne didn't recognize. They stopped at an innocuous wooden door, glancing around before opening it and gesturing for Corinne and Iliana to enter. It was a small storage room,

CHAPTER 10

shelves stacked high with cleaning supplies and a few gardening tools. An empty table stood below the only window in the room. Danai hoisted themself onto it and patted the empty space on their right for Iliana. She joined them with a sigh.

"How did you know about this place?" she asked, lifting her hand as Corinne held out her own.

"Nik found it."

"Why would Nik need a— oh, Goddess, never mind," Iliana groaned. "You two are worse than teenagers in love."

Danai's answering laughter faded as Corinne's magic illuminated her hands and arms. Iliana's eyes grew as large as serving plates as the light funneled into her hand, the angry red marks on her knuckles fading as they healed. It took longer than Corinne expected—there was a small fracture in one of the delicate bones of Iliana's hand. No wonder it had hurt.

She'd been reckless, impulsive in a way that drew the attention of the entire dining hall. Corinne breathed a little easier despite the situation—it seemed less and less likely that any of her three new friends here would be working with the Nightrenders.

When her healing was complete, Iliana sighed in relief, then sniffled as Corinne's magic faded.

"I'm sorry," she said, her voice thick.

Corinne met her tear-filled amber eyes, and she froze. She hadn't expected Iliana to cry.

"I didn't mean to drag you two into my foolishness."

Danai draped an arm around Iliana's shoulders. "It's okay. Do you want to talk about it?"

"My parents again, as always," Iliana said, sniffling again. "They say '*We* were twenty-seven when we had you and then Jaela, you should be grateful for where you are.' As if being the only person in the family making any real money isn't something that terrifies me every day. I feel like I can't breathe, Danai."

"I know," Danai said softly.

Iliana squeezed Corinne's fingers, making her realize she hadn't dropped Iliana's hand. She wasn't entirely sure what to do other than stand there and let Iliana cry until she felt better.

Corinne had carried many worries during her life, but money had never been one of them. The monastery was self-sustaining, providing plenty for its own people, and according to Vera, most villages hosted Lightguards at no cost, grateful for their presence alone.

"Thank you again," Iliana said finally. "Both of you."

Corinne knew she was supposed to be keeping these castle dwellers at arm's length, should be careful with whom she trusted. But when she left the storage room alongside Iliana and Danai, she feared they'd sidled closer to her heart than she'd expected.

CHAPTER 11

If Corinne never heard a knock on her door in the middle of the night again, it would be too soon. She forced her sluggish mind into focus as she answered the door.

"Apologies for waking you, Corinne," Captain Ekhana said. "But Cato is sick and I need you to cover for him."

Corinne nodded. "Of course, Captain. I'll be right out."

Yawning, Corinne donned her shirt, trousers, boots, and sword belt as quickly as she could. Her appearance mattered little when she'd just be standing guard outside Prince Aryel's door all night.

"Thank you, Corinne," the captain said, nodding to her as she stationed herself to the left of Aryel's door.

She settled in place and breathed evenly. It would be so much easier to remain awake if she could read one of the books Nik had given her, but that would defeat the purpose of her keeping watch. She'd gotten decent sleep the previous night at least, and hoped that and the hour or so she'd already gotten tonight would be enough.

The lock on Aryel's door clicked behind her, and she whirled to the side just as his face appeared in the doorway.

"Fuck, *you're* out here?"

Corinne gaped at him, summoning a bit of light to her fingertips so she could see him properly. He was dressed in a dark green shirt that cut in a deep V, and a silver chain around his neck mirrored its shape on his bare chest. His hair fell on either side of his face in a roguishly handsome way, and his facial hair was freshly trimmed.

"Yes, your other guard fell ill," Corinne said, remembering herself.

Aryel swore colorfully. He stepped out into the alcove and muttered to himself for a moment before putting his hands on his hips and staring at Corinne.

"I'm going out tonight," he said.

Corinne's throat went dry. "Where?"

He narrowed his eyes. "A gathering of nobles."

"Oh," Corinne said, relaxing. "In the castle?"

"No. In the woods."

"The *woods*?"

"Yes, Sunshine, it's where we go to get away from it all."

Helaera help her, she could not let him do this. "I can't let you do something so reckless."

"Oh, you can't, can you?" he asked, his voice low as he took a step toward her, bracing one hand on the wall to her right.

Corinne mustered her courage, not backing away. He couldn't intimidate her into directly disobeying the wishes of the queen.

"I'm sorry, Prince Aryel, but I will not have you getting into trouble on my watch," she said. "I…I will physically restrain you if I have to."

A wicked smile spread across his face. "Do you promise?"

Corinne wanted to melt into the floor. She had no witty retort, only a fierce flush that ran from her cheeks to the tips of her ears.

"I—"

Aryel sighed heavily, the mischief fading from his expression. "Don't worry about it. You win, Sunshine."

He stalked back into his room, closing the door behind him, and Corinne exhaled. She was confident that the queen and king would not punish her for physically restraining their son to prevent him from being foolish, but she didn't particularly want to deal with the complications of explaining herself either. What a relief it was that she'd been able to reason with him.

Only a few minutes had passed when a *slam* sounded from within his rooms, followed by a sharp yelp. Corinne burst inside, flying through the antechamber and into his bedroom, searching wildly for some intruder.

But no one was in his room—a bedsheet had been secured to the knob of one of his balcony doors, which had slid shut, leading over the railing and down the side of the castle. Corinne sprinted to the balcony's edge and looked down. Aryel was clinging to a stretched-out blanket he'd tied to the sheet, halfway down the wall.

"Have you *lost your mind*?" Corinne whisper-screamed at him, furious and terrified of attracting attention all at once. "What in Helaera's name are you doing?"

Aryel looked up at her as he scaled downward. "I'm...going to that party."

"Why are you so determined to put your safety at risk?" she hissed, and he lowered himself the final few feet to the ground. A light wood sprawled to the south just behind him, his footfalls softened by pine needles.

"If you're so concerned for my safety, then you'll just have to follow me, won't you?" he said.

Goddess, she wanted to wipe that smug smirk off his face. He started to walk off toward the pine trees, and Corinne stepped away from the balcony's edge, wringing her hands. She couldn't let him go alone, not when it was her duty to keep him safe.

Helaera help me, I beg of you. Corinne leapt over the side of the balcony and gripped the sheets. Goddess, she didn't want to fall. She made her way down as quickly as she could without losing her grip, all the while letting her ire grow.

Prince Aryel was the most insufferable, spoiled, impudent man she'd ever had the misfortune of meeting, and she would drag him back to the castle by that ridiculous silver chain around his neck if she had to.

She landed silently on the pine needles and hurried in the direction he'd gone, and for the first time in her life, she understood the impulse to swear. There were no inoffensive words that came to mind as she summoned light to her fingers and tracked her wayward charge through the woods in the middle of the night. A few voices carried through the trees up ahead, and she lowered her hand. A dim light flickered in the distance, casting shadows on the trees and silhouetting a figure only a few yards in front of her. She hurried after him.

Corinne didn't make it to the prince before he'd reached the edge of a clearing full of people sitting around a bonfire. He turned to confront her head-on as she got in his face.

"I'm not going anywhere, Sunshine," he said, his voice low. "So you can stay here and brood off to the side, or you can lighten up and have a drink. Dragging me out of here in front of a bunch of nobles' children is not an option."

It was like he'd read her mind. Corinne glanced behind him, fuming as she counted over a dozen attendees, some seated by the fire, some dancing, a few paired off and speaking in hushed voices.

"Fine," she said, meeting his self-satisfied gaze. "But you stay in my line of sight."

He huffed a laugh. "Fair enough."

Aryel swaggered off to retrieve a drink from a barrel that had been set up at the far end of the clearing, well away from the fire. Several nobles greeted him warmly, clapping him on the back or grinning. Corinne couldn't make out what they'd said, but Aryel laughed. She planted herself against a large tree, crossing her arms and scowling at the lot of them. If anyone caught her eye, they looked away quickly, whispering to their fellows.

Corinne studied them all, wondering which noble family each belonged to. Perhaps one of these nobles was the spy, and here Aryel was amongst them, not a care in the world.

Quiet footsteps approached from her left, and Corinne turned just as a familiar face smiled at her.

"You're Catherine, aren't you?" Lana asked, that golden hair of hers pulled back into a long braid.

She wore far more casual attire tonight than when Corinne had first met her, dressed in a fine purple tunic and black trousers. She was the daughter of Nora and Calin Riann, nobles with land to the southwest, far from the border to the Shadowlands. Unlikely to have connections to Nightrenders, but still, Corinne narrowed her eyes at her.

"Corinne," she corrected.

Lana's eyes widened. "Oh, I'm so sorry! I'm terrible with names."

Corinne looked away from her, finding Aryel again. He was seated on a large log with two other men, deep in conversation.

"You certainly can't keep your eyes off Aryel."

Corinne ignored the heat that crept up her neck, giving Lana a withering look. "It's my sworn oath to watch him."

Lana giggled. "Oh, come on, nothing's going to happen to him out here. Here." She held out a cup filled with Helaera-knew-what, and Corinne frowned at her.

"No, thank you," Corinne said.

Lana shrugged. "Suit yourself, Catherine."

Corinne's blood boiled beneath her skin. Aryel was a vexing brat, but something about Lana felt rotten. Even the tone of her voice when she spoke to Corinne was sickly sweet, laced with poison. Corinne tried to breathe deeply, returning her attention to Aryel.

He was walking toward her, his mouth twisted into a frown.

"Why don't you come sit with us?" he asked, nodding toward his friends. They gave Corinne a friendly wave, and she raised an eyebrow.

"Why?"

"Because watching you stand here like you're going to stab everyone is making it difficult to relax," he said, all antagonistic pretenses gone. "Come on. They're not going to bite you."

Corinne scanned the clearing once before uncrossing her arms. "All right."

They strode back to Aryel's friends, who greeted Corinne warmly.

"I'm Elys," one of them said, holding out his hand.

"Petros," the other man said as Corinne shook Elys's hand.

She couldn't recall their surnames since she'd read so many, but she would check her list again later. They both had the look of carefree noble sons; Elys with his light brown face peppered in freckles, offering a full-lipped smile, and Petros with an impressively straight nose and defined muscles rippling beneath sepia skin. Not that Corinne had met many nobles' sons, but if she'd been asked to imagine them, these two would be it.

"This is Corinne," Aryel said, and a low, slow warmth spread behind her ribcage. He'd never said her name before.

"How's it been following this one around?" Elys asked, slipping to the grass and fully lounging back, one arm behind his head, propped on the log.

Corinne took a seat on the log in front of them, folding her hands on her knees.

"A nightmare, I'd wager," Petros said, taking a sip of his drink. "It's why my father's never assigned me a guard; if I die, I die."

The three of them laughed, and Corinne allowed them a small smile. Very small.

She didn't contribute much to the conversation as it continued, but she was at least right in front of Aryel and wouldn't be subjected to more of Lana's attempted jabs.

"Corinne, have you tried the wine?" Petros asked, getting up to refill his own cup.

Corinne shook her head quickly. "Oh, no, I—"

"I'll get you a cup," he said, already walking off before she could protest further.

Aryel and Elys were arguing about what types of bird feathers made the best fletching.

"You only like peacock feathers for their visual appeal," Aryel accused, fully alert and engaged in the debate despite the two drinks he'd had.

Elys scoffed. "They're just as accurate as pheasant."

"Goose feathers," Corinne said, and both men turned to look at her. "They're pretty, durable, and hold up in the rain. They're my preference."

She wasn't sure if she should be insulted at the shocked admiration on Aryel's face, but it made that warmth behind her sternum tug at her again. What was wrong with her? Having his approval should be the last thing she was concerned about.

Petros returned with the wine, which Corinne took with a polite smile. As the three men continued speaking, she sniffed the contents of the cup. It was a rich, earthy smell, and somehow fruity at the same time. She looked over her shoulder at the fire, at the surrounding nobles who had become even less polished since she'd arrived. Their laughter was unhindered, their dancing unrefined. An ache formed in her chest, a foreign feeling of...longing? Envy? She couldn't name it. She turned back to the wine in her hands and, giving in to impulse, lifted it to her lips.

She choked and coughed, and Aryel, Elys, and Petros looked over at her, Aryel pausing mid-sentence.

"This is disgusting," she said, placing the cup on the ground, and Aryel's answering laugh rattled her bones.

"We don't drink it for the taste, Sunshine," he said, Elys and Petros chuckling along with him.

"No," Corinne said coolly. "You drink it for the excuse to act like brazen fools."

"Sounds about right," Petros said, lifting his cup so Aryel and Elys could toast with him before they all continued laughing.

Corinne sighed. In truth, it wasn't even as bad as the tea she drank each week. That ache in her chest built again as the merriment around her continued; she felt so starkly out of place, even sitting amongst them. Would it be so bad if she decided to drink? It wasn't like a single cup of wine would make her completely lose her wits. She lifted the cup from the ground again, glancing around, but no one was paying her any mind. She took another sip, and then another.

Her cheeks turned warm after she'd consumed half the wine, and her anxious alertness changed to calm observation. What had she been so worried about? This was a small group of people, they weren't that far from the castle, and she was one of the most skilled fighters in the land.

"Aryel."

Corinne's heart sank, her warm serenity vanishing. Lana had appeared to her left, arms crossed as she looked at the prince.

"We need to talk," she said, that airy sweetness from earlier gone.

Aryel's face went stony. "Fine," he said, handing his cup to Elys as he hauled himself off the ground.

Lana led him close to the tree line, just far enough that they couldn't overhear them. Corinne shifted positions, a little clumsily, so she could keep an eye on Aryel.

"He never should have gotten involved with her," Elys sighed, taking another gulp of his wine. "Told him she'd just break his heart."

Corinne tried to sound nonchalant as she asked, "Were they lovers?"

"I don't know if you could even call them that," Petros said with a snort, shaking his head. "He'd been going through a rough time, and she pounced on the opportunity to share the prince's bed. Always kept him at arm's length, though. She's done the same thing with other high-ranking nobles' sons."

Corinne watched in befuddlement as Aryel and Lana had what appeared to be a quiet argument. She didn't understand any of it—how could one let someone into their bed, to share that level of intimacy, and still keep them at arm's length?

"Why would she do that?" Corinne asked.

Petros shrugged. "Some people seek power and control in whatever way they can."

Lana's face softened as Aryel started to turn away from her, and she said something to make him pause. She grabbed the collar of his shirt, pulling him down to kiss him. All the warmth left Corinne's body as Aryel pushed Lana away, and he spoke loud enough that she heard this time.

"What the fuck is wrong with you?"

He stalked off, toward the back of the clearing, and Lana started after him, hand outstretched.

Corinne didn't recall getting up, but an instant later, her hand was around Lana's very snappable wrist.

"If you touch him without his consent again, I'll break your hand," Corinne said.

Her voice was not laced with poison; it was pure venom. She let some of her magic flash in her eyes for good measure, and Lana's face went stark white. Corinne released her and hurried after the prince.

She found him just a few rows of trees back, his pace brisk as he wove through the woods.

"Your Highness," Corinne called, but he didn't slow. She sped up until she was beside him. "We're going in the opposite direction of the castle."

"I know," he said, and Corinne didn't miss the note of pain in his voice.

"Then where are you going?"

"Into the city."

CHAPTER 11

"I really don't—"

"Please," Aryel said, stopping so suddenly Corinne almost dashed ahead of him. "There's a place I like to go there that helps me calm down. We can both sober up, and then we can go back to the castle. Okay?"

Corinne looked at him in the darkness, uncertainty prickling her insides, but the look on his face was so undressed, so genuinely imploring.

"All right."

She summoned a bit of her magic to her palm to light their way, letting Aryel lead, and soon the pine needles beneath their feet turned to the cobblestones of a back alley. Corinne would have been hopelessly lost weaving through all the little streets Aryel trekked.

She extinguished her light as they emerged onto streets lit with lanterns, and he led her toward an abandoned old shop of some kind. She half expected him to try the boarded-up front door, but instead he walked around the side and began climbing a steep, crumbling staircase. Corinne followed, careful where she placed her feet on the uneven stone. Soon they emerged onto a little rooftop. Aryel plopped onto the ground in the center of the roof and lay flat on his back, exhaling sharply.

"Care to join me?" he asked.

Corinne looked at the star-smattered sky. For a moment, it was as if she was on the roof of the dormitory at the monastery. But Vera wasn't here, and she had a job to do.

"It's best I stay vigilant for us both," she said.

Aryel's answering sigh sent a small flicker of guilt through her, but she was right to remain where she was. The wine had mostly worn off, especially after she'd used some of her magic. Perhaps Helaera's Sun burned away the effects of alcohol the same way it mended maladies of the flesh.

"Do you ever feel like you don't belong to yourself?" Aryel asked at length, his voice quiet but clear.

Corinne shifted where she stood, watching him in the darkness. He hardly moved, still gazing up at the stars with his hands crossed over his middle.

"I'm not sure I understand," she admitted.

Aryel sat up, resting his forearms on his knees and looking over his shoulder at her.

"I suppose someone who's dedicated their life to the Goddess wouldn't," he said. "You at least made the choice to give yourself to a higher calling."

She still didn't fully understand what he meant, but something about it made disquiet prickle up her spine. Perhaps it was her lack of sleep. Aryel looked at the sky again, letting out a long sigh.

"I shouldn't have come out tonight," he said. "Then I wouldn't have run into Lana again."

Corinne shifted where she stood. "Do you think she could be the spy?"

Aryel snorted a laugh. "She's manipulative and selfish, but she wouldn't dare. If I'm dead, there's no path for her to be queen."

Corinne grimaced. "She wants to marry you, after treating you like that?"

Aryel gazed at her for a long moment, and Corinne couldn't make out whatever emotion played on his face.

"She wants power and riches and utter devotion," he said. "I don't give a fuck about the first two, and I will not offer the third if it's not given in return."

"Yet she still hopes to marry you?"

"Apparently," Aryel muttered. "It doesn't help that my mother is friends with hers."

Corinne truly did not understand the point of it all. Danai was right—nobles and their games were not pleasant company.

Aryel stood once more, and Corinne forced herself back to alertness.

"All right," he said. "Let's head back."

Corinne could have crumpled with relief; she'd get him back safely, secretly, and hopefully tomorrow she'd have time to steal a few hours' sleep while he attended a large council meeting set to take place.

Goddess, she hoped he wouldn't be hungover for that.

Aryel led them through more winding streets and back alleys until they stepped into a larger square, headed for a part of the woods that was closer to the castle than where they'd exited.

CHAPTER 11

Halfway across the square, the hairs on the nape of Corinne's neck stood up. She whipped around, ready to draw her sword in an instant, but no one was there. She summoned light to her palm again, scanning the alley behind them as she walked on. Empty.

Shaking her head at herself, she faced forward again. Perhaps she was too sleep-deprived to be a reliable guard right now.

"Oof!"

Corinne bumped right into Aryel, who'd stopped midway down a short street. Her eyes locked on the silhouette ahead of them that had made Aryel freeze in place.

A figure stood at the end of the street, blocking their way forward with two daggers drawn.

Corinne moved at the same time they did. She shoved Aryel out of the way as another figure lunged from behind them, blocking that attacker's sword with her own while flinging a beam of light at the other. The one with two daggers rolled out of the way while the other reset, circling her and Aryel. Corinne didn't give them a moment's reprieve.

She sent another arc of light slashing toward the first assailant, hitting him squarely in the chest. He crumpled to the ground, and Corinne blocked the other's attempt to reach Aryel, grabbing his forearm and ramming her knee into his gut. He dropped the sword to the ground with a clatter, but quickly drew a knife with his other hand. Corinne shoved him away in time to avoid anything worse than a shallow cut to her side, and then thrust her sword through his heart.

He died with a sickening, bloody wheeze, and Corinne let his body slump to the ground, yanking her blade out of him with a ragged cry. Her arms still glowed with the markings of her magic as her chest heaved. *Aryel.* He was on the ground, propped on his elbows and staring at her and the dead man blankly.

"Are you hurt?" she asked hoarsely, and he didn't move. "Aryel?"

He blinked several times, the blank shock morphing to confusion, and then lucidity.

"No," he said. "I'm not hurt."

Corinne nodded, a strange calm spreading within her. She helped him up, her sword still drawn in her right hand, her magic still steady.

"Good. Come on, we need to alert the city guard and Captain Ekhana."

Every bit of tiredness had vacated Corinne's body. She was more alert than a bloodhound, picking up on any sound or shifting shadow in the woods as they hurried back to the castle. Aryel scaled the castle with the aid of his sheets and blankets first, and she quickly followed. The deep-seated irritation toward him from mere hours ago felt like it belonged to someone else.

As she vaulted onto his balcony, a voice drifted through her mind.

You wanted him to die.

Icy fear gripped her insides.

You wanted him to die, so you wouldn't have to deal with him anymore.

No. That wasn't true. It wasn't—

Why else would you have let him be so reckless?

Corinne began to tremble.

If he died, you'd get another assignment. It's what you want.

No. No. No. *No.* Stay the course. Be the Light. Be the Light be the Light be the Light be the Light be the—

"Are you all right?"

She should tell Aryel to get away from her, that he couldn't trust her, that she was an evil, wicked person—

"Hey." A pair of hands gripped her shoulders, and Aryel's face appeared before her.

When had she ended up on the floor? And—oh, Helaera above, that horrible gasping sound was coming from her.

"Breathe, Sunshine. It's okay. We're both okay."

She shook her head rapidly. "You don't understand."

"That two men just tried to kill me in the street and you saved my life by killing them? I think I understand that part."

"No," Corinne whispered, the guilt gnawing at her insides as the voice echoed in her ears. "No, no, *no.*"

"Okay, okay," he said. "Just breathe. What can I do to help?"

Corinne gasped again, a bit of clarity breaking through at the sound of his voice.

"Keep talking," she said. "Please."

"Talking, all right. Did you have fun tonight? You know, prior to the, uh, near-death experience?"

Corinne choked on a laugh. It felt hollow, like she was still half in reality, half stuck in the abyssal spiral of her thoughts. "Between climbing down the side of a castle and nearly breaking a noblewoman's wrist, I would say no, I did not have fun."

"Whose wrist did you—?" He paused. "Lana. What did you do to her?"

"I..." Corinne gulped down air, and suddenly she could feel how hard the stone floor was beneath her palms. "I grabbed her arm before she could go after you again and told her I'd break her hand."

Aryel huffed a humorless laugh, his eyebrows pinching in incredulity. "That might be the nicest thing anyone has ever done for me."

"That's a little depressing," Corinne said.

More of that all-consuming dread and guilt subsided. She was in Aryel's room, just inside the balcony doors, her bloodied sword on the ground beside her.

"You seem to be better," he said. He gave her a thorough once-over, and Corinne didn't even have the energy to be self-conscious. "Do you want to tell me what happened? You looked like you might faint or collapse from terror."

Corinne took a deep breath as she looked into his eyes. She *couldn't* admit it to him.

Then again, she was already on the floor in front of him, on the verge of a meltdown, and he'd hardly flinched.

"You'll think I'm completely mad," she said. *He'll think you're evil.*

Aryel raised an eyebrow. "I didn't think you cared what I thought."

"I don't," she said, sharper than she'd intended.

"Then try me."

Corinne stared at him for another moment, something within her aching to reveal this torment she'd endured in solitude for years now. Perhaps he would think her mad...but perhaps he wouldn't. If she didn't care what he thought, what did it matter anyway?

It was enough to bring the words forth.

"Sometimes," she said, her voice small. "Sometimes I have these... thoughts."

Aryel nodded slowly, still kneeling on the floor in front of her. "Thoughts?"

"Terrible thoughts," she said. "Like this voice that's me, but not really me. It terrifies me. It makes me feel like I'm a fraud, like I don't deserve to be a Lightguard, or deserve kindness, or friendship, or anything, really."

Aryel grew pensive for a moment. "And what thoughts were you having just now?"

Corinne swallowed hard. "I can't."

"Tell me," he said softly. It wasn't an order, but an invitation. "No judgment. I promise."

She could barely get the words out. "That it was my fault, that I let you go tonight because I wanted you to be in danger. That I...wanted you to die."

Aryel stared at her, eyes widening. Corinne's throat constricted. He was going to think she was a wretched human being.

His laughter shocked the despair right out of her. That encroaching darkness disappeared as if someone had lit a candle in the night of her heart. She could breathe again, its shadowy hand no longer clamped around her neck.

"How can that possibly be funny to you?" Corinne asked, bewildered.

"Because if you actually wanted me to get hurt or die, you wouldn't have followed my foolish ass over a balcony and then *saved my life* tonight," he said. "Just because a thought enters your mind doesn't mean it's true or real. Hells, sometimes I imagine pitching myself off the top of the castle, but that doesn't mean I actually want to do it. They're just thoughts."

A weight that she hadn't noticed was there lifted from her heart, leaving an ache in its absence that was both raw and a relief. *They're just thoughts.* Was it really that simple?

"Near-death experience and having to kill two would-be murderers aside," Aryel said slowly, "are you all right? We really need to go find Captain Ekhana."

CHAPTER 11

Corinne exhaled sharply. "We do. I'm well enough for that."

Aryel stood, offering a hand to help her up, and she lifted her sword from the floor, grimacing at the drying blood on the blade. That would be a challenge to clean.

But no—this was a Lightguard's blade. Corinne wiped what she could onto her trousers, then channeled a bit of her magic into it. The blade lit up, burning the remaining blood off. It looked freshly cleaned, as if she hadn't just rammed it into someone's chest cavity.

"I don't think I'll ever get used to that," Aryel muttered, shaking his head. "Let's go, Sunshine."

CHAPTER 12

"Unfortunately, there is no indicator of who those men were yet."
Corinne stood off to the side in the small council chamber, watching dawn break over the mountains through one of six windows. The king and queen sat at the table alongside the full six-member council and Prince Aryel, and Captain Ekhana stood as he reported the findings of the city guard.

"And there was no..." Councilor Dresden hesitated. "Dark magic involved?"

Captain Ekhana looked to Corinne, and all eyes followed his. She tried not to wilt under the gaze of so many powerful people.

"No," she said. "They were skilled fighters, perhaps trained assassins, but ordinary as far as I could tell."

King Theo sat in seething silence while Queen Erina fidgeted with the end of her braid, her face pale.

"Do we think they are connected to the threat we received three weeks ago or not?" she asked, her voice cutting.

"It's hard to say," Captain Ekhana said slowly.

"I don't want to be told what we don't know, and what cannot be done, Captain Ekhana," the queen said. "Have your guards continue

CHAPTER 12

their investigation." She turned to Corinne. "And you—send word to the monastery as soon as this meeting is finished."

Corinne nodded, hoping that afterward, she could finally get some sleep.

"I would encourage you all to be on your guard," King Theo said, standing, and the others followed suit. "Prince Aryel will not be leaving the castle grounds for the foreseeable future, and I suggest you all assign guards to your children as well. A threat to my family is a threat to us all."

Morning light crept slowly into the room as the councilors departed, and Corinne lingered behind, waiting as Aryel had a quiet conversation with his mother. Her cheeks warmed when she caught the last bit of what he said.

"...Can't she sleep a bit first? We've been awake all night—"

"If you were so concerned for her, you wouldn't have snuck out in the first place when I strictly told you not to," Queen Erina snapped. "She will keep watch over you, as is her duty."

Aryel sighed as his mother took his father's arm and left the room, leaving Aryel, Corinne, and Captain Ekhana alone.

"Do you know your way to the courier room, Corinne?" the captain asked.

She shook her head—that was not a place Orana had shown her.

He turned to a nearby guard, who stood at attention when he approached. "Please escort Prince Aryel back to his rooms."

The guard nodded, and Aryel shot Corinne an apologetic look before leaving. The fact that he'd at least tried to vouch for her made the entire situation a little less terrible. She rallied what remained of her energy and followed Ekhana into the corridor.

By the time they reached the courier room at the top of a tower in the east wing, Corinne feared her legs might fall off. She resisted the urge to ease her fatigue with magic; at this point, it would only tire her out further.

A small man with paper-thin peachy skin sat at a little desk in the circular room, riffling through a mountain of papers. Several servants cleared the room upon Captain Ekhana and Corinne's arrival, carrying notes they'd retrieved from the doves roosting in a small house-shaped structure by the singular open window.

"Good morning, Fael," Ekhana said, and the man looked up at him.

"Morning, morning, Captain. What can I do for you?"

"Corinne here needs to send a message to the monastery."

Fael looked around Ekhana's form to assess Corinne.

"Very well. Write your note and I'll get it sent out," he said, going back to his papers.

Corinne exhaled. She wasn't sure she could've handled prying questions.

Ekhana gestured to one of several small tables on their left, which had piles of blank parchment, quills, and ink, before departing.

It took Corinne far longer to draft the note than she'd expected. What was she to say? *The prince and I were at a party in the woods, and we got attacked in the city on our way back.* Guilt settled in her heart. What had she been thinking last night? She should have insisted they go back, should have dragged him away from that gathering, noble witnesses or not.

She kept the message simple and rolled it up after signing her name. Fael took it wordlessly. Despite her exhaustion, Corinne lingered, a thought nagging at her.

"May I ask you a question?" Corinne asked, and Fael raised an eyebrow. "The note received threatening the prince's life...did you all keep it?"

Fael shook his head. "The Lightguards requested it for investigation, so it's with them now."

Corinne nodded with a sigh—it made sense, even if she wished she could have seen it herself.

After thanking Fael, she set off to return to her station. *You can sleep tonight, Corinne,* she told herself. She could make it through, even if the thought of standing alertly outside Aryel's door for another full shift made her want to cry.

When she arrived at the alcove, though, it wasn't the guard Captain Ekhana had sent with Aryel that stood by his door, but Danai.

"Corinne," they said, eyebrows shooting up.

CHAPTER 12

"Danai, what are you doing here?" Corinne asked, her voice low as she approached.

"We heard what happened last night," Danai said. "I can stand guard here for a few hours if you want to get some sleep."

Corinne could have kissed them. "Are you sure?"

"Of course," they said, smile bright. "I got plenty of sleep last night, and today is my day off."

"Danai, you don't have to—"

"Just for a few hours," they said. "I'll wake you, I promise."

Perhaps it was her utter exhaustion that made her constitution so weak, but she agreed. "Wake me by midafternoon."

"Will do."

Corinne hesitated a moment before placing a hand on Danai's shoulder, and their mouth lifted in a lopsided smile.

"Thank you, Danai. Truly."

"You're welcome. Now go to bed."

Laughing a little, Corinne stepped into her room. She quickly scrubbed herself clean in the shower and buried herself in her blankets the moment she was dry enough, sleep taking her almost instantly.

ARYEL ONLY ADHERED TO HIS AFTERNOON AND EARLY evening schedule, attending an additional meeting with Councilor Toro before he was summoned to a dinner with nobles. Corinne didn't envy him, but she was grateful for her own reprieve—numerous guards would be present at that event, and another guard was set to take over the night shift upon Aryel's return. So she sat in her room in solitude, reading through the tome with noble family histories again, this time putting several faces to the names.

Petros and Elys belonged to families who didn't own land, but rather businesses in Vytanos. Corinne rubbed at her eyes as she glanced over the few names she'd written down of nobles with holdings closer to the Shadowlands. She hadn't met any of those mentioned, and it wasn't much to go on, anyway.

Perhaps Vera was right, and she shouldn't bother trying to figure out who the spy might be. Losing sleep over it would only make her struggle to carry out her duty. With a yawn, she closed the book and placed her list in her nightstand drawer before once again surrendering to the call of sleep.

The next morning found Aryel in a particularly foul mood. Before, she might have attributed it to his generally temperamental nature, but now she couldn't help but wonder if Lana or perhaps some other noble had mistreated him in some way at the dinner last night. He didn't snap at Corinne, at least, but he didn't speak to her, either. The tension in his body grew even more pronounced as they approached the throne room.

"I'll be back in a few hours," Corinne said, in an attempt to dispel some of that tension.

"Great." His voice was flat, emotionless as he stepped inside.

Corinne suppressed a sigh as the doors shut behind him. The empathetic Aryel from two nights ago had morphed back into the obstinate prince she'd come to expect. A bit of worry prickled at the back of Corinne's neck as she headed for the dining hall. She'd let her guard down in front of him in a way she hadn't with anyone except Vera. What if he no longer trusted her, thought she was unqualified to be not only his protector, but a Lightguard at all?

What kind of Lightguard collapses in panic after successfully executing their duty?

Corinne shook her head as she walked. *Stay the course. Be the Light.* Her heart slowed again after she'd repeated it to herself four more times.

The moment Corinne entered the dining hall, she regretted it. Of course, news of an attack on the prince would travel quickly, and the eyes and whispers that followed her as she hurried toward her usual table made her stomach turn. Danai, Nik, and Iliana were already seated, their conversation halting the moment Corinne sat down.

"Can I help you?" Iliana asked over Corinne's shoulder, narrowing her eyes at a guard who was gawking at Corinne.

They scurried off, and to Corinne's relief, others went back to their meals and conversations.

Iliana nudged Corinne's shoulder with hers. "Are you all right?"

Corinne met her gaze, then looked to Nik and Danai as a servant placed a plate before her. She wasn't certain she could even eat now.

CHAPTER 12

"I'm...well enough," she said.

She truly didn't know how to answer the question. Physically, she was perfectly fine, but the rest...she hadn't really let it sink in yet.

"What happened?" Danai asked at the same time Nik said, "You don't have to talk about it if you don't want to."

"What Nik said," Iliana said, shaking her head at Danai.

"No, I don't mind," Corinne said, keeping her voice low. She glanced around to ensure there were no other eavesdroppers or gawkers before explaining the prince sneaking out and the subsequent events of her evening two nights prior.

"See, this is why I'm not upset that I don't get invited to those gatherings," Danai said, stabbing a sausage with their fork. "All that theater, and for what?"

Corinne refrained from sharing the fact that she'd threatened a noblewoman, unwilling for that particular detail to be overheard. When she told them about the attackers, all three of them leaned in closer.

"Sounds like you took care of them easily," Iliana said. "Which isn't surprising. But Goddess, what a nightmare."

"I hope the guards can find out more," Corinne said, shaking her head. "If there are more assassins in the city or around Ashera. Or who is giving them orders."

"I'm sure they can figure out something," Iliana said. "Nik's father has trained them well."

"As soon as I find out anything, I'll let you all know," Nik said.

A servant approached from Corinne's right, and Iliana threw them a withering glare. The girl's face paled, but she quickly bowed and held out a rolled-up note.

"A message came for you, Lady Corinne," she said, her voice soft.

Corinne thanked her and took the note, bewildered. *Lady* Corinne? She was no noble. She looked to the others with a raised eyebrow, and they all laughed.

"I suppose she isn't sure what to call you," Danai said.

"What *does* one call a Lightguard?" Nik mused as Corinne opened the note.

> Corinne,
>
> This is harrowing news. You are hereby summoned to the monastery to report more on this incident. We will await your imminent arrival.
>
> Priestess Bria

Corinne's heart picked up speed. It didn't give her confidence that the Priestesses were so worried about the attack that they would call her away from her assignment. Though perhaps if she spoke with them directly, they could use her information to discover more about the plot against Aryel's life.

"Speaking of your father, Nik, I have to go find him again," Corinne said, sighing.

"Is everything all right?" Nik asked.

"I've been summoned to the monastery," she said. "I'll see you all later."

They each bade her good luck, and Corinne set off to find Captain Ekhana.

CHAPTER 13

It was a relief that the majority of the journey from Vytanos to the monastery was through the forest. By the afternoon, the sun was relentless, and as she trekked the final few hills toward the sprawling stone and red clay roofs, the air was thick with an impending thunderstorm. The last thing Corinne wanted was to get stuck on the road in the rain, so she pushed her horse as much as she could without tiring her out; she also didn't want this poor mare to feel as miserable as she did.

The Goddess was with her in that regard, at least. She made it to the gates of the monastery just as the first droplets of rain began to fall. The sounds of training, of shouts and shuffling feet, and the feeling of belonging greeted her the moment she stepped into the main courtyard. She was home.

As the sky opened and the deluge began, she handed her horse off to an attendant and darted for cover. She'd be expected by Mother Creita, she assumed, so she made her way to the side entrance of the sanctuary.

"Corinne."

Priestess Chala approached her, dark hair hidden beneath her white hood. Corinne crossed her arms over her chest in a show of respect, bowing her head.

"Come with me."

Corinne ignored the whisper of dread in her gut. This wasn't meant to be a lighthearted visit; she was here to report on what happened last night and receive instruction on how to proceed.

Chala took several turns Corinne didn't expect, heading for the dim back hallway behind the sanctuary's chancel. They weren't headed to Mother Creita's study, but rather the Hall of Mothers. Corinne swallowed against the sudden dryness in her throat when Chala stood back, directing her to enter through the old wooden doors.

The Hall was lit by torches placed at even intervals along the limestone walls. There were no windows here, only murals of High Priestesses who had come before Mother Creita. Once Corinne stepped inside, Chala followed, closing the doors behind her before stepping around Corinne. She took her place in one of the four chairs placed in a semicircle in the center of the room. A richly woven red and gold rug was placed in front of them all. The other Priestesses looked up at Corinne, white robes shifting, and Mother Creita beckoned her forward.

"Come, child," she said, her voice low and soothing.

Corinne approached and removed her sword belt, placing the blade beside her as she knelt upon the rug. She'd been in this room only once before, shortly after her arrival when she was a child. Today, though, something about it made her nervous.

"Tell us truly, Corinne Anastos, what happened two nights ago?" Mother Creita asked.

"Prince Aryel and I were attacked in the streets of Vytanos," Corinne said, her palms growing sweaty on her lap. "Two men, one with dual blades and the other with a sword. I subdued them quickly and escorted Prince Aryel safely back to the castle."

Mother Creita stood from her chair, taking a few steps forward. "Is that all?"

"Yes, Mother Creita. I sensed no presence of Arytalis on them, only human malice."

"That's a relief, at least." Mother Creita began to walk again, her bare feet padding lightly on the little carpet surrounding Corinne. "And before that? Why were you and Prince Aryel in the streets of Vytanos at that hour?"

Corinne's heart stuttered in her chest before taking off. "He snuck out of the castle and I had to follow him."

"And how long were you absent from the castle?"

Tears began to sting Corinne's eyes as shame took hold. "For several hours."

"And what, might I ask, were you doing all that time?" Mother Creita's footsteps halted after she'd fully circled Corinne. "Why did you not return the prince to the castle at once?"

The guilt would destroy her if she lied. Her tears fell in earnest now, a gasp falling from her lips.

"Forgive me, Mother Creita," she said, bowing her head. "There was a gathering in the woods, and I let him go. I sat amongst them and consumed wine. I let my judgment lapse and faltered in my purpose."

Silence met her confessions, anticipation heavy in the air.

"I have been ungrateful," Corinne said hurriedly, as if saying it faster would make it less egregious. "I have been selfish and lost sight of our vow."

"Oh, Corinne," Mother Creita said, heaving a sigh. She lifted Corinne's chin with a delicate hand. "Thank you for being honest."

She turned away, and two other Priestesses, Bria and Ronna, stood and walked toward Corinne, helping her to her feet. Corinne sniffed, her heart lighter after admitting her wrongdoings.

"Have you been in this room before, child?" Mother Creita asked, looking up at one of the murals on the wall.

"Only once, Mother Creita," Corinne said, her voice thin.

"Of course," the High Priestess said, nodding to herself. "I recall now. We had such hopes for you even then, newly freed from a home full of corruption and shame."

Corinne's throat constricted. Mother Creita's left hand lit up with her magic, the warm, yellow light casting a brighter glow than the torches around them. She took a deep breath.

"I hope you'll remember the honor bestowed upon you in this room all those years ago," Mother Creita said. "When we took you in, after Helaera spared you."

When she turned to Corinne again, her face was pained.

"And I think you know this must not go unpunished," she said, closing her eyes.

Bria and Ronna took hold of Corinne's arms, the latter shoving her sleeve up past her right elbow. Out of pure instinct, Corinne flinched, but they held her firmly. Ronna forced her right arm out in front of her just as Corinne sensed the heat Mother Creita had summoned to her palm. *No.* Her mind seized with panic.

"No," she said, her voice breaking. *Not this. Anything but this.* "Mother Creita, please, I—"

"You strayed from the path, Corinne, and this is the consequence," Mother Creita said, taking a step closer, and Corinne flinched again, fighting the hold the Priestesses had on her despite her better judgment. "Chala."

The third Priestess joined them in restraining Corinne, forcing her to her knees. Corinne's breaths came in rapid gasps.

"Please," Corinne sobbed. "Please don't. I'll do anything—"

"You strayed, Corinne. You don't want to be like your father, do you?"

"*No.*" The word ripped from Corinne's throat. "I denounce him, you know I do, I—"

"Our Goddess is mother to us all," Mother Creita said, and her markings brightened until they turned to flames along her arms. Corinne couldn't stop the tears from streaking down her face, couldn't contain her terror. "Her magic heals, but when needed, it also burns."

"No," Corinne begged as Mother Creita lifted her hand toward her exposed forearm. She lurched against the hold of the three Priestesses to no avail, her voice pitching higher. "No, no, *no, no—*"

The last word turned into a scream as Mother Creita clamped her hand on Corinne's flesh. Her vision went white, then flashes of fire danced before her eyes as she screamed and begged for her to stop. She was burning, she was inhaling smoke, she was stuck under a beam in a little house, and her mother's voice joined her own, screaming her name.

"*Mother!*" she cried. "*Mother!*" *Make it stop, please make it stop.*

"Mother Creita!" The voice near Corinne's ear was panicked, though she didn't know why.

All she knew was this burning, this heat that was spreading from her arm now to her chest, filling her lungs and choking her. The acute agony of the fire against her arm disappeared, and she was on the floor, her vision blurred by tears and the light reflecting off them.

"Sedate her."

Corinne gasped for air for a few more seconds before a hand touched her neck, followed by a sharp, hot prick, and she fell into darkness.

Evening sunlight filtered through the little window of Corinne's room at the monastery—or rather, her former room. Any tiny piece of her fifteen-year presence here had been wiped away, made neutral again for the next trainee to take up residence.

Numbness had settled within her moments after waking up, and she lay curled in on herself, clothed in only a loose tunic. She stared at her arm, at the ugly, puckered handprint they'd healed into a scar after she'd lost consciousness. It was the second magical scar she'd sustained; the other, on her left thigh, had been an accident. She looked at it now as well, the pink flesh a near-perfect circle, darker in the center.

Corinne's door opened, and she didn't move, hardly blinked. She did not want to talk to Vera, or to anyone, about what had happened. She just wanted to lie here.

"Corinne."

It was not Vera's voice that greeted her—Mother Creita stepped inside, pulling up a little wooden stool by Corinne's bed. Corinne dully met her eyes.

"I'm sorry, Corinne," she said, her face pained again, those green eyes full of empathy. "I did not want to do that, but you left me no choice."

Shame crashed into Corinne, ousting the numbness. She'd behaved like a wild animal, fighting the Priestesses in their own Hall against the punishment they'd prescribed for her transgressions.

"Forgive me, Mother Creita," she said, closing her eyes. The High Priestess placed a hand over Corinne's, then lifted her arm slightly.

"Let this be the last time, for both our sakes," Mother Creita said, and Corinne met her gaze once more. "You know the rules, but I will remind you not to heal this for a month."

Corinne nodded. Helaera's healing was a privilege, and Corinne did not deserve it until she'd paid her penance.

"Night is falling fast, child," Mother Creita said, lowering her arm to the bed and standing once more. "Retrieve some food and then be on your way; the royal family is expecting you back as soon as possible. I have sent a message already."

Corinne's limbs were wooden as she pushed herself up. "Is...is Vera here?"

The High Priestess turned just as she reached the door, shaking her head. "No, Corinne, she is at her post."

Corinne tried to ignore her disappointment, and shame overtook her again. Some minuscule, weak part of her had wished for at least one person to tell her they were sorry without the added admonishment of her deserving it. *Foolish.*

She dressed in the fresh clothes they'd laid out at the foot of her bed. She wouldn't be going to the dining hall—not with this glaring mark of her disgrace on her arm. The sun had begun to set when she exited the stables, her heart hardening in her chest with every step she took toward the monastery's gate.

She would not stray again. She would not falter.

Stay the course. Be the Light.

CHAPTER 14

Corinne's entire body was alight with awareness as she rode through the streets of Vytanos past nightfall. She'd been so tired she'd nearly given in to the temptation to sleep in a little village halfway between the monastery and the city. The moment she'd passed the city gates, though, she looked around every corner, watched every flickering shadow. There was no reason for anyone to come after *her*, but she was still on edge.

No one greeted her when she arrived at the castle. *Thank Helaera*. If she'd had to face anyone, she might have died from the shame of it all. She'd wrapped her arm carefully after leaving the monastery, hoping the bandage and her long ochre sleeve would conceal the burn scar.

Only a few servants traversed the halls as Corinne made her way to the south wing. At least she'd be able to sleep more before facing Aryel or anyone else again.

Cool air drifted through her curls as she walked across the breezeway, and she paused to look out at the city for a moment. Clouds parted in the night sky, revealing a crescent moon. It mirrored the Serra family crest perfectly tonight.

She'd disappointed the royal family, she'd disappointed the Priestesses, and she'd disappointed the Goddess. She'd gone from one of the most promising new Lightguards to a delinquent in a matter of weeks. Nothing had gone to plan since her Anointing. She looked over the edge of the breezeway to the stone path several stories below. Aryel's voice drifted through her mind.

Hells, sometimes I imagine pitching myself off the top of the castle...

She nearly laughed, and Corinne raged against the comfort that brought her. She had shared far too much with him, had become too comfortable and undisciplined. There was no reason for his laughter and his attempt to vouch for her yesterday to make her feel such warmth inside. *He is my charge, not my friend.*

Footsteps approached on the other side of the double doors to her right, and Corinne tensed when one creaked open slowly, a hand on the hilt of her sword.

But it was only Nik who emerged, his eyes sparking with familiarity when he spotted her.

"Corinne," he said, hurrying toward her. "I wondered if you'd be back yet and hoped I'd find you here. How was the monastery?"

Corinne steeled her heart against his question. She could not become distracted again.

"It was fine," she said. She straightened and inclined her head toward him. "Good night, Nik."

She left him there, trying to ignore the pang of guilt at the hurt on his face. It was in his best interest for her to distance herself from him. She couldn't be his friend, or Danai's, or Iliana's. If her heart wasn't strong enough to avoid softening around them, she would simply have to avoid them entirely. Remove the temptation to stray from Helaera's path.

She nodded to the guard posted outside of Aryel's door, confirmed she would take over in the morning, and disappeared into her room.

∼

THE SOUND OF RAIN PATTERING ON CORINNE'S WINDOWS AS she awoke early the next morning was more welcome than she expected. Rain meant she could avoid training with Danai and Iliana with greater ease, postponing the moment she would need to sever herself from them more explicitly.

Corinne showered quickly and pulled her hair back at the nape of her neck with a leather band. Rain also meant her curls would turn wild and get in her eyes if she didn't tame them preemptively. A few still hung around her face, but the weight of the rest of it wouldn't push those into her field of vision now.

She adjusted the sleeve of her shirt over the scar on her arm. Rain also meant she could wear long sleeves without overheating. A bandage, however, was too bulky beneath this particular material.

Breathe, Corinne. No one would see it. She stepped out into the alcove with a renewed sense of duty and determination, holding her head high after relieving the night guard by Aryel's door.

The prince emerged only minutes later. He stopped short at the sight of Corinne.

"Morning," he said. "I didn't know you were back."

"I returned last night."

"Are you all right?"

"I'm fine."

Aryel raised an eyebrow. "Are you sure?"

Where was this concern for her yesterday? "I'm sure. You're safe, and I'm fine, and you have meetings to attend."

Aryel snorted incredulously. "Come on, Sunshine, I think we're past the aloof stoicism at this point. You were a wreck on the floor of my bedroom three nights ago."

Rage flared up Corinne's spine. "That will not happen again, and if you try to use it against me—"

"Goddess, I'm not going to do *that*," Aryel said. "I'm just trying to make sure you're not—"

"Don't," Corinne said, her voice cutting. If he wasn't going to let it go, she'd have to draw this line with him, just as she had Nik, how she planned to with Danal and Iliana when the time came. "You got us into this mess, and I forgot my purpose. We are not friends; I am your sworn protector, and you are the Prince of Ashera."

Anger lit up Aryel's face. *Good.*

"As if the entire castle doesn't constantly like to remind me of that fact," he said.

"Perhaps because you need reminding."

He looked like she'd slapped him, and Corinne pushed the guilt deep, deep down. If this is what it took to get him to stop prying, then it was for the best. The hurt on his face morphed quickly into smooth neutrality. He opened his mouth as if to say something, thought better of it, and turned on his heel to hasten down the breezeway toward the main corridor.

He let the door slam in her face.

"Come, Corinne, join us today."

Queen Erina beckoned Corinne into the council room for the second time in two days, and Corinne kept her face as passive as possible. Today, she was the only additional presence in the room, no Captain Ekhana to act as support.

"What news from the monastery?" the queen asked, taking her seat at the head of the table.

King Theo sat at the opposite head, and the rest of the councilors joined them. Corinne kept a tight leash on her emotions as she thought back to her meeting with the Priestesses.

"They have simply reminded me of my duty," she said. "And asked for details of the attack. They had no knowledge of the attackers' identities."

Queen Erina sighed. "I don't know if that's encouraging or somehow worse than I thought."

"They held no dark magic," Councilor Toro said. He truly looked so like Danai, with the same open, kind eyes and sleek black hair. "And our city guard still cannot identify who they may have worked for. For all we know, they were simply back-alley murderers out for some coin."

"No, it's too convenient," Councilor Mika said, steepling her fingers in front of her mouth. "For there to have been a direct threat to the prince's life and an attempt on it less than three weeks later?"

"All the more reason to figure out who these men were!" King Theo slammed a fist on the table, startling everyone. "My son's *life* is in danger. Why are we surrounded by such incompetence?"

"The Priestesses have not been forthcoming, either," Councilor Orvos said. "They summon their Lightguard to the monastery only to send her back with no real answers or information?"

"What we *really* ought to be addressing is the likelihood that we have a spy amongst us," Councilor Dresden said, and the room fell silent. "Yes, we all know it, and no one has said it. But it could be someone in this very room!"

Corinne tensed, forcing herself not to reach for her sword. The silence grew for another long moment before the king shifted in his chair.

"A fair point, Councilor Dresden," King Theo said. "Then let us tighten security. All nobles will remain in the castle. All outgoing messages will be examined by our postmaster. We will close the gates and post twice as many guards along the perimeter walls. Same goes for the city walls. Twice as many."

Prince Aryel cleared his throat, making his presence known for the first time. "I really don't believe that's necessary—"

"And *you*, Aryel, will continue your combat training in addition to your regular duties." King Theo's gaze traveled to Corinne, and she felt the color leave her face. "I hear you led him in a training session a few days ago. Good. Keep that up daily."

Daily. Corinne bowed her head once and stared determinedly at the wall even as Aryel tried to catch her eye from the table.

"If we catch anyone trying to sneak away from the castle grounds without authorization," King Theo said, standing, and the rest of them stood with him. "Then we will know they are up to no good."

"A brilliant plan, my love," Queen Erina said, taking his arm as he walked past her place at the table.

The other councilors vacated the room, bowing to Aryel before they departed. The prince had returned to his seat at the table.

"Well," he said suddenly, standing. He didn't even turn to Corinne as he said, "You heard my father, let's go train."

Corinne hurried after him as he headed for the exit, once again letting the door swing back in her face.

"Your Highness, it's pouring rain outside," she said, keeping pace several steps behind him.

"There's an indoor sparring hall."

Of course there was. Corinne suppressed a groan and then chastised herself. *Stop being such an ungrateful wretch and do your job.*

When they arrived at the sparring hall in the west wing of the castle, Corinne's stomach plummeted. Danai was stationed just outside the doors, offering Corinne a bright smile and a nod. Their smile was so contagious it took immense effort not to return it, but Corinne bit the inside of her mouth and gave them a single nod of acknowledgment. She couldn't be Danai's friend, but she didn't need to be rude unless forced to. Danai's smile faltered a bit as she and Prince Aryel passed.

Two guards were training inside already, but vacated quickly at the prince's approach. It wasn't an ideal fighting area, with its wood flooring and far smaller perimeter, but it would have to do for today. The attendant on duty came forward to take Corinne's sword and belt off her hands. Aryel loosened the laces on his shirt at his wrists, rolling the sleeves up to his elbows the same way he had before. The sight of his arms, of the muscle flexing beneath his skin as he adjusted his sleeves, made her heart falter.

What in the name of Helaera was wrong with her? She shook her head as if to rattle those thoughts out of her mind.

"All right," Aryel said. "Last time I still hadn't figured out that hold."

Corinne nodded quickly. She could focus on that easily enough. Training was grounding too.

She stepped forward to demonstrate to Aryel again how to escape one of the more complicated holds she knew. It was unlikely some cutthroat would know such a maneuver, but if the original threat to his life had come from Nightrenders, they would be highly skilled.

He watched her with calm, quiet focus, and Corinne channeled her energy into the simple physicality of it all. She didn't miss his quips or exasperated sighs from the last session. No, that would be an absurd reason for this dull ache in her chest. She didn't notice the length of those dark eyelashes around his deep brown eyes, either, or the way his eyebrows pinched together slightly when he didn't fully understand something.

"Ready to try it?" she asked, backing away from him, and he nodded.

Corinne lunged at him, taking him to the ground as gently as she could—this was just practice for getting *out* of the hold, anyway, and she didn't want to hurt him. She wrapped her arms around his neck from behind and did the same with her legs across his torso, locking her feet at his left hip.

The prince froze for a moment, unmoving, and Corinne became acutely aware of his breathing and heartbeat, of her own as it hammered in her chest, pressed against his back. Another breath, and he still hadn't moved. Had she accidentally hurt him?

"Are you—?"

Aryel shoved her left elbow up with his hand, breaking her grip and quickly twisting his body so he broke her leg lock as well. The moment he was free, he leapt to his feet, and Corinne sat up.

"Good," she said, pretending she didn't see the light blush that had crept into his cheeks. "You'll want to practice being faster than that, but the execution was well done."

"Right," he said, shaking his head and blinking his gaze back into focus.

They drilled that same hold several more times before Corinne had him demonstrate the others they'd gone through the last time they'd trained. Nearly an hour had passed before Aryel finally admitted he needed a reprieve. He sat on the floor, forearms resting on his knees and his head bowed as he caught his breath. Corinne thanked the attendant when they approached to return her sword.

"Can you teach me how to wield a blade?"

Corinne glanced at Aryel as he stood. "You want to learn sword fighting?"

"Yes."

"Why?"

Aryel frowned. "So if we're ever attacked in the streets again, I'm not utterly useless."

Corinne could understand that, even if she knew it was more dangerous for him to get involved in a fight rather than let her handle it.

"All right," she said. "Next time."

"What, not now?"

Corinne looked him up and down, pursing her lips at his wilted posture, the clear fatigue he was trying—poorly—to hide.

"It's not wise to train when you're fatigued," she said. "Especially not with blades."

"You afraid to hurt me, Sunshine?"

Corinne mastered herself before her face could give her away. Why was she suddenly having *this* reaction to him? The faster she got these fleeting feelings of warmth under control, the better. She would just have to do what she'd done the handful of other instances she'd found herself attracted to someone—ignore the feelings until they faded.

"I would be a poor guard if I harmed the person I swore to protect," she said coolly. "So, yes, I'd like to avoid that. We'll start tomorrow."

Aryel's face morphed back into that mask of apathy, and Corinne took it as a victory.

It was a weakness she could not abide. Perhaps training with a blade was wise for that reason too—she could avoid touching Aryel almost entirely.

Corinne would discipline her mind against it all, against his maddening yet disarming teasing, against her own childish inclination to make friends here. When Vera returned the following week, she would have no further shame to shadow their conversation.

CHAPTER 15

The beginning of Corinne's third week in Vytanos brought hope—she completed her private ritual well before dawn, unable to sleep, and answered her door promptly when a kitchen servant arrived with the hot water for her tea. She knelt before her makeshift altar and methodically placed the dried leaves into a tiny pouch, humming to herself as she placed it into the steaming cup.

Careful, dear light, of the darkness that looms
Shadows will take you so swiftly
Keep your eye trained on the sun and the moon,
They'll guide you onward and with me

Before she could begin the next stanza, a shadow of her own crept into her mind, and dread washed over her.

You're only happy because you've gotten what you wanted.

Not now. *Why* did this have to happen now? She'd done so well these past few days, keeping stoic and solemn around Aryel, and avoiding Danai, Nik, and Iliana altogether. It hadn't been particularly difficult to do so, considering the tenfold increase of nobles in the castle.

Guards were working twice as much, and younger nobles completing their lessons and studies in the library had kept Nik busy.

You don't truly want to be a good person, you just want everyone to think you are.

Corinne gritted her teeth and tried to dampen the fear of spoiling the ritual. *Stay the course. Be the Light.*

You've tricked everyone into thinking you're a good person, when really you're selfish, and that scar on your arm proves it.

Corinne's heart was beating so rapidly she was sure it would fly out of her chest. *Stay the course. Be the Light. Stay the course—*

They're just thoughts.

The panic beginning to rage in Corinne's gut eased off, stopping her spiral into despair. Aryel's voice drifted into her mind again.

Just because a thought enters your mind doesn't mean it's true or real.

She let that knowledge wash over her, and her heart slowed. She took a deep breath and looked outside at the lightening sky. Aryel wouldn't be awake for hours, and she was far too restless to sit in her room.

Corinne grabbed her sword and belt as an idea struck her—she hadn't yet had the chance to venture into the gardens, and surely she could find some solitude and solace there at this hour.

Her optimism renewed, she headed for the east wing, taking the quickest route she'd memorized and mercifully avoiding a good number of guards and servants. Most were stationed outside of guests' bedchambers at this hour, she guessed.

The predawn morning air was cool against her cheeks as she stepped outside. Though most of the plants were purplish outlines of the various flowers and trees she'd seen on her first day here, the place was still absolutely breathtaking, and it smelled incredible. Corinne wandered down the center path and took a right at the fountain, following the stepping stones through a maze of flower beds. Perhaps there was a bench somewhere she could occupy for a few minutes.

The smell of wisteria hit her as she approached the willow trees along the southern perimeter of the gardens, and she closed her eyes for a moment. Her last memory of the monastery wasn't a pleasant one, but

CHAPTER 15

it was still her home, and that scent was a comfort to her the way her tattoos were, the way her mother's ring was.

Corinne turned a corner around a trellis holding up a tall, flowering vine, and stopped dead at the sight of two figures on a bench before her, so wrapped up in one another as they kissed that she could hardly tell it was two people. She yelped in surprise before she could stop herself, and the pair broke apart.

"*Corinne?*"

Danai was gripping the front of Nik's shirt with one hand and had started reaching for the hilt of their sword with the other.

"Oh," was all Corinne could manage. A flush spread from her cheeks down her neck. "I'm sorry, I—"

"It's all right," Nik said, gracefully removing Danai's fingers from his shirt. "No need to apologize. Danai and I just haven't had hardly a moment to ourselves since the castle locked down, and...well...we take what time we can get."

"Sorry, Corinne," Danai said, standing. "How have you been? We haven't spoken since you got back—"

Corinne shook her head, backing away. "I'm fine. Sorry to interrupt, I— see you around."

She hurried off despite Danai's protests. Perhaps it was better to just wait in her room and start her day once Aryel was awake. By the time Corinne's mortification wore off, she realized she wasn't on her way back to the south wing, but halfway down some corridor she didn't recognize. She began to double back—if she could retrace her steps, she could reorient herself.

"...the Lightguards are a source of endless frustration."

Corinne halted as she approached the spiral stairwell. Two voices drifted downward, footsteps growing nearer from a higher floor. She pivoted and pressed her back against the stone outside the landing, hoping they wouldn't exit at this floor.

"How is it they don't have more information for us yet? They have dozens of sentries at the Boundary, and have deployed dozens more to every village in the kingdom to keep an eye out for those Nightrenders," Queen Erina said.

Corinne held her breath as she reached her floor, not daring to move or blink when the queen stepped past her, Captain Ekhana trailing her.

"I understand your frustration, Your Majesty," he said, and the moment they'd cleared her, Corinne darted into the stairwell on silent feet.

Somehow they hadn't noticed her. *Thank Helaera.*

"That liaison of theirs is due back in a week," Queen Erina said. "She better have information for Corinne, or I'm going to request an audience with Mother Creita herself. They are not living up to their reputation."

Corinne swallowed hard. If the queen was unhappy with Mother Creita, if the Crown and the Lightguards were at odds, what would that mean for Ashera? The nation could not be sundered so. Corinne had to tell Vera what she'd heard, and hopefully Vera *would* have something from the other Lightguards to report. Corinne wished she herself could be more useful, but her duty was Aryel's protection.

Queen Erina and Captain Ekhana's voices faded as they disappeared around a corner down the hallway, and Corinne finally released a breath. Now she just had to find her way back to the south wing.

Another flight down, she emerged into a corridor she recognized and sighed in relief. No more solo excursions in the castle before dawn.

WITH OTHER NOBLES IN THE CASTLE, IT SEEMED ARYEL WAS more inclined to actually spend time in the library as his schedule dictated, and Corinne was stationed inside the doors instead of the hallway, given the larger presence of guards in the corridors. She was deeply relieved that Lana did not show up to these study-based gatherings, but she still had to face Nik's repeated apologetic looks thrown her way as he organized books in the various stacks or retrieved books for visitors. She tried her best to return them with a soft smile that expressed her indifference. He didn't owe her anything.

Aryel had begun taking his training more seriously, too, quickly mastering not only breaking free from holds but avoiding Corinne's attacks altogether. Goddess above, Corinne was grateful for that; she touched him far less now that he was improving each day, and she was confident in her waning attraction. There were still moments of weakness, like when he held a practice sword with greater confidence on their fourth session, arms flexing and hands gripping with the right balance between firm and fluid. It had passed quickly, though, and they spoke little.

"My mother wants you to attend the council meeting again today," Aryel said as they wrapped up their training session on the eve of Vera's next visit.

Corinne looked up from her sword belt as she fastened it back on her waist, stepping out of the grassy ring in the outdoor training yard.

"Do I need to say anything?" she asked, nervousness creeping into her voice before she could stop it. She'd done well these past two weeks, avoiding any show of vulnerability in front of him. *Don't ruin it now.*

"Not that I know of," he said. "But I just wanted to forewarn you that she'll ask you to stay."

Corinne knew she wouldn't be able to control her voice, so she simply nodded once in thanks.

"I'm going to bathe before the meeting," he said, heading for the castle doors. "Feel free to take time to do the same."

Unbidden, the shirtless image of him on her first full day at the castle appeared in her mind. Corinne shoved the thought away and forced her feet to move at a normal pace behind him.

"But no one is stationed outside your door," she said.

"Easily remedied," he said, offering no further explanation. He glanced over his shoulder, eyeing her up and down. "I can't imagine it's comfortable training out there with long sleeves on. You've been wearing those more recently, even though it's been warmer."

Corinne's heart stuttered in her chest. He'd noticed that?

"I'm perfectly comfortable," she said, hoping her voice didn't tremble.

"I doubt that."

"I don't understand why you're so concerned with my attire," Corinne snapped.

Aryel stopped, turning to look at her, and Corinne halted several steps away. She had the distinct feeling that he could see straight through her as he held her gaze.

"I...fine. You're right. Wear what you want."

Corinne tried to calm herself as they continued. There was no way he knew about her burn. She'd kept it well hidden since her return, and would continue to do so until she was permitted to heal it.

Part of the way back to his rooms, Aryel approached a guard patrolling a corridor, requesting her presence, and she agreed. Corinne supposed it was for the best—she couldn't stand around a council meeting smelling like sweat and grass.

She showered quickly and said a quick prayer by her little altar nightstand before venturing back out. Vera would be there in the morning, and Corinne would be able to speak with her about Queen Erina. She would have no further shame to conceal from Vera or any of the other Lightguards. She'd finally fallen into a pattern of self-discipline these past two weeks that was painfully rigid, and if Vera asked her about any of the people here, Corinne could confidently say she'd stayed the course.

On their way to the council meeting, Aryel caught the door from the breezeway before it swung back on Corinne, and she stopped short as he blocked her way through.

"Just so you know, you are a terrible actress, and I'm not falling for this pretense of cold indifference for one second, Sunshine," he said, his eyes locked on hers.

Corinne stared at him, heart in her throat, but he didn't wait for a response, just turned and kept on his path.

Stay the course. Corinne jogged after him. It wasn't a pretense; it was her finally disciplining herself. What did he know, anyway?

When they arrived at the council room, Queen Erina requested Corinne's presence, just as Aryel had warned her. In addition to the six councilors, three additional nobles were present. Corinne recognized them from around the castle but didn't know their names.

"Good people of the council," Queen Erina said, barely suppressing a smile as the door shut and the last councilmember was seated. Captain Ekhana stood opposite Corinne, just as he had the night of the attack in the city. "We have news of the would-be assassins' place of origin."

CHAPTER 15

The councilors and nobles all began speaking at once, and King Theo held up a hand. He motioned to Captain Ekhana, who cleared his throat, hands clasped behind his back.

"They hailed from Cara Talle," he said. Corinne's blood froze in her veins. "We are sending a dozen city guards there to investigate the entire locale."

"Given the sensitive nature of this information, we have not informed the monastery," Queen Erina said, her eyes landing on Corinne. "Too risky to attach it to a dove that may end up in the wrong location, or in the wrong hands. Your contact is due to arrive in the morning, no?"

Corinne nodded, pushing past her shock. "Yes, Your Majesty."

"Excellent. Please relay this information to her. I'm certain the Lightguards have a few of their own stationed there, if not nearby. We would greatly appreciate their assistance."

"I'm certain they would be eager and honored to do so," Corinne said.

Queen Erina's answering smile was tight, but soon her attention returned to the council, and they discussed the plan for the guards departing for Cara Talle.

Why, of all places in Ashera, did the men who tried to kill her and Aryel have to come from *her* home village? Helaera must truly be testing her resilience.

Just an afternoon, Corinne told herself. Just an afternoon and a sleep until she could speak with Vera.

"Cara Talle isn't particularly close to the Boundary, is it?" Councilor Dresden asked, reaching for the map of Ashera on the table and sliding it closer to himself. "Is it possible for Nightrender sympathizers to have breached so far into our borders?"

"We certainly can't rule it out," Councilor Toro said, frowning. "Which would be concerning."

"It could point to a far greater problem, and a far more complex plot than we first anticipated," Queen Erina said. "Which is why we must uncover the truth as quickly as possible. Captain Ekhana, how soon can your guards be ready to depart?"

"As early as first light, Your Majesty."

"Good. And the Lightguard messenger comes quite early as well."

Corinne breathed as evenly as she could throughout the rest of the meeting, trying and failing to focus on the conversation at hand. She was even more glad she'd been wearing long sleeves recently—it also meant none of them could see her Cara Talle tattoos. It was unlikely for someone to know their origin, but on the off chance....

She remembered little of living in her home village, and had only visited once to receive her tattoos when she'd turned eighteen. It was nestled in the woods to the north, near the smaller mountains of Ashera, and Corinne had traveled the additional day on horseback to gaze upon the sea for the first time. She'd watched the Lightguards at the nearby Boundary station place their hands upon the sand, just where the tide washed in, and send a pulse of magic into the earth. The entire shoreline had sparkled with a warm glow for several moments, a rippling wave of light reaching for the heavens, gleaming in the darkness of the night. She'd never seen anything so beautiful, and it was when she'd decided *that* was the posting she'd hope for. Imbuing the very earth of Ashera with her magic to keep her people safe...there could be no higher honor, no greater beauty.

"...And with the monastery's support, we could be rid of these threats as early as the prince's birthday."

Corinne's attention returned to the meeting, which was now nearly over. Thank the Goddess. All that remained of her day was Aryel's pianoforte lesson, which was more just him playing on his own for an hour or two. If he had an instructor, Corinne had yet to meet them.

Neither Aryel nor Corinne said anything on the trek to the music hall. Corinne's mind raced between Vera's impending arrival, Queen Erina's displeasure with the Lightguards, and the assassins' connection to Cara Talle. Perhaps the progress on discovering more about the assassins would appease the queen somewhat, but Corinne still needed to bring it up to Vera.

She'd need to address it carefully to ensure it didn't sound like *she* was blaming the Lightguards for a lack of information. It wasn't Corinne's place to question the Priestesses. An emotion Corinne couldn't place crept up the back of her neck as she recalled what had

CHAPTER 15

occurred nearly two weeks ago in the Hall of Mothers. Hopefully Vera wouldn't bring *that* up, if she even knew about it.

A familiar melody drifted from the music hall, pulling Corinne's thoughts back to the present. Aryel was playing that same piece he had the first time she'd heard him play, the one that had moved her to tears. She fought them again as the music swelled. If only she could sing something so lovely, just to be able to hear it whenever she wanted to.

Footsteps echoed up the stairwell at the far end of the hallway, and Councilor Toro Mykotas emerged, his sweeping charcoal robes billowing behind him. He approached Corinne with a smile—the same smile Danai always offered her.

"Hello, Corinne," Councilor Toro said. "I hate to be a bother, but is Prince Aryel in there?"

She nodded. "He is, Councilor."

"I would like to speak with him, but I don't want to startle him. Could you...?"

Corinne took a deep breath and turned, peeking inside the door. The pianoforte stood at the center of the hall on a massive dark blue rug. The light of the setting sun streamed through the window behind it, casting a soft yellow haze around Aryel as he played. His brow pinched slightly as he played through a rather intense passage, his mouth lifting on one side. It looked like Helaera herself was blessing him. He finished the song with a flourish along the highest keys, then noticed Corinne. He raised an eyebrow.

"Apologies, Your Highness," she said, forcing the words out as formally as possible. "Councilor Toro is here and would like to speak with you."

"Oh," Aryel said, placing his hands on his lap. "All right."

Corinne quickly turned back to the corridor, motioning for Councilor Toro to enter. He stepped past Corinne with an appreciative smile.

"Your Highness, forgive the intrusion, but I had a few follow-up questions after our conversation earlier this week, regarding the complaints several farmers in the east put forth..."

Stay the course, Corinne. Meeting with Vera tomorrow would help her keep her eyes on the path, and if she were honest with herself, she desperately needed a friend. A safe, familiar friend whom she could trust.

CHAPTER 16

Corinne hardly noticed the bitterness of the tea that morning, her mind preoccupied with the anticipation of Vera's arrival. She'd found herself awake well before dawn again, and hoped it wouldn't bode poorly for her alertness later that evening.

She turned her mother's ring over in her fingers as she waited, having retrieved it from the top drawer of her nightstand. She closed her eyes and pressed her lips to it, trying to quell her impatience.

When the knock came at her door, she jumped up from her bed, putting the ring away again. She paused as she reached for the door's handle. *Compose yourself, Corinne.*

Vera's face was such a welcome sight that Corinne immediately lost her composure and wrapped her in an embrace. Vera patted her back gently and urged her inside, shutting the door behind them.

"What news do you have to report?" Vera asked flatly, approaching Corinne's little altar and studying the empty teacup.

Had she done something wrong in her ritual? Corinne's joy faltered a bit, but she recovered quickly.

"I'm sure you noticed the castle has been locked down," Corinne said. She rattled off details of any additional protocols she'd seen put in place, the typical number of guards around the corridors, her training with Prince Aryel. "He's improved expeditiously, it's quite impressive. And they have found the place of origin of the would-be assassins who attacked us."

Vera turned, her brow furrowed. "They have? Why didn't they send a message?"

"The queen said it was too sensitive to send by dove." Corinne kept her voice devoid of emotion as she said, "They have connections to Cara Talle. The Captain of the Guard is sending a dozen guards there, and they wanted to request the aid of the Lightguards stationed nearby."

Vera pursed her lips, the expression so familiar Corinne's heart ached. She'd missed Vera especially these past two weeks.

"We'll have to get word to them as soon as possible," Vera said. "What else? Did you record the prince's movements like I asked?"

Corinne nodded, retrieving a piece of parchment from a drawer in her nightstand and handing it to Vera.

"I've also kept watch for any suspicious behavior from those in the castle's employ," she said. "But I haven't discovered anything yet—"

"That's not surprising," Vera said, examining the parchment briefly. "We think it's likely a noble."

"I've compiled a list of nobles as well," Corinne said, a bit of hope lifting her heart. "To see if any may have connections to Nightrenders."

"That's not your responsibility, Corinne," Vera said, her jaw tightening. "You could potentially rouse suspicions."

Corinne's hope deflated, more shame prickling up her body.

"Vera, I..." Corinne swallowed. "I overheard Queen Erina the other day speaking as though she were dissatisfied with the Lightguards' progress on finding the Nightrenders and their sympathizers."

Vera stared at her, her face passive. "I'll let Mother Creita know."

"Is...is there anything you can share with me to appease her?"

"It's not our job to appease the royals—it's our job to protect them in the name of Helaera. It seems they could use some prayer and self-reflection."

"I just thought the Crown and the Lightguards were meant to work together under Helaera's guidance," Corinne said, frowning.

"Don't worry about that. Just do what you were assigned to do, and we'll handle the rest."

CHAPTER 16

Corinne chewed her cheek. "Vera...what are you not telling me?"

"That's not your place to ask," Vera said, and Corinne's neck flushed.

She should have known better. After hesitating a moment, she stepped closer to Vera.

"How are you?" she asked. "I've missed you—"

"Please don't make me do this, Corinne." Vera interjected, her face finally cracking.

Corinne fell back a step. "I...what do you mean?"

"You are *disgraced*," she said in a hoarse whisper, like she was fighting tears. "I told you to keep your distance from everyone here, and you let this place lead you astray days later. *Days,* Corinne."

Cold, unyielding shame washed over her all over again.

"It was a mistake," she said quickly. "And I've recommitted myself, these past two weeks I have kept my eye strictly on the path—"

Vera was shaking her head, disgust plain on her face. "I hope you have been recommitted these past days, Corinne, but from now on, my visits are in service to Helaera only. I can't put my own soul at risk by being friends with someone like you."

Corinne had begun to tremble. "Vera, please, I-I'll pay my penance and—"

"I'm sure you will," Vera said. "But I was friends with someone who kept her duty in mind first and foremost. You faltered at the *first* true test of your devotion, and here you are still seeking to do things outside of what you've been assigned. Maybe you were right to doubt your place among the Lightguards."

Corinne couldn't speak, couldn't breathe. Surely this was one of her nightmares and she'd wake in moments.

"I'll send word to the Lightguards near Cara Talle," Vera said, her face smoothing over again. "And I'll see you in two weeks."

Vera left her without another word, shutting the door behind her with a soft click that hit Corinne's ears like an explosion. Her insides were hollow, as if someone had punctured her chest and emptied it of breath, of blood, of feeling. She collapsed to her knees on the floor beside her bed and let out a ragged sob.

The fragile beast within her that had craved empathy from her only friend over her punishment reared its head and roared its grief. No chance to let Corinne explain, no sympathy for her pain, even if she'd deserved it.

Corinne had always fought the voice in her head that whispered that she never deserved the honor of the Lightguards, but to hear it said aloud, by her oldest friend…perhaps it was right all along. Perhaps they weren't just thoughts, perhaps they were her truest, deepest self, and now the world saw her for what she was.

Selfish, prideful heretic. You don't truly serve Helaera. You serve your own whims.

She couldn't even fight it this time; she just let the despair take her, cutting into her body and leaving her raw. She didn't know how long she fell into the infinite spiral of her darkest thoughts, but a sharp rap on her door yanked her back to reality.

"You in there, Sunshine?"

Oh Goddess, it was late. Corinne scrambled clumsily to her feet, her muscles barking in protest after she'd been curled up on the floor for what must have been hours. She was already dressed, at least, and answered her door promptly. Aryel stood outside with a guard who looked deeply annoyed.

"My sincerest apologies," she said, "I lost track of time."

The guard mumbled something she couldn't hear and stalked off. Aryel watched him go and then turned back to Corinne. He started to say something, then stopped, pressing his lips into a hard line before nodding and setting off down the breezeway. *Thank Helaera.* She couldn't handle him pressing her right now. *Just get through the day.*

Just get through the day.

※

Corinne reported what Vera had said to Queen Erina and King Theo when she brought Aryel to the throne room that afternoon, and could hardly muster a smile at the queen's satisfactory praise. A day ago, she would have been relieved, pleased even—she'd delivered news that once again eased the relationship between the Crown and the monastery, even if Vera had said that wasn't her concern.

CHAPTER 16

It all rang hollow now.

Instead of training on her own or going to find a secluded spot in the library as she'd done the past two weeks, Corinne traipsed back to her room and climbed into bed. She wouldn't let herself sleep for fear of losing track of time again, so she simply lay there, watching through the window as the clouds floated low over the mountaintops in the distance.

Perhaps she'd gone about things all wrong after they'd burned her, holding onto the image of who she'd been, or wanted to be. Corinne, the most talented mage and fighter they'd seen in years. Corinne, the Lightguard who would be given an assignment of high honor. It was time for her to accept who she was, what she was.

Corinne, the daughter of a violent defector and murderer.

The trainee who'd started five years later than every other child in the monastery. In her pursuit of perfection and her determination to prove she could be the best of them, she'd fallen abysmally short, been exactly what anyone would've expected of a latecomer. Perfection and renown were not hers to achieve, it would seem.

Helaera, forgive my pride and foolishness.

She would have to claw her way back into the hearts of the Lightguards, earn their respect all over again, if that was even possible now. Regardless, that penance began here.

Eventually she forced herself to get up and shower for something to do other than wallow in her own self-pity. She even washed her hair, meticulously applying her favorite cream to her curls. Her hazel eyes were dull in the mirror, but the way her curls fell around her face after they'd dried for a while was quite beautiful. At least if she felt wretched on the inside, no one would know by looking at her. She adjusted her white and gold tunic and set off to retrieve the prince. Every passing face in the corridors felt like a ghost. Or perhaps she was the ghost herself.

Would the rest of her days here just be spent counting down the hours until she could be miserable in solitude?

"Ah, Corinne!"

Corinne halted down the last corridor to the throne room, turning toward Captain Ekhana.

"Captain," she said, nodding.

"There has been a change of plans for today," he said. "Several nobles' children are gathering with Prince Aryel tonight, so your shift will go a few hours later. The queen feels he's safest with you, and though they won't be leaving palace grounds this time, the last time he convened with these nobles..."

Corinne didn't need reminding. "Understood, Captain."

"Thank you, Corinne."

The warmth in his smile was genuine, and Corinne wished she could return it. She watched him direct his steps the same way he'd come, greeting another of his guards as he went. The guard caught her eye, then—it was Iliana. She offered Corinne a tentative smile and a small wave, her freckled face hopeful.

Corinne turned away and walked on.

CHAPTER 17

The small banquet hall where Prince Aryel and the other children of nobles gathered doubled as a lounge, almost half of the room a mass of plush couches and chairs. The fireplace that stood at the center of them all had been lit for the evening. It was just like their previous gathering, but not in the woods, and with far less alcohol.

Aryel sat by his friends Petros and Elys, two young women sat on the couch adjacent to theirs, and the rest of them were scattered throughout the rest of the room, either retrieving food and drink from a generous spread at the large table or milling about. On the farthest couch from Aryel, Lana sat next to another man Corinne hadn't seen before. He was sandy-haired and extremely tall, garbed in a light blue shirt that showed the hulking muscles of his shoulders and chest.

Corinne stood watch by one of the windows, facing Aryel, who glanced her way several times over the course of an hour. She was the picture of the enduring guard, of the humble, silent servant to the Goddess she ought to be.

The man sitting by Lana stood, swaying a bit. He looked about as drunk as Aryel had the first night she'd met him. Corinne hoped he was retiring—the last thing she wanted to do was call for a servant to clean up some drunken fool's vomit.

But the tall, muscular man did not head for the door. He sauntered right up to Corinne, a lopsided smile plastered on his chiseled, tanned face.

"You know, I wondered why Lana kept complaining about Aryel's celibate pious guard," he said, his speech slurred. Corinne froze as he got closer, and the smell of liquor hit her nose. "Makes sense now. You're awfully pretty for a Sword of Helaera."

Corinne couldn't move; she could only stare at the man in mild panic.

"Why don't you relax a little, eh?" he said. "Haven't you been tempted to indulge in the luxuries of the real world?"

Corinne's heart clenched. She *had* been tempted, and now she was scarred and shunned by her oldest friend. She needed to get away from this man, but she couldn't leave her post.

"Leave her alone, Janus."

Aryel's voice cut across the space between where he sat and where Corinne stood. He was reclined, a drink in his hand, feet propped on a short table between his couch and the other. The man, Janus, turned to the prince, and those nearby quieted, watching.

"What? I'm just trying to help her out," Janus said, bracing an arm on the wall behind Corinne. He was *far* too close. "She just needs permission to relax, get off her high horse."

Aryel hardly looked up from his drink as he said, "Or perhaps the concept of honor is so foreign to you it's impossible to imagine someone else may have a modicum of self-control."

Janus snorted, all humor vacating his face, and he pushed off the wall, mumbling to himself as he returned to his couch. Once everyone had resumed talking, Aryel caught Corinne's gaze, an apology in his eyes.

Her heart cracked. She looked away from him, tears forming in her eyes before she could stop them. *No, not now.*

"I think I've had enough for tonight," Aryel said suddenly. Corinne chanced a glance at him. He patted Elys on the back as he stood, placing his drink on the table. "I'll see you all tomorrow, I'm sure."

He headed quickly for the exit, and Corinne hurried after him. *Keep it together. Keep it together. Just a few more steps...*

The moment she cleared the door, tears began streaming down her cheeks. Goddess, she couldn't guard Aryel if she couldn't *see*, but she'd lost control entirely. Aryel stopped a few strides down the corridor, beckoning her through a doorway. They stepped into a room lit only by tiny candles on an altar at the front. Corinne hastily wiped at her face and realized they were in the sanctuary, surrounded by rows of chairs, stained glass windows depicting Helaera, and a vaulted ceiling with intricate stone carvings.

"I'm sorry about Janus," Aryel said, leaning on the back of a chair. "He's always been an ass." He studied her for another moment. "Are you going to tell me what's wrong?"

Corinne shook her head, making to take a step away from him, but he caught her arm, his fingers pressing into her scar through the thin fabric of her shirt. His eyes widened as he looked down. Before Corinne could pull away, he pushed her sleeve up, his hand brushing the damaged flesh. The handprint-shaped burn was stark even in the dim light of the sanctuary lanterns.

"Corinne," he said slowly. *Corinne.* Not *Sunshine.* "Who did this to you?"

Corinne pulled her arm away, cradling it to her chest. "I did it to myself."

"You burned yourself?"

"No, I—" She shook her head, rubbing at her eyes again. "Why do you care? Why did you defend me back there when all I've done is resent you since I arrived, and then all but ignored you these past two weeks?"

Aryel stared at her.

"Because you saved my life," he said after a beat. "And I know something happened to you at that monastery."

It wasn't any of his business what the Lightguards did with their own. She'd deserved the punishment for her carelessness.

"They burned me," she said anyway, her voice small. The truth poured out of her like a dam breaking, and the sheer horror on his face pulled at a thread within her, a thread she both feared and hoped would unravel something gnarled in her soul.

"You saved my life that night, Corinne," he said. There it was—her name again. "You didn't deserve that. Goddess, if I'd known they would do that to you...I'm so sorry."

"It was a fair punishment for my negligence," she said, closing her eyes. They flew back open at the sudden presence of Aryel's hands on her face.

"No, it wasn't." His voice was low, dangerous almost, but still gentle, and his eyes burned with an intensity she hadn't seen before. "What they did to you was *wrong*. It was needlessly cruel, and I can't think of anyone less deserving of such treatment."

Corinne could only blink at him through her tears. He brushed them away from her cheeks with his thumbs, and for a moment, his gaze shifted downward to her mouth. Corinne nearly stopped breathing. Surely he wasn't thinking about—

"I'm sorry." He released her, the whisper of his hands lingering on her cheeks. "I've been wanting to tell you that for two weeks, but you wouldn't let me say anything unless it was about training or council meetings or my schedule."

"Sorry for what?" she asked.

"For being a fucking ass to you since you got here," he said. "Sorry — swearing. I've been trying to limit that, by the way, not sure if you noticed."

A choked laugh burst from her lips. "We haven't been speaking enough for me to notice a difference."

"And whose fault is that?"

Corinne exhaled slowly, the tears finally subsiding. "I have tried to... be better. To ensure I am serving Helaera and being Her Sword and Her Light."

"Well," Aryel said, "I can say with full confidence that the barbaric thing they did to you had nothing to do with Helaera's Light."

Corinne wasn't sure if she wanted that to be true or not. It was a comfort for someone to tell her that her pain was a tragedy rather than a revelry of the Goddess, but was that the truth, or just what she wanted to hear in her weakness?

"Now that you're speaking to me again, why don't we start over, hm?" he said, holding out his hand to her. "I'm Aryel."

CHAPTER 17

Corinne stared at him, at his outstretched hand, and hope flickered in her chest. This kindness, his concern for her, felt genuine, and if she knew anything to be true, she knew Helaera honored such acts.

She placed her hand in Aryel's. "Corinne."

"You can also call me Ari," he said, squeezing her hand before dropping it and stepping into the corridor again, this time beside her instead of in front. "That's reserved for friends only, though, so no more icing me out, yeah?"

Corinne huffed, allowing that warmth she'd fought to spread within her. It almost felt the way her magic did, and surely something like that couldn't be entirely bad or unholy.

"All right."

CHAPTER 18

Early the next morning, Corinne knelt before her little altar and closed her eyes. It had only been one day since Vera's visit, and the conversation stung like a fresh wound. Somehow, though, Corinne also felt...lighter.

Vera's loss hurt, but the fear of wondering what others might think, the worry that Vera secretly believed she wasn't good enough, had vanished. Corinne knew exactly what Vera thought of her now, and it was likely anyone else who'd heard about her transgressions thought the same. All she could do was try to be better.

I can't think of anyone less deserving of such treatment.

More of that hope flickered within her. Aryel hadn't judged her that night she'd had an episode in front of him, and still had confidence in her abilities, in her goodness. Vera wouldn't approve of a close friendship with the prince and the others she'd met here, but Corinne had spent the past fifteen years pushing away everyone *but* Vera, and it had done nothing to prevent her from making mistakes.

What if she could allow herself to find comfort and confidence in others to find her way back to her purpose? What if she could strive to be the person they believed she was?

Corinne didn't execute the full weekly ritual; she'd done it only yesterday, and this was simply an additional communion with Helaera. Breathing in the fresh morning air wafting through her open windows, Corinne started to sing.

Fear not, my dear one, the sun will still rise
My Light will greet you when you open your eyes
You won't remember the shadows that fell
Hold tight in moonlight, and I'll keep you well

Normally when they'd sung this song at the monastery, a fiddle or flute or harp would accompany them, and Corinne could almost hear the instruments in her head as she sang the second verse.

Look not to futures that may not arise
Keep faith and look for my star in the sky
You won't be lost here, you've found a home
Wield now the sunlight, wherever you roam

The scent of impending rain hung in the air when Corinne stepped into the alcove and greeted the guard who'd been at Aryel's door overnight. The woman yawned and walked off, and Aryel emerged from his room several minutes later. He'd consistently been awake before noon for the past week.

"Hi, Corinne," he said, adjusting the cuff on his dark blue sleeve.

"Hi, Ari," she said, and his eyes lifted to hers, a lopsided smile on his face.

The flood of warmth behind her navel didn't scare her this time; she could do this. She was above temptation now, resigned to her life and her duty here.

She escorted Aryel to the kitchens, where workers tossed him a scone, fully expecting his visit. They tossed one to Corinne, too, and she caught it with a grateful nod. She ate it quickly, uncomfortable with having either of her hands occupied when she was meant to be guarding Aryel. It had been baked with raspberries, and she nearly sighed at the taste even as she practically inhaled it.

Goddess, Corinne, eat the roll, don't inhale it. The memory of Vera's lighthearted admonishment sent a pang through her heart. Had it truly been lighthearted then, or had Vera always seen her as some trainee in danger of straying? Had she lied all these years about not judging her based on who her father was, what he had done?

Aryel arrived at the library, and Corinne joined him inside despite the limited visitors within. It was still awkward to stand in corridors with twice as many guards walking around. Servant activity had also increased with all the nobles now staying on the grounds.

So Corinne took up a spot by the end of one of the stacks, with a full view of the library entrance and Aryel at a table piled high with books. His brow scrunched up as he read and then scribbled something down on parchment. What was he studying so intently?

A book tumbled to the floor to her left, and Corinne turned to find Nik crouching between the stacks to retrieve it. She hadn't even heard him approach.

"Hi, Nik," she said, and the surprise on his face when he looked at her turned her stomach. One day she would figure out how to avoid doing and saying the wrong thing so she could live without this constant shadow of guilt.

"Hi, Corinne," he said, straightening with the book in his hands. "Are we on speaking terms again, then?"

She grimaced. "I'm sorry. I was…it doesn't matter. I'm sorry."

Nik offered her a small smile, adjusting his glasses with one hand. "Don't worry about it."

"Helaera honors your capacity to forgive, and I'm grateful for it," Corinne said.

Nik approached her, patting her shoulder. "Wonderful. Now can you forgive Danai and me for scandalizing you in the gardens?"

An embarrassed laugh caught in her throat. "Only if you promise never to speak of it again."

Nik grinned broadly at her. "Deal."

Nik returned to his work, and Corinne stood steadily at her post as others filed in and out of the library over the next hour. Councilor Toro appeared, approaching Aryel and speaking with him at length, both of them occasionally pointing to the text of a book Aryel had open on his table. Corinne couldn't make out what they were saying, but it seemed they were trying to solve some sort of problem.

Nik was shelving several books in the stack next to Corinne when Councilor Toro noticed him and stood, bidding Aryel farewell.

"Nik," Councilor Toro said, his smile bright. "Danai tells me you've reached a breakthrough in your studies on ancient texts?"

"I wouldn't call it a breakthrough," Nik said. "Not yet, at least. But Danai is ever the optimist."

"That they are," Councilor Toro chuckled. "Very well. I'll see you the evening after next, then?"

"I'll be there," Nik said. He tilted his head toward Corinne. "I've told Corinne she ought to join us."

"I wouldn't want to overstep," Corinne said quickly, cheeks flushing.

Councilor Toro looked to her, an open smile on his kind face. "You would be most welcome, dear. Please do join us if you can."

The councilor bid them both a good day before departing, and Nik huffed a soft laugh.

"I told you there was no imposing on the Mykotas household," he said.

Corinne's smile faded as she turned her attention back to Aryel, who now looked worried instead of just perplexed as he stared at the books and parchment before him.

"Everything all right?" she asked, approaching his table.

He sighed, leaning back in his chair and rubbing his face. "The eastern farmlands did not yield as much as we'd hoped this past year," he said. "Their stores are running low. The lands in the west produced plenty, but figuring out a way to transport that food quickly and securely has been a challenge. We can't let this issue continue into the summer and autumn, or we will have a crisis come winter."

Corinne glanced at the maps, books, and notes strewn about the table. "And this is a new issue?"

"There was a similar problem about a hundred years ago, according to several accounts I've read," he said. "But we have a greater population now, and the location of the villages provides additional complications that our predecessors did not have to handle."

He pointed to the villages in question on the map, and Corinne frowned.

"Could the Lightguards not help?" she asked.

Aryel paused. "You think they could?"

Corinne shrugged. "They travel around more than anyone in the kingdom, and our magic could quickly remedy any ailments along the road and prevent animals from approaching the wagons of food."

Aryel blinked at her, one hand scratching his jaw as he considered it. "That would be brilliant."

"I can write to them if you'd like," Corinne said. "As soon as today."

Aryel gave her that lopsided smile again, and she ignored the flush that crept up her neck.

"Thank you, Corinne."

She offered him a smile and nod in return. "Those people are under the protection of the Crown and the Lightguards, and it's our duty to serve them."

His face turned pensive for a moment, and a bit of doubt crept along Corinne's skin. Perhaps it wasn't acceptable to describe the royals as servants to the people, and she'd somehow offended him.

"Let's hope that the other Lightguards are half as willing to help as you are," Aryel said.

As Aryel went back to poring over the books and papers, Corinne shook off the nagging fear that his skeptical tone was warranted. She'd send that message later, ask for the help needed, and perhaps help strengthen the tie between the Crown and the Lightguards as the two great pillars of Ashera.

Few others ventured into the library during Aryel's stay, and Corinne was grateful for the quiet as she returned to her post by the stacks. Perhaps the other nobles had all drunk themselves unconscious the previous night and were still recovering.

"Corinne?"

She turned at Nik's approach, offering him a little smile.

"Danai and Iliana will be outside training tomorrow at the usual time," he said as he placed another book away on a nearby shelf. He gave a little shrug. "Just in case you wanted to know."

More guilt settled in Corinne's gut at the thought, but she knew it wouldn't dissipate until she spoke to them.

She nodded once. "That is good to know," she said. *Stay the course.* "Do you...are they angry with me?"

"Angry? No," Nik said, placing his hands in the pockets of his tan trousers. "Perhaps a little confused. I'm sure you can clear things up."

Corinne wished she had such confidence. Knowing that she'd suspected them of spying at first, when in reality they'd been genuinely kind to her with no other motive...she had to try. *Helaera guide me.*

"I will try," she said.

CHAPTER 19

Corinne took a deep breath before stepping outside the castle doors onto the training grounds the next day. Heavy clouds obscured the sun, but she still had to squint in the diffused light of midmorning. A cool breeze ran through her hair and ruffled the long sleeves of her white tunic.

Aside from facing this conversation, she was in better spirits. Hopefully she'd taken a step in rebuilding her own honor by sending that message to the monastery yesterday. If she could contribute in some small way to serving both the Lightguards and the people of Ashera, that would be enough to start.

The smell of rain clung to the air, and very few guards were sparring or making use of the archery range. From here, though, Corinne could make out Iliana and Danai in the ring with sandy terrain. Her palms grew sweaty, but she pressed forward.

Iliana fell to the sand with an *oof* just as Corinne reached the ring's perimeter, and Danai held their sword to her throat with a satisfied grin. They both laughed, and Danai helped her up. Danai's smile faltered when they caught sight of Corinne, and Iliana's gaze followed.

"Hi," Corinne said feebly. *Great start, Corinne.*

"Hi, Corinne," Danai said, walking over to her. Iliana hesitated before joining them. "How are you?"

"I've been better," Corinne said. "But that's not why I'm here. I wanted to apologize to you both."

They exchanged a quick glance, their faces surprised but not unkind.

"I've been cold these past two weeks, and neither of you deserved that after your kindness toward me."

Danai's face softened into a smile. "Corinne, we know you've had a lot to face here. And we've all made mistakes."

"Yeah, did you miss the part where I punched another guard in the face during lunch?" Iliana quipped, and the three of them laughed.

"So...can we train together again?" Danai asked. "And will you join us for meals again?"

Corinne nodded, a weight lifting from her chest.

"Eugh, Danai, no more training in sand when we have a shift later," Iliana said as they stepped inside, headed for the dining hall. "I'll be shaking sand out of places I didn't even know existed for the rest of the day."

Danai's laugh was echoed by a loud clap of thunder from outside. "At least we got inside before that started."

"Corinne Anastos!"

The three of them whipped around mid-stride, facing a servant who scurried toward them, a stack of messages in hand. He wheezed as he halted, holding out one to Corinne.

"A letter came for you this morning," he said, and Corinne's heart leapt. Had the monastery gotten back to her already?

She took it, thanking him, and walked on with Danai and Iliana, unrolling it while they continued their conversation a pace ahead of her. Corinne read it quickly and stopped breathing.

I know your secret, Corinne Anastos.

There was no signature, no symbol indicating who it had come from. Corinne's head felt suddenly heavy, her lips and cheeks going cold. Who could know her secret? And why tell her if they didn't want something? Why just send her this cryptic note?

"Corinne?"

Danai and Iliana turned several paces ahead of her. She hadn't realized she'd stopped walking.

Stay the course. Be the Light. Stay the course. Be the Light.

Someone knows your secret and is going to tell all the Lightguards. You'll never regain their respect or trust.

No, she couldn't let that happen.

And you deserve it because you're a fraud and you always have been.

Corinne hadn't started gasping for air like last time; instead she was frozen, fear and dread spreading throughout her body, immobilizing her.

"What did the note say?" Danai asked, concern written on their face.

Corinne blinked, swallowed hard. "Not here," she managed to say.

Danai and Iliana exchanged another look before nodding to one another. She followed them to that same storage room they'd ventured to after Iliana's lunchtime brawl and, before shutting the door behind them, ensured no one else was outside.

"Corinne, what's going on?" Danai asked.

"Are you hurt?" Iliana asked, looking her over. Corinne shook her head. "Is someone you know hurt?"

"No," she croaked, and it forced her to take a gasping breath.

Danai gently took the letter from her hands.

"Can I look?" they asked, and Corinne nodded her assent. Danai's brow furrowed deeply. They handed the note to Iliana, who looked equally perplexed after reading it. "I don't understand."

"Neither do I," Iliana said. "So you've got a secret, and some anonymous fuck sends you a note about it? Without even threatening you or asking for something so they don't spill it? That makes no sense."

Corinne took a deep breath. "No, it doesn't."

"Well, we won't pry if you don't want to share," Iliana said. She glanced up at Danai. "Right, Danai?"

Danai lifted their hands in surrender, which coaxed a halfhearted laugh from Corinne. Iliana stared at the note for another moment.

"You know, my little brother makes his own ink," she said. "Talks our ears off all the time about how it's made, which types of ink come from which parts of Ashera. I bet he could tell us where this letter might've come from, at the very least."

A bit of the weight lifted from Corinne's chest. "Really?"

Iliana nodded. "I'll bring it to him when I go home tonight, if you don't mind."

"Please," Corinne said. "And thank you. Thank you both."

"It's your turn to need the storage room next time, Danai," Iliana said, slapping them on the back. "When do you think you'll have your own crisis?"

Danai let out a low whistle, shaking their head dramatically as they opened the door for Corinne and Iliana. "Hard to say. Maybe if Nik tells me to read that pirate book one more time."

"Oh, *The Sea of Starlight*?" Corinne asked, forgetting all else for a moment. "I love that one."

"Thank the Goddess for you, Corinne," Danai said, wrapping an arm around her shoulders as they walked. It was, admittedly, awkward, given that Danai was a head shorter than Corinne, but she didn't mind. "He'll finally have someone to ramble about it with."

Corinne knew Danai had meant it lightheartedly, but as they walked on, she found herself truly thanking Helaera for both Danai and Iliana.

Aryel's face was stony when he exited the throne room, and some of the lightness in Corinne's chest grew heavy again. He looked away quickly when their eyes met and started down the corridor. Corinne followed.

"What do you do in there for hours, anyway?" she asked, speeding up so she was nearly beside him. He wasn't going to ice *her* out after requesting she stop doing that herself.

Aryel's shoulders tensed, then loosened as he exhaled. "My parents and I discuss pressing matters, and then we treat with nobles," he said. There was an edge to his voice Corinne didn't like.

They passed by a group of guards, who each bowed to Aryel, and then turned a corner, headed for the stairs.

"Are the nobles difficult?" Corinne asked.

"Depends on who it is and what day."

Corinne frowned as they kept walking. "You just always seem to be in a foul mood afterward," Corinne said.

Aryel glanced at her sidelong. "Who wouldn't be after hours of speaking to people you don't wish to speak with?" he asked, entering the stairwell.

Corinne suppressed a sigh. He was being evasive, but she didn't want to press him into hating her again.

What if he never stopped hating you?

Corinne slowed, letting Aryel walk ahead several strides as icy dread gripped her insides.

He's just going to use your own weakness against you. He'll find out your secret and shun you for it too.

It wasn't true. Was it?

Stay the course. Be the Light. Repeat four times. *They're just thoughts.* Her pulse slowed again. Goddess, she wished that voice would simply leave her in peace for once.

She nearly scoffed aloud at the thought. Peace.

Would she ever know it?

CHAPTER 20

I *know your secret, Corinne Anastos.*
The voice drifted from the shadows of the castle corridor, stopping Corinne dead. A cloaked figure appeared at the stairwell a few feet ahead. A disembodied voice floated past her ears again.

Your father was a defector. A heretic. A traitor.

"What do you want?" Corinne asked, her voice breaking. She drew her sword, but the voice only laughed.

Admit it, to the world, to yourself—you will end up just like him.

"No," Corinne growled, gripping her sword more tightly.

She whirled around, but the corridor was empty. The cloaked figure at the stairwell entrance lifted their hands to lower their hood. It revealed a middle-aged face, hazel eyes, and cropped hair the same chestnut color as Corinne's. His expression was rigid, his eyes cold.

"Father," she whispered, the blood draining from her face.

"*Corinne!*"

She whipped around again, and this time, at the opposite end of the hallway, her mother was there, her dark brown curls falling into her eyes as she searched wildly for her daughter.

"Mother!" Corinne called, but she didn't seem to hear her.

Corinne looked back to her father just as he summoned his magic, and it wasn't just light along his arms and hands, but flames that licked up his skin.

No.

Corinne sprinted toward her panicked mother. She could save her. This time, she could save her. She *had* to.

Fire engulfed the entire corridor in an instant. Corinne screamed as it rose to her legs, and suddenly she was falling.

She wasn't in the castle anymore; she was in that tiny room in that little house, and it was burning. *She* was burning and choking on smoke. She couldn't move, so she just screamed and begged for help, begged for her mother—

"Corinne!"

Corinne's eyes flew open, greeted by disorienting darkness. Her magic was blazing from her hands and arms, up her shoulders, illuminating the panicked face a few inches from hers. Goddess, she was still burning, and Aryel was there. What if she hurt him?

The way her father had hurt her mother?

"Corinne, are you hurt? What can I do?" he asked, his hands on her upper arms.

Some small part of her realized if she was actually on fire, that would have caused him pain.

"Shower," she choked out. Aryel quickly helped her out of bed, supporting her weight as he guided her to the washroom. "Cold."

Aryel stepped into the shower with her, both of them fully clothed, and turned the tap to the coldest setting.

"You'll get wet," she said hoarsely.

"I don't give a fuck about getting wet, Corinne. Here." He helped her sit on the tiled floor and joined her there, his back resting against the wall as Corinne bowed her head beneath the frigid water.

It washed over the back of her neck, her head, her shoulders, soaking through her nightgown just as it had the last time.

Her magic finally calmed, the light fading until they were left in darkness. Corinne clumsily reached up to cut the water off. Aryel leaned forward, one hand on her water-slick back between her shoulder blades, right where her Sun of Helaera tattoo was.

CHAPTER 20

"How did you know?" she whispered, pushing back the wet hair plastered onto her face.

"You were screaming," he said, his voice strained. "The guard outside and I thought something had happened, and I had him unlock your door."

"You heard me from your room?"

"I would've heard you from down the breezeway."

Corinne dropped her face into her hands. "That is humiliating."

"D-don't worry about it," he said, leaning forward and shivering against her. "He won't say anything. Goddess, without your magic, it's freezing in here. Come on."

He helped her stand and retrieved two towels, draping one around her shoulders. Corinne shivered herself now, and more embarrassment prickled along her skin—beneath the soaked white fabric, her body was *very* much on display.

"I'll, uh, give you a moment," Aryel said, toweling at some of the water drenching his loose gray shirt. "I'm coming right back, but I'm going to put dry clothes on while you do the same."

Corinne mechanically dried herself off and retrieved a comfortable shirt and loose trousers, trying not to wilt from mortification. Plenty of people at the monastery had seen her entirely naked, but Aryel seeing even that much of her felt...different, somehow. Exposed. Yet it didn't bother her as much as it should have.

She quickly pulled on the dry clothes and squeezed as much excess water from her hair as she could. When a soft knock sounded on her door, she called, "Come in."

Aryel stepped inside and shut the door behind him, a small candle in his hand. He placed it on the table right by her door.

"Feel better?" he asked as Corinne stood there, her right hand clutched around her left arm.

She shivered again. "Y-yes," she said.

"Do you want me to stay for a bit?"

Corinne stared at him, at his tousled black shirt and loose tan trousers.

At his earnest face.

"Yes," she said, her voice small.

She padded over to her bed and climbed beneath the blankets, and Aryel sat on the rug beside it, his back propped against her mattress.

"Is this okay?" he asked, looking over his shoulder at her. "Me sitting here?"

She nodded against her pillow, and he faced her room again. Corinne studied the outline of his profile in the flickering candlelight, his still-damp hair.

"Was that...were you having more of those thoughts?" he asked.

Corinne exhaled slowly. "Those happen more regularly," she said. "And sometimes I can't calm myself down. The nightmares are rarer. Well, they used to be. I've had this happen twice since I've been here."

Why was she telling him this? It was like being around him put her in some kind of trance where she had to tell him the truth about everything.

Almost everything. Only Corinne, the Priestesses, Vera, and whoever had written her that note knew about her father.

"Do you want to talk about it?" he asked. "Will that help?"

Corinne breathed deeply. "My mother died when I was ten, in a fire. Sometimes I still dream about it."

Aryel turned to look at her again, horror etched into his face.

Corinne closed her eyes as she said, "Fifteen years later and each time I have a nightmare about it, it's like I recall every detail *so* clearly. I nearly died too, but my magic saved me."

"Goddess, Corinne," Aryel murmured, and she opened her eyes. Tears shone in his in the dim light. "I don't know what to say."

"What is there to say about tragedy?" she said, shrugging a shoulder. "All we can do is hope it does not befall us or those we care for. And if it does, hope it does not visit us twice."

Aryel turned away from her again, silent for a long moment.

"You nearly died in a fire as a child," he said slowly. "And those— and they *burned* you as punishment for some perceived mistake?"

The small, weak child tucked deep in her heart cried out for this understanding, reveled in the barely suppressed rage in his voice. But Corinne pushed her away.

"It's a typical punishment for a Lightguard who has strayed," she said. Exhaustion tugged at her now, heavy in her heart and her head.

CHAPTER 20

"That doesn't mean it isn't deeply fucking wrong. Sorry," he added.

Corinne closed her eyes again, smirking. "S'fine, Ari."

He said something else, but Corinne didn't catch it as she drifted into the waiting arms of sleep.

∼

Sunlight warmed Corinne's face, and she opened her eyes slowly. Aryel's right arm was draped close to the edge of her bed, his head resting atop his shoulder. It would be so easy to reach out and glide her fingers along his skin, grasp his hand in her own.

Coming to her senses, Corinne shifted in bed, sitting up. Aryel stirred, then, inhaling sharply.

"Goddess," he said, stiffly rolling his shoulder and neck. "That's going to be sore."

"I can help," she said. She started to reach for his neck, then hesitated. "Can I?"

"Please."

Corinne placed her hand on the back of his neck and summoned her light. She sent the gentle warmth into his stiff muscles and felt him relax as they released. It only took a few seconds for her magic to do its work, but then her light drifted downward, seeking something else to mend. She didn't see it, but she sensed bruising on his upper right arm. It was easy enough to heal, so she let her magic soothe that little injury too.

"Better?" she asked.

Aryel turned to face her as she removed her hand. "Infinitely. Thank you."

Corinne sat frozen under his gaze for a few more moments before reality crashed into her.

"Oh, Goddess," she said, her face going red as she flew out of bed, pacing to her window and back. "You were in my room overnight."

"Yes," he said, standing slowly.

"People will...*assume* things," Corinne said, wringing her hands, and understanding lit Aryel's face.

"No one is going to assume anything," he said. "Hey."

He stepped into her path, and she halted right before running into him. He gently removed her hands from her horrified face, holding her wrists.

"Listen, Sunshine, the only person who knows I stayed in here last night is the guard stationed out there right now," he said. "He's not going to say a damned thing, so please breathe."

Corinne chewed her cheek but nodded. He was right. No one ever came to the alcove unless summoned.

Except for Nik. Or—goddess above—Lana, that one time. Still, it was unlikely, so Corinne calmed herself.

"I'll meet you outside in a few minutes," he said. "I've got an early meeting with Councilor Toro today."

Corinne nodded and remembered just before he walked out.

"About Councilor Toro," she said. "I've been invited to dinner at his home tomorrow evening."

Aryel smiled softly. "His family are good people. You should go."

"Are you sure? I don't want to inconvenience anyone."

"I'll talk to Captain Ekhana today when we train," he said. "Should be easy enough to find someone to cover for you for a few hours."

Corinne returned his smile. "All right. Thank you."

"Anything for you, Sunshine," he said, winking, leaving Corinne somehow both annoyed and flattered at the same time.

CHAPTER 21

Corinne shifted her weight from one foot to the other as she stood by the castle gates with Danai, Nik, and Iliana, waiting for Danai's father to arrive so they could leave. She'd forgotten about the stricter rules surrounding the entering and leaving of the grounds; she hadn't left since they'd been enforced.

Danai and Nik exchanged updates about their respective days with an occasional contribution from Iliana, and Corinne was the first to notice Councilor Toro's arrival. He stepped outside the castle and walked toward them with a stack of books in his hands, which Nik and Danai both offered to take.

"Thank you," Councilor Toro said. "Shall we be on our way, then?"

The guards let them through without trouble, assured that Corinne, Nik, Iliana, and Danai would be returning later that night. They took an immediate right down a wide street along the castle's perimeter wall.

As the evening sun shone down on the cobbled streets and clay roofs, Corinne realized she'd never actually been in Vytanos during the day. The stone and stucco buildings were a mix of tans, blues, and grays on this street, shops closing up for the day, and most homes were at least two stories high. The rooftop Aryel had climbed the night they'd been attacked was back the other way, in the southwestern part of the city.

They headed north for two more blocks before coming upon a two-story stone house covered in flowering vines and accented by two wrought-iron window fixtures. A small but beautiful garden was walled in around the front side, with a little stone path leading to the door. The roof, from here, at least, seemed to be open, with more flowering vines wrapped around a wooden pergola.

Councilor Toro opened the gate and held it for Danai and Nik so they wouldn't drop his books, and Iliana and Corinne followed. The moment she stepped inside, Corinne's mouth was watering at the aromas in the air. The foyer was dark, leading down a narrow hall that opened into a large kitchen with wide, short windows. A small woman with raven hair identical to Danai's looked over her shoulder from the stove where she was stirring one of three pots. Ingredients and already-prepared food items lay behind her on an island counter.

"I hope you're all hungry," she said, flashing a bright smile. The warm sepia skin of her face was caked in flour on one side. "Oh, a new face?"

"Amma, this is Corinne," Danai said, beckoning Corinne forward. She stepped toward the woman a little timidly, her face warming. "She's a Lightguard."

Danai's mother's mouth popped open, and she let her spoon drop to the side of the pot she'd been stirring.

"It's an honor to have a Lightguard in my home," she said, stepping forward to take Corinne's hand. "I'm Selana."

"The honor is mine, Selana," Corinne said, and she meant it.

A month ago, Selana's reverence might have felt deserved, even expected. Now it felt unearned, but Corinne would do her best to be worthy of it.

"You all can wait upstairs," Selana said. "I'll call you down when it's time to help haul everything up there."

"Thanks, Amma," Danai said.

Nik stepped forward to accept a kiss on the cheek from Selana, and a quick whispered exchange resulted in a cackle on her part. Iliana stole a small square of flatbread from the counter and popped it into her mouth, holding a finger up to her lips at Corinne before following Danai and Nik toward the stairs.

They passed by the second floor, which was a short hallway with two doors on either side, and emerged onto the rooftop with the pergola. It was even lovelier than Corinne had expected it to be, covered in greenery and a mix of deep fuchsia, violet, and yellow flowers. A large wooden table stood at the center, already set with small plates and utensils. One side boasted a bench like those in the castle dining hall, and the other had four identical wooden chairs.

Corinne could've stayed up there for days, but what truly took her breath away was when Danai beckoned her over to the stone railing on the far side. They had a view of the entire city, even better than the view from the breezeway close to Aryel's rooms. It was somehow both in the city and above it all, and the forests and hills beyond its gates stretched for miles. The mountains rose tall to the north and south, resolute against the deep azure sky.

"Gorgeous, isn't it?" Danai asked wryly. Nik and Iliana had taken seats at the table already, making themselves comfortable. "The castle has some views, but this is my favorite in all of Vytanos."

"And you grew up here?"

Danai rested their arms on the railing. "I did. I'm very fortunate."

"Corinne, have you told Nik that you've read that pirate book yet?" Iliana called, and Corinne turned to meet Nik's excited gaze.

"You've read *The Sea of Starlight*?"

Corinne joined Nik at the table, and Iliana and Danai gaped at them as they went on at length about the novel.

"Is it offensive that I'm surprised a Lightguard is so well-read?" Danai asked when they both took a breath, and Iliana smacked their arm.

"Since when are you concerned with being offensive?" Nik asked, rolling his eyes.

"When you think about it, Lightguards are keepers of stories," Corinne said, smiling softly. "We know all of Asheran history and all the legends of the gods."

"Can you tell us a story?" Danai asked, and Nik's eyes brightened.

"I..." Corinne looked at their expectant faces and sighed. "What kind of story?"

"Whatever first comes to mind," Danai said, settling in their chair and leaning their head on Nik's shoulder.

Even Iliana couldn't hide the curiosity on her face.

"All right." Corinne lifted her right hand, palm aligned with her forehead, fingers gracefully curved, and summoned a small bit of light.

The three of them watched her, frozen in place. She closed her eyes.

"We honor the Goddess Helaera for Her Light, which gives us life and warmth and guides us wherever we go. May she speak through my voice and attend my heart."

Corinne lowered her hand, holding a glowing orb of light in her palms by the center of her chest, and opened her eyes again.

"Tales of light are often spun out of darkness. When mortals had only walked the earth for a century, the goddesses Helaera and Arytalis worked in tandem. Sisters, daughters of the Sky herself, Day and Night shepherding the turn of the earth and the passing of time.

"But wicked things can fester in the dark. Arytalis grew jealous of her sister, of the mortals' love for her when they feared the dark and the night. So Arytalis granted humans her power, hoping such a gift would bring them to understand her. The humans wielding those shadows wrought only more fear, though—violence against their fellows, corruption as they sought dominion over those without magic. Helaera confronted Arytalis about this mistake, and the night goddess denied any wrongdoing.

"Desperate to prevent the Nightrenders from annihilating the other humans and each other, Helaera chose a select few to be granted her power, the power of sunlight, of warmth, of healing. Lightguards, she named them—divine protectors. They defended

the nonmagic humans for a time, until once again, Arytalis grew bitter with jealousy. Her rage strengthened the Nightrenders, who hunted the Lightguards to near extinction.

"In a final attempt to salvage humankind, Helaera gathered the Lightguards and nonmagic folk and drove her great spear into the earth, carving out a piece of it where the mortals could be safe. Along its perimeter, she infused a shield of divine Light. Thus Ashera was split from the Shadowlands, and thus we have dwelt for a millennium, the Boundary kept intact and ever watched by Lightguards."

When Corinne finished, her light receded, and she was met by utter silence and blank stares. Discomfort crept up her spine; had she said something to frighten or offend them? It was the most commonly told story she knew, but perhaps the origin of Ashera was not so widely known outside the monastery.

"That was *brilliant*," Nik said breathlessly, and Danai blinked before they started applauding softly. "Truly, Corinne, thank you for sharing that. I've never heard a story orated that way."

"Oh," Corinne said, flushing. "Well, you're welcome."

"Danai!" Selana's voice rang out from downstairs. "Time to eat!"

Thank Helaera for that. Corinne rose with the others to hurry downstairs and help retrieve the platters of food. It was an incredible assortment of colors, and she tasted at least one of everything while they ate together; grape leaves wrapped around a mixture of rice and goat cheese, roasted chicken and garlic, and the best flatbread she'd ever had.

She wasn't able to contribute much to the conversation outside of jokes about training and guard duty, but the peace that befell her as she sat there with Danai's family and her friends took her by surprise.

The moment she noticed the contented warmth within her, though, it began slipping away. Danai and Iliana had begun good-naturedly arguing about the merits of participating in street fighting for pay when Corinne quietly slipped over to the roof's railing again. Nik and Councilor Toro remained deep in quiet conversation over wine.

Corinne leaned on the railing as the sun set over Vytanos, fighting the growing sense of dread in the pit of her stomach, forcing herself to breathe.

"Everything all right, dear?"

Selana appeared beside her, dark brown eyes full of gentle knowing. It was a mother's look, a look she hadn't seen in many years but recognized all the same. Corinne couldn't find the words.

"I knew another Lightguard once," Selana said, leaning beside Corinne and looking out over the city. Corinne's surprise was enough to make the turbulence within her settle somewhat. "She was from my home village, Orynas. We'd been best friends as children, and wrote to each other once we both learned how, but her letters dwindled as the years passed. She returned as a young woman, gleaming sword and honed magic. It was one of my greatest sadnesses that she no longer wished to be my friend."

A knife twisted in Corinne's gut. *I can't put my own soul at risk by being friends with someone like you.* "I'm sorry that happened to you."

Selana looked at her sidelong, and her gaze pierced right through Corinne.

"My sadness was primarily for her, my dear," she said. "She had achieved all she set out to, and yet I could see how detached she had become, how she was never at peace with herself."

Corinne looked out at the city again, a lump forming in her throat. "It...it's not right for me to feel so content when I'm so far from the goddess. So far from the other Lightguards."

Selana faced her fully now, tucking one of Corinne's curls behind her ear.

"Oh, Corinne," she said. "You of all people should know Helaera is close no matter what. And that peace you feel? That's part of Her Light too. You should run toward those who give you such peace, not push them away."

Corinne's stomach unclenched. *That's part of Her Light too.*

They're just thoughts.

She'd have to decipher it all later, because it was true—she'd been taught her whole life that Helaera was goodness and comfort and light, and she felt all those things around Danai, Nik, and Iliana.

CHAPTER 21

Her heart took off as she gazed out at the city. She felt those things around Aryel too.

"Come, dear," Selana said, patting Corinne's hand. "I've made some dessert for us all."

Corinne returned to the table just as Danai emerged from the stairwell with a tray of fruit tarts. They all dug in the moment everyone was served, and Corinne closed her eyes as the sweetness washed over her tongue.

"*Fuck*, that's delicious," Iliana groaned.

Corinne nearly choked on her food, and Selana cackled as Danai slapped a hand to the table and said, "HA! Pay up!"

"Oh, hells," Iliana said, rolling her eyes as she dug into her pocket to extract a silver coin.

Danai snatched it, shaking their head in mock disappointment.

"We all promised not to swear in front of you tonight," Nik explained across the table, chuckling. "And that we had to pay if we did."

Corinne couldn't help it—she burst out laughing, and once she'd started, she couldn't stop. The others joined her, hardly able to finish their dessert.

Cheeks sore and stomachs full, Corinne and the others helped clear the table and clean the dishes before departing. Councilor Toro remained behind, not obligated to return to the castle that night. Danai and Iliana bemoaned their impending night shifts as they walked, but Corinne hardly heard them, unable to relax until they'd reached the castle gates. Being in the city at night had every one of her senses on high alert. At least tonight she wasn't sleep-deprived or under the influence of alcohol.

The guards at the gates promptly let them inside after verifying they recognized each of them, and Corinne exhaled.

Danai let out a dramatic sigh as they approached the entrance hall. "Well, good night, you all. Same time next week?"

"As always," Nik said, yawning.

"Good night," Corinne said. "Thank you for inviting me."

"You're welcome any time," Danai said, draping an arm over Iliana's shoulder as Nik kissed their cheek.

"Nik, tell your father we hate him," Iliana said as Danai dragged her off down the corridor.

"I'll be sure to do that," Nik called after them. He huffed a laugh, a hand on his hip. He looked to Corinne. "I'll see you tomorrow in the library, I'm sure."

Corinne nodded. "See you tomorrow."

CHAPTER 22

Corinne couldn't find it in herself to be disappointed that she was also headed for a night shift—being able to go to the Mykotas's for dinner had placed another bandage over her battered heart, and it was easier to breathe now. She thought of the Lightguard who had been childhood friends with Selana, and hoped that, wherever she was now, she had found that peace she'd lost.

A thread tugged in her heart again, threatening some untangling she wasn't ready to face.

Corinne pushed through the doors that led out to the breezeway. Halfway across, muffled shouting reached her ears, and her heart stopped at the same moment her feet picked up speed. The guard standing outside Aryel's door was unperturbed, meeting Corinne's alarmed gaze without so much as a blink.

"...A disgrace to us *and* the nation!" The shout came from within Aryel's rooms, and the voice was horribly familiar.

The king. Corinne released the grip on her sword hilt and straightened.

"You can go," she said to the guard, jerking her chin toward the breezeway.

He nodded once and walked off. Corinne braced herself as she took up her post and the shouting continued.

"...I mean, *really*, Aryel, have you taken your position seriously for even a moment?" This time it was Queen Erina's voice.

Corinne swallowed hard as she stared at the wall.

"Even when you aren't engaging in constant debauchery, you manage to be an utter disappointment!"

"Well, perhaps if you were better at your job, *Father*, we wouldn't be in this predicament in the first place!"

The answering *crack* and cry struck Corinne's chest like a bolt of lightning. *Stay put. Don't move.* Whatever else was said in the following moments was too low for her to distinguish. Footsteps rapidly approached the door, and Corinne stood as still as she possibly could as King Theo and Queen Erina emerged, the king wiping the back of his right hand on his cloak.

"Oh, good," the king grunted, catching sight of Corinne. "You can fix his face."

The shock wore off in an instant, replaced with broiling rage.

The queen took King Theo's arm as they headed for the breezeway. It seemed to take them an eternity to walk across it and disappear through the doors. Corinne held her breath as she waited a few more seconds, just to be certain they were gone.

She turned to face Aryel's door. Another moment, a forced inhale, and she knocked softly and waited. No sound. No answer. She knocked again with a little more conviction.

"Ari, it's me," she said, her voice cracking beneath the combined weight of ire and concern.

The door opened, and Corinne gazed in horror at the nasty cut across Aryel's cheek for only a moment before he threw his arms around her, his face tucked into the crook of her neck. Corinne returned his embrace, letting him collapse into her for a few seconds of silent comfort.

The mysterious bruises he'd hidden. His changes in demeanor after being around his parents. The fact that he'd noticed when she'd started wearing long sleeves to hide an injury.

Anger gripped Corinne by the throat with frightening intensity, and

CHAPTER 22

she tamped it down hard. Aryel didn't need her fire right now, but he did need her light. She leaned back and peered at his downcast face.

"Let me look at that," she said quietly, her fingers brushing his jaw.

She took his hand and led him back over the threshold, allowing his door to shut behind them. Aryel didn't say a word as she had him sit on the couch in his antechamber. She removed her sword belt and placed it on the little table before sitting beside him.

That fire blazed inside her again when she gently reached for his face, turning his head so she could clearly see the injury. Blood trickled down his left cheek into his facial hair, leaking from a jagged cut surrounded by an angry red welt that was on its way to becoming a dark bruise. Corinne's fingers alighted with her magic, and Aryel closed his eyes as she placed her glowing hand on his cheek. He breathed slowly as Corinne's magic mended the cut, the broken blood vessels beneath.

"This has happened before," she said, her voice trembling.

"Yes," Aryel said, his eyes opening slowly. The twinkle within them she'd grown so accustomed to had vanished. "For a few years now. This is the first time he's cut me, though. Forgot to take his rings off."

Corinne's rage flared so high her light pulsed, her eyes flashing.

"Easy, Sunshine," he muttered, resting a hand on her glowing forearm. "It just happens sometimes. I should know better than to fire back at him."

Corinne shook her head, angry tears threatening her eyes.

"You do not deserve this," she said, her voice a hoarse whisper as she finished his healing. She didn't immediately remove her hand from his face, even after her light receded.

"I know," he said, smiling sadly, his fingers sliding up her arm to take her hand. She let him, unable to break his gaze. "That's how I knew you didn't, either."

Corinne couldn't ponder that right now, and she needed to calm down. What was she going to do, go hunt down the king and break *his* hand for daring to strike his son?

The thought was appealing.

"I don't understand," she said. "You have been working so hard, I've seen it, with Councilor Toro and your studies and training—"

"None of that makes a difference when I've spent years

disappointing them in one way or another," Aryel said, leaning back on the couch and staring at his ceiling. He still hadn't let go of her hand. "But I...I still try. If not for them, for the nation." His gaze shifted to Corinne again. "For...people like you. You make me want to try. You make me want to be a better person, Corinne."

Her? The mediocre Lightguard whose oldest friend had abandoned her out of shame and disgust?

No one had ever said such things to her. It meant more to her than he would ever know, even if she hadn't earned such regard.

Aryel sighed and finally released her hand. "I suppose I should sleep."

"I'll make sure no one disturbs you."

A little smirk graced his face. "Are you going to deny the king himself entry if he were to return?"

Corinne narrowed her eyes. "Perhaps."

Aryel huffed a humorless laugh and stood. "Don't do anything that stupid on my behalf."

"He'll strike you again over my dead body," Corinne said, standing as well, her face inches from Aryel's as that fire broiled in her again. "I've sworn to protect you, and that is what I will do under any and all circumstances."

Something serious and earnest settled in Aryel's eyes, and the flames within her winked out, replaced by glowing embers. It was a slow wave of smoldering heat that rolled through her at that look from him, at the realization that they were so close her breath could mingle with his.

He blinked and stepped back, rubbing the side of his neck with one hand. "Thank you, Corinne," he said, gesturing vaguely to his face. "For...just, thank you."

Corinne nodded, quickly retrieving her sword and fastening her belt again. Why did her name always sound particularly lovely when he said it? *Stop it, Corinne.*

"I'll be outside if you need anything," she said.

Seemingly unable to form words, Aryel nodded once, and Corinne took up her post outside, her mind reeling and her heart torn.

Another thread loosened within her.

CHAPTER 23

Corinne had all night to decide that she hated King Theo. She hadn't hated many people in her life; just her own father, and Aryel when she'd first arrived in Vytanos. But with every passing moment as she stood watch overnight at Aryel's door, her hatred grew, and so did her determination to keep her vow to Aryel last night.

The king would not touch him again. Not while she lived.

The door to Aryel's room opened earlier than expected, and Corinne turned to greet him, trying to hide her fatigue. Once she'd eaten something, she'd be good as new.

"I'm sorry you didn't get to sleep," he said, though by the dark circles under his eyes, he'd hardly slept either.

"I'll be fine," she said. She nodded toward the breezeway. "Breakfast then library?"

He took a deep breath, closing his eyes. "Breakfast then library."

The kitchen workers knew Corinne by name now, greeting her as they greeted the prince and tossing her a cinnamon pastry she'd come to consider a favorite. She savored its taste as best she could with how quickly she had to devour it.

This early, the library was sparsely populated, and Aryel studied in solitude. From where she stood by the stacks, she couldn't make out what books he'd laid out, but she expected it was more research for the ongoing issue in the western farmlands. Corinne's heart sank when she recalled the letter she'd sent. She still had no reply from the Lightguards, and still no idea who had sent her that cryptic note.

I know your secret, Corinne Anastos.

It had been four days, and she'd received nothing else, had noticed nothing out of the ordinary at the castle. What possible reason could someone have to anonymously tell her they knew about her father, other than scaring her and putting her on edge?

Her throat went dry. Could it perhaps be the same group who had threatened Aryel? They'd sent an anonymous cryptic note as well. She wished the note was here instead of with the Lightguards so she could determine if the contents or even the handwriting shared any similarities.

A servant entered the library and approached Aryel, snapping Corinne out of her wild musings. The young man bowed to the prince and said something Corinne couldn't quite hear. Aryel scowled and tipped his head back as the servant departed, pinching the bridge of his nose.

"What is it?" Corinne asked, approaching his table.

"I've been summoned to the throne room early," he said, dropping his hand and closing the book in front of him. He offered her a rueful smile. "At least you can go get some sleep now if you'd like."

Corinne couldn't return his smile, even ironically.

With a great sigh, Aryel stood and headed for the exit. He didn't know it as they walked, but Corinne's chest had turned to iron. She would not be going to sleep while he was in a room alone with his parents. She wasn't going anywhere.

The doors to the throne room opened upon their arrival, and Corinne stepped through without being summoned this time. Aryel was halfway down the aisle before he looked over his shoulder, noticing Corinne hadn't left. Confusion crossed his features, but he faced forward again, approaching the dais and his enthroned parents.

"You may go, Corinne," Queen Erina said, waving her hand as Corinne halted several steps behind Aryel.

Corinne remained rooted to the spot.

CHAPTER 23

"There's no need for you here," King Theo said, almost impatient.

Corinne stepped forward until she was at the base of the dais, beside Aryel. She knelt and said, "The prince was injured on my watch last night. I failed in my duty to protect him, so I will keep a closer watch from here on out."

A muscle twitched in the king's face. "And how was the prince injured?"

Corinne looked at the king with theatrically widened eyes, forcing herself to not glance at Aryel. "He would not tell me, Your Majesty. But I can assure you, whatever it was will not happen again. You have my solemn vow."

Something sinister stirred in the king's eyes, and Corinne relished in his struggle to restrain it. *Coward.* She hoped he saw that word in *her* eyes as she held his stare, unyielding.

"Very well," the king finally said, feigning boredom and leaning back in his throne.

In the brief moment their eyes met when she stood and turned, the look of utter disbelief and gratitude on Aryel's face slammed into her, and she knew she'd done the right thing. Even as her heart raced, even as a little fear trickled down her spine, the victory of standing up to the king filled her with satisfaction. *You will not touch him again.*

"Aryel, we must begin preparing for your birthday festivities," Queen Erina said, clapping her hands together in a lackluster attempt to dispel the tension. Corinne took up her post at the right front side of the dais so she had a clear view of Aryel on the opposite side. "The ball will go on as usual, but we must make sure it's all especially thrilling since the nobles have been cooped up in the castle. We will spare no expense."

Corinne quickly realized why Aryel dreaded these meetings with his parents so much; they spoke about every possible detail of event planning, requests of nobles, issues facing the kingdom, and hardly gave him the opportunity to contribute to the conversation. By the second hour of it all, Corinne's head was spinning. It didn't help that she hadn't slept, but there was no way on Helaera's earth she was leaving Aryel alone in the presence of his father again. That guard last night had seemed entirely unbothered by the raised voices in Aryel's room, and she didn't trust any of those present now to protect him the way she would. She didn't answer to the king and queen the way they did. She answered to Helaera.

During the third hour, nobles began to arrive to treat with the king and queen. Aryel stood off to the side of the king's throne, hands clasped behind his back, face stoic. Corinne watched every noble carefully, trying to guess the parents of the noble children she'd seen. When a woman of exceptional beauty walked in, light brown skin covered in freckles, Corinne knew she must be Elys's mother. A woman with ivory skin and silvery blond hair was on her arm. They offered a report on how their lands were faring in the east and thanked the king and queen for their hospitality. *Every* noble thanked the king and queen for their hospitality. How genuine was that gratitude when none of them were permitted to leave the castle?

Corinne was ready to drop dead on the carpet when the doors opened again and two more nobles walked in. No, three—one walking behind. Tiredness vacated Corinne's body at the familiar shimmer of golden hair. *Lana.*

"Ah, welcome, Nora and Calin," Queen Erina said, the warmest greeting she'd offered any nobles thus far. "And Lana, you look radiant as ever, my dear."

Corinne fought the urge to slap the simpering smile off Lana's face as she thanked the queen with a curtsy, the hem of her emerald dress briefly pooling around her on the floor.

Queen Erina and King Theo stood from their thrones and walked down the dais to speak with Lana's mother and father more conversationally, strolling about the room. Lana started toward Aryel, then caught sight of Corinne and scowled. She carefully continued forward. It was only then that Corinne recalled what Janus had said to her several days prior.

I wondered why Lana kept complaining about Aryel's celibate pious guard.

Corinne had been so upset and overwhelmed in the moment that she hadn't realized...was Lana *jealous* of her?

That couldn't be true. Corinne didn't think herself unattractive, but she certainly didn't wear beautiful dresses and flowing fabrics that

CHAPTER 23

accentuated her body and curves. The nightgowns she wore left little to the imagination, sure, but no one ever saw her in those.

Except Ari. Corinne ignored the heat that flooded her cheeks and focused on the quiet exchange happening between Lana and Aryel. He hardly moved as they spoke, and Lana, to her credit, didn't get particularly close to him. Based on his facial expression, however, he wasn't enjoying the conversation. Corinne tensed when his face went from mild annoyance to flushed anger. Lana looked over at Corinne, offering her that same disparaging once-over she'd given the first time they'd met before walking away and joining her parents and the king and queen.

What had she said to him? Corinne tried to catch his eye, but he wouldn't look at her.

Lana and her parents left shortly after that, and the king and queen returned to the dais.

"Whenever you *do* decide to marry, Aryel," Queen Erina said, "I encourage you to consider Lana."

Aryel's answering smile was tight. "Yes, Mother."

"I believe that's enough for today," King Theo said. "You may go."

Corinne bowed to the king and queen before departing with Aryel, glad he seemed determined to walk out of that goddess-forsaken room as quickly as possible. The moment the doors shut behind them, he turned to Corinne.

"Walk with me," he said in that gentle tone of his that made it an invitation, not an order.

She took several steps forward until they were side by side, and he started down the corridor, away from the guards by the throne room doors.

"You did not have to do that, Corinne," he said, his voice low as they walked.

"Yes, I did," she said, her eyes trained ahead. "I meant what I said last night, and I will keep my vow to you and to Helaera in keeping you safe."

Aryel paused as they reached the stairwell. She waited for him to say something, but all he did was hover just a step away from her, his expression conflicted.

"What did Lana say to you?" Corinne asked. "You seemed upset."

His face went violently red, and he averted his eyes again. He cleared his throat and said, "Nothing important."

Corinne was burning with curiosity, but she didn't push him. After another moment of awkward silence, he started down the stairs, and Corinne joined him.

"Are you hungry?" he asked suddenly, turning to her, and Corinne stopped short before she ran into him on the landing.

She *was* hungry, since she'd missed the usual time to eat with her friends, but she couldn't sit down for a meal while guarding him.

"I'm fine," she said.

Aryel raised an eyebrow. "It's midafternoon," he said. "Let's at least run by the kitchens."

Corinne sighed and nodded. It wouldn't hinder her any more than their quick breakfasts, she supposed.

Halfway down the next corridor, Danai appeared, their face brightening at the sight of Corinne.

"Corinne!" they called, then blinked, realizing who was walking in front of her. They bowed quickly. "Your Highness."

Aryel stopped, and Corinne halted a step behind him. "You're Danai Mykotas, right?"

"That's me, Your Highness."

"I've been working closely with your father lately," Aryel said. "He speaks very highly of you."

Danai beamed. "Glad to hear my father doesn't speak ill of me to the Prince of Ashera."

Aryel laughed, and it sent that little bit of warmth through Corinne again.

"If you needed to speak with Corinne, don't let me stop you," Aryel said.

"Right," Danai said, turning to her. "A servant was looking for you in the dining hall a few minutes ago. You've received another message."

The blood drained from Corinne's face as Danai produced the letter themselves, holding it out to her. What if it was another cryptic note of some sort? Would they threaten her this time? Provide some ultimatum?

She took it with a shaking hand, trying to ignore Aryel's gaze on her. She hadn't told him about the previous message. Mustering her courage, she broke the seal and read through it quickly.

> *Corinne Anastos:*
> *Please inform the Royal Family of Ashera that the Lightguards will provide aid in transporting food to the northeastern villages in need. Six Lightguards have been sent to Orynas to await instruction from the village elder.*
> *May Her Light guide us,*
> *Priestess Ronna*

Corinne's heart leapt. "Ari," she said, turning to Aryel. "The Lightguards have sent six to Orynas to help transport food."

The spark in Aryel's eyes returned fully as he held out his hand, and Corinne handed him the letter. He let out a disbelieving laugh, one hand going to his forehead.

"That's incredible," he said, his eyes meeting Corinne's again. "You're incredible, Corinne, I—we need to go find Councilor Toro."

"He's in the library right now," Danai said.

Corinne quickly pulled Danai into a hug. "Thank you, Danai."

With that, she and Aryel hurried off to find Danai's father.

CHAPTER 24

Corinne slept so deeply that night she had neither dreams nor nightmares, at least as far as she could recall when she awoke in the morning. In a panic, she bolted out of bed—it was already past dawn, and she only had a few minutes to complete her weekly ritual. She wrenched her door open and retrieved the pot of hot water on a tray at her feet. A kind servant must have left it there. Had she slept through their knocking?

The tea was even worse than usual, barely warm and poorly steeped, but she choked down as much as she could and said her prayers. What was the tea's purpose anyway? She could tell stories of the goddesses, recite words of wisdom from Helaera's teachings, and recall dozens of songs, but the origins of the tea were murky at best. She'd simply had a cup of it every week since her first day at the monastery. *I'll have to ask Vera to remind me.*

Corinne's stomach dropped. Vera wouldn't want to speak to her, and certainly wouldn't want to know if Corinne had forgotten one of the basic tenets of their most essential ritual.

Perhaps Corinne had truly never deserved the high praise and approval of the Lightguards. What kind of servant of Helaera was she, to fail so miserably, so quickly, on her first assignment, and to forget such core pieces of her own culture?

The Lightguards agreed to your idea, she reminded herself, and some of her anxiety dissipated. That was a step in the right direction.

Tucking her grief over Vera away for later, Corinne showered and dressed quickly, headed for breakfast with her friends. Aryel had requested his overnight guard remain for an extra hour to allow Corinne to sleep a bit more, and she hadn't had the heart to tell him she'd be up before dawn for her ritual anyway. Her body had other plans, though, it seemed, and she'd gotten at least a bit of extra rest.

Nik was the only one in the dining hall when she arrived, greeting her warmly as he put down his book.

"Morning, Corinne," Nik said, and Corinne thanked the servant who placed a plate in front of her, unaware how ravenous she was until the bacon and freshly baked bread were just below her nose. "I hope you slept well."

Corinne began to nod as she chewed her food, and nearly choked when Danai slid onto the bench beside her with a *thump*.

"Corinne and Prince Aryel are friends now," Danai announced quietly, and Iliana plopped onto the bench beside Nik with a sigh.

"Sorry, Corinne, I tried to rein them in before we got here," she said.

"Oh, please, you were just as intrigued as I was."

"Sorry to interrupt, but might we get Corinne's input on the matter?" Nik asked, pointing his fork in her direction.

They all turned to her expectantly. Goddess, *please* let her not blush in front of them.

"We've become...friendlier," she said slowly.

"You called him by his nickname," Danai accused. "And my father told me last night that the three of you planned routes and logistics for that food transport for hours after I handed you that message."

Corinne took another bite of bacon, a bit of heat creeping up her neck. After another moment of painful silence, she exhaled.

"Fine, yes, I've learned more about him," Corinne said. "And we could be considered friends. But I am still his guard first and foremost."

"So what's he like?" Danai asked, nudging Corinne's ribs gently. "Is he really the party man we've heard whispers about?"

"Danai," Nik groaned.

"Indulge me this once, I beg you," Danai said to Nik, clasping their hands together. "All I've gotten is crumbs from this other councilor's son he f—uh, slept with once."

Corinne's entire face heated. It was none of her business who Aryel had slept with, but something unpleasant pinned itself behind her sternum. She kicked herself internally.

What reason did she have to be jealous, especially over some tryst that had occurred before they'd even met? They were barely friends, after all. She was his guard.

"Perhaps he was," she said, distracting herself from such ridiculous emotions. "Perhaps he still is, but I…I can't say I entirely blame him for it."

Even Iliana leaned in with interest now. "Why is that?"

Corinne looked at their eager expressions and frowned. She'd said too much.

"I—"

The appearance of a servant at the end of their table saved her, capturing their attention. The woman bowed briefly and addressed Corinne.

"The queen has summoned you to her study, Lady Corinne," she said, her voice high and melodic.

All her friends' eyes immediately returned to her as dread settled within.

"Thank you," Corinne said, barely managing a smile.

"Why does the *queen* want a private audience with you?" Danai asked quietly.

To berate her, to chastise her for staying with Aryel yesterday, to throw her in the dungeons for daring to stand up to the king.

Instead of voicing every horrible scenario that entered her mind, she said, "I don't know."

"Then why the hells do you look like you're going to be sick?" Iliana asked. "What's going on, Corinne?"

She shouldn't—couldn't—tell them about King Theo's treatment of Aryel. That was not her pain to share.

"I...can't say," she admitted. "But I may have...*subtly*...defied the king yesterday. To his face."

The silence that met her was loud. Corinne fidgeted on the bench, knowing she needed to leave soon and terrified to go.

"It was in the name of protecting the prince," she said quickly, her voice a near whisper.

Danai draped an arm over Corinne's shoulders. "You," Danai said, looking her right in the eye, "are the bravest fucker I've ever met."

Corinne snorted a laugh, and when Nik reprimanded them, Danai said, "What? It made her less nervous! I'm *helping*."

It had, admittedly, helped, and Corinne patted Danai's shoulder gratefully as she stood and bid them farewell. They offered her wishes of luck as she headed off to meet her fate.

Queen Erina's study was up a level from the throne room, and Corinne hoped she hadn't kept her waiting too long. She braced herself. *Stay the course. Be the Light.* She was here to protect Aryel. That was her sworn duty to the Lightguards and to Helaera.

She knocked, and a soft "Enter" sounded in reply.

"Ah, Corinne," Queen Erina said, not standing from her large light wood desk as Corinne stepped inside.

The walls were all dark blue and covered in artworks of moons and stars. She tried not to think about how they resembled some of Aryel's tattoos.

"Please sit."

Corinne took a seat in one of two chairs across from the queen, trying her best to maintain her posture as she sank into the deep cushion of the golden fabric. Gold curtains hung by the large window behind the queen as well.

"I thought a lot about what you said yesterday," she said, folding her hands on her desk.

Corinne ignored the rapid increase of her heart rate. *Stay the course. Be the Light.*

"I do think it's quite necessary for you to be present to protect Aryel whenever possible. With that in mind, at his birthday celebration, I expect you to keep close watch over him throughout the festivities."

Corinne stared at the queen's placid expression for several moments before realizing exactly what she'd said. "Of course, Your Majesty."

"Good," Queen Erina said, offering Corinne a tight smile. "And we can't have you dressed in your normal attire. Would you prefer formal trousers and a shirt or a gown? The tailor can do either."

Corinne had never worn anything formal besides armor. The closest the Lightguards got to formal attire was the robes the Priestesses or Acolytes wore, but that wasn't garb Corinne was permitted to wear.

"I—a gown, I suppose," she said, still stunned.

"Excellent. She'll need a few days to make the gown, but Goddess knows she's busy all day today with mine. You'll report to her first thing in the morning so she can take your measurements."

"Your Majesty, I have not—"

"Oh, but of course, you've never worn such things before," the queen said, her eyebrows shooting up. "I can assure you our dressmaker is *incredibly* skilled; she will make certain the garment is created with ease of movement in mind. Nothing too extravagant."

"I...thank you, Your Majesty," Corinne said.

The queen merely smiled again. "That's all, dear," she said. "I know you must return to my son soon."

Corinne stood and bowed, hardly daring to believe her luck as she headed for the exit.

"Corinne?"

She turned, and the queen was standing now, her face flickering with pain for a moment before she mastered it again.

"Thank you," she said. "For protecting my son when I have failed to do so."

Corinne didn't expect the anger to burn in her chest again, but it smoldered for a moment before she forced herself to smile softly. "It's my duty and honor to protect him, Your Majesty."

Corinne sketched another bow before leaving the room, her heart hammering behind her ribcage.

CHAPTER 25

Corinne stared at the dressmaker's door from down the corridor, fighting the panic that she'd tried to quell with every step. The previous day had passed without incident, other than Aryel being a little quieter than usual while they trained. He'd continued to improve with swordplay at an impressive rate.

Upon waking, however, Corinne recalled that she needed to report to the dressmaker. And that taking her measurements meant disrobing.

She fought tears as she gripped her right forearm, the light fabric of her long sleeve the only barrier she had to hide her scar. She didn't have any bandages on hand, and how would she explain wearing one as a healer, anyway?

"Oh, hi, Corinne—sorry!"

She flinched and whirled around to face Nik, who she hadn't heard approaching. He nearly dropped the books in his hands at Corinne's reaction.

"Is everything okay?" he asked, adjusting his now-lopsided glasses.

Corinne tried to rein in her distress, but it broke free at the genuine kindness on Nik's face.

"I'm supposed to go to a fitting," she said quietly. "But I don't want to...I can't take my shirt off."

Nik placed his stack of books on the ground by the wall. He held out a hand, golden rings glinting in the morning sunlight filtering through a nearby window. Despite realizing his gaze had slid to where her left hand clenched her forearm, Corinne loosened her grip and placed her right hand in his.

"You know, I'm not an expert on Lightguard culture," Nik said. "But I was curious after you returned from the monastery and stopped speaking to us all. I found a few books and read about ways they punish their own when they apparently stray from their teachings. I also noticed you stopped wearing tunics or shirts without sleeves."

Corinne fought the tears that threatened to breach the surface. *He knew.* He'd cared enough to discover why she'd pulled away from them all, and he'd known this whole time.

"Is it your arm?" he asked, his voice soft.

Corinne managed a nod.

"Faye, the dressmaker, is very kind. I believe if you tell her you're simply not comfortable removing your shirt, she won't press the issue."

A bit of Corinne's heart unclenched. "You're sure?"

Nik nodded with a small smile. "I'm sure she'll still need to get close, but with the style of summer dresses especially, she won't need your full arm measurement anyway."

Corinne took a deep breath. *Summer dresses.* She would need to find a solution to wearing a dress with shorter sleeves before the ball, but she could worry about that later.

"Thank you, Nik," she whispered.

"Happy to help," he said with another smile. "Also, Faye is kind, but she doesn't like getting off schedule, so I'd head inside if I were you."

He squeezed Corinne's fingers once before letting her hand drop, bending to retrieve his books. Corinne bid him goodbye before turning back toward the dressmaker's door. *Just stand your ground, Corinne. Stay the course. Be the Light.*

She'd lifted her hand to knock when the door swung open and a short, pale woman with round cheeks appeared, immediately craning her neck to look at Corinne. She placed her hands on her wide hips and raised her dark brown eyebrows.

"Goddess, you'll need a lot of fabric."

CHAPTER 25

Faye shuffled Corinne inside quickly, directing her toward a small raised platform in the center of the green-carpeted room. A large multi-panel mirror had been erected in front of it, below one of the four windows on the far wall.

"I don't often have to make gowns for people as tall as you," Faye said, wrapping her peppery brown hair in a twist before placing an ornate, sharp stick through the center to hold it in place.

She walked over to a wall that was absolutely cascading with rolls of fabric. Corinne stared at them all, admiring several bright greens and blues that reminded her of the mountains and the sky. Faye extracted a small square of white gossamer material, followed by a swatch of gold fabric, before returning to Corinne and holding them up to her face.

"You'll look perfectly lovely in your normal colors," she said, eyes sharp and assessing. "The gold with those eyes of yours...stunning, really."

Faye said it with such casual certainty, and both satisfaction and guilt rose within Corinne at once. She shouldn't want to feel as beautiful as the noble guests who would be in attendance, but the idea of feeling both powerful in her physical strength and in her appearance was undeniably alluring.

"Yes," Faye said, mostly to herself. "I think the idea I had in mind will work nicely. Let's take your measurements, then, and you can be on your way."

Corinne swallowed hard. "I...would it be all right if I leave my shirt on?"

Faye lifted her eyebrows again, but she shrugged a shoulder. "Whatever makes you comfortable, dearie," she said. "Just know it may take me a little longer."

Corinne nodded quickly. "Of course. Whatever you need."

Faye measured what Corinne imagined to be every possible inch of her, making use of a white ribbon with little notches and numbers drawn on it. She stood in stoic silence the entire time Faye worked, relieved that Nik's advice had worked, and grateful that Faye moved with quiet efficiency.

"Wonderful," Faye murmured, making a final note on a little piece of parchment. "That's all, dearie. Come back morning after tomorrow and I'll have a preliminary fitting, make sure everything is working well, and it should be done the morning of the ball."

Corinne exhaled. "Thank you."

"Of course," Faye said, nodding once.

THE MORNING SUN PROMISED OPPRESSIVE HEAT FOR LATER in the day as Corinne headed across the breezeway toward the alcove, the air heavy with humidity. She hoped Aryel would be open to training indoors—sparring outside in a long-sleeved tunic would be brutal, even in the milder summer heat of the mountainous Vytanos.

She waited outside his door after relieving the overnight guard, still hardly daring to believe her luck in finding Nik before her fitting. A bit of guilt still weighed in her gut; was it right for her to feel relief in hiding her shame as a Lightguard, finding comfort in a friend helping her hide it?

That's part of Her Light too.

How could Helaera's light be in the vulnerability she exhibited around her friends, around Aryel, and also in the discipline of the Lightguards? Corinne's head spun, but she couldn't let the uncertainty spiral in her thoughts, not right now.

She shook her head and realized Aryel had not emerged yet. Normally by now he'd woken...perhaps something had happened, and he'd been out drinking late last night. Corinne's heart sank. He hadn't done that in a few weeks, now.

Steeling herself, she knocked on his door. He didn't answer. Corinne said a silent prayer before turning the knob anyway; they would be late if he didn't wake soon.

"Aryel?" she called, peeking her head inside.

Beyond his antechamber, his room was dim, the curtains on his windows and balcony drawn. Corinne cursed herself and stepped inside.

He was lying in bed in a heap, only half of him covered by the blankets. Corinne tried not to stare at the smooth skin of his back, at the intricate lines of his tattoos, at his dark, tousled hair on his sleeping face. *Helaera help me.* She stepped forward and nudged his shoulder.

CHAPTER 25

"Ari," she hissed. He stirred only slightly, so she nudged him harder. "Ari, wake up!"

His face scrunched up, and he inhaled sharply. "Corinne?"

"You're going to be late for your meeting with Councilor Toro," she said, ignoring how her heart skipped a beat at him murmuring her name.

Aryel groaned, finally opening his eyes.

"Fuck," he said when his gaze landed on Corinne, scrambling upright in bed. He yanked a large pillow in front of him, holding it on his lap. "Goddess, Corinne, can you give me a moment?"

Cheeks flushing, Corinne backed away. "I— sorry. I'll be outside."

Corinne hurried out of his rooms, letting her back hit the door after it shut and wishing to the goddess she'd just melt into the stones below her feet. Walking into his room uninvited had been deeply foolish. Now she'd crossed a boundary and made him uncomfortable, made him upset with her after they'd made such progress.

Before she could gather herself, the knob turned on the door, and she went tumbling backward as it opened. Aryel caught her before she'd fallen too far, his arms wrapped around her waist, her back against his chest.

"You and doors, Sunshine," he said, helping her stand upright again. "Your mortal enemy, it seems."

The humor in his eyes dispelled her worry somewhat. She cleared her throat. "Sorry if I intruded."

He shrugged, but Corinne didn't miss the slight blush in his cheeks. "No apology necessary. Sorry I snapped at you a bit. I'm not particularly pleasant right after I've woken."

Corinne was tempted to remind him of the second time they'd met, when he'd called her *my own personal hell* just after Orana had gotten him out of bed, but refrained from doing so.

"I'll keep that in mind," she said instead, and he offered her a smirk.

∼

THE MEETING WITH COUNCILOR TORO WENT AS SMOOTHLY as Corinne might have hoped; the Lightguards in Orynas had arrived the day prior, and she helped Aryel draft a letter of instructions for them. If all went as planned, food would be on its way to the northeastern villages in a matter of days.

"I am ever grateful to both of you for your assistance," Councilor Toro said, closing a book and standing from their shared table at the library. "And I'm certain the Asherans in the northeast will be grateful as well."

Aryel shook his head. "Food isn't a gift. I wish this hadn't been an issue in the first place, but I certainly don't want accolades for providing such basic necessities to my people."

"Even so," Councilor Toro said. "I thank you. Perhaps when this mess with the castle lockdown has ended, you and Corinne both could join us at my home for dinner."

Aryel's eyes darted to Corinne before returning to the councilor. "I'd be honored."

Corinne imagined it as she and Aryel made their way to the training grounds—that warmth and laughter and feeling of utter belonging at the Mykotas's home, this time with Aryel there. Would it not be strange for the prince to be in such an informal setting?

"Oh, Ari, wait—" Corinne jogged a few steps toward him as he paused halfway down the corridor. She lowered her voice, waiting to speak until after a servant had passed them by. "Would you mind training indoors today?"

His brow furrowed. "Is it supposed to rain?"

"No," Corinne said, averting her eyes as she adjusted her sword absently. "But the heat will be a bit unpleasant."

When she met his gaze again, understanding lit his eyes, then softened them. "Indoors, then."

It was a swordplay training day, and Corinne tossed a practice sword to Aryel after passing her real one to the attendant. They ran several drills in a row, ones he'd mastered previously, but today they weren't as cleanly executed.

"You're thinking too much," Corinne told him after he'd missed a parry that would've been a potentially fatal mistake. "Follow your intuition. You've done this before."

CHAPTER 25

Aryel lowered his practice sword and heaved a sigh. "My intuition seems broken today."

"You had trouble sleeping," Corinne said. It wasn't a question; she'd seen how tired he was even after waking late that morning.

Aryel sat on the floor of the training ring, placing his practice sword down beside him, and Corinne followed suit. He stared at her for a moment, his expression conflicted.

"I always have trouble sleeping around my birthday," he said finally. "My mother dreams up more extravagant festivities every year, it seems."

Corinne frowned. "Shouldn't you be able to do what you wish to do?"

Aryel huffed a humorless laugh. "Not if you're a royal heir. At the ball, it's expected that I dance with any unmarried noble who asks."

"That sounds...exhausting."

"It is." Aryel groaned. "And I'm certain Lana will take the opportunity."

"She won't if I have anything to say about it," Corinne said, eyes narrowing.

"What will you do?" he asked, grinning. "Dance with me all night so she can't?"

Corinne averted her gaze. "Maybe I would...but I don't know how to dance."

Aryel got up and walked over to where she sat, offering his hand. "I can teach you."

Corinne's face heated. "Oh, no, I—"

"Come on, Sunshine," he said with a soft smile. "I've been embarrassing myself for weeks in these training sessions, and now I can finally teach you something."

Hesitation still prickled up her spine, but she acquiesced, taking his hand and letting him help her stand.

"Have you at least seen dancing before?" he asked, and Corinne nodded.

"I've seen dancing in several villages. And that night at the party in the woods."

"Ah, right. Well, formal dancing is a bit different." Aryel held out both of his hands now, which Corinne tentatively took. "You'll put a hand here." He lifted Corinne's right hand to his shoulder, then held up her left in a soft grip. His now-free hand went to her lower back, gently pulling her closer, their chests almost touching.

Her breath hitched, and either Aryel didn't notice or pretended not to, his brown eyes trained on their feet.

"This is the simplest one and the most popular," he said. "Start by just mirroring my steps."

Corinne forced her mind to focus on his instructions for how she should step and not on the smoldering heat spreading from her core outward. *So much for avoiding touching him.* His thigh going between her legs as they stepped forward and back, moving to imaginary music, didn't help her rationalize the skip in her heartbeat either.

"You're picking this up quickly," he said, releasing her back to allow her to step outward once before pulling her back into his body. "You must be naturally good at everything, huh?"

Corinne huffed a laugh as she forced her gaze away from his, glad for the distraction. "I once thought so."

He leaned back, his hand coming to rest on her waist, and Corinne hoped to Helaera her face wasn't blatantly red. "What do you mean?"

Corinne sighed as they continued to move, the steps slowly becoming more natural. "I thought I was destined to become one of the greatest amongst the Lightguards. I was the best of my trainee class, and they told me all my life I was bound for a life of honor in the eyes of Helaera. But..."

The words caught in her throat. *But I've disgraced myself, been burned and abandoned by my only friend.*

"But I was too prideful, and now I'll have to start over," she said instead. "Find my footing and regain their respect with humility and devotion to the Goddess."

"Prideful," Aryel muttered, his eyes on something over her shoulder. "You deserve to feel confident in your own abilities."

Corinne wasn't sure how to respond. She opened her mouth to say something, but the door to the training hall flew open, and she and Aryel jumped apart.

"Corinne!"

CHAPTER 25

Danai rushed forward, the alarm on their face sending Corinne's heart into her throat.

"It's Iliana," they said. "She just arrived at the castle in a panic, her brother is injured, and she's asking for you."

Corinne turned to Aryel, who retrieved her sword from the attendant and handed it to her before gesturing toward the door.

"Let's go," he said.

CHAPTER 26

They followed Danai quickly out of the training hall and into the corridor, dodging servants and guards as they went. Iliana was pacing the entrance hall when they arrived, her cheeks wet from tears and her attire casual—she was not on duty today.

"Corinne," she said, running up to her and taking her hands. "My little brother, Aeson, he fell from a horse a few hours ago and hasn't been responsive since. We don't know what to do, and I thought maybe you could...oh Goddess." Iliana's gaze landed on Aryel standing by Corinne, and she sketched a haphazard bow. "Apologies, Your Highness, I didn't know—"

"Don't worry about it," Aryel said quickly. "Corinne, are you able to help?"

"It depends on the severity of his injury and how long it's been," Corinne said. "Where is he?"

"At our home," Iliana said, more tears spilling over her cheeks. "In the lower part of the city. Please, Corinne, I don't know what else to do, I'm terrified he's going to die."

Corinne's chest felt like it would tear open. She looked to Aryel—for permission? For encouragement? Perhaps both.

"I'll go with you," he said. "Fuck the lockdown mandate."

CHAPTER 26

Aryel called for horses to be prepared for them while Iliana thanked him profusely. Corinne was hardly present anymore; she thought through all scenarios of the boy falling, where he may have sustained an injury to prevent him from waking, what kinds of injuries would be irreparable. *Don't think on that.*

After a quick argument between Aryel and the guards at the castle gate, the iron opened with a mighty groan, and the four of them set off into Vytanos, racing the sun.

Corinne, Aryel, and Danai brought their horses to a halt behind Iliana as she dismounted by a small cottage surrounded by similar homes. A girl with hair the same color as Iliana's rushed out of the house.

"Go," she said, taking Iliana's reins. "I'll take care of the horses."

Corinne followed Iliana inside, tailed closely by Aryel and Danai. They stepped into a small kitchen with five people inside already— Iliana's other siblings, Corinne assumed, and her parents. Her father, auburn hair graying at the roots, looked at the figure lying on the table that had been cleared before him. Her mother, who looked exactly like Iliana would in twenty years but with dark brown hair, approached them quickly.

"Amma," Iliana said. "I brought Corinne with me—she's a Lightguard."

Her mother's eyes widened, and Corinne's mouth went dry. "Come."

Corinne approached the table, bracing herself for whatever she was about to see. The boy lying atop it couldn't have been older than fourteen, all gangly limbs and still baby-faced. There was a nasty gash on his browbone that had begun to swell. That was a good sign, at least— external manifestation of the damage was better than internal. His right leg, too, was smeared with blood and bruising and appeared to be broken at the shin. Corinne removed her sword and turned, handing it to Danai. With a deep, steadying breath, she summoned her light.

The little gasps around the room hardly registered as she reached for Aeson's head, placing her glowing hands on either side of it to allow her magic to assess the damage. Corinne closed her eyes. Head injuries were always more complex than anything else, requiring precision and expert control alongside the energy expended to heal. Her light began to heal the outer wound almost immediately, but there was certainly more beneath the surface, and that would take longer. She steeled herself as she opened her eyes again and looked to the others.

"This will take me a few hours," she said. She caught the eye of an even younger boy, likely around eight years old, who was now clutching Iliana's arm.

"Will he wake?" Iliana's father asked, his voice breaking.

Corinne smoothed her face into a mask of calm before looking at him.

"I can't say for certain," she said. "But it's a good sign that he's breathing normally and that some of the damage is external."

"Let's let her work," Iliana's mother said.

They all returned to their respective places, except for Iliana's other brother, who remained by her as she sat in a chair by the window. Danai joined another one of Iliana's siblings on the floor, and Aryel found a chair nearby, another one that had likely been pushed away from the kitchen table.

Corinne placed her hands on Aeson's head again and began her work.

BY THE THIRD HOUR OF HEALING, CORINNE'S ENERGY WAS fading quickly. She'd managed to heal most of the internal damage in Aeson's head and moved to the boy's leg—bones were easier than head injuries, at least, but they still took time. The marrow reknitted as Corinne's magic guided it back into place. To keep herself focused and awake, Corinne began humming softly to herself, the melody of an old healing song she'd heard from the Attendants in the monastery.

"Your voice is pretty."

Corinne glanced up and saw another of Iliana's sisters standing across the table, her dark hair in two braids. She looked to be the youngest of them all, her head barely passing the table's edge.

"Thank you," Corinne said. She might have engaged with her more, but she had to commit her concentration back to Aeson's healing.

"Mira, why don't you and Jaela go check on the horses?" Iliana's mother, Isa, suggested.

The little girl padded off to join Jaela, who had been the first one to greet them upon their arrival.

At long last, Aeson's muscle was repaired over his freshly-healed bone, and all that was left was the flesh wound. It normally would've taken Corinne less than ten minutes to heal such a wound, but with her magic depleted, it was another half hour. She leaned back once she'd gotten it to a shallow cut, her light snapping back into her, and tiredness weighed heavily on her entire being.

"Is that it? Is he healed?" Isa asked, stepping forward with hopeful eyes.

Corinne breathed deeply. "He has a few minor injuries still, but nothing as severe as before."

"He still hasn't woken," Iliana's father, Petyr, said. "Can you not wake him?"

"Atta, Corinne has done enough," Iliana said from the chair she'd slumped in, her voice strained. Her younger brother had fallen asleep in her lap.

"No, I can try," Corinne said.

Rallying the dregs of her magic, she reached for Aeson's head again and closed her eyes, letting the warmth of her light bring his mind back toward consciousness. She could sense him teetering on the edge of awareness and pulled him toward it.

With a sharp inhale, the boy stirred. Corinne looked at him just as his eyelids fluttered open, his amber irises the same color as Iliana's.

"Aeson!" Isa cried, rushing forward.

Corinne's magic receded, and she backed away to allow space for his family to approach him, each of them teary and joyful. Contentedness settled in her chest as she watched them, but her mind was slow to understand why, behind them, Danai and Aryel were staring at her with worried expressions. Perhaps she looked as exhausted as she felt...

Her face went cold, blackness dotting her vision, and she hit the floor.

～

"Do you think we could carry her back to the castle?"

"On horseback? That's a terrible idea, Danai."

"Well, she can't stay here all night without getting into trouble…"

"Hauling an unconscious Lightguard through the streets of Vytanos isn't an option."

Corinne's eyelids felt like they were weighed down by bricks as she awoke. She squinted in the candlelight that flickered nearby and couldn't make sense of where she was. A bed lay beneath her, a window was just ahead, displaying that dusk had fallen, and surrounding her in a tiny bedroom were Danai, Iliana, and Aryel. Her friends stood on either side of the window, arguing quietly, and Aryel immediately got to his feet from where he'd been sitting beside the bed.

"Corinne," he said, drawing Danai and Iliana's attention as well.

Her head swam as she sat up. "I fainted?"

"You passed out after healing Aeson," Danai said. "And you've been asleep since."

"How long has it been?" she asked, glancing out the window again.

"About four hours," Aryel said.

Goddess. It had been a long time since Corinne had overextended herself like that.

"My parents insisted you rest here," Iliana said.

"That was kind of them."

"It would've been kinder if they hadn't first insisted you wear yourself out," Iliana said, stepping forward with her arms crossed. "I'm so grateful to you, Corinne, and I'm sorry they pushed you."

Corinne shook her head. "I'll be fine." She made to stand up, and her head swam again, throwing her off-balance.

Aryel caught her before she stumbled too far. She was just so *tired*. She needed to lie back down.

CHAPTER 26

"We have to get you two back to the castle," Danai said, their brow furrowing. "But she's in no state to ride."

"Last thing we need is someone else falling from a horse," Iliana said.

"She can ride with me," Aryel said. He looked at Corinne, who was still leaning on him for support. "If that's all right with you."

Corinne was so exhausted she couldn't find the will to feel guilty about needing and wanting his help. "That's fine. We need to get back."

Danai, Iliana, and Corinne, with Aryel's help, left the little bedroom and ventured into the kitchen again, greeted by Iliana's family. Iliana shooed away her four siblings, demanding they give Corinne space. Aeson, propped up in a chair with his leg elevated, stood gingerly.

"Thank you, Corinne," he said, his face going beet red.

"You're welcome," she said, smiling softly, and after waving off Isa and Petyr's profuse apologies, they stepped into the evening air.

Aryel and Danai helped her onto his horse after he'd already mounted up. Corinne leaned back against his chest, her head tucked into the crook of his neck, sighing at the warmth of his body. She could feel guilty about this later too.

"I'll bring your horse back to the castle in the morning," Iliana assured her, and Corinne managed a nod.

The ride back to the castle was slower than their urgent gallop to arrive earlier that day, and Corinne fought to remain awake. Aryel rode with careful skill through the streets behind Danai, ensuring Corinne remained upright and avoiding the most crowded areas of Vytanos. Stars had begun to appear when they approached the castle gates.

"Corinne," Aryel murmured in her ear. "If you can sit up straighter as we arrive, that would appear better for us both."

The dutiful voice in the back of her exhausted mind nagged at her. *He's right.* With great effort, Corinne straightened, forcing her eyes open with false alertness.

"Your Highness," a guard at the gate said, bowing. "Welcome back."

They opened the gates promptly, and Danai handed their horse off to a stable hand before hurrying to help Corinne dismount. Aryel thanked the guards as they closed the gates again, jumping down and hovering near Corinne as she called upon every ounce of her will to take a step forward. *A few more minutes,* she told herself. *Then sleep.*

"Aryel!"

Corinne's head snapped up. The king and queen were storming out of the castle entrance, headed right for them.

"Where in the name of Helaera have you been?" King Theo demanded, an ugly snarl on his face.

Corinne fought the urge to unsheathe her sword as he got within a foot of Aryel.

"A castle guard's brother had an accident," Aryel explained calmly. "They needed Corinne's help, and instead of forcing her to remain here, I went with them. She saved the boy's life."

"And what of *your* life, Aryel?" Queen Erina asked.

Corinne was glad for the shadowy light of the nearby torches; she was certain her face clearly displayed her disgust. If she cared so much for her son's safety, why did she enable the king's abuse of Aryel?

"I was with Corinne and two of our most highly skilled guards in a residential home all day," Aryel said. "I was perfectly safe."

That sinister, dangerous anger flashed across the king's face, and Corinne took an involuntary step forward.

"I assure you I wouldn't have allowed the prince to join us if he was in any danger," Corinne said, masking her aggression with a little bow. It took enormous effort to straighten herself again. "Thanks to his willingness to accompany me, everyone knows the generosity and selflessness of the Crown."

Corinne didn't know where such savvy had come from, but her subtle manipulation worked; King Theo's face smoothed over as he considered it.

"Very well," he said. His eyes roved over Corinne, and she fought a grimace. "I expect Captain Ekhana has dismissed the guard who was standing outside your empty bedchamber, Aryel, so she will be on duty tonight."

Aryel stiffened beside Corinne, and she knew they both recognized that for what it was. Punishment.

Corinne could have cried; there was no way she could stay awake all night, but she couldn't admit that to the king, or in front of all the surrounding guards. The king turned on his heel and headed back

CHAPTER 26

inside, the queen close behind, and Danai stepped closer to Aryel and Corinne.

"I'm sorry, Corinne," they said quietly. "I'm on duty tonight, otherwise I'd offer to take over for you."

"My father can kiss the ground of the fifth gates of hell," Aryel muttered, his voice low enough that no one else could overhear. "I'll make sure Corinne gets the rest she needs."

Danai looked between Aryel and Corinne, and something a little devious sparked in their eyes. But all they said was, "Thank you, Your Highness. I'll see you tomorrow, Corinne."

Corinne bid them good night, then followed Aryel with every air of alertness she could muster. They made it up to the second floor before she nearly collapsed.

"Just a little farther, Sunshine," Aryel said, wrapping an arm around her waist and helping her walk. "Breezeway is just ahead."

"Ari," she huffed when he pushed the doors open. "How am I going to—?"

"We'll stay in your room like we did that one night," he said. "I'll be in your direct vicinity if something impossibly horrible should happen, and you'll wake up immediately if I'm in danger. Simple."

"That seems foolish," she said, but she didn't fight him when he pushed her door open and stepped inside with her.

"Well, there's no way for you to stand outside my door all night without collapsing." He helped her to the bed, and Corinne didn't bother removing anything except her boots before curling up onto the mattress. "See? You're already halfway asleep."

"Fine," Corinne sighed, her eyes drooping shut. "But wake me *immediately* if someone approaches outside. Or if something impossibly horrible happens."

Aryel chuckled, and Corinne smiled into her pillow.

"Sleep well, Corinne."

CHAPTER 27

Corinne couldn't stop staring at herself in the mirror.

Five days—it had only taken the dressmaker five days to make this gown. It was more exquisite than any attire she'd ever worn, the flowing white fabric accentuating the curve of her breasts, the inward dip of her waist. Gold-embroidered flowers decorated the bodice and the top half of the off-shoulder sleeves. Faye had indeed made it in a way that her movement wouldn't be terribly restricted, which Corinne was grateful for. But she stared and stared at the nasty handprint-shaped scar on her forearm, fully on display with the thin sleeves that stopped just past her elbows. She wasn't supposed to heal it for another week.

You just want to hide it.

Corinne shook her head. Perhaps some part of her did want to hide this shame from the world to save herself the embarrassment, but most people wouldn't know its significance, anyway. It would only lead to awkward questions she did not want to answer.

She was protecting the Lightguards from the scrutiny of those who would not understand their ways. She could always recreate the scar, as horrific as that would be.

Corinne looked outside for the fifth time in an hour, both eager for the sun to go down and dreading it. She and Aryel hadn't spoken much in the days following her healing Aeson, him being busier than ever with party preparations. They'd skipped training while he attended meetings or fittings or gatherings of nobles, and aside from a few light exchanges as she escorted him from place to place, Corinne had kept her distance. She wasn't sure how else to deal with this physical pull she felt toward him, that temptation with him stronger than it had ever been with anyone else.

Stay the course, Corinne. Or, rather, find the course again. She would do this last disservice, this last bending of a rule tonight in the name of protecting the Lightguards, and then she would keep her eyes on the path.

With a deep breath, she summoned her light. It concentrated in her right forearm over her scar, smoothing over the puckered, discolored flesh. Corinne winced as deep aches of pain spread through her arm. Magic injuries did not heal as easily or painlessly as nonmagic ones, the scar on her thigh a testament to that. *Helaera forgive me.*

Several minutes later, the burn was gone. Corinne eased the sharp lance of guilt through her gut by assuring herself she would recreate it at the next opportunity.

The sun was fully set now. Corinne checked the ties on her golden sandals before venturing outside, feeling rather naked without her sword on her hip. But the queen had insisted she not carry it tonight; it would be improper while wearing such a gown, and the priority was for Corinne to be nearby but not draw too much attention as Aryel's sworn protector. She was powerful enough with only her magic, anyway.

A guard stood outside Aryel's door, nodding to Corinne once. She turned and paced a bit toward the breezeway as she waited. Aryel had insisted on being left alone most of the day in preparation for the evening, and Corinne couldn't blame him.

She turned quickly when the door opened, her hands clasped behind her back. Aryel emerged in a deep blue shirt covered in silver embroidered moons and stars, tucked into loose black trousers that flowed to the floor around his black-sandaled feet. The deep V of the shirt's collar allowed his tattoos to peek out more than they usually did.

Corinne kicked herself internally for gawking at him right as she noticed his lips part slightly as he looked her up and down.

"Evening," Corinne said, glad for the darkness should her face give anything away. "Happy birthday."

Aryel took a moment too long to respond. "Thank you."

"Shall we go?"

He merely nodded, quietly dismissing his guard before joining Corinne. They set off side by side, and he held the door for her as she swept through, mindful of her skirts. The dress might support her free movement, but it still wasn't nearly as practical as trousers. She'd thought it more closely resembled what a Lightguard may wear, like their robes, but perhaps that choice had been a mistake.

"You look lovely," Aryel said quietly, and Corinne's stomach flipped pleasantly, her neck warming.

"Thank you," she said. They continued on in excruciating silence for another corridor before Corinne asked, "You're twenty-eight today?"

"I am," he said. "This will be the tenth year my mother has thrown festivities like this."

"I don't envy you," Corinne said, her body relaxing some as they eased into normal conversation.

"What do Lightguards do on their birthday, anyway?"

"Most years we are allowed to spend the day as we please." Corinne lifted her skirts as they started down a stairwell, holding the railing with her other hand. "But our twenty-fifth year is sacred—it's the year we are old enough to accept the oath to Helaera and become Anointed. For mine last year, I spent the day in the mountains praying."

"I would much prefer that to this."

Corinne laughed. "It was certainly more peaceful. And it's always beautiful up there in autumn."

"So your birthday is in autumn?"

"Mid-autumn," she said. "When the leaves have changed."

"That's my favorite time of year," he said.

They reached the first floor, and the buzzing sound of a crowd drifted to meet them from down the corridor.

Aryel turned to Corinne. "Remember, you don't have to dance with anyone unless you wish to," he said.

"How would I dance with anyone if I'm supposed to be watching you?" Corinne asked, lifting an eyebrow.

Aryel grinned wolfishly. "Excellent point. I suppose you can only dance with me."

"Only if you need rescuing from someone else," Corinne said, rolling her eyes.

"I almost certainly will," Aryel said, setting off again, this time a few paces ahead of Corinne as they approached the ballroom. He glanced over his shoulder. "Good thing I taught you how."

Corinne shook her head. If she recalled the steps from days ago, it would be a miracle.

Two guards stood on either side of the ballroom doors, opening them with a bow at Aryel's arrival. A wall of sound rushed into them, music and chatter and shifting feet, and Corinne forgot how to breathe as they stepped inside.

Floor-to-ceiling windows offered views of Vytanos and the star-smattered indigo sky above the surrounding mountains. Paper lanterns with cutouts of crescent moons were placed in the windowsills, and every sconce had been lit along the walls. Dozens of people were already milling about, holding wine or some other sparkling liquid in narrow glasses, and crystal chandeliers—Corinne counted eight—hung from the ornately carved ceiling. At the far end of the long hall, two thrones stood before a window, and upon a slightly lower dais to their left was a little stage where an octet of musicians played stringed instruments, drums, and a flute. Directly to her left by the entrance was a massive table piled with food and rows of drinks.

How on Helaera's earth was Corinne going to keep track of Aryel amidst all *this*?

"Come on, Sunshine," Aryel said, beckoning her forward.

Corinne almost didn't hear him over the noise. She forced herself to focus and followed him off to the left side of the crowd. Many nobles greeted him as he passed, offering birthday wishes, and he accepted them graciously but continued forward. Corinne kept her eyes trained on his back, ignoring the stares that followed her. It didn't matter what any of them thought about her—she was here to do her duty and guard Aryel.

Aryel continued forward until he'd reached the far side of the ballroom, passing the musicians and approaching his parents. Queen Erina stood with a bright smile at his approach, descending the dais to embrace her son.

"Happy birthday, Aryel," she said. She wore a deep blue gown with silver stitching that matched the embroidery on Aryel's shirt, and delicate silver organza sleeves that cinched at her wrists. Her crown was more ornate tonight, the crescent moons and stars sparkling with iridescent deep purple stones. "Do enjoy the festivities tonight."

King Theo stood from his throne as well, and Corinne tensed, nearly reaching for a sword that wasn't there. His attire was coordinated with his wife's and son's, deep blue and embroidered, but the neckline of his fine shirt was not nearly as low as Aryel's. He stepped down from the throne with a box in hand, holding it out to Queen Erina as he stopped before Aryel.

"Happy birthday, Aryel," he said, unsmiling.

The queen opened the box, and the king retrieved a crown from within. It wasn't as intricate as his own, nor was it encrusted with fine stones, but the silver had been woven together beautifully, dipping at the front into a delicate crescent moon.

Corinne's muscles went taut as Aryel bowed before his father, allowing the king to place the crown on his head. Rationally, she knew the king wouldn't dare harm his son in such a public setting, but seeing him so close put her on edge anyway.

Once the crown settled on Aryel's head, the moon resting in the center of his forehead, he straightened again. Several nobles, who had been nearby, watched the exchange between the king and prince but did not approach or say anything.

"It suits you so well," Queen Erina said, clapping her hands together with a smile.

She approached the musicians, waving at them, and they ceased playing at once. The murmurs of the crowd dissipated gradually, and Corinne turned, realizing that every eye in the room was now upon the royal family. She swallowed and forced herself to breathe. So many people facing her direction made her feel like a weight had been placed on her chest. *Just keep an eye on Aryel. Stay the course. Be the Light.*

"Friends!" Queen Erina called, her voice echoing around the room. "Thank you for joining us tonight as honored guests. We know this year's celebration of our prince's birthday is a little unusual, so we wanted to provide you with a night you surely won't forget. And since you're all already staying in the castle, you are welcome to remain at the festivities for as long as you wish!"

An appreciative chuckle rumbled through the crowd. Corinne forced herself to take a breath again. It was likely they'd be here very late into the night, and she couldn't get overwhelmed when the party had barely begun.

"A toast," the queen said, raising her glass, and everyone in the room did the same. "To Prince Aryel Serra, Heir to Ashera. May Helaera bless him with another twenty-eight years and more."

Murmurs of "May Helaera bless him" sounded from nearly everyone in the room. Corinne fought the urge to cringe—such a public display of prayer in such a debaucherous setting made her skin crawl. Though...it was not the place of everyday people to know the ways of the Lightguards and act as true servants of the Goddess.

The music began again, a lively tune with a soaring flute, and many of the guests parted from the room's center to make space for others to begin dancing. A young woman in a burgundy gown approached Aryel almost immediately, her face shy but hopeful, and he offered her his hand. As they joined several others on the dance floor, Corinne scanned the crowd beyond. She spotted Petros and Elys, both with noblewomen on their arms, and Lana stood farther back by her parents and Janus. Corinne looked away from them, returning her attention to Aryel and the noble girl dancing with him.

"Having a good time?"

Corinne turned, her heart leaping at the sight of Danai grinning at her. They were dressed in attire similar to Aryel's, a low-cut forest-green shirt and flowing black trousers. Their hair was braided into a twist at the nape of their neck, their eyes outlined in black kohl.

"Danai," Corinne said, glancing at Aryel again, just to be safe. "You look beautiful."

"Don't they?"

Nik appeared out of the crowd, grinning and placing a hand over Danai's shoulders before kissing their temple and handing them a glass of wine. Nik's shirt and trousers were all black, simple but elegant, and silver hoop earrings in his ears matched the frames of his glasses.

"I didn't know you two would be here," Corinne said, watching as another noble approached Aryel. She breathed a sigh of relief when she realized it was Petros.

"Nobles and councilors received an invitation," Danai said. "And permission to bring a guest."

"Oh." Corinne looked to her friends again. "I'm glad they did that. Have either of you heard from Iliana?"

"She's still on leave until tomorrow," Nik said. "But Aeson is doing well."

"Thank the Goddess," Corinne said.

"I suppose you're not here for your own enjoyment this evening," Danai said, taking a sip of wine and glancing over at the prince.

"No," Corinne said, watching as Aryel and Petros danced and laughed.

A bit more of the tension within her eased; at least he was smiling and spending time with friends.

"Well, even so, you look absolutely stunning," Danai said.

Corinne blushed furiously. "T-thank you."

"I'm sure Prince Aryel agrees with me."

"*Danai,*" Nik hissed, pinching the bridge of his nose.

Corinne coughed once. "The prince has no need to take notice of my appearance."

"Corinne," Danai said incredulously, raising an eyebrow. They lowered their voice. "He was beside himself at Iliana's after you fainted. And he's looked at you about five times since we started speaking."

Sure enough, when Corinne turned to the prince again, Aryel's eyes were on her. He looked away when their eyes met, his attention back on Petros, who spun him around unexpectedly, drawing another laugh from him.

"I promised him I'd keep an eye out for any unsavory nobles,"

Corinne said. "He's probably checking to make sure I'm paying attention."

"I'm not—" Danai cut off at a squeeze around their shoulders from Nik. They sighed. "Fine. Shall we join the dancing?"

"It would be my pleasure," Nik said, taking Danai's empty wine glass and passing it to a servant who was walking through at that very moment. "Thank you."

The servant bowed, and Nik pulled Danai onto the dance floor. Corinne remained on the outskirts of the room, making her way around nearly half the perimeter of the dancing before the music shifted. A noble girl in bright orange approached Aryel then, and another fast-paced tune began. Corinne didn't know how they kept up with the steps to such a dance, but a small part of her now wished to learn. Everyone was grinning or laughing as the song continued, and Corinne found herself humming along to the music, the melody easy enough to pick out.

"Is that gown Faye's work?"

Corinne looked to the noblewoman who had addressed her and recognized her as Elys's mother. Her dress was the color of steel, the fabric tight and flattering against her ample curves.

"Yes," Corinne said, remembering herself.

"Exquisite," she said. "And your tattoos...are you from Cara Talle?"

Corinne forced herself not to react. "That's where I was born, yes, but I was raised in the monastery."

"I see," she said. "Well, the ink is lovely. My father was from there."

Corinne plastered a polite smile on her face and nodded. The woman walked off, and Corinne returned to her task. The song ended on a low, soft chord, and many of the dancers dispersed, ready for a reprieve after several numbers. Aryel did the same, greeting a few nobles as he made his way to Corinne.

I'm sure Prince Aryel would agree. Why had Danai put that notion into her head?

"Holding up all right?" Aryel asked when he reached her, and Corinne followed him to the food table close to the ballroom entrance.

"Well enough," Corinne said. "You?"

"Wonderfully," he said, retrieving a small baked pastry of some kind and popping it into his mouth. He leaned against the table, surveying the room. "You know you can eat if you'd like to."

Corinne's eyes darted to the bite-sized delicacies on the table, unable to deny she was hungry. She reached for one of the same little pastries Aryel had eaten. Biting into it was like heaven; it was some miniature savory pie with cheese and herbs. Aryel laughed quietly beside her, and she looked at him, perplexed.

"They're good, aren't they?" he asked.

Corinne smiled sheepishly. "How do you not eat fifty of them?"

"Oh, trust me, if I had my way, I would," Aryel said. "But I'm afraid that's not considered appropriate."

Corinne ate another one, shaking her head. "You should be able to eat whatever you want. It's your birthday."

"I agree."

Another song began as Corinne finished a third bite-sized pie, and Aryel straightened.

"I love this piece," he said. He turned to Corinne, hesitating a moment before holding out his hand. "Dance with me?"

Corinne glanced around briefly. "No one else is approaching you."

"I know," he said, his mouth tugging upward on one side.

"I thought you said—"

"Come on, Sunshine," he said. "It's my birthday."

Corinne stared at him for several more thundering heartbeats. She would regret this.

She placed her hand in his and let him lead her to the dance floor.

"This one has the same counts as the one we practiced," he said, taking her right hand, lacing his fingers through hers.

Corinne placed her other hand on his shoulder, careful to avoid his bare skin where his shirt dipped. Her mind went entirely blank for several moments when he tugged her closer by the small of her back, his fingers pressing into her.

"Just follow my lead."

Corinne didn't have a choice, anyway—once the intro to the music led into the main piece, they were moving. She couldn't think about anything but following his steps, the feeling of his hand on her back, the brush of his thighs against hers. It was slow and simple enough, but

CHAPTER 27

Corinne's heart was beating so fast she might as well have been doing the livelier dances from earlier. She looked up at Aryel after a few moments and found that same look in his eyes from the night she'd healed his face.

Her stomach flipped again.

Had Danai been right? She'd fought her own attraction to him so doggedly that it hadn't really occurred to her that *he* might feel the same way around her. The way he moved with her as they danced, his touch gentle but steady, his hips so close to hers as they swayed—

Oh, Goddess above. *Control yourself, Corinne.* But that look in his eyes was like a battering ram to her bastion of self-discipline.

Before Corinne could regain her composure, he twirled her outward, the skirts of her dress spiraling around her legs elegantly. He pulled her back toward him the next moment, and a little smile tugged at her lips. She took a breath and glanced over his shoulder.

Her smile disappeared.

Four new guests had just arrived, three garbed in white robes with gold accents. Corinne froze in place seconds before the music ended, and Aryel glanced down at her.

"Corinne? Is everything all right?"

Her blood had turned to ice in her veins. She released Aryel, dropping her hands, and he dropped his in turn, his gaze following hers as partygoers shuffled around them, either entering or leaving the dance floor.

"Oh, hells," he muttered. "Are those...?"

"Lightguards," Corinne whispered.

Mother Creita's eyes landed on her, then, as if she'd heard her. Her disapproving expression turned absolutely livid for a half second before she smoothed her face into a mask of serenity again. Behind her stood Chala and Bria, and beside them was a familiar face that once would have brought Corinne great comfort, and now only sent a knife of grief between her ribs.

Vera. She was due at the castle the following morning, but Corinne had hoped tonight would distract her from that fact.

Corinne stood as straight as she could as Mother Creita and the others approached her and Aryel, trying to hide her arm behind her skirts. The crowd around them parted easily for the Priestesses and Vera, a few of them watching with interest while others ignored them after a cursory glance.

"Corinne," Mother Creita said, her voice smooth.

Corinne bowed. *Please don't look down. Please don't look down.*

"Mother Creita," she said. She gestured to Aryel. "This is Prince Aryel Serra."

"It is an honor to meet the heir of Ashera," Mother Creita said, bowing, and the others did the same.

"Likewise," Aryel said. "An honor to meet the Lightguards responsible for treating Corinne with such love and respect."

Even if her fellow Lightguards didn't catch the edge to his voice, Corinne did. *Don't be a fool, Ari.*

"Please," Aryel said, gesturing away from the dance floor as people gathered to start another number. "Allow me to introduce you to my parents."

Mother Creita nodded once, and they all followed Aryel off to the side of the room to avoid stepping through a sea of dancers. Corinne remained to their right sides as much as possible, still hiding her arm.

Queen Erina stood from her throne at their approach.

"Mother Creita," she said, a saccharine smile plastered on her face. "Welcome to Vytanos."

"You honor us by inviting us into your home, Your Majesty," Mother Creita said, smiling in return.

Corinne tried to breathe as evenly as she could. Vera wouldn't look at her, but she had no way of knowing whether the others had noticed the missing scar on her right arm. How long did they intend to stay at the ball? Surely no more than a few minutes.

"Corinne has been a glimmer of hope and comfort in these trying times," Queen Erina said, snapping Corinne's attention back to the conversation at hand. "We are ever grateful that one of Helaera's Swords has offered her service to us."

"Of course, Your Majesty," Mother Creita said. "Corinne is one of our strongest and most devoted. She is held in the highest regard even amongst those at the monastery."

Corinne forced her face to remain neutral. The lie hurt far more than the truth. Beside his mother, Aryel caught her eye and held her gaze. He breathed in slowly, reminding Corinne to do the same, and her heart slowed, at least a little.

"Well, please enjoy yourselves," Queen Erina said, gesturing to the dancing and food. "We have more than enough to share."

"Your generosity is unmatched," Mother Creita said with a bow. "But this is no place for us. We will retire for the evening."

"Of course," Queen Erina said. "There are servants outside who can show you to your rooms for the night. I look forward to our meeting tomorrow."

Corinne hadn't known Mother Creita would come for a meeting here, hadn't been informed that they would be in attendance tonight. They truly didn't trust her anymore, even with the most innocuous information.

Still, perhaps luck was on her side. The Lightguards made to leave.

Mother Creita was nearly past Corinne when her hand lifted from her robes and gripped Corinne's right forearm so hard she nearly cried out.

"We will discuss this later," she hissed in Corinne's ear.

Ice overtook Corinne's insides again when the High Priestess released her. She'd been such a fool to think they wouldn't notice, to think that wearing this gown, indulging in this party, dancing with Aryel wouldn't result in further punishment.

It seemed she would never regain their trust or respect, if she'd even had it in the first place.

"Aryel, I'd like you to speak with Lady Vivre," the queen was saying as Corinne turned to Aryel again. He hadn't taken his eyes off her and now tore his gaze away to focus on his mother. "She has been rather quiet since her arrival at the castle, and I want her to feel welcome."

"Yes, Mother," he said. He threw an apologetic glance in Corinne's direction, and she clenched her fists.

Control, Corinne. You have a duty to fulfill. She was to watch and guard Aryel tonight, and that was precisely what she would do.

Aryel didn't approach the noblewoman his mother had mentioned right away; instead, he headed straight for Nik and Danai, who were sitting by a small table in front of a window. They spoke briefly before both of her friends stood and immediately headed in her direction.

"Hi, Corinne," Danai said, their voice gentle.

"Hi, Danai." It was all she could manage.

"Mind if we stand with you?" Nik asked.

Corinne shook her head, and they did so, taking up a post on either side of her.

The knot within her began to loosen and unravel again. She hadn't done anything to deserve such kindness from them, or from Aryel, and yet here they were, standing steadily beside her.

"Oh my," Nik said quietly. "I believe Lana's had too much to drink."

Corinne looked over to the food table, where Lana was indeed swaying as she made her way to Janus. She flopped into his arms, several people around them scattering. Janus spoke briefly to her parents before escorting her from the room.

"Truly unfair," Danai said, shaking their head. "When I get that drunk, it's *a dishonor to my family* and a week's worth of double shifts."

Corinne couldn't help but chuckle, and Danai nudged her side gently.

They remained where they were for three more songs, the latter two with Aryel dancing with other nobles that didn't require Corinne's intervention. Before the next piece began, Aryel hurried away from the center of the room.

"I think I'm ready to retire," he said breathlessly, hands on his hips. "Are you two going to stay a while?"

"We may have another drink," Nik said, shrugging as he stepped forward and reached for Danai. "I hope your birthday was enjoyable, Your Highness."

Aryel grimaced. "Please, call me Aryel. And thank you both for coming."

Danai and Nik bowed before departing, smiling at Corinne as well.

"Shall we?" Aryel said, jerking his head toward the exit.

Corinne nodded. She'd made it.

CHAPTER 28

Aryel managed to slip out of the ballroom with minimal farewells, and the quiet of the corridor was more welcome than Corinne expected. Once they were out of sight of the partygoers and guards, Aryel slowed until Corinne was walking beside him again instead of behind.

"Are you all right?" he asked.

Corinne took a shuddering breath. "I'm a little shaken."

Before Aryel could respond, voices drifted down the hall, and they slowed, listening. His eyes grew wide, and he pulled Corinne behind a statue, holding a finger to his lips.

"...don't know *why* I can't go back—"

"Because you are *drunk*, Lana."

"I feel fine! I need to dance!"

"You need to sleep."

Lana's and Janus's voices drifted closer, and Corinne clapped a hand over her own mouth, trying not to laugh. Aryel did the same, his eyes sparkling with mirth.

"Aryel looked amazing tonight," Lana slurred. "But he couldn't keep his eyes off that goddess-damned guard of his all night."

"Yes, you said that earlier."

Corinne's heart skipped a beat. Their voices faded again as they ventured down another corridor, and Aryel peeked out from behind the statue. He sighed and emerged fully before looking at Corinne again.

They both burst out laughing. She hadn't laughed this hard since that night at the Mykotas's house, the tension in her chest dispelling, at least a little.

"Come on," Aryel said, still grinning as they headed off again.

"You know, you were about that intoxicated the first night we met," Corinne said, recalling that moment all too well as they approached the breezeway doors.

"Don't remind me," he said. "I will never be able to undo such a terrible first impression."

"Hmm." Corinne opened the door for him, leading them outside. "I don't know, I think it just shows how far we've come since then."

Aryel laughed once. "I suppose that's true."

They stepped into the alcove, and Aryel swore softly.

"I'm sorry, Corinne, I forgot a guard wouldn't be posted out here until later," he said.

"That's fine," she said. "I can wait."

He stopped by his door, and she took her usual place beside it, waiting for him to step inside. For a long moment, he stared ahead, and then he turned to her, pinning her in place with that same look in his eyes from earlier.

"I know Lana was drunk," he said. "But she wasn't wrong."

Corinne's pulse jumped at the change in his tone. "About what?"

Aryel took a step closer, and Corinne didn't back away when he brushed one of her curls away from her cheek. "About me not being able to take my eyes off you all night."

That warmth Corinne had fought so hard returned, spreading from her center outward.

"Truly, Corinne, are you all right?" he asked, searching her face.

She inhaled deeply, forcing herself to focus. "They noticed my burn is gone," she said, holding up her arm, and Aryel took it in his hands gently, his fingers brushing over her newly healed skin. She fought a shiver. "I don't know what they'll do. I didn't know they'd be there."

"I didn't either," he said. "I'm sorry."

CHAPTER 28

"It's not your fault."

Aryel lapsed into silence for a moment. "It could be."

Corinne's brow furrowed. "What do you mean?"

"Tell them I made you heal it. Tell them the royal family insisted. It would invite odd questions for an injured Lightguard to be protecting the prince, wouldn't it?"

Corinne could only stare at him. Emotions barreled into her, so many she couldn't name just one. Before she knew what she was doing, she stepped forward, pressing her lips to his cheek.

The look of blank shock on his face when she leaned back brought her to her senses, and panic overtook her in an instant.

"Oh, Goddess," she whispered, turning away from him. She started for her own door, appalled at herself, cheeks burning. "I'm sorry, I—"

Aryel's hand closed around her wrist, and he pulled her back to him, bringing her face to his. His lips found hers like the answer to a secret question in her heart, soft and insistent and sure. And Helaera help her, Corinne gave in to it.

She'd never kissed anyone like this before, but somehow it was like she'd kissed Aryel a thousand times, like his lips were meant for hers. She wrapped her arms around his neck, her body arching into his, her lips parting when his tongue brushed the seam of her mouth. The world disappeared, leaving only him, his hands gripping her waist as he pushed her back against the wall. Corinne wove her fingers into his hair, and he inhaled sharply. She'd never wanted—needed—anyone this desperately.

Corinne slid one hand downward, brushing the roughness of his close-shaved facial hair before pressing her palm to his chest. The bare skin she'd carefully avoided earlier was warm beneath her hand, even smoother than she'd imagined. Every moment she'd touched him and forced away her desire now boiled over, like she couldn't touch enough of him fast enough. The look in his eyes that night she'd healed him, the soft hitches of his breath when they trained, the blush in his cheeks... how had she not seen *so* clearly that he wanted her too?

Or perhaps she had, and she'd denied it up until this moment.

Aryel threaded his fingers into her curls on one side, gently tilting her head to kiss her jaw on the other, then her neck, and a small whine escaped her. *Goddess, that's embarrassing.* His body pressed hers into the stone, and still Corinne wanted more, her hands moving to his back like she could somehow pull him closer.

Muffled footsteps sounded, followed by the opening of a door, and Aryel's mouth went to her ear.

"Sorry, Sunshine."

His weight disappeared in an instant, but he pulled her forward off the wall before releasing her in one swift movement. The guard appeared only a moment later, bowing to the prince and a bewildered Corinne.

Focus, Corinne. Don't be a fool. She hoped she didn't look as disheveled as she felt.

"I can take it from here, Lady Corinne," the guard said, and she nodded gratefully, heading to her room as quickly as she could without seeming suspicious.

She glanced at Aryel before stepping inside. He was at his door now, too, staring at her with baffled wonder.

"Good night, Corinne," he said, those dark eyes boring into hers.

She swallowed hard as he disappeared into his room. Once inside her own room, she sank onto her bed in a trance, staring at the ceiling, one thought repeating in her head.

What have you done, Corinne?

CHAPTER 29

Corinne let the hot water of the shower run over her as she stared at the wall, her mind uncharacteristically at ease. She should feel immense guilt for what had happened last night, but the water was warm and pleasant on her skin, and it was a new day.

A silhouette appeared through the steam, and Aryel stepped into the shower, entirely naked. Corinne's breathing picked up as he wrapped his arms around her, planting a kiss on the side of her neck. She melted into his touch, letting him press his water-slick body into hers against the shower wall, her eyes drifting shut. He kissed her shoulder, then her chest, his mouth traveling lower toward her breasts. He closed his lips around her nipple, flicking it with his tongue—

Corinne woke abruptly, her entire body heated. She was still in her gown from last night, and *goddess*, her upper arms had alit with her magic in her aroused state. She scrambled out of bed and all but ripped the dress off before heading straight for the shower, trying to scrub away the images from the dream.

It was much harder to dispel the memories of the night before, the very real feeling of Aryel's hands on her waist, her back, in her hair, his mouth moving desperately against hers—

Stop, she commanded herself, squeezing her eyes shut in the stream of water. She turned the tap to cold, shocking her body back into a neutral state.

A knock sounded from her room, and Corinne nearly slipped in the shower, scrambling to turn it off.

"Corinne? Are you in there?"

Vera. *Goddess, help me.* "One moment!"

As fast as she could manage it, Corinne dried herself off and threw on fresh clothing. She forced herself to take a breath before opening her door, fully prepared to face Vera's judgment for her limp, wet hair and disheveled appearance.

Vera's eyes grew wide the moment Corinne opened the door, but she said nothing at first, merely stepping inside. As soon as the latch clicked, Vera whirled on her.

"Corinne," she choked out, gesturing up and down at her. "What has *happened* to you?"

Corinne hardly dared to breathe, terrified that Vera would somehow be able to tell that she'd kissed the prince last night.

"I—"

"You said you would recommit yourself," Vera said, her voice pained. "And last night we arrive to the sight of you *dancing* with the prince, your burn healed early. Have you no shame, Corinne?"

Corinne's entire body felt like she'd stepped into that icy shower again. "I feel more shame than you could possibly imagine. I feel it all the time."

"Well, you do a poor job of showing it," Vera snapped, crossing her arms. *Tell them it was me.* Corinne opened her mouth, the lie ready to spill forth, but Vera continued. "And that request for the Lightguards to transport food? What are we, pack mules? You have dishonored and humiliated us all."

The typhoon of shame within Corinne came to a sudden halt. "I... but those people needed help, and we could provide it—"

"That is the Crown's responsibility," Vera said. "The only reason Mother Creita agreed to it was to not create tension between the monastery and Vytanos."

"How is that any different from the protection we provide them in the villages? At the Boundary?" Corinne asked.

CHAPTER 29

"Because *we* decide, with Helaera's guidance, what is part of our duty." Vera walked to Corinne's window, casting a disdainful glance at the gown still in a heap on her floor.

The grief in Corinne's heart grew tenfold. The Lightguards were *displeased* with her for requesting their aid for the people of Ashera.

"You have strayed too far, Corinne," Vera said, facing her again. "You are *just* like your father."

Vera, more than anyone, knew how much that would hurt her, how deep that wound ran. The words severed something within Corinne—something that caught fire.

"I am *nothing* like him," Corinne bit out, angry tears stinging her eyes, and Vera balked. "If you believe that, then you never really knew me at all."

Vera stared at her, blue eyes turning icy. "Perhaps I didn't. I never expected you to fall so far from grace, yet here we are."

Without another word, Vera stalked past Corinne, wrenching her door open and letting it slam behind her. Corinne's anger flared for another moment before she caught sight of her nightstand by the window, her makeshift altar, and her heart stopped.

She'd forgotten to do her ritual this morning.

It was too late to do it now, the sun fully risen and Aryel soon to wake. A leaden feeling settled in her stomach. She'd never forgotten it, not once in fifteen years.

Vera is right—you have strayed too far.

Corinne felt like her chest would cave in. Hot panic raged within her once more, and she curled in on herself as her mind bombarded her with evidence of her own immorality.

You healed your burn. You wore extravagant clothes. You danced with the prince. You kissed him.

No...

Heretic deviant just like your father you want to hurt those you care about you want to stray from the Light you are selfish you had tricked them all but now they know—

"No," Corinne whispered, her head bowed as she began to tremble. *I've tried.*

Have you tried? If you had, you wouldn't have strayed.

Stay the course, she told herself. *Be the Light. Stay the course. Be the Light. They're just thoughts.*

Even Aryel's words couldn't entirely ease the onslaught of dread, not when Vera had just confirmed her worst fears about herself yet again. Corinne didn't truly believe she was like her father, but what if she'd just convinced herself she wasn't to ease her own conscience? Perhaps she deserved to feel so wretched all the time, and this was her fate.

Still trembling, Corinne retrieved her sword belt and sheathed her blade at her hip. She couldn't rationalize the fear drilling into her gut; all she knew was she'd forgotten her weekly ritual and something terrible was going to happen because of it. She imagined telling Danai or Nik or Iliana about it, but they wouldn't believe her, wouldn't understand.

Ari might.

Corinne's chest ached. She couldn't talk to Aryel about it, either. Not while the Lightguards were in the castle. If that meant pushing him away again to protect him and herself, then so be it. The Lightguards had already found out about her healing the burn early; if they discovered she'd let someone touch her like he had...

Corinne shivered. They'd punished her for far less.

She'd never heard of a Lightguard breaking that rule before. If they found out, she'd simply have to accept whatever penalty they deemed necessary, and there was nothing she could do about it. Perhaps she would end up burned twice over, handprints on both her arms. What would the Lightguards think of her? Would they discharge her of her duty here? Would she simply live in perpetual disgrace at the monastery, a cautionary tale for others?

And what would her friends here think?

Corinne breathed in, some of her fear dispelled. Danai and the others wouldn't judge her, of that she was sure. And Aryel...he would be furious on her behalf if they hurt her again.

That's part of Her Light too.

That knot in her chest that each of her friends had pulled upon began to loosen even more. She'd felt the tug of the thread again last night, when Nik and Danai had stood beside her, when Aryel had asked if she was all right. When he'd so readily offered to lie to protect her.

If they truly scorned her, if earning their love and respect was no longer possible, what would she do? She wouldn't belong anywhere, would have no purpose.

But she wouldn't be entirely alone. The thought both comforted and terrified her.

That's not what I want. She wouldn't be like her father. She wouldn't become a defector. Defectors were the most egregious affront to Helaera, and their magic became corrupt without the Goddess's blessing. She could not, would not allow herself to lose control in that way, to potentially hurt others.

Her insides roiling and her heart uncertain, she stepped outside to face the day.

CHAPTER 30

When Aryel stepped out of his rooms, Corinne forgot how to breathe, the air pressing on her lungs as the door swung shut behind him. Even if she planned to keep him at arm's length, she couldn't simply ignore him entirely. She forced herself to meet his eyes.

"Hi," he said, his posture stiff as he hovered about a foot away from her.

He looked like he hadn't slept any better than she had.

"Hi," she said, her tone just as flat and awkward as his. *I dreamed about you naked.*

"I—" He cleared his throat and blinked. She'd never seen him so at a loss for words, and for some ridiculous reason, Corinne found it excruciatingly endearing. "We should go, I suppose."

Corinne merely nodded, waiting for him to move. She followed him at her normal distance today, but when they reached the door, he paused, facing her.

"Are we going to talk about last night?" he asked, his voice low, his face uncertain.

Corinne's heart sank. Did he regret kissing her? Had he decided she was just some dull, inexperienced girl who couldn't hold his attention?

CHAPTER 30

Perhaps it was for the best. So why did that possibility hurt so much?

"Not while there are Lightguards in the castle," she said, her voice barely above a whisper.

Understanding settled in his eyes then, and he nodded.

Corinne breathed a little easier as they headed for the council chamber. She could avoid that conversation until Mother Creita and the others left, at least, and hopefully come up with a way to keep the kiss secret without the guilt eating her alive.

She wasn't sure what she'd have done if Vera had asked her outright about her relationship with the prince. Would she have confessed to kissing him? To wanting to do more than that? It was infinitely more difficult to ignore her body's reaction to his proximity now that she knew what it felt like for him to touch her the way he had in the alcove.

She shook her head as she walked. *Control, Corinne.*

As they stepped through the doors to the council chamber, Corinne pushed down every last emotion that had rattled her bones since waking. She couldn't entirely dismiss the unyielding dread, but she would not reveal a flicker of anything in front of the Lightguards.

Aryel greeted Councilor Toro and the others already present while Corinne took her place by the window. The Lightguards arrived shortly thereafter, and Corinne crossed her arms over her chest in a show of respect, which they returned.

Lies and deceit for appearances. If the others felt about her the same way Vera did, they held no respect or admiration for Corinne anymore.

A small part of her whispered that her respect for them had faltered too. She pushed that thought away; she had to find out whether Mother Creita truly believed that the aid they were offering the northeastern villages was beneath the Lightguards.

The king and queen arrived, and everyone in the room stood. Queen Erina greeted the Lightguards with overenthusiastic warmth.

"Shall we begin the meeting with a prayer?" she asked, and Corinne fought a grimace. It was just as uncomfortable in a group as it was when she'd done this to Corinne at their first encounter. "Mother Creita, I would be delighted if you'd lead us."

"Of course," the High Priestess said. She lifted her hands before her, palms facing the ceiling, and everyone at the table gazed in awe at the markings that began to glow along her hands and arms.

Everyone except Aryel, whose eyes went directly to Corinne. That look confirmed it—he knew. He knew it was Mother Creita who'd left that handprint on her arm.

"Goddess Helaera, Mother of us all, keep watch over your humble and faithful servants," Mother Creita said. "The Crown seeks to work alongside your Hands and your Swords. You have given each of us your blessing, and we ask now for your guidance and protection."

"May Helaera guide us," the Lightguards said in unison, Corinne included, and the others echoed them.

Everyone took their seats, and Corinne forced her eyes away from Aryel, looking instead to Captain Ekhana across the room.

"Thank you," Queen Erina said, inclining her head. "Let us proceed."

This time it was Priestess Chala who spoke, leaning forward with her hands clasped upon the table. "We remain confident that no Nightrenders have breached the Boundary, but that does not mean others who may act on their behalf have not slipped through. Several of our own have received additional threatening notes, and two of them have once again mentioned Prince Aryel."

Corinne's heart clenched. She'd known that was the entire reason for her assignment here, but hearing that more threats had been made on Aryel's life invoked a fear she hadn't felt before. It was personal now. She cared about him.

She cared about him more than she'd realized, more than she should.

"We remain vigilant," Chala said. "While we cannot provide additional Lightguards to the castle, we have agreed we will remain here for the next week to work with your castle and city guards. We are happy to provide assistance in shoring up security measures."

"Your presence and aid are deeply appreciated," King Theo said.

"What is it they want with Prince Aryel?" Councilor Toro asked. "We know he has been threatened several times now, and even attacked, but why?"

"We've always known this day would come," Mother Creita said, standing from her chair, her robes flowing elegantly as she paced toward the wall on Corinne's left, studying the portraits hung there. "The heretics of the Shadowlands tried to eradicate us centuries ago, and they are now attempting the same again. They ascribe to prophecies and divinations we do not abide or place trust in, but it is possible that such false spirituality could lead them to act without a cause we can identify."

"So you're saying they want our heir dead simply for conquest?" King Theo asked.

Mother Creita nodded, her eyes sliding to Aryel, and Corinne tensed. "As the sole heir to Ashera, Your Highness, you are the primary threat to their aims."

"Then I suppose it's a true blessing from Helaera that Corinne Anastos is here to protect me," Aryel said. "I'm indebted to the Lightguards for sending her here."

Corinne couldn't help it—she looked at him, but his eyes were burning a hole into Mother Creita. Her name, her full name, on his lips as he declared his gratitude for her presence to the Lightguards in the room was somehow more intimate than his hands on her waist, his tongue in her mouth—

Corinne fought the urge to scream aloud. She had to get ahold of her own thoughts. This was no time to revisit the kiss, to deal with the reaction of her body.

"You are most gracious, Your Highness," Mother Creita said with a serene nod to Aryel. "We are honored to provide such protection through Corinne."

Corinne's face heated, a mix of embarrassment and anger, but she breathed through it. She breathed through the rest of the meeting, trying to focus on the logistics the Lightguards discussed with the royal family and councilors. Once it was adjourned, Corinne watched the Lightguards, her mind wandering back through what Priestess Chala had said about the threatening messages.

I know your secret, Corinne Anastos.

Corinne quickly approached Aryel as he stood from the table, doing her best to ignore the slight flush to his cheeks as she leaned close.

"I need to ask them something," she said quietly. "I won't be long."

He nodded, and Corinne followed them into the corridor.

"Mother Creita," she called, and the Lightguards all turned.

Mother Creita waved the others on at Corinne's approach. Corinne inclined her head.

"You want to do this here?" Mother Creita asked softly, her voice dangerous. "Now?"

Corinne swallowed hard. *Tell them I made you heal it.* "No. I wanted to discuss a different matter."

The High Priestess looked her up and down. "Very well."

"I also received an anonymous threatening note," she said. "It wasn't about Prince Aryel, though."

Mother Creita nodded solemnly. "What were the contents?"

"Just one line," Corinne said, her voice barely audible. "*I know your secret, Corinne Anastos.*"

With a frown, Mother Creita said, "That...is quite cryptic. As were the others. Be on your guard, Corinne. We don't know what their intentions truly are."

Corinne bowed her head. "Yes, Mother Creita."

"Join us tomorrow after your duties have concluded," Mother Creita said. "We will offer you one chance to explain yourself."

Corinne didn't trust her voice, so she merely nodded again. The High Priestess set off once more, following the other Lightguards.

SOMEHOW, CORINNE MADE IT THROUGH THAT DAY AND THE next without falling apart. Nothing extraordinary happened as a result of her missing her ritual, and Aryel was on his best behavior, quieter than usual but not cold. She was left in peace to focus on the pressure of the Lightguards' presence without him further complicating things.

Part of her wanted him to complicate things anyway. Especially when she noticed every breath, every movement he made in response to her now, and she kicked herself mentally again. She was supposed to be the virtuous one of the two of them, and here she was, having lewd dreams and fighting unholy desires every time he was near.

"You're going to meet them?" he asked, his eyebrows nearly

shooting into his hairline as Corinne escorted him to his rooms that evening.

He stopped in the corridor leading out to the breezeway, and Corinne shushed him before nudging him forward through the doors. She let them shut and then faced Aryel again, the balmy Vytanos air drifting through his hair.

"I have to," she said, keeping her voice low. "To explain." She held up her arm, still free of the scar in her sleeveless tunic.

She'd missed wearing such attire, not realizing how much of a relief it would be until she'd been able to do so the past two days.

Aryel's eyes hardened. "I meant what I said, Corinne. Tell them it was me."

Corinne took a steadying breath. "Okay."

"I'm serious," he said, taking a step closer to her. "Don't give them the chance to hurt you like that again. You did nothing wrong."

The realization that she agreed with him made her feel lightheaded.

"I'll tell them," she whispered.

Aryel moved closer again, and Corinne backed up until she hit the door. He stopped, closing his eyes for a moment.

"I just want to be clear," he said, his voice strained as he looked at her. "If you felt in any way obligated to...reciprocate...the other night, I'm sorry. I never want anyone to feel like they have to do what I want just because I'm the prince."

"Ari, we can't talk about this right now," Corinne breathed, her chest aching. Had he been worried about *that* this whole time? The conflict in his eyes pulled the next few words from her. "That's not at all how I felt."

The tension in his shoulders melted away, and he took a slow, deep breath. He stepped closer again, startling her as he braced his hands on the door on either side of her head.

"Then I'm going to kiss you again before I leave Helaera's earth, Corinne Anastos," he said quietly, those beautiful eyes holding her captive.

She shouldn't want this, but every part of her seemed to glow with him so close, as he confirmed that he didn't see their kiss as a mistake.

He wanted her as much as she wanted him.

Aryel turned away from her as though nothing had happened, ever the impeccable actor, and Corinne clumsily gathered her scattered thoughts. *Goddess help me.* She had a meeting with the Lightguards to attend, and she needed to embody the same collected exterior Aryel had.

After he disappeared into his rooms and another guard arrived to relieve Corinne, she dashed inside her room to change her clothes and muster her courage. None of her shirts or tunics were just right for what she wanted—they were either too plain, or too wrinkled, or too flattering. Knowing she was short on time, she settled for a bone-white tunic with sleeves that went down to her elbows and a gold hem. She quickly shook out her curls and splashed a bit of water on her face, staring at her hazel gaze in the mirror for a moment, hands gripping the edges of the stone sink. *Stay the course. Be the Light.*

You did nothing wrong.

That's part of Her Light too.

Corinne was going to lie to the Lightguards for the first time in her life. She would simply have to beg Helaera for forgiveness—in the end, Corinne answered to Her. Surely the Mother of Ashera would understand why she couldn't bear to be burned again.

Why she now questioned if she'd deserved it the first time.

That revelation settled heavily on her heart. *Helaera guide me, I beg you.* Corinne straightened, retrieved her sword, and set off.

Orana met Corinne by the entrance hall, ready to escort her to the guest chambers the royal family had given the Lightguards. The matron of servants looked absolutely exhausted.

"How are you?" Corinne asked as they began walking, and Orana blinked at her in surprise.

"I'm well, thank you," she said, leading Corinne toward the north wing of the castle.

"I know it can't be easy managing all the extra nobles in the castle," Corinne said. "I hope you've been able to get ample rest."

Orana was quiet for a moment as they ascended a flight of stairs. "You are kind to say so, Corinne."

CHAPTER 30

They continued on in silence until they reached a door on the third floor, unremarkable and at the end of a short hallway.

"Have a good evening," Orana said with a soft smile and left Corinne to stand before the door with a thundering heart.

She forced air into her lungs, then out again, then knocked.

"Enter."

Corinne stepped inside, her stomach dropping. The Lightguards had rearranged the large room—four beds lay within, and two couches, but they had been shifted aside to make room for a semicircle of the Priestesses, resembling the Hall of Mothers. Mother Creita sat in a chair directly ahead, Chala and Bria on the right and left of a folded rug in the center. Vera stood by the window behind Mother Creita, her arms crossed and her expression stony. The normal lanterns were lit in the room, but they'd found candles somewhere too, setting them out to form a more distinguished semicircle with the missing Priestess.

When Mother Creita beckoned her toward the room's center, Corinne let the door shut behind her and forced her heavy feet to bring her forward. Her instincts screamed at her to get as far away from that center rug as possible, recalling all too well what had happened the last time she'd been in such a position. But there was no way they would punish her here, not when so many would hear her screams.

Doing her best to hide the trembling in her legs, Corinne removed her sword and knelt, placing the blade beside her.

"Corinne Anastos," Mother Creita began. "We hoped not to be here again, but you have much to explain."

"I'm here to beg your forgiveness," Corinne said, her voice shaking. "And Helaera's."

Mother Creita and the two other Priestesses nodded. "Proceed, then."

The tears came too easily, not entirely false. "They made me heal the burn early, Mother Creita. They insisted I attend the ball to keep watch over the prince, and he did not want the questions the scar would invite from all the attendees. I had no choice but to obey."

The High Priestess's expression softened somewhat, and some of Corinne's fear melted away. "Very well. We'll have to rectify that at some point, but I can understand it was forced upon you. Do you agree, my sisters?"

Priestess Chala and Priestess Bria looked to Corinne, then back to Mother Creita before nodding their approval. Corinne didn't allow herself to dwell on her relief.

"And what have you to say about the participation in party activities?" Mother Creita asked. "I assume the attire was also forced upon you, but surely the dancing was not."

Corinne let more tears fall. "It was for the prince's protection, Mother Creita. He and the king and queen don't entirely trust some of the nobles. We agreed I would intervene should any of those nobles try to get too close to the prince." She hung her head, allowing her shoulders to slump. "It was all a farce, and I did it in the name of duty, but it was shameful nonetheless."

Corinne didn't dare lift her head as she waited for them to respond. *Please. Please, Helaera above.*

"Your contrition is admirable, Corinne," Mother Creita said. "And as Helaera forgives her children, so we forgive our own as well."

Corinne looked up, hardly able to breathe.

"While you remain here, if you continue to show the utmost devotion to your purpose, we will stay the reinstatement of your punishment and consider your penance fulfilled. But this is your last chance," Mother Creita warned, standing from her chair and walking toward Corinne. She took her chin in her fingers, lifting it, and Corinne fought the urge to recoil. "Remember who you are, Corinne. You can still prove yourself to us and Helaera."

"Thank you," Corinne whispered, closing her eyes.

The High Priestess removed her hand and stepped away, and Corinne got to her feet. Behind her, Vera wouldn't meet her eyes, turning to face the window with her arms still crossed. Vera had made it very clear to her that their friendship was over, but this displeasure with Corinne's atonement sent another knife through her heart. How had they ever been friends if a single mistake from Corinne could make Vera hate her so completely, abandon her without a flicker of remorse?

"Mother Creita, I have a question, if you'll allow me to ask it," Corinne said as the others rose from their chairs.

CHAPTER 30

"Ask, child."

Corinne swallowed. "The aid I requested we provide...was I out of line in asking for such a thing?"

Mother Creita pursed her lips. "Not out of line, precisely, but I'd hoped you would have known such tasks are not ones that should fall to us. If we provide such services to the Crown, it may become too reliant upon us for things the royal family should do itself. It diminishes our purpose and our reputation."

"Is it not a service to the people, rather than the Crown, Mother Creita?" Corinne asked, her brow furrowing. A bit of fear twisted behind her sternum as the High Priestess narrowed her eyes.

"We are here to protect and fortify the Boundary, and to provide basic protection to villages around Ashera," Mother Creita said. "You would do well to spend more time in prayer, Corinne. Don't lose sight of the path."

Corinne nodded, and as she crossed her arms over her chest to bid them farewell, one thing became clear, settling into her bones.

She did not agree with Mother Creita. She and Vera had very different ideas about what mattered most in serving Helaera, in being a Lightguard.

You just want an excuse to be selfish and do what you wish.

Corinne let the dread and fear prickle through her chest and constrict her throat as the thoughts followed her out the door and down the corridor.

Perhaps it was true. Perhaps she had strayed and dishonored herself, but Helaera knew her heart, and that had to count for something.

She'd been prideful. She'd healed her burn. She'd pined after Aryel. She'd lied to the Lightguards. She'd kissed a man and might've done more. If she was damned, she was damned.

A fire within began to burn alongside the fear, a radical acceptance of her fate.

CHAPTER 31

By the sixth day of the Lightguards' stay in Vytanos, Corinne wondered if she'd ever feel at peace again. They were due to leave in the morning after holding a ritual in the sanctuary, and then she could breathe again. Maybe.

Because after they left, she'd have to face Aryel. This past week had felt like the days following her visit to the monastery, except this time the silence between them wasn't what she wanted. Still, the anticipation of speaking to him more freely again was both comforting and terrifying.

I'm going to kiss you again before I leave Helaera's earth, Corinne Anastos.

"Corinne!"

Her head snapped up as she stepped outside onto the training grounds, finally able to train outdoors in sleeveless shirts again. Danai waved her over to the grassy ring, and she smiled for the first time in days, jogging to greet them and Iliana.

"How's your brother?" Corinne asked, stepping into the ring.

Iliana jumped down from the fence where she'd been sitting. "He's doing well," she said. "We'll never be able to repay you for that, Corinne."

CHAPTER 31

"You don't owe me anything," Corinne said, shaking her head. "Our healing is a gift from Helaera."

Iliana smiled before throwing her arms around Corinne, who returned her embrace.

"Did you two want to train?" Corinne asked when Iliana released her.

"Sure," Danai said. "Or we could talk about why you and the prince have barely looked at one another since the ball."

Corinne's entire face heated. "The Lightguards are in the castle, and I have to remain disciplined."

"You've spoken freely to us and Nik," Danai said, shrugging one shoulder.

"Danai," Corinne said, certain her entire face was red. "I beg you not to press me on this right now."

With a sigh, Danai acquiesced. "All right. I'm sorry."

"Oh!" Iliana exclaimed, startling both Corinne and Danai. "Corinne, I forgot to tell you that Aeson tested that ink from the note."

Corinne had nearly forgotten about that entirely in the wake of Aeson's injury, and in the revelation that she wasn't the only Lightguard to receive such a cryptic message recently.

"What did he find out?" she asked.

Iliana frowned. "He said it was likely ink that originated in central Ashera. That's unfortunately where most ink is made here."

Corinne's brow furrowed. Of course it wouldn't be that simple.

"I found out other Lightguards received strange notes as well," she told them. "Which isn't good, but it does make it feel less targeted."

"Strange," Danai said, brow furrowing. "Perhaps they don't actually know your secret. Or whether you even have one. Perhaps it was a guess to scare you."

"Perhaps it was," Corinne said, considering that for the first time. "Their investigations are ongoing. They're also conducting the preparations and plans for shoring up castle defenses as well."

"Oh trust me, we know," Danai said, grimacing. Iliana nudged them sharply.

"What?" Corinne asked. They both looked at one another, hesitant. "Please tell me."

"They've recommended Captain Ekhana make changes to guard shifts and rotations," Danai said. "They insist they're based on their expert experience in guarding the Boundary and the villages all around Ashera, but they are overly complex and it's giving everyone a headache."

"What Danai is trying to say is castle and city guards don't have the intelligence to protect people as effectively as Lightguards," Iliana said, trying to hide a grin.

Danai groaned and plopped onto the grass. "Perhaps so! All I want is to do my job and protect the castle," they said. "And still have time to spend with my family and Nik."

Corinne frowned. She and the other Lightguards had taken their oath, fully aware of the commitment and dedication it required. Guards here having to adapt to such duties without the proper training seemed unfair.

"I can see how that would be frustrating," Corinne said, unable to think of anything else to say. Danai and Iliana couldn't disobey orders any more than she could.

"Well, nothing we can do about it," Iliana said. "Other than vent our frustrations by hitting something. Or each other."

Corinne and Danai both laughed. She stood back and watched first, letting the two of them spar before she got involved. Iliana's ferocity still impressed her every time she saw her fight or sparred with her, and the two of them only got better each time they trained. Corinne leaned on the fence, a smile settling on her lips.

"They're quite skilled, aren't they?"

Corinne flinched violently and whipped around, not having heard Aryel approaching. He stood back, his face contorting with suppressed laughter.

"Sorry," he said, though he didn't look sorry at all.

Corinne cursed herself, her entire body warming.

"Prince Aryel," Danai said breathlessly, jogging to greet him, Iliana close behind.

"Just Aryel, please," the prince said.

"Only when Captain Ekhana's not around," Danai said conspiratorially. "He'd have my head if he heard that."

CHAPTER 31

Aryel laughed. "Fair enough."

"Did you come out here without a guard?" Iliana asked.

"One of them escorted me from the throne room," he said. "Then once I walked out here, I told them I'd be perfectly safe with you two and Corinne."

"No one safer," Danai said, nodding sagely. "But now that you're out here, did you want to train with us? We hear Corinne's been working with you as well."

Corinne pinned Danai with a look that promised murder, but they merely smiled at her innocently.

"Why not?" Aryel said, leaping lithely over the fence.

Iliana called for the attendant nearby, requesting several practice swords.

"Iliana and I just had a turn, so you two first," Danai said, gesturing to Corinne and Aryel.

Aryel's eyes met hers briefly before he took the practice sword and headed for the center of the ring. Corinne watched as he rolled up the sleeves on his tan shirt, baring his forearms, and another deeply inappropriate dream she'd had this week surfaced in her memory.

Helaera smite her. She handed her sword to Iliana and took the practice one before stalking after him.

"A true spar this time?" Aryel asked, one hand on his hip. "Not just drills?"

"Fine by me," Corinne said, dropping into her stance. "Whenever you're ready, Your Highness."

Aryel quirked an eyebrow. "Back to that, are we, Sunshine?"

Corinne didn't say anything, merely waited for him to strike, and when he did, she was ready. Thank Helaera sparring was such second nature to her.

Or it was, at least, until she caught a glimpse of Aryel's smile as they fought, and her steps faltered. A quick counter on his part nearly made the sword fall from her hand, but she recovered, regaining her balance and composure. Almost.

"Feeling a little off today?" he asked, grinning wolfishly, and Corinne lunged at him. He dodged just in time.

"I could put you on your back if I really wanted to," she said, circling him.

"I would *very* much enjoy that."

The implication threw Corinne so thoroughly that her mind went blank, and when he attacked again, they both went tumbling to the grassy earth. He pinned her, the practice sword at her throat.

"Get it together, Sunshine," he said, breathing hard as he hovered over her.

His eyes darted to her mouth, and for a wild moment, Corinne wondered if he was going to kiss her right there in the open.

Danai and Iliana cheered from the edge of the ring's enclosure as Aryel got up, offering Corinne his hand. She took it, dazed.

"We can tell them you let me win," Aryel muttered, pulling her upright.

Corinne returned to her senses and scowled.

"You promised no more jokes about nudity," she hissed.

"I didn't say a thing about nudity," Aryel said, his voice even lower. "Not my fault if that's where your mind went."

Oh, it was *entirely* his fault, but Corinne couldn't say so as Danai and Iliana approached them.

"Impressive," Danai said to Aryel. "Corinne's taught you well."

"She has," Aryel said. "Perhaps one day I'll actually beat her without her letting me."

"That's my goal as well, but I'm not getting my hopes up," Iliana said, stretching. "Corinne, are you up for another spar?"

If it would distract her from the images Aryel had conjured in her head, she was up for anything. She and Iliana sparred several rounds while Danai spoke with Aryel on the edge of the ring. Corinne threw herself into it entirely, letting her mind focus on the task of fighting. They were both sweating profusely by the time they finished, lying on their backs in the grass as they caught their breath.

"I like him," Iliana said, turning her head toward Corinne. "The prince, I mean. He's different from what I expected."

Corinne met her amber gaze, then glanced past her at Danai and Aryel.

"He's different from what I expected too."

CHAPTER 31

When they finally peeled themselves off the ground and headed for the ring's perimeter, Danai smiled brightly at their approach.

"You know how it's more difficult for us to have our weekly dinner at my parents' house?" Danai asked. "Since we're both off duty tomorrow, Aryel's invited to host us here."

Iliana's eyes brightened. "That's kind of you, thank you."

"Any friend of Corinne's is a friend of mine," Aryel said. "And to be quite honest, I'm rather sick of nobles at the moment."

"Me too," Iliana said, then her eyes widened, realizing what she'd said. "I mean—"

But Aryel just laughed. "I completely understand. So, my chambers tomorrow evening? Please bring Nik with you as well."

"I'm supposed to be on duty then," Corinne said.

Aryel shrugged. "You can guard me perfectly well while joining us," he said, a twinkle in his eye, and that low, slow heat crept into Corinne's abdomen again.

"It's a plan, then," Danai said brightly. "And speaking of food, I'm starving. Anyone else want to get lunch?"

CHAPTER 32

Corinne stared at the steaming tea in front of her, placed on the table by her door instead of the nightstand by her window. There was no need to use the makeshift altar when the ritual was taking place in the sanctuary this morning, led by the visiting Lightguards. She was still expected to drink the tea, but its bitter smell was especially rancid today. She got dressed and refreshed her hair before returning to the drink, and still, she couldn't bring herself to lift it to her lips. It was almost time to leave, anyway.

She left it on the table and stepped outside. Something about leaving it still made her uneasy, but...she'd been perfectly fine last week. She still couldn't recall its purpose, anyway, so maybe it wasn't as important as it had always seemed.

Aryel would be escorted to the sanctuary alongside his parents after the Lightguards arrived, so Corinne merely glanced at his door once before heading there herself. She just had to get through this morning, and then the Priestesses and Vera would be gone.

And then dinner this evening. She still had no idea what she was going to say to Aryel when they had that inevitable conversation. Would she reject him like she should? Would she tell him it was too complicated? Would she kiss him again?

CHAPTER 32

I'm going to kiss you again before I leave Helaera's earth, Corinne Anastos.

Terrifying, yet...exhilarating. She couldn't bring herself to feel guilty about her desire, either, but then guilt over her lack thereof settled in her gut. It was one of the most basic rules of Lightguards after they'd taken their oath—no romantic relationships. Her heart belonged to Helaera.

Was that what this was, though? All she knew was Aryel wanted her *physically*, and she wanted him that way too. If that's all it was, perhaps it wasn't so bad.

Corinne shook her head as if to clear it. She could worry about that later. For now, she needed to get through this ritual and give the Lightguards no other reason to doubt her while she untangled the conflicted mess that was her soul.

The sanctuary was beautiful in the early morning light, the stained glass casting rainbows on the stone floor and walls. The Lightguards were already there, the Priestesses in white robes with golden tassels, and Vera was dressed similarly to Corinne in a white shirt with gold laces and matching trousers. Corinne joined Vera on the front row of the chairs set out while the Priestesses prepared the altar at the front.

"Good morning, Corinne," Vera said. Her tone was pleasant enough, but Corinne recognized it as the voice she used when she was being forcibly polite.

"Good morning."

"When I return in two weeks," she said quietly, "I hope to find you truly recommitted. But if I don't, I will not protect you or cover for you."

So Vera was threatening her now. Simmering anger rose out of the chasm of grief within her. No fear, only disappointment that Vera truly wasn't the person she'd always thought she was. It didn't make it sting any less, but she kept her face smooth, her body language relaxed.

"May Helaera guide us both, then," Corinne said coolly.

"Would you two mind lighting the candles?" Priestess Bria asked, turning to Vera and Corinne.

They both silently agreed. Vera headed for the candles up front, so Corinne walked to the back of the sanctuary. With a sigh, she pinched the wick of a tall white candle between her thumb and forefinger and summoned a bit of her magic.

It sparked higher than she'd intended, making her jump. She blinked, glancing at the others, but they hadn't noticed. Terror crawled its way up her body. Was her magic becoming corrupt? She'd thought Helaera had not turned on her, but now...

Trembling, she turned to the next candle a few feet away, releasing a bit less magic into her fingers this time. Normal spark. She exhaled, the fear quelling. She was still in full control. She hadn't really used her magic much these past weeks, at least not as regularly as she had at the monastery. As much as she enjoyed training with her friends, she really ought to do some solo work as well so she wouldn't get rusty with the light.

Nobles began to arrive as she and Vera finished lighting the candles. Corinne returned to her place at the front and kept her eyes forward after taking her seat. The room grew warmer as more and more bodies filled the space, and everyone stood suddenly at the arrival of the king and queen.

Aryel was with them, trailing behind as they made their way to the front row. Of course they would sit up here by Corinne. Of course Aryel would sit in the seat directly to her right. To his credit, at the sight of Vera, he did nothing but nod at Corinne in acknowledgment before taking his seat.

Goddess, he looked unnecessarily handsome in a deep red shirt. Corinne mastered herself as the ritual began. They spoke the normal prayers, engaged in a call and response with the gathered crowd, and finally sang. No one but the Lightguards were expected to know the songs, so Corinne joined her voice to the four others as Mother Creita began.

Careful, dear light, of the darkness that looms
Shadows will take you so swiftly
Keep your eye trained on the sun and the moon,
They'll guide you onward and with me

CHAPTER 32

Careful, don't stray into darkness that looms
Shadows can hide you from sunlight
Stay in the glow of midnight and noon
They'll keep you stronger in my sight

With a final prayer led by Mother Creita, the ritual was finished. Corinne knew she wouldn't truly breathe until everyone had dispersed and the Lightguards had departed, but she'd made it through the most challenging part. Many nobles approached the Priestesses to offer their gratitude and appreciation. One even pulled Vera aside, an older man who appeared to be asking her a number of questions.

"I could listen to you sing all day."

Aryel hadn't turned to her, hadn't even leaned in, but the chatter in the room drowned out his words for all but Corinne. His eyes were on the Priestesses and nobles up front, soon joined by his parents. Corinne didn't know what to say, or if she should say anything.

"See you at dinner, Sunshine," he said, joining his parents when they beckoned.

Her heart felt like it was melting in her chest. *Aryel Serra, what have you done to me?*

Slowly, excruciatingly slowly, the nobles departed, leaving the Lightguards on their own. Corinne and Vera put out the candles while the Priestesses gathered the items on the altar into a satchel. Vera took the bag once it was full and set off with Bria and Chala. Mother Creita approached Corinne.

"May Helaera guide you, child," she said. "Danger lurks here, I can feel it. Stay vigilant."

Corinne crossed her arms over her chest, this time allowing her markings to alight.

"May Helaera guide you," she said in turn.

Mother Creita placed a hand on Corinne's shoulder, and she fought to remain still, that instinct to flinch away still alive within her. But the High Priestess merely squeezed her shoulder before dropping her hand again and gliding toward the sanctuary's exit.

Corinne remained in place for a few more heartbeats before she looked to one of the stained glass windows that depicted Helaera. The Goddess's golden hair flowed around her gracefully as she bestowed her healing light upon people below, their hands uplifted. Corinne stepped forward as if in a trance, pressing her palm to the golden light on the window.

"Forgive me, Mother Goddess," she whispered. "Guide my heart."

CHAPTER 33

"Do you think he has a fountain in his rooms?"

Danai had asked about a thousand questions on their way to Aryel's rooms that evening, holding onto Nik's arm and nearly trembling with excitement.

"He doesn't," Corinne said, leading the way toward the breezeway doors.

She'd met her friends in the entrance hall several minutes prior. Once she'd been certain of the Lightguards' departure from the castle, she had taken advantage of her afternoon off duty to read and then train.

Her magic wasn't out of her control, but it felt larger, somehow, requiring less effort to use and maneuver. She'd felt abnormally powerful and sure. Perhaps it had built up within her during the weeks she'd spent here.

"You've been in Prince Aryel's rooms?" Iliana asked, raising an eyebrow.

Corinne's face flushed. "Yes. Madam Orana brought me in there on my first day."

She'd been in his rooms several times since then, but she didn't need to tell them that.

Corinne held open the doors to the breezeway, and they stepped through, admiring the view. Danai and Iliana were still in their guard attire after working all day, and Nik wore his usual plain dark shirt with laces at the front. He and Danai paused at the railing of the breezeway to point at something in the distance, and Corinne smiled as she passed, entering the alcove to dismiss the guard on duty. He gave her a nod and greeted Danai and Iliana on his way across.

Aryel's door opened, and he peeked outside, grinning and waving them over.

"I hope you all are hungry," he said, stepping aside to allow them through his doorway. The smell of food hit Corinne's nose immediately, and her mouth watered. "I may have gone a little overboard with my requests from the kitchens."

When Corinne stepped past the antechamber and into his main room, she nearly burst out laughing. The dining table was piled with food, not unlike the spread that had been at the ball a week prior. Two carafes of wine sat by a three-tiered tray of meats and cheeses, and on a large platter to the left, those tiny herb and cheese pies were stacked in neat rows. Aryel approached Corinne's left as the others began to retrieve plates of food.

"I don't think there are fifty of those," he said, pointing to the pies. "But you can have as many as you like."

Corinne laughed. "I'll certainly take you up on that."

Danai, Nik, and Iliana poured glasses of wine for themselves, and Aryel encouraged them to sit on the couches by the unlit fireplace. His balcony doors were open to let in the cool evening air. Corinne carefully placed at least half a dozen of the pies on a plate alongside a selection of fresh fruit. She balanced it with expert focus as she made her way to the couches and chairs, adjusting the sword at her hip before taking a seat in a chair that sank lower than she was expecting. If she'd had any wine in her hands, it certainly would have sloshed out of its glass. Aryel followed them over with his own plate, handing Corinne a cup of water before gingerly taking a seat in the chair across from hers, at the end of a short, narrow table.

"How was the ritual this morning?" Danai asked, placing their wine glass on the table before lounging back with their plate.

"Uneventful," Corinne said. "Nothing particularly special. But I'm used to them."

"What did you think, P—Aryel?" Danai asked.

"Certainly different from what I expected," he said. "I particularly enjoyed the music."

Corinne's face heated.

"That's right, you play pianoforte, don't you?" Nik asked, and Aryel nodded.

"He plays it beautifully," Corinne said, and it was Aryel's turn to blush. She hid a smile. "It brought me to tears the first time I heard it."

"What a shame there isn't one in here," Danai said.

"Thank the goddess," Aryel muttered, popping a grape into his mouth. They all laughed, and he raised his glass, which also only contained water. "To the Lightguards' departure. May we all find a bit more peace."

"To our favorite of the Lightguards," Iliana said, raising her glass and smiling at Corinne.

The others followed suit, and they all drank.

The same warm contentedness spread throughout Corinne's body as she sat and dined with her friends and Aryel that had enveloped her at the Mykotas's house.

This feeling...it *was* part of Helaera's Light, part of the Goddess's goodness. Aryel's glances in her direction as the evening wore on still made her pulse quicken, but she felt overwhelmingly at ease with every person in the room. She'd known them all for just over six weeks, and they had been there for her in ways others never had. In ways Vera never had.

Danai was standing by the table, picking at the remainder of the food, when Corinne stood, shaking her head at the heated debate Iliana, Nik, and Aryel were having over which fruit was best in baked desserts.

"They're all wrong," Danai said, sighing as Corinne approached. "It's obviously peaches."

"I'd have to agree with you," Corinne said seriously, and Danai chuckled.

She wrapped her arms around them, and they froze for a moment before returning her embrace.

"What was that for?" they asked as Corinne released them.

"For bringing me into your life," she said, trying not to get overly emotional. "I'm so glad you approached me that day on the training grounds, Danai."

They beamed at her. "I had a feeling about you, Corinne. And I was right."

"Danai, Corinne! Settle this for us, would you?" Iliana called. "Blueberries or raspberries in baked goods?"

"Peaches," Corinne and Danai said in unison, and they both laughed.

Iliana shook her head while Nik finished off his wine. Aryel caught Corinne's eye, his smile soft.

What if he's just pretending?

A bit of cold crept into the warmth within her, but she didn't dwell on it. *They're just thoughts.*

"As much fun as this has been, I am exhausted," Iliana said, stretching on the couch before standing. "And Danai and I have early shifts tomorrow."

"Don't remind me," Danai groaned.

"Thank you for inviting us," Nik said, turning to Aryel.

"I'd be happy to host any time," he said. "Especially given the extra difficulties in leaving the castle."

"Then we look forward to the next invitation," Danai said, walking back to the couch to offer Nik their hand.

Aryel stood as the three of them headed for the door, and Corinne's heart picked up speed. *They're leaving.* Should she stay in here? Take up her post outside his door?

Uncertain, she followed them all toward the antechamber, bidding her friends good night. She was about to walk through the door herself when Aryel placed his arm across the opening.

"You don't need to stand outside my door, Corinne," he said.

Her breath froze in her throat as the door closed and his eyes blazed into hers.

"The Lightguards are gone," he said, dropping his arm.

"Yes."

"Can we talk freely now?"

CHAPTER 33

Corinne still hadn't breathed. "Yes."

He fixed her with that fiery gaze as he moved closer. "You really didn't feel like you had to kiss me back?"

"No," she said, her voice barely audible.

"So if I told you that you've been all I could think about for weeks," he said, so close now, one step and she'd collide with him. "That all I've wanted to do since the ball is kiss you again...would you tell me not to?"

Corinne's heart was sure to stop.

"We shouldn't," she breathed as he closed that gap further, the desire in his eyes nearly incinerating her.

He brushed her cheek lightly with the back of his fingers. "Then tell me to stop."

She almost did, the word hovering on the tip of her tongue.

Corinne surged forward, the lingering taste of that word obliterated as she grabbed the front of his shirt and kissed him.

Aryel wove his fingers into her hair, his mouth earnest and desperate against hers. Everything was *him*—his mouth, his hands, his body pressing into hers, sending waves of fiery warmth up her skin. His tongue brushed her upper lip, and it drew a soft whimper from her as her lips parted.

His hands traveled to her waist, pulling her with him into his bedroom, away from the table and lounge areas and toward his bed. He unfastened her sword belt with deft fingers, his lips still on hers, only stepping away from her for a moment to prop the sheathed blade by the head of his bed. It was wrong, heretical to allow a man to remove it from her person for *this*...whatever this was.

But Corinne let him, and he placed it with such care before taking her face in his hands and bringing her lips back to his. Something wild tugged behind her navel as she gripped his shirt and tumbled with him onto the mattress.

Was she really going to do this?

"Told you I'd enjoy you putting me on my back," he said, biting her lip lightly.

The subtle sharpness shot more desire through her center, and any sliver of doubt vanished.

She leaned back, breathing heavily. "I can't believe you said that during training."

"Really? I thought you knew I was a heathen."

"I know you're a terrible student."

"I beg to differ."

Aryel used one of the maneuvers she'd taught him to flip them over, capturing her lips greedily with his own. Gripping her waist with one hand, he pinned her wrist to the bed with the other. Normally she would've countered, instinct leading her to gain the upper hand, but... she *liked* this, being beneath him, relinquishing a bit of control. She didn't know what that said about her, but right now she didn't care.

Corinne slid her free hand to the neckline of his shirt and tugged him closer before slipping her fingers past the fabric, hungry for more of his skin against her own. Aryel kissed down her jaw to her neck until he reached her ear with a low chuckle.

"You want my shirt off, Sunshine?"

Corinne's breath hitched when he nipped at her ear. That pleasant tug in her abdomen sent heat tingling downward, to her core and between her thighs.

"Yes," she said breathlessly.

Aryel kissed her jaw and pushed upward off the bed until he was standing. He grabbed the hem of his shirt and quickly pulled it over his head before discarding it on the floor.

Corinne sat up, gazing at the tattoos on his chest and shoulders, more of that need settling in her lower abdomen. *Goddess,* he was beautiful.

She stood, too, running her hands up his muscular chest, tracing one of the moons inked onto his skin. Aryel's hands glided from her hips up her torso, tracing tingles up her sides, and he leaned in again to press his lips to hers. He kissed her slowly, deliberately this time, his fingers grasping the fabric at her lower back.

Gathering her courage, Corinne stepped back from him and began pulling the hem of her shirt up. Aryel placed his hands over hers gently.

"Can I help?" he asked.

With a tentative smile, Corinne nodded, releasing her shirt. He continued the work she'd started to pull it over her head, and when it

CHAPTER 33

was off, he tossed it to the floor to join his own. She shivered as he slipped a hand beneath the fabric wrapped around her breasts at the back, loosening it until it fell away too. His expression as he took in her bare torso, her breasts, was nothing short of reverent.

Corinne placed a hand on his face, brushing her thumb over his cheek before pulling him in to kiss him again. A newfound boldness overtook her as she reached for one of his hands and guided it upward, placing it on her left breast, over her thundering heart.

His breath came out in a huff as he yanked her closer by the small of her back with his free hand. When he ran his thumb over her nipple, she whined, nearly startling herself.

Corinne drew back, covering her face with her hands and letting her forehead hit his chest.

Aryel breathed heavily for a moment, wrapping his arms around her. "Are you all right?"

Corinne shook her head. "I don't know what I'm doing, and I'm making the most *ridiculous* sounds."

"Corinne," he said, removing her hands from her face. She peeked up at him. "I would sell my soul to hear you make those sounds again."

She blinked. "Well...we can't have you doing *that*."

"No," he said, one corner of his mouth lifting as he tucked a curl behind her ear. "Far simpler to use my hands and mouth to make that happen."

Corinne's breath shuddered out of her as more heat flooded her abdomen, her thighs. Aryel's mouth found her neck again, and she wrapped her arms around him, relishing the heat from his chest pressing directly against hers. He pushed her back onto the bed, pausing before she could kiss him.

"We go only as far as you want to," he said, his face serious as he hovered over her, one arm braced above her head. "If you change your mind at any point, if you want to stop, we stop."

Corinne nodded, her breathing uneven.

She hadn't really thought it all through, only that she wanted him, and he wanted her, and she trusted him to soften the landing as she fell into impiety and whatever that meant for her afterward.

Corinne lost herself in him, in his mouth claiming hers, the feeling of his hands roaming over her breasts, down her stomach. Lower.

"Can I take these off?" he asked, his lips close to her ear, his fingers at the waistband of her trousers.

"Yes," Corinne said.

He worked quickly to unlace them, and Corinne wiggled out of them once they'd loosened around her hips, tossing them to the floor by her shirt. He laughed, his fingers brushing her lower abdomen, and Corinne thought she might die with need, an ache building between her thighs. He paused again, though, as his fingers glided over her left thigh, over the scar she'd almost forgotten was there.

"Corinne, what—?"

"Not now," she whispered. She didn't want *that* to tarnish this moment. "I'm fine, Ari. It's old."

He searched her face for a moment. "All right."

Corinne tugged him downward, impatient to taste his lips again, and his fingers continued their light, teasing dance around her lower abdomen and thighs. He stopped as his hand drew closer to her center.

"Can I touch you?" he asked.

Corinne nodded, breathless.

"I need to hear you say yes, Corinne."

"Yes," she said, almost begged. "Please, Aryel."

When he kissed her this time, his hand slipped between her legs, and she thought she might truly catch fire. His fingers brushed her clit before running down to her entrance and back up. Corinne had done such things to herself before, but to be touched by someone else...she forced herself to remember how to breathe. Breathy whimpers huffed through her lips as he continued, his mouth finding her neck again. Her mind became a haze.

One of his fingers slipped inside her, then, and a low moan rumbled in her throat, vibrating against his mouth. Something tightened in her lower abdomen as she dug her fingers into his back. He added another finger and then withdrew them to draw circles over her clit again, and her hips lifted of their own accord.

"Corinne," he said, and Corinne opened her eyes, unaware that they'd rolled shut in the first place. "Would you mind if I used my mouth?"

"I...are you not using it already?" she asked.

A smirk graced his lips. "I meant in place of my fingers."

Oh. *Oh.* Corinne stared at him. "You want to do that?"

Aryel leaned in, his breath cool against her ear. "If you'll let me."

The thought of how he'd kissed her, his tongue and lips in place of his fingers...Corinne nearly stopped breathing. "I wouldn't mind."

With a wicked grin, Aryel kissed her once more, then shifted downward, trailing his mouth along her collarbone, her breasts, her stomach, lower until he settled at the edge of the bed. His lips traced over her scar, too, lingering to kiss it so gently, before his head dipped between her muscular thighs.

The first brush of his tongue nearly shattered her. It was an echo of what he'd done with his fingers, but somehow more indulgent, the strokes languid and intoxicating, then faster. Corinne reached for something, anything to grip onto as he brought her ever closer to climax, her moans pitching higher each time. One of her hands found his, and the other ran through his hair, tugging at the roots in encouragement. Nothing on Helaera's earth could have made her stop him right now, not when her muscles began to tense, that tightening returning in her lower abdomen.

"Ari," she panted, and his grip on her right thigh tightened. "I—"

Before she could say anything remotely coherent, she came undone entirely, back arching as release overtook her in waves. He guided her over the edge and back downward with his mouth and fingers, and when she blinked herself back to reality, uncurling her toes, he lifted himself up, returning to the bed beside her.

"Holy Goddess," Corinne whispered, and Aryel laughed softly, kissing her neck.

She'd experienced climaxing a number of times, but *that*...her whole body had come alive. A bit of guilt began to settle in her bones, but it couldn't overshadow the warmth that had flooded her entire being.

Aryel got up to retrieve a damp towel from his washroom, wiping his fingers and face before handing it to Corinne. It was hard to miss the straining bulge in his trousers as he climbed into bed again. Corinne swallowed hard, but he didn't make to remove them, simply sidled closer to her.

"You—" Her voice failed her, and she cleared her throat. "You don't want me to...?"

Aryel propped himself on his elbow, brushing her cheek with his fingers again before leaning down for a soft, chaste kiss.

"Trust me, Corinne, I want you to do whatever you want to me," he said. "But if you're worried about returning the favor, don't be. You have no idea how much I enjoyed that."

A bit of the pressure in her chest eased. "Really?"

"Really. The rest can wait."

"If you're sure—"

"Listen, Sunshine," he said softly, holding her gaze in the darkness. "I've imagined making you come like that all week. I am more than happy for tonight to just be about you."

Corinne was silent for a long moment, her mind scattering again. How was he able to just *say* such things when even dreaming about him mortified her? She lay there as he glided his fingers along her chest and neck, her thoughts a blur until they landed on something he'd said earlier.

"Weeks," she said, turning over so she wasn't facing him. "You said I was all you could think about for weeks."

"Yes," Aryel said, tracing the tattoo on her back. He pressed his lips to it, and Corinne's eyes fluttered shut. "Since you got back from the monastery and wouldn't talk to me or anyone else."

That guilt overtook her again, and tears filled her eyes, her breath coming out in a shudder. Aryel wrapped an arm around her middle and drew her close, so her back was pressed against his chest.

"What is it?" he asked, his breath cool on her cheek.

The tears wouldn't stop now, one falling across the bridge of her nose and onto the sheets beneath them.

"I've been terrified my whole life of being like my father," she whispered hoarsely. "He was a Lightguard who defected. He abandoned the ways of the Goddess and kept me from the other Lightguards as a child, and then he...one day he lost control, and his magic turned to fire."

CHAPTER 33   243

Aryel squeezed her tightly, no doubt certain what came next.

"My mother died. I almost died. The Lightguards took me in and gave me a home, but I always felt like I had to be perfect, or else they would find out where I came from, see me for what I was. If I wasn't perfect, if I wasn't the best of them, I was nothing but the daughter of a defector."

Aryel ran a hand up her arm, tracing soothing circles along her skin, over her tattoos.

"That's why I tried to stay away from you," she said. "And from Danai and Nik and Iliana."

His fingers drifted downward again, lightly brushing the scar on her thigh, tracing the marred skin.

"Fire," he said quietly. "Lightguards can summon fire?"

"Only particularly powerful ones."

"Have you summoned fire before?"

Corinne shuddered. "Once. Before I lived at the monastery. Without Helaera's blessing, our magic is dangerous to ourselves and others."

They lapsed into silence for a moment, and Corinne focused on the feeling of his chest rising and falling against her back.

"I don't want to cause you pain, Corinne," Aryel said finally. "And I don't want you to feel like you have to abandon yourself and the Goddess. But I—"

He cut off, burying his face in her hair.

"I know it's only been a few weeks," he said. "And I know you're the one protecting me, but I would do anything to keep you safe. I would do anything for you."

Warmth enveloped her so entirely it triggered her light, her markings beginning to glow along her hands and up her arms, all the way to her chest. Aryel leaned back, and she turned to face him finally, watching every emotion play across his face in the light of her magic. He took one of her hands and pressed his lips to the back of it, his mouth cool against her heated skin.

Corinne could only stare at him, at how beautiful he was in the glow. This wasn't unholy or heretical. This was devotion and care and ease between two people who had spent their lives feeling like they would never be good enough.

That's how he made her feel, she realized. Like she was enough. Like she was the sun.

"Ari," she whispered, and he met her eyes. She wasn't sure what she wanted to say, but her bravery faltered, and her magic faded again. "Can you get my shirt?"

One side of his mouth lifted. "I'll get a fresh one."

He quickly kissed her cheek before climbing out of bed to riffle through his wardrobe, returning with a loose black shirt.

"I can't wear that outside," she said, her brow furrowing. It would barely cover her to her thighs.

"You won't need to," he said. "I told you you don't have to stand outside my door."

Corinne took the shirt uncertainly, and he sat on the bed, one hand cupping her face.

"Please stay, Corinne," he said.

She couldn't deny him anything when he looked at her that way. "All right."

While he retreated to his washroom to change into looser trousers for sleeping, Corinne slipped his shirt over her head. It was the softest fabric she'd ever felt, falling over her bare skin like a gentle caress. Tiredness settled deep in her bones as Aryel returned to bed and pulled her close again, her back against his chest like before.

She closed her eyes and fell into the bliss of feeling truly safe for the first time in her life.

CHAPTER 34

Corinne's eyes flew open, and she was disoriented for a moment at the sight of Aryel's bedroom ceiling. A breeze blew through the room from the open balcony doors. Aryel was still asleep beside her, one arm draped over her middle, but something had woken her, put her on edge. She sat up, scanning the room, and Aryel stirred, his hand grasping at the fabric around her waist.

"Sleep, Sunshine," he murmured, eyes still closed.

Movement to her right. The gleam of a knife and—cold metal at her throat. A rough hand grabbed her by the hair and hauled her away from Aryel, who sat up with a jolt as she yelped. Aryel froze as Corinne tried to focus her panicked thoughts.

A man's voice, low and sinister as he forced her upright near the edge of the bed, crept into her ear. "Make a sound and she's dead."

Aryel raised his hands slowly, his eyes widening at the knife pressed against Corinne's neck. She grasped at the man's arm, and he pressed the blade harder into her skin.

"They said you'd be alone," the man growled, his breath hot against Corinne's ear. "I wasn't paid to kill two, so come quietly and I'll let her live, Prince."

"All right," Aryel said carefully, locking eyes with Corinne. "I hear you. Don't hurt her."

"Are you with the Nightrenders?" Corinne growled.

The man's grip on her hair tightened.

"I'm not telling *you* anything, noble trash," he sneered.

So he didn't know who she was. *What* she was.

Focus, Corinne. A breath in. On her exhale, she moved.

Her magic burst to life, and she sent it blasting into the man, who swore and stumbled backward, releasing her hair and dropping the knife. Corinne leapt from the bed, light blazing at her fingertips as she stood between him and Aryel. She didn't give him time to react—she hurled another blast of light at him, and he dodged, rolling on the floor and nearly colliding with the wall.

Corinne ran at him, ducking a second knife he'd pulled from his belt and swiped at her. She caught his arm, but he was faster than she expected, using her momentum to send them both to the floor. He gained the upper hand and plunged the knife downward.

The furious face of a young man scowled at her, lit by her magic as she gripped his arm to stop the knife from piercing her heart.

"You all said he'd be alone!" he hissed.

Corinne snarled up at him, preparing to hurl him off her, but a pair of hands grabbed the man's shirt and yanked him backward.

Corinne landed a kick to his sternum as Aryel heaved their assailant away from her. He gasped for air but still tried to stab the prince, who danced out of the way just in time. Corinne flung light at him again, this time landing a blow squarely in the center of his chest. He crumpled to the ground.

"Corinne!"

She turned to her right as Aryel tossed her sword to her. The moment she caught it, her magic illuminated down the blade. Doggedly, the man got to his feet again and ran at Corinne.

She caught him on the tip of her sword. It ran him through with ease, and the knife fell from his hand, blood blooming along his front and dribbling from his mouth. Corinne yanked her sword out of him and let his body slump to the floor. Blood pooled across the stone.

He twitched, then stilled.

CHAPTER 34

Her arm went limp at her side, her sword suddenly impossibly heavy, and she stumbled. Aryel was at her back in an instant, arms around her middle as he helped her gently sink to the ground.

He was here to kill Ari. And might have succeeded had Corinne not been there. She began to tremble as she stared at the dead man, gripping Aryel's arm to remind herself he was there, he was safe.

Reason slowly returned as she forced herself to take one, two, three breaths. She was covered in blood, her magic still glowing along her skin, and she was wearing nothing but Aryel's shirt as he held her in the darkness.

"Are you hurt?" he asked.

"No," Corinne said hoarsely. "You?"

"No."

They sat in silence for a few more moments before the reality of everything barreled into Corinne like a tidal wave.

"Ari," she said, her voice thick. "We can't hide this."

He took a moment to respond, his heart thudding against her back.

"Put your own clothes back on," he said, tugging her upward with him as he stood.

"They'll find out," Corinne said, panic squeezing her chest. "The Lightguards, your parents—"

"No, they won't," he said, taking her face in his hands. "We'll tell them I woke and called for help. You were outside my door."

With a shaky breath, Corinne nodded. She quickly retrieved her shirt and trousers from the floor, as well as the wrap for her breasts. Aryel's shirt barely reached her mid-thigh, and she quickly pulled it off.

"Here," he said, holding out his hand, and Corinne handed him the shirt, her eyes lighting on his forearm.

"You *are* hurt," she said, pulling her trousers on as quickly as she could.

Blood ran down his skin from a slice across his forearm.

"It's nothing," he said, tugging the shirt over his head and grimacing at the blood on it.

Corinne wrapped her breasts and redonned her shirt, trying not to think about how her clothing had come off. The bliss of that moment was so far removed from the present that she felt queasy.

"Okay," Aryel said once they were both fully clothed, looking down at the dead assassin. "I called for help, you rushed in, fired your magic at him, and ran him through."

Corinne's mouth twisted as she nodded, fighting panic and dread again. She reached for Aryel's injured arm, turning him toward her. Without a word, she called her magic to her fingers and let it run into him, healing it in moments.

"Thank you," he whispered, touching his forehead to hers.

"We have to alert the castle guard," Corinne said, her voice small.

"All right," he said, breathing deeply. He leaned in to kiss her, just once, and it wasn't fiery or passionate this time, but more like a reminder that she was there, that they were both alive and both still *them*. "Let's go find Captain Ekhana."

"Double the guards at every entrance, and have them do a sweep of the perimeter," Captain Ekhana barked to several subordinates. "Find out how someone got into the castle undetected *now*."

Corinne fought the instinct to take Aryel's hand as they followed Captain Ekhana through the corridors, headed for the prince's chambers with two other guards behind them. The king and queen had been sent for, and soon everyone in the castle would know an assassin had breached the walls and tried to kill the prince.

Corinne was sick with rage and disbelief. All the extra security measures, including the new implementations from the Lightguards, and still someone had slipped through and climbed the wall leading to Aryel's balcony. She couldn't dwell on what might have happened if she hadn't been in Aryel's bed, if she'd insisted she stand outside his door.

"Are either of you injured?" Captain Ekhana asked, opening the doors to the breezeway for them.

"I had a small cut, but Corinne healed it," Aryel said.

Ekhana nodded, allowing Aryel to lead the way to his chambers and inside. The captain stepped around Aryel's bed and stared down at the dead assassin.

"Goddess," he muttered. He turned to the guards who had followed them. "Get this body out of here."

They came forward immediately, heaving the body between them. Sticky, half-dried blood remained on the stone floor.

A shriek made Corinne turn abruptly, and the king and queen stepped into Aryel's bedroom. Queen Erina had a hand clapped over her mouth. Her eyes darted from the dead man to Aryel, and she rushed forward to embrace her son.

"I'm fine, Mother," he said quietly, wrapping one arm around her.

King Theo watched with rageful eyes as the guards toted the dead assassin out of the room. "What in the name of Helaera happened?" he demanded.

"I woke up right before he attacked me," Aryel said as his mother released him. "I avoided injury besides a cut to the arm before Corinne rushed in."

"Captain Ekhana, *how* did this happen?" the king asked, his voice rising. "We have made every effort to increase security of the castle, have we not?"

"We have, Your Majesty," Captain Ekhana said, bowing. "But clearly something has failed. We will not rest until we discover how this man entered the castle grounds undetected."

"It was bad enough that Aryel was attacked in the streets, and now this," the king said. "You implemented the suggestions of the Lightguards, yes?"

"Yes, Your Majesty."

"Summon them back immediately," King Theo said, and Corinne's heart sank. "I demand an explanation for this. You." He looked to Corinne, and she stopped breathing. "I thought your kind was supposed to be unmatched in your power to protect and fight. Has our faith been misplaced?"

"She just saved my life," Aryel said, stepping in front of Corinne, his hands clenched into fists at his sides. "For the second time."

"She wouldn't have had to if someone hadn't made a grave error," King Theo said, his voice menacing. "I *will* find out who is responsible, and they will face punishment. I want everyone in the council room now."

The king stalked off, slamming Aryel's door as he went. Queen Erina hesitated, her face pale.

"Perhaps take a few minutes and clean yourselves," she said, gesturing at Corinne and Aryel's bloodstained appearances. "Captain Ekhana, I want two extra guards trailing Aryel alongside Corinne at all times."

"Yes, Your Majesty," Ekhana said with a bow. Queen Erina headed outside, and the captain sighed. "I'm sorry. To both of you."

"This wasn't your fault, Captain," Aryel said.

"Well, we'll hopefully discover the truth soon enough," Ekhana said. "I'll have two guards remain here while Corinne gets that blood off."

Swallowing hard, Corinne nodded. Aryel's fingers brushed her arm lightly as she passed, following Ekhana. She let herself hold his gaze for a second longer than was wise before the guards stepped inside. Aryel disappeared into his washroom, and Corinne made for the door.

"...want her there *now*. I don't care about blood."

Corinne halted by Captain Ekhana in the alcove, met by the king and queen having a quiet exchange. Their heads turned, and the king beckoned to Corinne.

"I don't give a damn about bloodstains, and I expect as a warrior you shouldn't either," he said. "You can bathe later. Council room, now."

Corinne bowed once and followed the king and queen, Captain Ekhana just behind her. The blood on her body and clothing wouldn't hurt her, but it did turn her stomach to leave it there. She glanced at the sky as she walked down the breezeway; it had started to lighten, dawn fast approaching. Corinne steeled her heart against whatever the day would bring.

CHAPTER 35

"And you're certain there was no trace of dark magic?" Councilor Dresden asked.

Corinne had answered the same question about five times now, and exhaustion was sinking into her bones. She craved a moment to heal some of her fatigue, but she couldn't simply start glowing in front of everyone in the council chamber.

"I'm certain," she said. "He was stronger than an average fighter, but he was no Nightrender."

"Still, if he held his own against a Lightguard, that is great cause for concern," Councilor Orvos said.

"He didn't hold his own," Aryel said, his tone as exasperated as Corinne felt. "Corinne killed him in about thirty seconds."

He lied so easily about it, and shame washed over her. She would've killed him in that time if she hadn't been caught unawares.

Still, she may not have gotten to Aryel in time if she hadn't been next to him in the bed. She held onto that knowledge to keep the guilt at bay while the council continued to question her about every little detail regarding the assassin. Captain Ekhana had not returned to the council room yet after he'd left an hour prior to check on his guards' investigation of the body.

"We've been at this for hours," Aryel said, standing and cutting off another question from Councilor Dresden. "I'm taking Corinne to get something to eat."

Corinne could have cried with relief. Her stomach had been growling for an hour. Aryel turned to her and nodded, and she stood from her chair. King Theo's face was murderous as they headed for the exit.

"Aryel!" he barked, following them into the corridor. "You were not given leave, and neither was she."

Aryel stepped around Corinne and stood only a few inches away from his father.

"You dragged her in here before dawn and have allowed everyone to hound her with questions since," Aryel said. "She's still covered in blood after killing a man to protect me. I know this may be difficult to grasp, but she is not your guard, she's *mine*, and I won't have her treated with such indignity."

Corinne's heart jumped into her throat. *She's mine.*

"Tread lightly, boy," King Theo growled.

"What are you going to do, Father?" Aryel asked, his voice low and taunting. "Strike me in front of everyone in the corridor? Where the councilors can hear?"

The king looked ready to implode with rage, his face bright red. Aryel turned on his heel and headed down the hallway, one hand at Corinne's back to steer her alongside him.

"That was foolish," Corinne muttered as they started down the stairwell.

"Perhaps it was," Aryel said. "But I don't care."

Corinne couldn't voice her gratitude in that moment, not when two guards were trailing just behind them, but she hoped Aryel knew what that had meant to her.

Though she wanted nothing more than a few minutes alone with Aryel without guards tailing them, it was still a relief to venture to the kitchens in relative silence. After thoroughly washing her hands, they sat at the end of a long servants' table in a room off the main kitchen while Corinne ate a plate of bacon and scones, even more ravenous than she'd realized. Aryel started to say something several times, but stopped himself before voicing it. He folded his hands on the table, and she wondered if it was to keep himself from reaching for hers.

Not being able to touch him openly was going to be torture, especially if the Lightguards were on their way back. How had one night made her so keen to be in his arms whenever possible? The safety she'd felt had been shattered, but she still craved the comfort of his embrace. Her mind drifted to the scar on her thigh again, the way he'd touched it and kissed it with such tenderness.

It was no longer possible for her to pretend Aryel hadn't stolen a piece of her heart. She'd broken that rule entirely and betrayed her oath to Helaera.

And yet...she did not feel remorse. Caring for someone else didn't weaken her or pull her away from the Goddess. If anything, caring for Aryel would make her even more devoted to the oath she'd sworn to Helaera, the assignment she'd been given here.

That's the only reason he's kind to you.

Nausea rolled through her.

He just wants to keep himself safe. He doesn't really care about you.

It was ridiculous to have such a thought after he'd just stood up to his father, blatantly risking his safety for her. But the voice was insistent—it felt so *true*. She looked at him, accidentally catching his eye, and concern lit his features. Abandoning caution, Aryel placed his hand over hers on the table.

"Breathe, Sunshine," he said, his voice so low she barely heard him. "Let thoughts be thoughts."

The queasiness eased immediately, and Corinne breathed again. After a moment, Aryel removed his hand smoothly, picking at a splinter in the table.

"How did you know?" Corinne asked softly.

"You started to get that look," he said. "It's like your light fades a little bit."

Corinne's chest ached with the need to pull him close. Goddess, she wanted to disappear from the world with him, to take a shower and then sleep the rest of the day with him beside her.

"Corinne Anastos?"

She and Aryel both looked at the doorway leading into the kitchens, where a servant stood with his hands clasped.

"Yes?" she said.

"I've been sent to inform you the Lightguards are here. They're waiting at the entrance hall."

Aryel didn't hesitate to join her as she stood and made her way through the corridors and up the stairs. The two guards Ekhana had assigned them followed, silent but watchful. Corinne tried to force her breathing to even out as they approached the entrance hall, but her heart still picked up speed when they arrived and she spied Mother Creita, Priestess Chala, and four other Lightguards, including Vera. Why did she have to show up every time and bear witness to Corinne's strife?

"Corinne," Mother Creita said, hastening to her. She placed a hand on Corinne's face, her expression morphing into disgust. "They sent for us hours ago, have you not had a chance to rest and bathe?"

Corinne shook her head, and anger lit in Mother Creita's eyes. Behind her and Aryel, more footsteps approached, and the king and queen appeared.

"What is the meaning of this?" Mother Creita hissed at them, and Corinne blinked at her. "Why has she not been given time to rest?"

"We have been investigating the attack," King Theo said gruffly.

"And you believe interrogating Corinne for hours will result in answers?" Mother Creita demanded.

Corinne looked between her and King Theo, unsure which of them was more apt to blow up from anger.

"The Crown and Council will question whomever we deem necessary," King Theo said. "Perhaps you all can offer an explanation for how this assassin was able to breach our walls in the first place. He got *directly* into the prince's rooms."

Mother Creita took a deep breath, tension lingering in the silence.

"My apologies," she said. "We have come here to aid in your investigation, and if you'll allow us, we will leave five Lightguards in place while Corinne returns to the monastery. We are recalling one Lightguard from every village, and she needs to share the details of this

CHAPTER 35

attacker, and the two previous ones, so we know what to watch out for outside of Vytanos."

Corinne wasn't sure she'd heard correctly. *While Corinne returns to the monastery.*

"That seems like a reasonable plan," Queen Erina cut in before her husband could reply, inclining her head to Mother Creita. "We are still waiting to meet with Captain Ekhana about details regarding this latest assassin."

While the king and queen continued speaking with Mother Creita, Corinne turned to Aryel. She broke his gaze quickly when she noticed Vera's eyes on her. *Breathe, Corinne.*

Were they going to reinstate her burn when she arrived? Perhaps not, if they intended to have her speak before dozens of others to relay what she'd seen here.

"Aryel, come," Queen Erina said as Mother Creita walked past Corinne again, returning to the other Lightguards. "We will meet with them shortly."

Aryel hesitated a moment before following his mother and father toward the entrance hall's exit. He lightly brushed Corinne's fingers with his as he passed, the contact so subtle she wondered if she'd imagined it. Corinne gathered herself after he'd disappeared, turning to the Lightguards.

"...We'll go, and Chala can help Corinne."

The others began to follow the royal family as Corinne approached Mother Creita and Priestess Chala.

"Mother Creita," Corinne said, inclining her head.

"You've done well, Corinne," the High Priestess said.

"Thank you," Corinne said, though it meant little. "How long will I be at the monastery?"

"No longer than a week, I'm certain," Mother Creita said, placing a hand on Corinne's face again. "We'll have a new assignment for you very soon."

Corinne blinked at her. "A new assignment?"

"Yes, of course," she said. "You have shown your devotion here, and we will need others like you outside Vytanos now that we'll have five Lightguards in the castle."

Corinne tried to speak, to say something, but she couldn't trust her voice.

"You don't look pleased, child," Mother Creita said, her brow furrowing. "I expected you would be honored."

"I am, Mother Creita," Corinne said quickly. "I just...I wasn't expecting to leave so soon. I...have become fond of this place."

I've become fond of Ari and my friends.

"As many do where they are assigned," Mother Creita said sagely. "There are far more places for you to grow a fondness for, Corinne." She looked around for a moment, then stepped even closer, lowering her voice. "There are things we have not yet told you regarding all this, and I see now that was a mistake. But we will, upon your return to the monastery. Do not speak of it to anyone here."

Corinne's heart somehow sank even lower. "Mother Creita, I don't understand."

"I know, but you will soon. Now, go with Chala. You can clean up, and she will help you with your things."

"I'm to leave now?" Corinne barely kept her voice from breaking.

"Yes, child, and make haste. I must go now and meet with the royal family and their Captain of the Guard. Chala?"

Priestess Chala stepped forward with a soft smile, gesturing for Corinne to lead the way.

CHAPTER 36

Corinne wasn't sure how long she stood in the shower, her mind racing. The blood had come off easily enough, and now she let the water rush over her until it ran cold, as if it could drown her before the grief would.

Aryel. Danai. Nik. Iliana. She was leaving them all, and she doubted she'd have the chance to say goodbye. She closed her eyes and cut the water off. She stood on a precipice of despair, and she couldn't let herself tumble down if she was going to keep a collected exterior in front of Chala. Surely there was *some* way to convince them to let her stay here.

Guilt and shame tore at her insides. *You've strayed and chosen hedonism over devotion.*

Corinne dried off and dressed in a trance, Chala helping her with the armor—it was easier to wear it rather than travel with it for hours. A lump formed in Corinne's throat when she thought about her arrival weeks ago, and how she would've given anything on that day for another assignment.

Now she would give anything to stay. She felt like her chest would cave in every time she pictured Aryel's face.

But what had she been thinking, anyway? Aryel was the prince, and she was his guard. Whatever this was between them might not be heretical in the eyes of Helaera, but it certainly wouldn't be acceptable to the Lightguards, and the king and queen would surely dismiss it as another of the prince's fleeting indulgences, if not a sordid scandal. Corinne was not a suitable partner for the heir of Ashera.

That truth hurt more than she expected it to, nearly knocking her breathless as Chala fastened the ties on her pauldron.

"There you are," she said. "The rest of your things are packed and ready. We should head to the stables."

To the stables. Corinne fought back tears.

A knock came at her door, and Corinne walked to answer it with heavy feet. The sight of Danai, Iliana, and Nik on the other side nearly made her knees buckle.

"Corinne," Nik said, his face full of empathy.

Danai wasn't their usual bright, chipper self, their eyes immediately going behind Corinne, no doubt landing on Priestess Chala.

Corinne stared at them all. *Do not cry.*

"Who is this?" Priestess Chala asked, approaching the door, and Corinne cleared her throat.

"Danai Mykotas, Iliana Calais, and Nik Ekhana," Corinne said, forcing a neutral smile to her face. "Danai and Iliana are guards who have partnered with me in my mission here. Nik is Captain Ekhana's son and a librarian of the highest order."

Priestess Chala gave them all a polite smile and nod. "May Helaera bless you all."

"We hoped to see Corinne off," Nik said. The deference in his tone was impressive.

"Then you have arrived just in time," Chala said. "I'm afraid she must depart at once. Come, Corinne."

The Priestess handed Corinne her bag before stepping past her friends and into the alcove. They waited until she'd just disappeared around the corner onto the breezeway before all three of them threw their arms around Corinne at once. Her armor made it terribly awkward, but she cared little.

"I don't know when I'll see you again," she whispered.

CHAPTER 36

Danai squeezed around her ribs. "One day," they said. "We promise."

"Can we write to you?" Nik asked.

"Of course you can," Corinne said, her voice strained.

They released her, and Corinne hastily wiped a tear away, offering them all a sad smile before hurrying after Chala.

She couldn't stay. But the ache to do so built behind her ribs as she walked through the corridors behind Priestess Chala. Aryel's face floated through her mind again, and she thought she might choke.

She *had* to find a way to return. Perhaps her new assignment would be a traveling one, and she could make detours in Vytanos like Vera had.

"Priestess Chala," Corinne said as they approached a staircase. "Is there not still a threat here? Is it truly wise for me to leave now?"

"That's why we have the others staying, dear," Chala said, taking Corinne's hand and squeezing it. "You heard Mother Creita—you're needed at the monastery to help lead others. You've overcome many trials here and now Helaera calls you to an even greater purpose. We honor your efforts, Corinne. You're on the right path to redemption."

Corinne swallowed hard, and that ever-present knot in her chest squeezed at her heart. It was everything she'd ever wanted—to be respected and held in high esteem by her people, by her family. What kind of Lightguard was she, to be so fickle that a lifelong aspiration now fell flat as it was laid before her?

But if they found out about her sleeping with Aryel, it would all crumble at her feet. He wouldn't tell anyone what they'd done, but could she live with herself amongst the Lightguards, knowing the disdain they would have for her if they knew the truth? She would be right back where she'd started, terrified every moment that someone would discover a shameful secret.

The sun was high in the sky when she and Chala reached the stables. Corinne stood numbly behind the Priestess as she argued with the stablemaster over a suitable horse for Corinne. One hadn't yet been prepared and saddled for departure.

"...*Yes*, I will show you which is preferred. Goddess, this should have already been communicated. Wait here, Corinne."

Corinne managed a nod, deeply apathetic about Chala's choice of horse. The stablemaster led her down the stables, pointing to several stalls, and Corinne stayed rooted to the spot.

A low whistle had her turning her head to the right, and Corinne's heart cracked open. Aryel stood in the doorframe of a storage room filled with grooming supplies. She looked to Chala and the stablemaster, well out of earshot now, and hurried over to him.

"Ari, what are you doing here?"

He shut the door behind her and pulled her close. "I had to see you. I paid off the stablemaster to distract her for a few minutes."

Corinne huffed a humorless laugh, wrapping her arms around him for a moment.

"How long will you be gone?" he asked, leaning back.

"I don't know," she whispered.

Aryel's brow furrowed, and her heart fractured further. "What do you mean?"

"They're giving me another assignment."

The shock that played across his face sent knives into her chest. "Why?"

"They said I excelled in my duty here, and they wish to assign me elsewhere in Ashera."

"That makes no sense," he said, shaking his head. "There's still a threat here. Why are they making you leave?"

"They—" Corinne cut off. *Do not speak of it to anyone here.* She fought the compulsion to obey that command. "They said they have important information to tell me when I return. I have to go."

"The hells you do," Aryel said, his hands going to her face. "I'm sure my parents could convince them to keep you here—"

"Ari," Corinne said, wrapping a hand around one of his arms. "I can't just disobey them. They're...they're all I have."

He looked almost as if she'd struck him. "That isn't true."

"But it is. I'm a Lightguard."

"You're more than that," he said, his eyes burning into hers. "Corinne, I...last night was not just a fleeting tryst for me. I meant everything I said. I want to keep you safe, and you are not safe with them."

CHAPTER 36

Tears welled and spilled over before she could stop them. "I...I don't know what to think or what to believe anymore."

"Believe me when I say I want your happiness," he said. "And it's okay if you're afraid. I care about you so much it scares the hells out of me."

This man was going to break her into a thousand pieces. "Aryel—"

"Corinne," he said, touching his forehead to hers. "Please. Stay."

She sobbed quietly. "What would this have become, anyway? I'm your guard. You're the *prince*."

"Fuck my title. All I know is you're the most extraordinary person I've ever met," he said, his voice thick. "And I've never wanted anything more than to find out what this could become."

Corinne knew she shouldn't, knew it would only make things more painful, but she lifted her chin to press her lips to his. Aryel threaded his fingers through her hair and kissed her back like his life depended on it. How was it possible to feel such joy and grief at the same time? Aryel cared for her just as much as she cared for him, was ready to do anything for her.

Corinne had much to untangle in her own heart, but she knew he'd have a place in it from now on. She held on to that, to the hope that she could return before long, that she could figure out some way to keep him in her life, as she pulled away from him.

"I have to go," she said, the words like poison on her tongue.

Before he could convince her to linger any longer, she opened the door and hurried out of the storage room.

"Corinne."

After checking that Priestess Chala was still speaking with the stablemaster out of earshot, Corinne turned to Aryel. The tears in his eyes ripped her heart in half.

"Stay safe," was all he said.

"You too." *Everything you feel, I feel it back.*

Corinne wasn't sure how she could commit her heart to Helaera if there wasn't much of it left. As she left the stables, the largest pieces of it remained with two guards, a librarian, and a prince.

CHAPTER 37

It was a blessing from the Goddess that Corinne's journey away from Vytanos was on her own. The moment she cleared the city gates, she let the tears fall, let herself sob freely atop her horse. Chala had insisted she be given a speedy mount and instructed her to make haste as Mother Creita had, but Corinne was in no hurry to reach the monastery.

How she'd longed to return weeks ago. Now, not even the sight of the mountains and sky along the road could touch the growing misery in her heart.

Was this her punishment for opening her heart to non-Lightguards? For kissing Aryel, for letting him touch her, taste her the way he had? That shame she'd kept at bay washed over her in full force. She gritted her teeth against another sob, wiping at her eyes.

Helaera, please. I don't know what to do.

The Goddess had never spoken to her, not directly, but she'd felt Helaera's presence in her magic, in the sunlight, in the songs of the weekly ritual. Every Lightguard knew it wasn't in Helaera's nature to physically appear before mortals and speak to them, but she wished desperately for once that Helaera would do so now and give her direction. She needed *someone* to help her make sense of it all. She needed a mother.

It wasn't Mother Creita who flashed in her mind at that thought, but Selana Mykotas.

That's part of Her Light too.

If Corinne was so sure that her newfound friendships were blessed by Helaera, what did that mean for her return to the monastery, where every face would bring her anxiety and insecurity? She would never know peace beneath the certainty that they would hate her if they knew who she was and what she had done.

She rode on, her thoughts spiraling as she reached the crest of a hill. A small voice in her head, gentler than the one that usually plagued her, whispered to her, rising above the turbulence in her mind.

What if you left?

No, she couldn't do that. Helaera may not have judged Corinne unworthy for her actions these past weeks, but the Goddess did not abide defectors. Corinne couldn't lose her connection to the Light.

A distant, low rumble sounded, and Corinne sniffed, looking at the sky above her. There wasn't a cloud in sight. Another, louder this time. She blinked in the sunlight and turned, scanning the sky beyond the mountains, but there was nothing but endless blue. Shifting in her saddle, she looked to Vytanos, now several minutes behind her.

The city's sprawling rooftops looked ordinary, running up the various hills and cliffs toward the castle. The castle—

Corinne stared at it, not immediately believing her eyes. She blinked several times, but no, she hadn't hallucinated it.

A plume of smoke was drifting from the north wing, minuscule from this distance, and at its base, by a window, raged the orange glow of a fire.

The castle was on fire.

Corinne wheeled her horse around and took off back the way she'd come.

∼

Vytanos was in a panic all the way out to the gates. Even galloping as fast as possible, it had taken an excruciating number of minutes for her to get back. Corinne steered her horse through the streets as quickly as she could without trampling anyone. The citizens were all rushing to their homes, city guards barking orders to get to safety. Corinne could think of nothing but reaching the castle.

Please. It was the only prayer she could offer the Goddess, too terrified to give thought to what she was pleading for.

By the time Corinne reached the upper city, the only people remaining in the streets were occasional guards. She pushed her horse faster.

It was pure chaos at the castle gates, people running outside, some wailing, some shouting at guards or nobles shouting at each other. Hundreds of servants had gathered to stare at the growing cloud of smoke emanating from the north wing. Corinne jumped down from her horse, the crowd too dense to ride through, and began shoving her way toward the entrance.

"The prince?" she asked a servant, who stared at her like she had two heads. Corinne turned to someone else. "Have you seen the prince?"

The servant shook her head, and Corinne pressed onward. She spotted Captain Ekhana by the doors to the castle entrance, and beside him was—

"Nik!" Corinne cried.

He turned immediately, spying Corinne as she made her way through the shifting crowd. He hurried down the few steps to meet her as she cleared the mass of people.

"Corinne, I thought you'd left?"

"I heard the explosion and wasn't far," she said. "Nik, where is everyone? Danai, Iliana, Aryel?"

"Danai is helping a few other guards gather water," Nik said, twisting the laces on his shirt nervously. "No one knows what happened. We haven't seen Iliana, and the explosion occurred in the north wing, they think in the throne room."

Corinne's heart stopped.

"No one has been able to reach the royal family," Nik said, his voice barely audible, his eyes pained.

CHAPTER 37

Corinne looked to the castle entrance, where another wave of nobles poured out.

She sprinted for it.

"Corinne!"

She ignored Nik's protests, dodging nobles, guards, and servants alike as she entered the castle. She knew the way to the throne room now like it was second nature, dashing through corridors and up flights of stairs. Halfway down a hallway on the second floor, she skidded to a halt before two figures staggering their way toward her. One was nearly doubled over coughing, auburn hair falling into her face.

"Iliana!" Corinne rushed forward.

Another guard Corinne didn't recognize was helping Iliana walk as she coughed, a nasty burn on her left leg.

"Corinne," she said, her face partially dusted with soot. "The third floor of the north wing—it's on fire, it keeps spreading, no one can get to the throne room—"

Corinne bent to help when Iliana coughed again, but she waved her off.

"*Go*, Corinne," she wheezed. "I'll be fine."

"I've got her," the guard said.

Corinne nodded and sped off again, heading for the next stairwell.

She could smell the smoke now. Memories crept in from the back of her mind, and she shoved them away. *Ari. I have to find Ari.* She dashed up the stairs. The air grew hotter as she reached the third floor, and when she emerged onto the landing, a scene straight from her nightmares awaited her.

Fire licked up the walls mere yards away, debris littering the corridor that led to the throne room. The open area before the doors was nearly obscured by smoke. Panic rose in her chest, but she pushed forward, engaging her magic to protect her lungs and eyes at least somewhat. She kept as low as she could without losing too much speed.

A massive *pop* sounded just above her, and before Corinne could get out of the way, a piece of the ceiling crashed downward. She tucked her head beneath her arms, but the impact still sent blinding pain through her shoulder, her arm, her entire left side. The weight didn't disappear, pinning her beneath it.

Smoke, burning, a beam on her legs—

Corinne!

Fire was everywhere. Corinne was ten years old again, her body barely sustaining itself, barely keeping her alive as everything burned around her. As *she* burned.

As her mother died.

Corinne!

Mother!

Her mother screamed, and Corinne let out a guttural cry. No, she had to save her this time. She couldn't let it happen again. She had to save her. She had to—

Save *him*.

Reality returned, Corinne's eyes flying open. She had to save Aryel.

But charred beams of wood lay on top of her, pressing her to the floor, flames beginning to lick at her skin through her armor. She cried out, her light flaring and then dimming again. She couldn't do this, not while fire crept ever closer, heated the metal of her armor, began to burn her. Tears filled her eyes as the pain overtook her. She was going to die here, and Aryel...who knew if he was even still alive.

No.

Corinne called upon her light again. It began to heal her, bolster her strength, and she shifted beneath the debris, jostling some of it off her. She closed her eyes and gritted her teeth.

Helaera, I beg you. Lend me your strength. Help me save him.

Her magic answered her tenfold, its glow rivaling that of the fire surrounding her. The flames suddenly seemed less hot, less wild, and Corinne remembered what her father had been, what he could do that so few Lightguards could.

That power had been his demise, but perhaps it could be Corinne's salvation.

She reached for the fire within, then recoiled at the heat and curled in on herself again. She breathed in. No smoke in her lungs, no unbearable burning. She could do this. *I can do this.* Helaera had not abandoned her.

This time, instead of cowering and shrinking away, Corinne let her light burst outward with another cry. Fire erupted from her markings,

CHAPTER 37

incinerating the debris on top of her, incinerating the straps of her armor and the fabric of her hauberk. Slowly, she got to her feet, her body healing itself and her mind refocusing. Fire danced up her hands and arms, and Corinne stumbled forward a step before reaching for the metal plates at her shoulders and neck and ripping them away. She gripped the chainmail and lifted it over her head, letting it fall in a heap to the charred floor. The greaves on her legs fell away as she burned those straps, too, leaving her in only her gold tunic and black trousers.

The flames of the corridor made a path for her as she pushed forward again toward the throne room. Her steps were clumsy at first as her pain faded, and then she was running headlong for the throne room.

The doors had burned to ash, and fire raged within, but most of the smoke was floating toward the northeast side of the room, likely toward the window Corinne had seen from a distance. The flames tugged at her, the feeling filling her chest, calling to her wildly.

Aryel. She had to find Aryel *now*.

She dashed into the throne room, the flames once again clearing before her. It was nearly impossible to see with all the smoke and fire, the debris falling from the ceiling. Still, she pressed onward, heading for the dais, for where Aryel usually stood.

Something nearly tripped her, and she looked down in horror at the body of a guard. Whoever it had been was now burned beyond recognition. Fear gripped Corinne's throat, and she hurried onward.

"Aryel!" she called. "Aryel!"

Corinne's fear grew as she drew closer to the dais and stepped around more bodies. *What* had done this? After tearing her gaze away from the vacant stare of a minimally burned but still-dead guard, she caught sight of a moving figure by the base of the dais steps. She rushed forward and leaned down, reaching for the woman's shoulders. It took her a nauseatingly horrible moment to recognize Queen Erina as she gasped for breath, half her face burnt raw. The larger figure behind her, burnt and slumped on his throne, did not stir.

The king was dead.

"Aryel," Queen Erina choked, grasping weakly at Corinne's sleeve. "The window."

Corinne's head whipped around, finding a shattered window, and sure enough, her eyes landed on a silhouette on the ground beneath it.

"Leave...me," the queen croaked. "Save...my son...save..."

Corinne met the queen's eyes, the right bloodshot and unfocused, surrounded by melted skin. Even if she had time, Corinne did not have the strength to heal the queen and Aryel both.

"I will," she vowed.

She released the dying queen and ran for Aryel.

Please. Please.

She fell to her knees beside him. The left side of his face and his arm were covered in shards of broken glass, blood streaming down his skin and staining his clothes. His leg was badly burned, the fabric of his burnt trousers stuck to the glistening, raw skin along his thigh.

Corinne reached for his neck and nearly sobbed at the presence of a faint pulse. Her strength was dwindling, but so was his grasp on life, so Corinne gathered her light in her palms and pressed them to his chest. *Lungs first, then the burn on his leg.* She couldn't let herself get to the same point of exhaustion she had when healing Aeson, but she had to heal him enough to get him out of here alive.

The sound of a wheezing cough as he awoke was the most beautiful thing she'd ever heard.

"Ari," she sobbed, her hands going to his face.

His eyes took a moment to focus, bloodshot and halfway open. "Corinne," he rasped, then cried out as he shifted.

"Hold on," she said quickly, placing one hand over his burn. With the other, she carefully removed the glass from his face, making him hiss in pain.

She let the magic flow out of her with calculated precision, or as much as she could manage, and some of the agony on his face faded.

"We have to move," she said once she'd partially healed the burn. It would have to do for now. "Grab onto me and stand with me on three, all right?" She gripped the front of his tattered shirt, ignoring the insistent warning of exhaustion in the back of her mind, and he gripped her shoulders. "One...two...three."

With a cry, Aryel managed to sit up, then stand with her. Corinne bore the brunt of his weight, draping his arm over her shoulders as she guided him out of the throne room as quickly as possible. She glanced back at the dais, and her heart lurched at the sight of the queen no longer moving.

Just a few more steps and they'd be out of the worst of the fire. The flames were closer than before with Corinne's magic weakened after healing Aryel, but they managed to get out of the throne room without sustaining any more burns.

The flames outside had nearly gone out, and Corinne almost collapsed as Aryel's knees gave way. She kept him from tumbling to the floor, helping him lean on a pile of debris that looked sturdier than others. She held his hand tightly, allowing him a moment to breathe. They still had to get out of the north wing, get off the third floor.

"Corinne," Aryel said, his voice strained.

She met his eyes, startled by the fear she found there.

"Please tell me you didn't know."

Her brow furrowed. "Didn't know—?"

Footsteps hurried toward them, and Corinne whipped around, squinting at the three figures approaching. She could have sobbed with relief.

"Vera," she choked out, her hand tightening on Aryel's behind her. Two other Lightguards flanked Vera, all of them glowing with their magic. "Thank Helaera."

"Corinne, what are you doing here?" Vera asked, her eyes wide.

"I heard the explosion and saw the fire from beyond the city," she said. "Please, Vera, we have to get Aryel out of here, I was only able to partially heal him."

None of the Lightguards moved. What was wrong with them? Did they not hear her? Corinne stared at them, at the pain on Vera's face, and the swords in their hands—and the blood on the blades.

"Corinne, please don't make me do this," Vera said.

"Do what?" Corinne asked, her voice rough.

Aryel took a shuddering breath behind her, tugging weakly at her hand. "They set the fire," he told her. "They locked us inside. My parents—"

"They're dead," one of the Lightguards by Vera barked. "And you will be soon."

No. No, they *couldn't* have...

Vera took a step forward. "Corinne, we can explain. Just hand over the prince and we can talk."

Corinne didn't move, still grasping Aryel's hand. That hateful, pitying look was plastered across Vera's face. She turned to look at Aryel, who was watching the Lightguards with hatred in his eyes.

"Stay behind me," she said, her voice hard. He looked up at her, and before he could respond, she faced the Lightguards again, releasing his hand and drawing her sword.

It ignited.

"Corinne," Vera said. "You don't know what you're doing."

Corinne didn't move, but she kept her eyes on Vera and the others, ready for them to attack.

"You have one last chance," Vera said, her stance shifting. "Stand aside."

Corinne raised her sword. "No."

The pity vanished from Vera's face, replaced by unbridled rage. A half second later, a burst of light flew at Corinne, which she caught and hurled back at the Lightguard on Vera's right. Vera charged forward, and Corinne blocked the slash of her sword with her own, the impact reverberating up her arms. She forced Vera back and barely dodged another magic attack from the third Lightguard. Another minute of dodging, countering, and taking the brunt of everything they threw at her, and Corinne stumbled backward, crashing into Aryel. Even in his weakened state, he helped steady her as the Lightguards stalked closer.

"Corinne," he said hoarsely, gripping her arm. "You don't have to do this. Save yourself."

"I am saving myself," she ground out, and lunged at them again.

She landed a blow to one of the Lightguards that sent him crumpling to the ground. All she had to do was hold off Vera and the other one.

He ran at Aryel, and Corinne flung her magic at him, forcing him back at the same moment Aryel launched a shard of glass at him. It hit its mark, grazing the man's cheek.

The moment of distraction gave Vera an opening to deal a nasty slice to Corinne's side. Corinne hissed in pain; she didn't have the energy to heal it right now.

"You can't win this fight, Corinne," Vera growled.

Corinne's magic attempted to heal her anyway, and even the effort of pulling it back in cost her. Her vision started shifting. *Just a few more moments. A few more attacks.* Shaking her head, she took a defensive stance again.

A magic attack from Vera's ally clipped her shoulder, throwing her off-balance. A moment later, Vera had her on the floor, pressing her face to the charred carpet.

"Corinne!" Aryel's voice sliced her open more sharply than Vera's blade had.

All she could see was the Lightguard bearing down on him as he attempted to reach her. She tried to rise, tried to force her muscles to engage. An inch off the floor, pain shot through her skull, and darkness swept in.

CHAPTER 38

Softness caressed Corinne's body, the warmth of morning sunlight kissing her skin. She breathed in the scent of summer air and sweet orange blossoms. Her eyes opened slowly, her mind taking a moment to make sense of her surroundings. She was in her room in the castle, and by the look of the beams of sunlight shining through her window, it was midmorning.

Corinne stretched in her bed, then froze, looking down at her hands.

Her wrists were shackled.

Memories flooded her all at once, and she flew out of bed, her chest heaving as her heart took off. She was wearing a clean tunic and fresh trousers, and after quickly assessing the state of her body, she found her injuries were gone. How long had she been asleep?

She had to get out of here, had to find Aryel and figure out what was going on. As quickly as possible with her shackled wrists, she tugged on her boots and looked for her sword, but it was nowhere in sight. Corinne marched to her door and tried the knob. Locked.

"Let me out!" she shouted, pounding on it with her fists. No one answered her, but she knew someone had to be outside. "Vera! Mother Creita! *Let me out!*"

CHAPTER 38

The door opened a moment later, and Corinne stepped back as Vera, Priestess Bria, and Priestess Chala entered her room, shutting the door behind them again. Vera crossed her arms as she stood by the window.

"Really, Corinne, have some decorum," Priestess Bria said.

"Where is Prince Aryel?" she asked, her eyes darting between the three of them.

Vera's arms dropped, her face going blank. The Priestesses stared at Corinne for a long moment.

"Corinne," Chala said slowly. "What is the nature of your relationship with the prince?"

She didn't have time for this. "Please just tell me if he's alive."

"So the noble girl was right," Priestess Bria said, her eyes igniting with anger. "We did not want to believe it."

"What noble girl?" Corinne demanded.

"A very lovely young woman named Lana told us the prince was making advances toward you," Bria said. "We were concerned for you, being exposed to such temptation."

"Lana is a snake," Corinne spat.

"And yet it seems she spoke true."

"Then why tell me I had redeemed myself?" Corinne asked. "If you thought I had succumbed to such temptation?"

"We hoped our commendations would bring you back to us," Chala said. "But you have betrayed us all, Corinne."

"*I've* betrayed *you*?" Corinne nearly choked on the words. "Since I was a child, you all promised me safety and honor amongst the Lightguards, and then you throw me into an assignment without telling me anything important, and the moment I make a move slightly outside of your secret plans, you burn me and shame me back into submission. All for *what*? Power? Conquest? The things *you* taught me that we have abhorred since our inception, which you claimed Nightrenders were doing. Was that even real?"

"Vera," Bria barked.

Vera stepped behind Corinne, grabbing one of her arms and kicking the back of her legs. She collapsed to her knees, and Vera drew her sword, holding it to Corinne's neck.

Corinne breathed heavily, her skin shifting against the blade as she looked up at the Priestesses.

"You were kept in the dark for your own protection," Bria said, disgust on her face. "We thought you would be devoted no matter what. But you strayed days after your arrival, and while we thought you had begun redeeming yourself, you were betraying us again. You're no better than the hedonistic nobles who throw themselves at royalty like irreverent lechers."

They truly didn't understand, Corinne realized. Perhaps they'd never felt what she felt for Aryel, had never known the light that bloomed inside her when he laughed, the peace within her when he was near.

"You dare lecture me on irreverence," Corinne said, her voice low, Vera's sword still hovering by her throat. "Have the Lightguards overthrown the Serra family, then? Have you broken our Creed?"

"Have you whored yourself to a Goddessless prince?" Chala snapped.

Corinne looked right in her eyes as she said, "Maybe I have."

Bria stepped forward to grab the back of Corinne's collar and upper arm.

"We've tried to be gentle with you, Corinne," Chala said, her eyes flashing. "But you've strayed further than we'd realized. To the dungeons, then. To see your *prince*."

Even as dread prickled along her skin, Corinne's heart leapt. *Ari is alive.* She waited for Bria to force her to her feet, for Vera to remove her sword, but instead, a sharp jab similar to what she'd felt at the monastery pierced her neck, and darkness swept in.

∽

"Corinne."

Consciousness dragged Corinne back to reality, her eyes pounding in her skull as she forced them open. Torches on the dark stone walls lit the room, not a window in sight between the floor and the high ceiling. Before her, a figure crouched in white robes—Priestess Ronna, her dark hair in a neat braid over her shoulder.

CHAPTER 38

"She's awake," Ronna called, standing.

She moved aside, revealing the rest of the room, including Mother Creita in the center beside—

"Aryel!" she choked out.

He was slumped in a chair, unconscious, his hands and ankles bound to the arms and legs by thick rope. Corinne made to stand, to reach him, but her shackles were chained to the wall behind her, only allowing her enough lead to take a single step forward. She summoned her light to bolster her strength, but her power hadn't fully recovered since the fire.

"Let's not be brash, Corinne," Mother Creita said, drawing a knife and holding it to Aryel's throat.

Corinne's light winked out, fear clawing at her.

"Why are you doing this?" she asked, her voice small.

"The royals have been an abomination to Helaera for a century now," Mother Creita said, her green eyes wide, the knife still at Aryel's throat. "It is our duty to protect the people of Ashera and to bring them Helaera's Light. These heretics are a disgrace to the Goddess."

"Was any of it true, then?" Corinne asked, her voice shaking. She hated that part of her still wanted to believe Mother Creita, believe that the Lightguards were serving an honorable purpose. "About the Nightrenders? The threat from beyond the Boundary?"

"It's only a matter of time before they *do* threaten us," the High Priestess hissed. "That's why we needed to act. The Lightguards will install a more devout rule in Ashera, and we will protect Ashera and ourselves whenever the Shadowlands come for us. And *you*, Corinne, must give up this childishness. This heretic is not worthy of your devotion."

Corinne stared at her, at Aryel.

"You made me think I had strayed," Corinne said, the break in her voice not contrived. "Forgotten our ways and disgraced myself and the Goddess. But *you*—" She broke off, unable to form words that captured her disbelief. "Lightguards do not seek thrones."

Mother Creita sighed. "I feared you would say that. You have such *potential*, Corinne, and here you waste it. But we can help you return to the path, to the Light. We want to welcome you back."

The tangled knot of Corinne's soul finally unraveled, the bonds of fear and shame falling away.

She didn't want to go back.

Mother Creita's hands lit up as she touched Aryel's neck, and he woke with a ragged inhale, disoriented. Most of his injuries from the fire had been healed. Had they had him down here since then? Had they hurt him?

His exhausted eyes landed on Corinne, and the fear that immediately replaced the flash of relief on his face tore into her.

"Corinne," he said, his voice rough.

Mother Creita flicked the knife across his upper arm, and he swore.

"No talking unless I ask for a response, Prince," she said, her voice cold. Corinne's magic flashed along her arms as rage ignited in the pit of her stomach. "Keep yourself in check, Corinne, or I'll do worse than cut him."

Corinne forced down her anger, cursing the shackles on her wrists. Ronna stood several feet away by a heavy wooden door, calm and silent.

"As I said, the royals are heretics, and this one is no different," Mother Creita said, placing a hand on Aryel's shoulder. He flinched, but didn't say anything. "You, Corinne, are the daughter of a flamewielder, and you are worthy of so much more."

"My father was a violent defector who killed my mother," Corinne said, her voice trembling again.

Defector. The word echoed in her mind, insistent, reaching for her.

"Yes, but he was still powerful, and he passed that power down to you."

"I've only harnessed the flames once," Corinne said, shaking her head.

"So I've heard," Mother Creita said. "Now tell me, Corinne, have you been drinking your tea?"

Was she truly trying to shame her over *that* right now? "What does that have to do with anything?"

"Everything," Mother Creita said, stepping past Aryel and removing her hand. He shifted as he looked to Corinne, but his bindings were secure. "It's a suppressant, child. To keep the flames in check until you were fully trained."

CHAPTER 38

"I've been fully trained for years," Corinne said, even as her mind reeled.

A suppressant?

"Mentally trained. This assignment was your true final test," Mother Creita said. "It made sense at the time to use this to test the true depth of your devotion. You never know with the daughter of a defector."

Defector. Defector. Corinne raged against the shame and torment those words wrought upon her heart. She would not let that fear cage her anymore.

"Perhaps we should have told you of our plans all along, and you would not have strayed," Mother Creita said. "But there's still time to redeem yourself, Corinne. Denounce the prince and take your rightful place among us. Lend us your considerable power, and Helaera will bless you in ways you could scarcely imagine."

Corinne looked to Aryel again, and the trust in his eyes bolstered her courage.

"No," she said.

Mother Creita sighed again. "You make this so difficult."

She turned and swiped her knife across Aryel's arm again, and he yelped in pain. Mother Creita stepped behind his chair, grabbing the collar of his shirt and holding her knife to his cheek.

Corinne pulled at her shackles, her magic flickering again.

"You see how freely he bleeds, mending so, so slowly?" Mother Creita asked, her voice breathy and awed, and Corinne nearly shuddered at the shift in her tone. "We're tasked with protecting nonmagic mortals, Corinne, and only those who deserve it. They're weak, fragile creatures, a few of them worthy of our protection, but none worthy of our hearts."

Watching her drag the knife across Aryel's face as he gritted his teeth against a scream broke something in Corinne.

"*Stop,*" she said, her voice strained as she pulled at the chains.

"Denounce him and recommit yourself," Mother Creita said.

"Corinne, don't let them—" Aryel's voice cut off in another cry as the High Priestess cut his face again, crossing the first slice in an upward motion.

"I said no talking," Mother Creita hissed. She straightened and then sighed, and Aryel locked eyes with Corinne again as blood trickled down his face, his arm. "Ronna? Fetch our guest, please."

Corinne and Aryel turned as Ronna approached the door, torchlight flickering across her face as she unlocked it. A familiar face appeared that made Corinne's heart sink to her toes.

"Come, child," Mother Creita said, beckoning.

With hands folded delicately in front of her dark green gown, Lana stepped forward into the dungeon chamber. Aryel looked perplexed, but Corinne knew why she was here. *Snake.*

"Hello, Corinne," she said tightly, coming to stand before her. Not close enough for Corinne to reach her. Wise.

"Tell her what you told us, child," Mother Creita said, her voice gentle.

Lana took a deep breath. "I met them a few days after the ball, and learned many things I hadn't known before about being devoted to the Goddess. I also learned how forbidden it is for a Lightguard to have any sort of romantic relationship. I was worried about you after seeing Aryel's advances toward you."

"Oh, *fuck* you, Lana," Aryel said, and Mother Creita held a knife to his throat again.

Corinne held her breath as Lana continued.

"I told the Priestesses what I had seen," Lana said, sniffing. Corinne wished she were a step closer so she could throttle her. "But it seemed nothing happened while they were here, and I thought perhaps I was mistaken, perhaps you hadn't fallen for his act."

Corinne's eyes darted to Aryel again. His gaze was desperate, imploring as Mother Creita kept the knife firmly against his neck.

"But now it's clear you have," Lana said. "You were in his room that night of the attack, weren't you?"

Corinne's face flushed. How did she know that? No one had been around—

You all said he'd be alone.

"The assassin," Corinne breathed, looking to Mother Creita, who gazed back at her with disdain. And the two before, and the cryptic note.... She looked to Lana again. "You helped them."

CHAPTER 38

"I used to sneak into his room often," Lana said with a sigh. "It was easy to share the best way to remain undetected." She took a step closer, her smile rueful. "I know Aryel, Corinne, perhaps better than most. He doesn't care about you, he only cares about himself. Once he's tired of fucking you, he'll toss you aside like the others. Like me."

He just wants to keep himself safe. He doesn't really care about you.

Corinne had let that voice convince her to mistrust herself too many times. After everything they'd been through these past weeks, after she'd seen Aryel risk his own safety for her, the thought was laughable.

"If I ever see you outside this dungeon," Corinne said, her voice low, "I will do far worse than break your hand."

Ire lit up Lana's features, her demure facade disappearing. "Fine. Enjoy suffering for a worthless man."

She turned on her heel, fists clenched. "Priestesses," she said with a quick nod, and strode from the room.

"This is disappointing, Corinne," Mother Creita said, but Corinne was more focused on the spark that had returned to Aryel's eyes, even with that knife at his throat. "I'd truly hoped you would see the truth about him before tonight."

"Why tonight?" Corinne asked, tensing.

Mother Creita's face shifted into that horrible, pitying look she'd given Corinne after burning her.

"We only kept him alive this long to help prove to you that he isn't who you think he is," Mother Creita said. "We hoped to spare you pain, but perhaps pain is the only way you will learn. We offer his life to Helaera at sundown."

Corinne's lungs emptied, and Aryel paled.

"You will return to us one way or another," Mother Creita said, her voice hard. "He will die in the name of the Goddess, and you will watch."

Corinne's magic burst to life. "*No.*"

"Ronna," the High Priestess called, and Ronna approached Corinne quickly.

"No!" Corinne growled, firing a blast of light at the Priestess, who dodged easily given Corinne's shackled hands.

She avoided Ronna's attempts to grab her, even with the chains, until a terrible cry pierced the air. Her head whipped to Mother Creita, who had a glowing hand on Aryel's arm, burning him.

"Stop!" The plea ripped out of her, joining Aryel's cries. "*Stop!*"

"Then stop resisting!" Mother Creita called.

Corinne's magic faded as she fell to her knees, and Mother Creita removed her hand from Aryel's skin. His chest rose and fell rapidly, his face contorting in pain.

"Corinne," he panted, but she didn't hear if he said anything more as Ronna forced her into unconsciousness again.

CHAPTER 39

For the third time that day, Corinne woke to a living nightmare.

She was in a dark cell, being hauled to her feet by two sets of hands before she'd even reached full consciousness. They dragged her into the dungeon corridor, her hands still shackled in front of her.

"If you resist, Mother Creita has promised to draw out the prince's death."

That was Vera's voice in her ear.

Corinne's mind sharpened as they trekked down the corridor toward the stairwell. The cells were mostly empty. What had become of Iliana, of Nik and Danai, and all the other guards?

"How long was I unconscious after the fire?" Corinne asked quietly.

She glanced to her right to find Priestess Bria grasping that arm.

"Just a day," Vera said.

"And the Lightguards have successfully staged a coup?"

"Not a coup," Bria said. "A liberation and return to the values of the Goddess."

Corinne didn't bother to argue. "What about the castle guards? Where are they?"

"Some surrendered, others were killed," Vera said, and Corinne's heart lurched.

They could all be dead.

And she was about to watch Aryel die.

"The people of Ashera will turn against you all," Corinne muttered.

"The people of Ashera know us as heroes who put out the fire set off by violent assassins," Bria said. "We are providing the nation stability during a time of tragedy and uncertainty."

Corinne clenched her teeth. The Lightguards would go on as beacons of righteousness in Ashera, and no one would know they'd killed the royal family themselves.

Emerging onto the ground floor of the castle, Corinne fought to keep her magic under control. It hummed beneath her skin, aching to be unleashed. But she didn't know where they were taking her, didn't know if she could get to Aryel before they all converged on her if she tried to escape. Lightguards were all over the castle, roaming the corridors, eyes following Corinne as they marched her toward...where *were* they going, anyway? They weren't headed for the entrance hall.

Corinne tensed when they approached the doors to the gardens, two Lightguards opening them to let them outside. Her racing heart skittered to a stop.

A short wooden platform had been erected right in front of the central fountain, almost like a little stage, surrounded by roughly a dozen Lightguards standing in a circle. Mother Creita stood atop it, sword in hand, and Aryel was on his knees to her left, his hands shackled like Corinne's.

Corinne lost her grasp on her composure the moment she locked eyes with her irreverent, heathen brat of a prince.

She fought Vera and Bria's holds, her markings flaring along her skin. She grappled with them for a moment before a voice cut across the gardens.

"Enough, Corinne!" Mother Creita bellowed. "It's your choice: he will die by the sword, or by fire."

Fear tore its way up her body, and Vera and Bria took advantage of it, forcing her to her knees. Corinne looked to the platform again.

Mother Creita's left arm was alight with her markings, flames beginning to form along them. In her other hand, the sword she held glowed. Corinne's insides blazed.

That was *her* sword.

Corinne's magic flared brighter, her power building within, and she fought Vera and Bria again with a snarl.

"Chala," Mother Creita barked, and the other Priestess came forward, relieving Vera to grip Corinne's arm with greater strength.

They let some heat into their hands, searing into her arms, and she fought back a cry. The Lightguards all around them didn't say a word, their faces either stoic or pitying as they looked at her. She didn't care about any of them, her eyes glued to the man she couldn't bear to lose.

"Ari," Corinne sobbed, her magic flickering again as the burning intensified.

"It's okay, Sunshine," he said, his eyes holding hers as if there weren't a dozen feet between them.

The idea that the light in them was about to go out...

"We gather today to finalize the cleansing of our realm," Mother Creita began.

No. Corinne would not allow it.

She let out a cry, all fury and fear and desperation, startling both the Priestesses holding her and cutting off Mother Creita's speech. Bria and Chala summoned actual flames to their hands, now, and Corinne's vision went white.

It wasn't despair that accompanied Corinne's agony this time, but pure, white-hot rage. She screamed her throat raw as they drove their magic into her flesh, vaguely aware of someone calling her name.

"Corinne! *Corinne!*"

Somewhere in the torrent of agony that drowned all rational thought, Corinne knew that wasn't her mother screaming for her. Reality blurred as images of a burning house flashed before her eyes, then a man struggling against the hold of a woman in white, a sword at his throat. Just when she thought she'd lose consciousness, something nagged at the back of Corinne's mind.

No matter how hard she'd tried to avoid it, fire was part of her, hers to wield. Helaera's Light was a gift she'd been given, and it was not meant for this—to cause her this pain.

They're just thoughts.
That's part of Her Light too.
I had a feeling about you, Corinne.
Stay the course. Be the Light.
You're more than that.
"*Corinne!*"

Corinne reached for the magic burning into her, reached for the fire, and *pulled*.

The pain eased, and power flooded into her chest, her lungs. With a sharp exhale, she let her magic ignite along her skin, the light turning to flames. The Priestesses stumbled back, yelping in pain, and Lightguards all around them began moving in a panic as the flames grew hot enough to melt the shackles from Corinne's wrists. The burns on her arms faded away painfully but quickly, and she rose to her feet, her tears evaporating in the heat.

She sent a kick directly into Bria's ribcage, leaving a charred slash across her white robes, and the Priestess collapsed to the ground. Chala's own magic lit her body, far more dimly than Corinne's, and she launched an arc of fire at Corinne. She ducked it easily and prepared to counter, throwing two slashes of flames at Chala, who dodged one but hissed in pain when the other hit her in the side.

Behind them, a Lightguard lurched in place, an arrow protruding from his shoulder, and everyone froze. He looked up right as another arrow flew and lodged itself in his eye.

Shouts erupted as more arrows flew, and Corinne glanced over her shoulder, greeted by the appearance of castle guards armed with bows and swords as they poured into the gardens.

An instant later, Corinne returned her attention to Chala, taking her down with a ruthless blow to her chest, and then sprinted for the platform.

Mother Creita was dragging Aryel away down a side garden path, sword at his throat as she shouted orders at the Lightguards.

Corinne did not slow.

Two Lightguards blocked her way, and she wove between them, dodging their attacks with ease, harnessing their magic as they hurled it at her. The fire welcomed the additional light and heat even more easily than her normal magic did, almost hungry for it. She kept it close as she raced down the path and around the fountain, not wanting to set the gardens and everyone in them ablaze.

Several Lightguards chased after her, but she evaded them easily enough. She knew this place, and they did not.

But where was Mother Creita? Corinne couldn't hear anything over the shouts and screams from behind her. Goddess, she hoped her friends were alive and would stay that way.

When she emerged from between two flowering trees, another Lightguard was there. She took him down before he'd even realized who she was. The hem of a white cloak caught her eye from around the next corner, and she dashed for it.

She skidded to a halt as a burst of light flew inches past her head, whipping around as Vera bore down on her. She caught Vera's next attack and hurled it back at her tenfold. Vera barely dodged the pillar of fire aimed for her face.

"You were supposed to be as devoted as me!" Vera shouted, her face contorted as she ran at Corinne again, sword drawn.

Corinne ducked beneath the blow and sent her flying backward with a blast of flames to her chest.

Vera shrieked as it burned a hole through her tunic, her sword clattering to the ground.

With a deep inhale, Corinne sent a blast of her magic into the stones, and the earth shook beneath them, upending the stones and toppling several nearby trees so Vera had no clear path forward. She screamed in rage, and Corinne ran off, gritting her teeth.

And you were supposed to be my friend.

She was approaching the garden perimeter. Surely Mother Creita couldn't have gotten far trying to drag Aryel with her.

"Aryel!" she shouted, unsure which direction to take when she reached a fork in the path.

"Corinne—!" His voice cut off with a cry, but it was enough.

Around the next corner to her right, beneath one of the pergolas, Mother Creita held Corinne's sword at Aryel's throat as she gripped his shirt. Aryel pulled at her arm, but with the High Priestess's magic bolstering her strength, the blade didn't budge.

"Careful, Corinne," Mother Creita said soothingly. "If you're rational, I'll let him live."

Corinne pulled her fire inward, but she remained tensed to attack. Shouts and clanging metal rang out over the trees and flowers from the central garden.

"Let him go," Corinne said.

"Perhaps I will...if you rejoin us."

Corinne began to gather heat in her left palm, concentrating it as much as she could. She channeled every bit of her rage, her grief, her confusion and disappointment into it.

"Let. Him. Go."

"Don't you want to be the highest blessed—"

Corinne let all that magic in her palm reach a peak, until it felt like her hand was going to explode from the pressure, and then she twisted, throwing out her arm. A spear of fire, so hot it was white, shot from her hand and slammed into Mother Creita's face, inches from Aryel's neck.

The High Priestess let out an earsplitting scream, releasing him and Corinne's sword as she cradled her face, and Corinne was already moving.

She grabbed Aryel, melting the shackles on his wrists before reaching down to retrieve her sword. Mother Creita had collapsed to her knees on the stone path, still screaming and writhing when Corinne took Aryel's hand and *ran*.

CHAPTER 40

As they emerged back at the center of the gardens, a Lightguard sent a castle guard sprawling to the ground, magic hitting them in the chest. Corinne threw out a blast of fire, blocking them from going after another guard a few feet ahead.

They turned to her and growled. "Traitor!"

Yes, Corinne thought as she leapt forward and overpowered the woman. *I am.*

Defector. Defector.

It was a bloodbath as Lightguards and castle guards fought in the gardens, the latter group directed by Captain Ekhana, who was bellowing orders as he fought off a Lightguard himself.

"Corinne!"

She whirled. Nik was standing several yards to his father's left, close to the castle wall with a bow in hand. Corinne and Aryel ran for him, ducking as more arrows flew over their heads, taking out two other Lightguards nearby.

"Nik," she shouted over the fighting, then sent an arc of fiery light toward a Lightguard who ran at them from behind.

Another Lightguard stared at her in a daze before falling to his knees and muttering prayers.

Corinne blinked and returned her attention to Nik. "Danai and Iliana?"

"Fighting inside," he said. "A handful of guards and servants avoided capture or worse, and my father was able to get everyone here just in time."

Captain Ekhana caught sight of them then and hurried in their direction.

"Get the prince out of here *now*," he said. "Take Danai and Iliana with you if you can find them."

"I'll go too," Nik said.

Captain Ekhana looked to his son for a moment before pulling him into a fierce, quick embrace. "Get somewhere safe," the captain said. "And don't come back unless Toro or I send for you."

Nik nodded and, alongside Corinne and Aryel, ran for the castle doors. They slowed as they entered and found it mostly quiet down the first corridor, but the sound of shouts echoed from up ahead. Corinne brandished her sword and took Aryel's hand again, noticing the burn on his neck for the first time, and a bit of the fire in her quelled.

She'd done that. She'd hurt him.

"Come on," he said, squeezing her hand and pushing onward.

They ducked around several skirmishes as they approached the entrance hall, dodging the body of a falling Lightguard from one of the stairwells. Corinne wanted to scream at them all to *stop*, that this wasn't the way, wasn't what Helaera wanted, but no one would listen to her. Not her, the traitor. The defector.

Just like your father.

Corinne shook her head as they emerged into the entrance hall. She could deal with that later.

Several Lightguards took notice of Corinne, then Aryel, and hurled magic at them. Without even blinking, Corinne let her flames engulf the light. The Lightguards gaped at her, stunned. Two more fell to their knees like the one outside, but Corinne couldn't hear if they were praying or not.

"Corinne!"

Danai and Iliana, more than any other guards, were holding their own against the Lightguards, fighting off two particularly vicious ones by the doors.

"Danai! Iliana!" Corinne shouted.

Both of them disengaged from the fights they were in, dodging flares of light, and hurried for the entrance. Corinne covered their retreat with a blast of fire, forcing their attackers to back down.

They burst through the doors, and another magic attack immediately hit Danai's shoulder, sending them reeling back. Iliana caught them while Corinne leapt down the stairs to face the two Lightguards waiting by the gates.

Their magic didn't touch her—it only served to feed her own as they attacked. The flames climbed higher around her as they fought, until finally she landed a blow to one's head, sending them crumpling to the ground. She twisted, catching the other's sword with her own. They growled at her as she grabbed their forearm and shoved them back with a burst of fire, disarming them and knocking them unconscious. Corinne flipped their sword in her right hand, and both hers and the new one ignited with the flames of her magic, rivaling the brightness of the setting sun.

Aryel and her friends were staring at her when she turned to face them. She breathed heavily as the flames danced around her, framing her body in their wild glow.

"Goddess above," Danai said.

Corinne ensured the Lightguards were subdued before dampening the fire again and beckoning the others forward.

"Where can we go?" she asked as they ran through the castle gates.

"My house," Iliana said.

Wordlessly, they all agreed and followed Iliana into the streets.

◊

IF CORINNE HAD THOUGHT THE JOURNEY TO ILIANA'S FELT long on horseback, it was nothing compared to walking, or rather sneaking, through the streets. Every passing second heightened her worry that they would be caught, even as twilight fell.

For the most part, though, the streets were empty, shops closed and curtains drawn. A face appeared in a window every now and then, only to disappear quickly. The occasional Lightguard strode past, and Corinne held her breath each time, certain they were about to be discovered.

She'd tapped into a depth of her power she hadn't known was possible, but that didn't mean she was immune to exhaustion. If another group of Lightguards attacked them, she might be overwhelmed.

"One more street," Iliana whispered as they crouched behind a cart full of hay in an alley.

If they could make it to Iliana's undetected, hopefully the night would be quiet, allowing them time to plan for what came next.

After ensuring the street was clear, they darted out from the alley and hurried for the wall of a shop, shaded by a green cloth awning. Only a few more steps until they'd be in front of Iliana's, and Corinne could let herself breathe. She looked to Aryel, whose face was drawn, and a pang of nausea rolled through her at the sight of the burn on his neck.

Two of Iliana's siblings were out front when they reached her house, immediately running to the door at their approach. The five of them scrambled inside as quickly as possible, Petyr and Isa shutting the door behind them and drawing the curtains.

"What's going on, Ili?" Petyr asked.

"The Lightguards have turned on us, Atta," Iliana said, her voice strained. "Can we hide here for the night?"

"Of course," he said, looking at the faces of each guest in his house. All five of Iliana's siblings were scattered about. "I assume Corinne is not amongst those who've turned?"

"No," Iliana said. "I'll explain, but we all need to rest a moment."

Danai flopped into a chair by a tiny fireplace, and Nik leaned on the arm of it, one hand on their shoulder.

Isa insisted Corinne make use of the bedroom she'd slept in two weeks prior if she needed to rest, and shuffled her along despite her halfhearted protests. Aryel followed shortly after, Isa bowing deeply to him and reiterating what an honor it was to have him in her home.

"Apologies that we don't have enough comfortable seating in the front area, but this should do just fine," Isa said. "Just yell if you need anything. I'll make everyone some food."

Aryel looked rather queasy as he sat on the bed. Corinne approached him hesitantly, her eyes locking on his burn again.

"Let me heal that," she said, taking a step toward him, and he looked up at her with exhaustion and grief in his eyes.

"Are you going to pass out if you do?"

Corinne shook her head. "But it...won't be pleasant. Magic wounds are painful in healing."

He took a deep breath. "So I've discovered."

Corinne's stomach lurched. She knelt before him, taking his hands in hers.

"I'm so sorry," she whispered.

"I'll be fine. Go ahead."

Bracing herself, Corinne summoned her light and placed her hand gently on his burn. He hissed in pain, and when her magic really began its work, he bit back a cry.

"I'm sorry," she breathed. "I'm sorry."

It only took a few minutes to heal, and he endured it remarkably well. He sighed in relief when Corinne was done, her light fading again.

"I'm sorry," she said again.

Aryel took her hand. "Stop apologizing for saving my life, Sunshine," he said. He gave her a weak smile. "Or Sunfire, more like."

Corinne fought the urge to burst into tears. She didn't deserve to fall apart in front of him, to seek comfort from him after all he'd just been through. She started to stand, but he took her face in his hands.

"Corinne," he said, and she tried blinking away her tears before looking at him again.

But tears welled in his eyes now, and he pushed himself off the bed and onto his knees, clutching her to him. She held him just as tightly as the relief of it all, coupled with the grief, washed over her.

He was alive despite all they'd done to him, all they'd tried to do. Her people had betrayed her and hurt her in ways she could never forgive. Corinne didn't know when she started crying, but she'd dampened the tattered, bloody fabric on his shoulder.

She couldn't wrap her mind around it all, how everything had changed so drastically in only a matter of days. In only a matter of hours.

"Thank you," he said, his voice barely above a whisper. "For coming back for me."

Corinne squeezed him tighter. "You don't need to thank me. I'm your guard."

He leaned back, brushing her hair out of her face and wiping away a tear on her cheek. "We both know you're more than that, Corinne."

Her heart thudded so hard in her chest she wondered if he could hear it.

"I'm just yours, then."

Her words hung between them, carrying the weight of what she didn't say, and Aryel began to respond when a voice called to them from the front room. They released one another and stood, headed into the little hallway.

The smell of food hit Corinne's nose, and it was only then that she realized how hungry she was. She and Aryel joined the others at the table as Petyr placed bowls of stew before them. She dug into the hearty broth and bread like a woman starved. Aryel slid his over to her while the others talked quietly, and Corinne looked at him, perplexed.

"You should eat," she murmured.

"I can't," he said, shaking his head. "Not right now."

Corinne understood the feeling. "At least try the stew. You need to keep your strength up."

Aryel huffed softly through his nose, a little smile tugging his lips upward. "Always looking out for me."

"Yes," Corinne said simply, taking another bite of her bread. "And that's a promise."

That got a small laugh out of him, and it brought a little warmth back to her heart. Corinne caught Danai looking at her a moment later, a wry smile on their face, and her cheeks flushed.

A sharp rap on the door startled all of them, Corinne ready to draw both swords at her hips.

"It's Toro!" a voice called, and Danai leapt up from the table.

"Atta," they said, hurrying for the door.

CHAPTER 40

Councilor Toro stepped inside quickly, greeting Isa and Petyr with a nod while wrapping an arm around Danai.

"I'm sorry to barge in like this," he said, breathless. His robes were dirtied on the hem, his hair haphazard. "I guessed you all might come here." His eyes landed on Corinne and Aryel. "You both need to get out of Vytanos as soon as possible. The Lightguards are launching a search of every inch of the city at first light."

Corinne felt the blood drain from her face. Leave the city, and go where? She couldn't return to the monastery, and Lightguards were stationed in every village in Ashera.

"I'm going with them, Atta," Danai said.

Councilor Toro smiled sadly. "I thought you might say that." He reached inside his robes and extracted a rolled-up bit of parchment, carrying it to the table. He smoothed it out, looking to each of them. "I can show you a route out of Ashera."

Silence fell over the room. *Out of Ashera.*

"Are we to just leave the nation to the Lightguards?" Aryel asked, his voice hard.

"For now, you're to stay alive," Toro said. "We'll do our best to keep everyone safe, Prince Aryel. But we need time to plan."

Aryel paled but nodded.

"Those villages in the northeast," Toro continued. "They never received that aid, so I'm sure they hold little love for the Lightguards by now. It will be safer to travel through there to reach the Boundary, specifically just beyond Balae."

"The Boundary?" Nik asked. "Are you saying we breach it? How is that even possible?"

Toro's eyes flicked to Corinne now. "Corinne can create an opening."

Corinne stared at him. He wanted her to break through the Boundary and send them to the Shadowlands?

"I've outlined everything here," he said, handing Corinne another folded bit of parchment. "I have connections with a light mage in the Shadowlands, in a city called Ohrai."

"There are Lightguards in the Shadowlands?" Corinne asked.

She wasn't sure how much more she could take. Had every part of her life up until this point been a farce?

"They don't call themselves Lightguards there, but yes," Toro said. "I've been trying to discover more about them for quite some time, but for now, all I know is you can trust this one. Her name is Rasi. I've sent word for her to expect you."

"What about Nightrenders?" Corinne asked. "Will they not attack us there?"

"Rasi has not told me much about them yet," Toro said. "If I've learned anything since beginning my correspondence with her, it's that the Shadowlands are not entirely what we've been led to expect."

"And you're certain we can trust Rasi?" Iliana asked.

Toro nodded. "She was my wife's dearest friend when they were children."

Selana's friend from her story, that night on the Mykotas's roof. She'd defected.

A Lightguard defector in the Shadowlands.

Corinne's head swam.

Danai and the others talked plans for travel while Corinne tried to let everything she'd just heard sink in. Hands trembling, she opened the parchment Danai's father had given her, quickly reading over the instructions. She read the same sentence five times before giving up on truly grasping it right now.

"...If you leave before dawn, you can reach Balae by nightfall," Toro said. "Many Lightguards have been recalled from their stations for this attack, so it's my hope you can avoid them. Even so, as long as none of them spot and recognize Corinne, it's unlikely any of them would know what the rest of you look like."

A mix of shame and hatred washed over Corinne, ousting the confusion and uncertainty for a moment. Any Lightguard who saw her was almost certain to recognize her. She was the top trainee of her class, the most talented mage they'd seen in twenty years at the monastery.

Oh, how she wanted to crawl out of her own skin and shed the disgust she felt toward herself. How proud she'd been, how hopeful in her place amongst them. Now, that notoriety was a danger to her and those she cared about.

CHAPTER 40

But she couldn't let them go without her. She couldn't let the Lightguards hurt any of them again.

Corinne would make them pay. They'd lied to and manipulated her for the past fifteen years, and they'd hurt and tried to kill Aryel.

The Lightguards had been the opposite of what she'd always trusted, committing acts of violence and selfishness she could scarcely comprehend. And she'd devoted her life to them.

"I'm sorry," she said, and every eye in the room turned to her, their conversation stopping abruptly. Her face contorted as a deep ache settled in her chest. "I'm so sorry."

"Corinne," Toro said, smiling sadly at her as Aryel took her hand from the table, lacing his fingers through hers. "You don't need to apologize to anyone here. The Lightguards hurt you too."

Nik stepped around the table to sit on Corinne's other side, patting her shoulder.

"Why don't you all try to get some rest?" Toro said as Danai rolled up the map and placed it in a pack they'd found. "You have a few hours before the Lightguards begin their search."

"I think we ought to leave now," Iliana said. "Before they have more time to shore up defenses. I'm sure they already have their own guards stationed at the city gates."

"I'm sure they do, but it won't make much of a difference whether we leave now or in a few hours," Danai said. "We should take advantage of the opportunity to rest. Especially Corinne. We don't have a chance of escaping without her magic."

As they all looked to her, Corinne took a steadying breath.

"A bit of rest," she agreed. "And then we get out of Vytanos."

THE CALAIS HOUSE WAS SILENT AND DARK AS THEY ALL tried to get a few hours of sleep. Corinne was on the couch at everyone's insistence, but she found herself unable to find sleep despite not being on the floor. Danai and Nik were curled up beneath the window on the large rug of the living area, and Iliana was in one of the back bedrooms with her siblings. Aryel was on the floor in front of the couch.

A quiet, shaky breath from beneath her sent a pang through her heart. Corinne reached downward, her hand finding Aryel's shoulder, then his chest as it shook with silent sobs. He gripped her fingers and sat up, facing her with tear-stained cheeks, and Corinne pulled him toward her in a silent invitation.

He climbed onto the couch, twining his legs with hers and wrapping his arms around her. She brushed the tears from his cheeks with her thumbs and pressed her lips to his forehead, her heart breaking as he tightened his hold and shook with another quiet sob.

She wished desperately that she could tell him it was okay, but the best she could do was hold him close and whisper, "I'm here. I've got you."

She didn't know how long they remained like that in the dark, but she drew soothing circles on his back until his shaking subsided and his breathing evened out. She said a prayer to Helaera for his safety before closing her eyes as sleep finally took her.

CHAPTER 41

Corinne's few hours of sleep were plagued by nightmares, but they were restful enough that her magic had rejuvenated. Her entire body hummed with power like never before, a source of light and heat ready to be summoned. She'd always been this powerful, this connected to Helaera's Sun, but the Lightguards had taken that from her, too, with that bitter, poisonous tea. And her first thought when she'd felt such strength, *her* strength, was utter terror, fear that Helaera would spurn her.

"You ready, Sunfire?"

Aryel was dressed more plainly than Corinne had ever seen him, leaning on the doorframe of the bedroom in an unremarkable tan shirt and brown trousers. The Calais family had generously provided them with old clothing before their journey. Corinne had rigged a sword belt at her waist to carry both her blade and the one she'd taken from the other Lightguard, heavy but grounding. Her own shirt was tan, too, a color she hadn't worn since she was a child. It felt strange to don colors besides white and gold, but it was best for her to appear as ordinary as possible while they traveled.

Not that it would matter until they actually got out of Vytanos.

"Ready," she said. And she was. *I can do this.*

They ran through the plan again with the others, voices hushed and hurried around the table in the kitchen. Each of them had a pack that was, for now, mostly empty; it was a risk to hope they'd be able to secure supplies outside of Vytanos, but they had no other choice. They'd all refused to take anything else from Iliana's home, and every shop in Vytanos was closed.

Iliana's family bid her a tearful farewell, and her younger sisters, Mira and Jaela, both hugged Corinne's middle before she left. Touched, Corinne waved at them all as they stole outside into the darkness of the early morning.

The city gate wasn't far from Iliana's house, and after darting through two streets free of Lightguards, Corinne let the wild hope that they could avoid them entirely delude her for a moment. Iliana crouched at the exit of an alleyway, turning to them to nod before venturing into the street.

Danai grabbed her tunic just before she emerged, spotting a figure at the last moment.

All five of them froze. The figure's white hauberk and cloak were unmistakable.

Whoever it was continued on their way, not noticing the five fugitives in the shadows.

Corinne let out a silent breath and followed them all quickly into the open, glancing behind them to ensure no one had spotted them. They darted into another narrow alleyway, the main road just ahead. Iliana dashed toward it on silent feet to peer at the gate, then returned to where they all hid behind emptied fruit crates.

"Three Lightguards," she whispered. "One on the wall, two by the gate."

"Can we handle all three?" Nik asked.

"It's what we expected," Danai said. They looked to Corinne. "You sure you want to do this?"

Corinne's gaze hardened alongside her heart. "Give me a few moments."

As she stood and stepped out of the alleyway, she begged Helaera for forgiveness, then approached the gate with wobbling steps. The Lightguards tensed immediately, their attention fully on Corinne.

"You're out past curfew!" one of them, a man, barked. He drew his sword, his markings illuminating.

Corinne held up her hands and swayed. "Ssssorry," she slurred. "I hadn' heard about the curfew!" She stumbled forward a few more steps, falling into the man, who caught her out of shock more than anything. "Can you gimme directions? I think I'm lossssssst."

The man holding her upright gaped at her in disgust. "Is she ill?"

"She's drunk, Ro." The other Lightguard, a woman, approached. "Ma'am, can you tell me where you live?"

Corinne slid her eyes to the other Lightguard, and panic seized her.

The woman stopped in her tracks, eyes widening. "Corinne?"

Before either of them could react, Corinne straightened, twisting the man's arm and forcing him to his knees. She drew her swords, her magic flaring to life along her arms and down both blades. Fire licked up her skin, but she kept the temperature from getting too hot, a level of control she hadn't expected. She crossed the blades at the Lightguard's throat before her, and he froze.

"Not another step, Tia," she said, eyes flashing. "You, stand slowly."

The man kneeling before her did so, his hands raised in surrender.

The Lightguard on the wall jumped down, poised to attack, and Corinne pivoted toward her, drawing a bit of blood from her captive's neck. Her beautiful face was filled with shock and contempt. *Sana.*

"Open the gate," Corinne said. Tia and Sana merely stared at her for a moment, and Corinne called more fire to her, the flames growing along her markings. "Now."

Sana scrambled backward, keeping an eye on Corinne.

Corinne barely moved as the gate creaked and groaned, the portcullis lifting with agonizing slowness.

"My friends are going to walk through," she said. "And I'm going to follow them. You attack any of them, and he's dead."

Tia's throat bobbed as she swallowed, lifting her own hands away from her sword.

Corinne whistled, and four figures appeared in her periphery, each with weapons drawn. Even Nik had a small knife in hand, though he'd protested when Danai had given it to him.

Warm night air blew through Corinne's hair and made the fire along her arms dance as she watched Danai, Nik, Aryel, and Iliana quickly dart through the city gate. Corinne slowly walked backward with her captive Lightguard, never taking her eyes off the two others, until she reached the opening.

She breathed in and then shoved him forward, withdrawing the swords.

He twisted, hurling magic at her, but Corinne ducked just in time. The Lightguard started after her, but just as Corinne prepared to counter his attack, magic slammed into his back, sending him careening to the ground.

Tia stood at the gate, one glowing hand outstretched, her eyes wide and her chest heaving. Sana was on the ground beside her, unconscious. Tia's eyes met Corinne's.

"*Go, Corinne!*" she mouthed.

Heart racing, Corinne tore her eyes away from Tia and sprinted after her companions.

CHAPTER 42

Despite the late hour in Balae, summer heat hung heavy on the air, and Corinne wondered despairingly when she might be able to bathe next. She leaned against the outside of a shop in the village with her arms crossed, keeping watch with Iliana and Aryel while Nik and Danai purchased supplies. Aryel had readily handed over several rings alongside the small bit of coin Danai's father had given them to purchase whatever they may need.

Villagers passed on the narrow street without offering them so much as a glance, headed into pubs or cafés for the evening. She wished they could afford to sleep in the inn across the way for the night, but they were limited on both funds and time. They'd been traveling since before dawn from Vytanos, and while they'd avoided any further confrontations since the city gates, they were all hot and exhausted by the time Balae came into view.

Keep it together, Corinne. Once they had their supplies, it was on to the Boundary.

"By the way," Aryel said, leaning close. "This morning? That was the worst drunk acting I have ever seen."

Corinne snorted. "Blame yourself, then. I just acted the way you did when we met."

Aryel stared at her for a moment, eyebrows raised, and Corinne held his gaze. He broke first, looking back to the street with a chuckle. "Goddess, no wonder you couldn't stand me."

Corinne laughed softly, and he nudged her shoulder with his. Their laughter faded gently into the silence of the night.

"If my entire life had to fall apart," he said, voice even lower, "I'm glad you're here to help me carry the pieces."

Corinne looked at him again, her chest blooming with some emotion she couldn't name. "Ari..."

The door to the shop opened with a creak, and Danai's laugh floated outside as they traded jokes with the shopkeeper. Iliana reached to help with the packs Danai and Nik carried.

"You could charm a brick, Danai," Iliana said, heaving a pack over to Aryel and then one to Corinne.

It was significantly heavier now, but nothing she couldn't handle.

"It's a gift," Danai said. "If we let *you* talk to strangers, we'd get run out of every town."

Once they'd each shouldered their packs, they set off down the little road through the center of Balae again. Corinne tensed every time someone passed, but the most reaction they received was a friendly nod or a raised eyebrow at Corinne's waist. Carrying two swords around wasn't exactly nonthreatening, she supposed. At least no one noticed exactly what kind of swords they were. She had the cover of nightfall to thank for that.

"How far to the Boundary from here?" Danai asked.

"About an hour east," Corinne said, and though no one complained, she could feel everyone's energy wilt around her.

Not that she blamed them; she was exhausted, too, but she had to keep her mind sharp. The only way they'd get through was if she could follow Toro's instructions.

They looked like they'd been torn from a book, and Corinne had memorized the movements and words to go with them hours ago. She'd been confused at first before realizing they were some strange, alternate version of the Lightguard's Creed. She chanted the words to herself as they left Balae, breathing easier the moment they were no longer surrounded by people.

The forest ahead brought welcome coolness as they stepped into the trees, and Corinne conjured a small orb in her palm to light their way.

"Goddess, it's creepy in here," Iliana said, shivering as they walked. "Can someone talk about something?"

"Too tired to talk," Danai said, yawning.

"That's a first."

"Fuck off," Danai said sweetly, then grimaced. "Sorry, Corinne."

"Don't worry about it," she said, heaving a sigh.

She strode on with them in silence for a few more moments. The unsettled feeling Iliana had mentioned started to prickle along her spine now too.

"Can you tell us another story, Corinne?" Nik asked, also yawning.

A deep ache formed in her chest at the thought of the stories she'd grown up hearing and sharing.

"I could sing something," she said instead.

Nik offered her a smile, nodding, so she took a breath and started to sing.

Fear not, my dear one, the sun will still rise
My Light will greet you when you open your eyes
You won't remember the shadows that fell
Hold tight in moonlight, and I'll keep you well

Corinne wondered if she imagined Aryel's breathing evening out and slowing beside her. She continued the second verse with crickets as her accompaniment.

Look not to futures that may not arise,
Keep faith and look for my star in the sky
You won't be lost here, you've found a home—

Corinne's voice nearly broke on that line. She took another breath and finished the song as the trees began to thin.

Wield now the sunlight wherever you roam.

"That was lovely, Corinne," Nik said.

"Thank you," she said past the sudden lump in her throat.

She didn't have a home anymore, not really. And she was about to break through the very Light she'd always sworn to uphold and protect.

The second half of the hour passed quickly as Nik and Aryel traded knowledge about the speculated topography of the Shadowlands. It couldn't be horribly different from Ashera, if Corinne thought about it logically, but the truth was, that knowledge had been lost to time.

A deeper silence took hold as they cleared the forest and entered a grassy field. In the distance, pinpricks of light were visible in towns perched in the mountains to the north and south. The orb of light in Corinne's hand shimmered, and something pulled at her from the east.

A few yards ahead, it was nearly impossible to see, but every few seconds a faint iridescent ripple ran through the air toward the night sky, disrupting the view of trees beyond it.

The Boundary. Corinne had only seen it once before, watched as those Lightguards had placed their hands to the earth to reinforce and strengthen it.

The others lagged behind as they drew closer to it, allowing Corinne to lead the way. She pressed a hand to the parchment in her pocket that Toro had given her. When she was only a foot away, she lowered her other hand, letting her light go out and dropping her pack to the grass.

She could *feel* the power it radiated, the Light that had been created by Helaera and fortified for generations by Lightguards. Tentatively, she reached for it, only the tips of her fingers grazing it at first. Immense power and pressure flooded her hand, and she yanked it back.

"Are you all right?" Danai called.

Corinne turned to face her companions, several feet behind her now, as she cradled her hand. She nodded once and turned back to the Boundary.

Corinne summoned her light and began to speak.

"Light by Light and stone by stone—"

She crossed her arms with her palms facing her shoulders, a slight modification of the Lightguards' greeting, and her magic flared.

CHAPTER 42

"Through this world I will atone—"

Her arms caught fire, and the Boundary shimmered.

"This I vow, to guide the land—"

Corinne centered her hands vertically, right above left, each palm facing the opposite direction, fingers pointed toward the Boundary. Pressure built in her chest the way it had in her hand in the gardens. She gritted her teeth.

"And sunder walls that I have sown."

Corinne thrust her arms forward toward the Boundary. It shuddered, and light burst out where Corinne's hands broke through it, nearly blinding her. The energy within the Boundary began to pulse, and a heavy wind picked up, but she held fast, twisting her hands around to grip onto it. With a cry, she braced her legs and began to pull apart with all her strength.

Her hair whipped around her as her magic flared ever higher. She'd never felt so much power concentrated in one place, in herself. The Boundary began to tear upward, golden light at the split. It pulsed again, and Corinne gasped at the answering flare of magic she felt in response. Emotions that weren't her own flooded her mind—panic, disbelief, fear, awe, anger.

Lightguards. Some were close by, and they knew where she was now. Corinne pulled harder, her magic blazing as she forced herself to focus.

"Come on!" she called beneath one of her arms.

The opening wasn't large enough for anyone to get through yet, but they needed to be ready.

Aryel's face appeared beside her, his hair wild in the wake of the outpouring of power. "Corinne, are you—?"

"Lightguards coming," she managed. "Be ready to move."

Just a few more inches. A few more. *Another few moments,* she told herself.

Her arms began to tremble with the effort. The Boundary was both feeding and sapping her power, an endless cycle of energy pouring into and out of her. She sensed more Lightguards now, more rage. Corinne forced it open wider.

"Go!" she shouted.

Iliana dove through first, shortly followed by Nik, then Danai. Aryel put a hand on her shoulder, and her flames danced along his fingers but did not burn him.

"I'm not going through without you," Aryel said.

"I have to go last," Corinne growled. "Go before I force you through, Ari."

"Corinne—"

"I'm right behind you. I promise."

Another half second of hesitation, and Aryel ducked through it, never taking his eyes off her. Corinne's relief nearly made her lose her grip.

The blast of magic that hit her back, however, did make her lose her grip.

The opening started to reseal itself as Corinne whirled around to face her assailants. Another arc of light flung her backward into the Boundary. She fell to the grass, then drew both her swords as two Lightguards began attacking her with the full force of their strength.

The Boundary's energy still flared within her, though, and she sent a wall of flame raging toward one of them, blocking their ability to get to her. The other let out a scream of rage, forcing Corinne to dance away from their flurry of attacks. Corinne knew she was short on time; she wasn't sure she had the energy to reopen the Boundary if it fully sealed itself shut again.

When the woman attacking her sent a powerful vertical blow toward Corinne's head with her sword, she moved just in time and took the opening to strike, bringing the Lightguard to the ground with her and pinning her there.

"*Defector!*" she spat. "You're no Lightguard!"

"You're right," Corinne said, her magic starting to flare higher again as she disarmed the woman. "I'm more than that."

She drove the woman's sword into her shoulder, and the Lightguard

CHAPTER 42

screamed. It wasn't enough to kill her, or even subdue her for long, and Corinne leapt off her, grabbing her pack from the ground and tossing it through the now-smaller opening before sheathing her swords again. She gripped the torn edges of the Boundary and nearly collapsed at the sudden influx of power. The flames on her arms grew higher.

There was movement behind her, then an angry cry, just before she threw herself through the opening.

The pressure reached a peak and then eased all at once. She slammed to the ground, palms grasping at leaves on a forest floor. She blinked a few times before realizing it wasn't as dark outside as it had been moments ago, appearing much closer to dusk.

A pair of hands helped her up, and Aryel pulled her into an embrace. Behind them, the Boundary was still intact, the tear resealed, the grassy field and the Lightguards nowhere in sight. Danai, Nik, and Iliana stood several feet away, brushing leaves and dirt from their clothes.

"You scared me for a moment," Aryel said into her hair.

Corinne patted his back. "I promised, didn't I?"

Aryel leaned back to look at her, the light from Corinne's markings dancing in his eyes. She breathed deeply, shuddering a bit as the remnants of the Boundary's power faded.

Danai, Nik, and Iliana's conversation cut off abruptly, and a moment later the thudding of hooves reached Corinne's ears. Aryel gripped her arm as the others closed ranks behind them. Five, no, six figures mounted on horses appeared in the forest clearing, circling them before coming to a halt. Even in the shadowy light of dusk, it was clear they each held weapons, blades at their sides and bows in their hands.

An icy breeze washed over Corinne from directly in front of them, and between two of the riders, a figure appeared. A tall, slender woman with ivory skin and eyes as dark as her short, raven-black hair stepped forward, dressed in fighting leathers with three silver stars embroidered on the chest. Darkness crept up her arms in gentle wisps above geometric markings on her skin, as dynamic as the night sky. Corinne had never seen anyone like her, but she knew in her bones what this woman was.

Nightrender.

"Hello there, sun walkers," she said, her voice low and melodious. "Welcome to Zovalos."

To be continued

AUTHOR'S NOTE

Thank you SO much for reading Lightguard! I wanted to add a quick note here regarding the OCD representation in this book.

If you've seen OCD portrayed in popular media and are less familiar with the disorder, you may not be aware that it can be nearly invisible, and isn't simply "liking things a particular way."

As a result of her intrusive thoughts, Corinne has almost purely mental compulsions, i.e. repeated phrases/prayers. This is not the lived experience of everyone with OCD, but it is my own lived experience, and it was important to me to portray it in this way. If you'd like to learn more about OCD and all the different subtypes, you can find some general information here:

https://www.treatmyocd.com/learn/blog

It was also important to me that while Corinne begins to learn better ways to manage her intrusive thoughts, her OCD is not "fixed" by love or magic or anything else. Book 2 will continue to explore how she manages it all and grows.

ACKNOWLEDGMENTS

This book came out of absolutely nowhere, and I'd firstly like to thank Maggie, Kim, and Hannah for enabling me in taking on this "Detour Duology" between publishing the books in the Heirs of Esran series.

Thank you so much to Jeanine, my editor, and Nay, my proofreader, for helping make this book shine and sparkle. And of course thank you to Maggie, Sierra, Kim, and Kaila, my alpha readers, and Sam, Hannah, Maggie, Marwa, and Katie, my beta readers.

To Kim and Hannah, for always being there to field questions, do gut checks, and yap about all things authorly. This industry is tough, and friends like you make it easier to weather anything life throws at me.

To Holli, for dealing with all my "mini-podcasts" about whatever I'm working on, and whose light and love is endlessly inspiring.

To my mom, who listened to me word vomit this book's entire plot after it came to me out of the blue in March, and who listens to me and supports me no matter what as I continue to discover and share pieces of myself.

And of course, always, to my dear readers: your support and excitement to dive into my worlds is the greatest gift.

About the Author

Hayley Turner is a writer and composer from North Carolina. Her favorite stories blend fantasy, magic, romance, and epic adventures for an overall "fairytale for adults" feel, and that's exactly what she seeks to capture in her own books. When she isn't writing books or music, she can be found playing videogames, eating good food with even better friends, or cuddling with her dog, Leia, or her void goblin cat, Nyx.

Also by Hayley Turner

The Prince of Terrana

The Princess of Maremer

www.ingramcontent.com/pod-product-compliance
Lightning Source LLC
LaVergne TN
LVHW091710070526
838199LV00050B/2342